PROPHECY

Also by C.A. Fox
PARADOX, Book One
PRAXIS, Book Three

PROPHECY

C.A. FOX

Book Two of the PARADOX Trilogy

Surrogate Press®

Published in the United States by
Surrogate Press®
an imprint of Faceted Press®
Surrogate Press, LLC
Park City, Utah

SurrogatePress.com

CAFoxbooks.com

ISBN: 978-1-964245-12-6

Library of Congress Control Number: 2024922343

Book Cover design by: Michelle Rayner, Cosmic Design
Interior design by: Katie Mullaly, Surrogate Press®

This is a work of fiction. Any resemblance to actual persons living or dead is simply coincidence.

For David Staley

"...ultimate answers cannot be given,
they can only be received."
Tom Robbins, *Jitterbug Perfume*

THE KNOWNLANDS

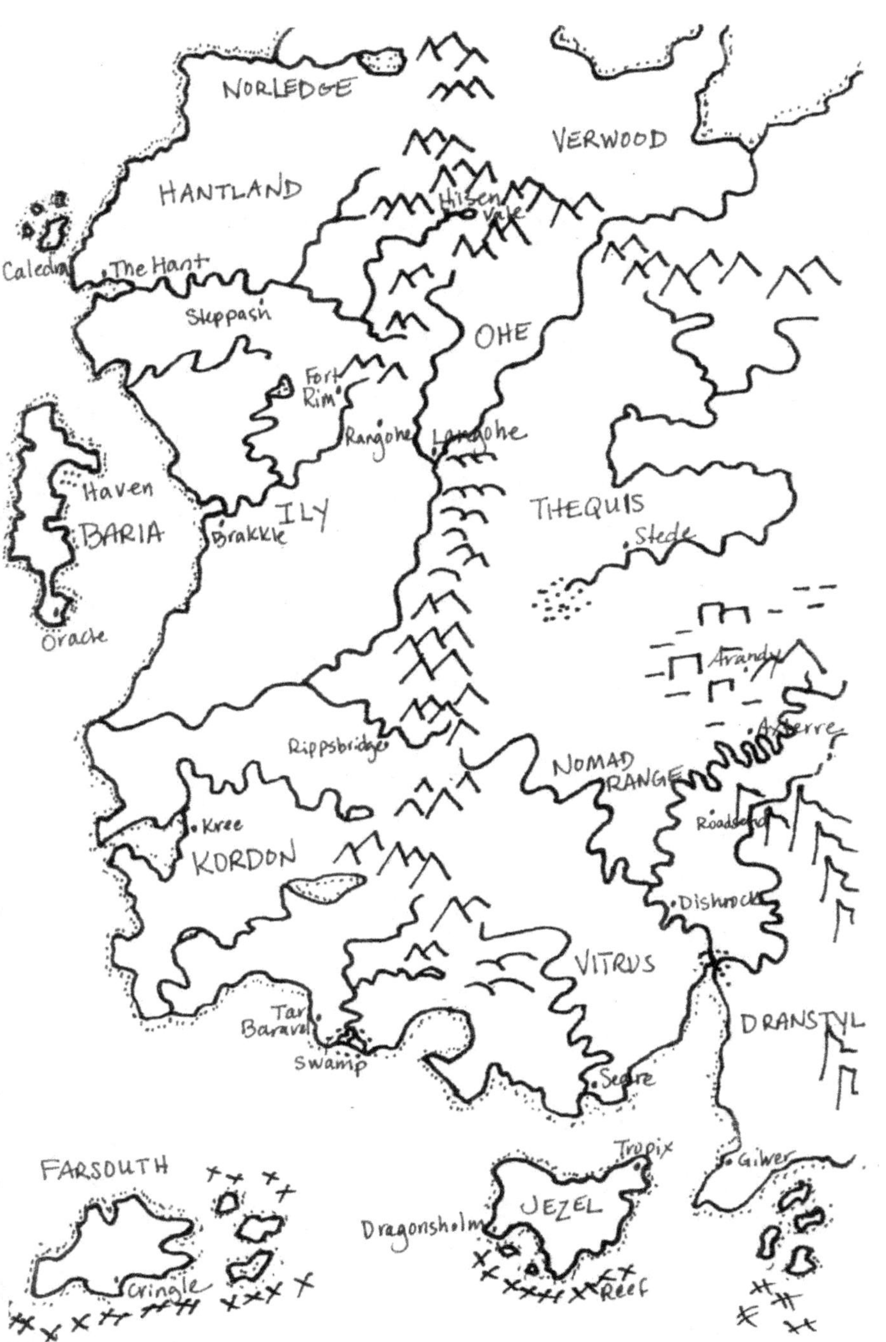

Prologue

The Duke of Midipex did not linger in Rippsmarch to hunt with his king. Claiming that his duties as lord chancellor demanded his presence in Kree, he and a few of his secretaries galloped out of Rippsgate heading south, following the messenger who'd been dispatched a day earlier. He hoped the rider had found Dowager Stylla still enjoying the company of his uncle at Pexbury.

When Midipex arrived at Pexbury two days later, he was relieved to see the dowager's royal banner still snapping in the brisk wind above the small turret of his uncle's townhouse.

The duke requested an immediate, private meeting with the dowager, taking only the briefest minute to clean himself and his clothes at his own palace.

She received him in a study, over-furnished in a style that had been popular two generations ago. The duke's uncle was nowhere in sight, but the dowager, her hair loose and somewhat windblown, sat writing at a heavy darkwood desk.

"Your majesty," he bowed.

"Hello, Thorag." She looked up and did not ask him to sit. "Explain to me how you've let him slip away again."

"Rippsmarch let him slip away, Ma'am. He was gone before the king and I got there."

The dowager shook her head. "Surely you have people in Rippsmarch."

"The wrong people," the duke said dryly. "Admittedly."

She sheathed her quill. "Did he accuse you?"

"No. Rippsmarch and his family wouldn't have been able to hide information like that. Tallyn is confused, but she doesn't have any concrete answers."

"Yet." The dowager snapped and smiled with some pride. "She's too smart for you, Thorag."

The duke made another small bow. "We will make the most of the confession. It helps that he gave it to Rippsmarch, because everyone knows Oklan is sympathetic to him."

The dowager's fingernails beat a slow tattoo on the polished desk. "That's useful, if you can catch him again."

"We shall be prepared." The duke watched the dowager for a moment. "Prepared, perhaps for extreme measures."

The dowager's fingers stopped drumming.

"He's moving about the Knownlands," the duke explained. "And the Oracle seems somehow involved. We must assume that he will show up in Kordon eventually."

"I never want to see that mother-killer again."

"Yes, Ma'am." The duke's fluty voice was soothing. "When we began the effort to remove the Barians from Kordon you specified that we were not to kill them. But their obstinance, and Javix's unauthorized return leaves us with few options."

Dowager's Stylla's light blue eyes met those of the duke. Her lips formed an implacable line. Then she smiled. "You're asking me to approve outright murder?"

"Only if he provokes us by returning to Kree," the duke answered.

The dowager turned back to the papers on her desk. "I don't know why you seem to be asking my permission, Thorag. It's your skin at risk."

Thorag Addle, Duke of Midipex and Lord Chancellor of Kordon stared at her back for just a moment. "I am merely working to ensure that you do not have to suffer his presence, your majesty."

"Indeed. My lord." She did not turn around.

The duke took his leave. He concluded some business with his agents in the town and galloped out of Pexbury without ever visiting his wife and son.

J avix Sharkin, Prince of Baria and Kordon, fell to his knees in the crusty snow. The pegasus that had carried him for the last thirty-six hours away from the Kordish hinterlands and across sea had landed softly enough, but Jax's muscles, exhausted from the long ride, failed to support him as he slid off the back of the winged horse.

It didn't matter. Tears of grief and relief filled his eyes. He smelled Baria: the pine, the late spring snow, and the sea, at last! The sea. He lifted the crunchy snow to his face and rubbed the hard, cold crystals over his unshaven cheeks.

"My lord." Juna, the priestess who had liberated him from the dungeon in Rippsgate and brought him here, reached out a hand to help him to his feet.

Jax stood and turned to face the white temple of the Oracle. He squinted as the sun rose over the building, blinding him. Something had been singing in his heart from the moment he had swung himself onto the pegasus in the darkness outside the Earl of Rippsmarch's castle. All through the long hours of two nights and a day he had ridden through the sky sustained by that unvoiced melody. Now the song in his heart reached such a level of elation and joy that he had no doubt about the small gray figure that seemed to come towards him out of sun.

He knelt again on purpose this time.

The Oracle crouched down to look Jax in the face. "Thank you for coming, Javix Sharkin." They spoke in Islish in a voice that was neither male nor female, neither old nor young.

Jax did not suppress the irony from his voice. "I am happy to oblige, Your Eminence."

"Eminence? Is that how they taught you to address the Oracle?"

Jax nodded.

"It sounds like something in the landscape," the Oracle muttered.

"What would you prefer?" Jax asked, standing.

"*Oracle.*"

"Very well, Oracle."

The creature looked up at Jax out of wrinkle-lined gray eyes. "Yes. Names are important, aren't they?"

"I believe so."

The Oracle considered the lad's smile thoughtfully. "You, Javix, need a bath. We don't have time for that now, but we can get you some breakfast."

With an undeniable sense of homecoming, Jax followed the Oracle through the purple doors and into the temple.

The Oracle led him to a round, airy room with vast windows overlooking the sea. Jax had never seen such wide panes of glass, and he marveled at the view that glittered in front of him, but which he could not hear or smell or feel.

Grunting softly, the Oracle dropped in a low chair and gestured for Jax to do the same. A priestess handed Jax a steaming mug of tea. Another placed a plate of buttered toast and hard-cooked eggs on a small table next to his chair. That he could smell, and it was heavenly.

"Eat," invited the Oracle.

Despite his hunger, Jax forced himself to eat with some decorum and not just shove the food into his mouth. After all, he was in the presence of what had once been the most powerful force in the Knownlands. As Speaker for the Goddess, the Oracle had priests or priestesses in every court throughout the Knownlands. While they rarely meddled in secular politics, the Oracle exerted their considerable magic and influence if the goddess' *Rote and Rede* was ignored or violated. Over the last century or so, however, the Oracle seemed less active. They no longer left their temple here on Baria. In fact, Jax remembered Lord Admiral Hix blaming the Oracle's inactivity for the trolls' continued use of slaves.

He gulped the hot tea and choked on the burning liquid.

"There is need for haste," the Oracle said dryly, "but choking yourself to death won't help us."

"I beg your pardon." Jax sipped the tea more carefully, struggling to organize the myriad reactions coursing through him. Attenuated by lack of food and sleep and overwhelmed with the awe of the sparkling day, the warmth of the room, the delicate perfume of dried herbs, he struggled to keep his thoughts in Islish, which he hadn't spoken in four years. The pressure of Oracle magic rubbing against his Dragon force didn't help.

With a steadying breath, he raised his eyes to look at the Oracle and found himself trapped in a deep gray stare. He felt the presence in his mind and instinctively fought against such an invasion.

The presence withdrew suddenly and released him.

"We don't have enough time for words," snapped the Oracle. "We need to see your memories."

"You might have warned me, *Oracle*." Jax snapped back.

"Humph. You are saucy. No wonder you get in so much trouble."

"Part of my charm."

Again, the Oracle noted that odd, grim smile. "We don't have time for your charm right now, Prince Javix. We need to see where you've been, since you can't be found in a scry."

"How did you find me in Rippsmarch's prison, then?"

"Spies. The priests and priestesses have been watching for you. We never expected to find you in Kordon."

"So you knew I'd been accused of treason there?"

"Of course."

This time Jax felt their magic as something much more compelling than a tickle, and the demand was undisguised.

"Look into the eyes, Javix."

Unwillingly, Jax lifted his sea blue eyes to the iron gray vice of the Oracle and recoiled physically as the presence again entered his mind. The tea spilt, unnoticed.

It was a violation. He could hide nothing. All of his feelings, anger, despair, lust, confusion, and fear accompanied each image the Oracle wrested from his memory. Tactile sensations were as fresh and as exposed as the day the whip cut into his back or the evening the fairy queen ran her fingers along his face. He wanted to vomit again with revulsion as the ghost of the Axterran Oracle impaled his heart with its misty finger.

Suddenly he was free. "Did you enjoy that?" he gasped.

"You saw the Oracle! The last Oracle of Axterre."

"I saw their ghost."

"And they saw *you!*" This was an accusation.

Jax pushed his fingers through his dirty hair. "Look, Oracle. What is this all about? I'm seen; I'm not seen. You've just helped yourself to things I didn't want anybody to see."

Something glinted in the Oracle's gray eye. It waved a hand and more tea appeared steaming in Jax's cup. "Compassion. Is that what you want?"

"Courtesy would be enough."

The Oracle snorted. "Very well, *your Highness*. You, Prince Javix Brondon Fellix Sharkin of Baria and Kordon, Viscount Norbay, and Vice-Admiral of the Barian Fleet, you have been summoned to perform a service for the goddess."

Jax sipped the tea and hoped the voice would stop. It did not.

"You will go to Sageham, to Castle Caledra. You will find the Weaver and take her to Kree. You must do this now, before the Spring Rising."

Jax sat back in his chair. "Oh. Is that all?"

"Don't be flippant, young man. The fate of the Knownlands depends on the Unseen Paradox."

"That sounds like a character in a tarot deck."

The Oracle smiled. "Indeed. A prophecy."

"I am not a playing card." Jax rose to his feet.

"And this isn't a game."

Jax turned away from those gray eyes and looked out at the sea. He spoke to the window. "Did you notice this as you pillaged through my memories?" From his pocket he pulled the folded paper that Lexyl had given him far away on a hot desert afternoon. He could almost feel grains of sand sift from the paper as he handed it to the Oracle. "I want to go to my brother. I think the sealord needs me."

The Oracle looked at the paper and gasped. The script on the page flared into red flames.

Jax backed away until he came up against a wall.

The flames subsided and the Oracle looked at him through the thin veil of smoke. "This has been looked for. It's time to remember."

"That's what the fairy queen said."

The Oracle stood up and shuffled over to Jax, holding out the piece of parchment. A new verse had appeared above the other:

> *Oracle, speak Mother's truth:*
> *Dragons come with claw and tooth.*
> *Your purpose for one thousand years:*
> *Is to remember fires and tears.*
>
> *A paradox who can't be found.*
> *The Mother stirs and shakes the ground.*
> *Oceans rise to touch the trees,*
> *And bring a ruler to his knees.*

Jax took a breath to try to steady himself. "If the oceans rise, all of Baria could be in danger. My duty lies there."

The Oracle's gray eyes considered Jax coldly for a few moments. "Your duty is larger than Baria. You are the Paradox, Javix Sharkin. You, who are both islish and landish; you, who have been both prince and slave; you, who are both cursed and blessed by the Holy Mother."

"Mostly cursed."

The Oracle ignored this comment. "The fairy queen recognized you. As did the Oracle of Axterre."

"No. I have been a slave long enough. I am not your invisible errand boy."

The Oracle just stared at him with those implacable gray eyes.

With increasing desperation, Jax argued: "It's a two-day sail from Baria to Sageham with a fast ship and the best winds. The Rising's no more than a week away. It wouldn't be safe to set out on a journey to Kree via Sageham even if I started today."

"You will start today."

"No." Jax repeated calmly, shoving down the panic rising from his gut. "I can't go to Sageham. I have Dragon force. I'll be cross magicked at the dock. And there is no Weaver."

"There will be."

"I can't go to Kree either, unless you want your Unseen Paradox to suffer a lengthy and quite visible death. Surely you can find someone else to do your bidding."

The sun, streaming through the wide windows struck the Oracle's iridescent eyes. They reached a bony finger toward Jax. Trapped already against the wall, he held his breath, remembering the last time an oracle had pointed at him. The finger touched him, and warmth flooded his hungry stomach.

"Nobody is free, Javix Sharkin."

"Only the dead," he choked.

"Only the dead," the Oracle agreed.

Jax squirmed away and walked across the room. The warmth from his stomach was spreading in a lovely way throughout his body. "Goddess damn me," he muttered.

"We believe you have been told that the goddess doesn't damn anything."

"Well, something does." Jax ran his hands over his face. "Look, what's the rush? You took long enough to find me. The fairy queen was talking in these same riddles last summer. Why can't all this wait a few weeks until after the Spring Rising?"

"So much was lost," the Oracle sighed. "We are running out of time. The fairy queen is right: The Cycle is coming due. But no one remembers what to do."

"Do about what?"

"The Millennial Cycle. It's nearly come round. It wasn't until people came here looking for you and we couldn't find you that we realized that the Cycle was due."

"People came looking for me?"

The Oracle nodded. "They did. A prince can't just disappear. Sealord Bryx came. And later, Klaris de Farsouth. But it was the Highlord who reminded us about the dragons."

"*What* about the dragons?"

"That it's time."

"Time for what? Goddess, do you always speak in circles?"

"Yes, of course."

Jax closed his eyes.

"Look at us, Javix Sharkin. The Weaver and you, you who are the Paradox Who Can't Be Found, the two of you have important work to do if we don't want another dragon interregnum."

Jax knew his history. Nearly a thousand years ago, giant, fire-breathing dragons had flown to the Knownlands, bringing death and devastation. After staying one hundred years here on the Head of Baria and on the Island of Jezel far to the south, they flew away and had not been seen since. Only their magic remained deep in the rocks on the Barian Head, amid the jungles of Jezel, and in the blood of those born with Dragon force.

"The dragons are coming back?" It would be horrible.

"They always have," the Oracle grumbled. "Now stop arguing and go fetch the Weaver off of Sageham and get her to Kree."

"Of all places."

The Oracle ignored him. "Your Dragon force is inconsequential. Your political problems are another matter."

"But not *inconsequential.*"

"Look, Javix. Exasperating as you are, you will do this. You must." The Oracle pulled a golden medallion on a long golden chain from a pocket of its gray robe.

"This marks you as our special servant," the Oracle explained, looping the chain over Jax's head. "No one in the Knownlands will dare harm you."

"You don't think?" Jax wriggled his shoulders. "I've had about enough of chains."

"Eh. Life is full of them. Come now. Juna here will take you home."

"Home?"

"To Haven."

"Of course," Jax said flatly. "Look, Oracle, what do I tell Sealord Bryx? I'm pretty sure he'll have other plans for me."

"You'll think of something. You always do."

"I wish I had your confidence." Bitterness rose in Jax's throat. Gone was the singing joy. Gone was the sense of resolution to be the prince he was born to be that he'd finally found after his exile and the long journey across the Knownlands with Marith. Once again, he was no more than a slave, bound by myths, and ghosts, and his own paradoxes.

The Oracle watched as the prince leapt onto the pegasus' back and maneuvered his legs around its large white wings. When the Oracle looked up into Jax's face, the sun again glowed through the gray iridescent eyes. "None of us is free, Javix, but you are the master of your own destiny."

This made sense to Jax when the Oracle said it, but as his winged horse leapt into the sky and he saw the Floating Islands of Haven and the forest of ships' masts rising in the distance, the words seemed trite and contradictory.

2

The pegasi flew through the clear winter air and arrived at Haven as the sun was setting behind the dark, pine-covered mountains of Baria, sending long icy shadows over the roofs and masts of the port. Jax's long anger against the brother who'd apparently abandoned him to the trolls, compounded with his sense of being ill-used by the Oracle, was as cold as the evening air.

As they dismounted on the winter-brown lawn surrounding Valla's Palace, Juna noted the hard look in the prince's eyes, but she said nothing. Naturally, Jax started toward the arching bridge that linked the palace grounds to the Floating Islands.

Ever since their flight from the dragons and the destruction of the city of Nec, the Barians had lived on the six Floating Islands. Now moored together and anchored in the bay, these vessels formed the capital city, housing the people and the government. Each "island" was governed by a noble family, but all had joined under the leadership of the Sharkin rulers of Helm.

Looking for the sealord, Jax headed for the Floating Island of Helm, where he expected to find Bryx in the Cabyn, the traditional palace of the Sharkin Sealords and Seaqueens from time immemorial.

"This way, please, my lord," Juna said quietly, gesturing away from the Floating Islands to the white marble palace that sat amid the smoothly manicured grounds. "Sealord Bryx rules from Valla's Palace."

Jax turned to follow Juna. "I guess that's no surprise."

Bryx had always preferred to have solid ground beneath his feet. Like their Kordish mother, Bryx was never comfortable on a boat. Sealord Rax had built the marble palace for his beloved Valla and consented to live there when he was in Haven, although he carried on the business of ruling from the Cabyn on Helm.

When Valla died at Jax's birth, Rax moved back to the Cabyn with his two sons. Jax remembered tagging along with Bryx on one of his frequent trips to Valla's Palace. The older prince had curled up in a large armchair and stared at Jax. "I wish you hadn't been born."

Jax had heard this many times before, and he banged his toy sailboat against the chair where Bryx sat.

"Don't!" spat Bryx.

"I didn't mean to kill her!" Jax shouted.

"But you did." Bryx's voice was hard and cruel. "It doesn't matter what you *meant*, what matters is what you *did*."

Jax had clutched his toy boat and run crying from the palace to Nanny Grosmith, who stood on the lawn chatting with a cook.

"I didn't mean to kill her," Jax sobbed into Nanny's bosom.

Nanny had heard all this before. Her soft heart broke yet again for the motherless half-islish princes. She gathered little Jax in her arms and carried him away from the white marble palace. "There, there, my prince. No one blames you."

"Bryx does."

"He'll grow to understand."

Jax did not know if Bryx had grown to either understand or forgive him for killing their mother. He wasn't sure he'd forgiven himself. He hadn't returned to Valla's Palace since that day. Now as he followed Priestess Juna across the crunchy brown grass, he realized that he did not know much about his brother at all and wondered if he ever had.

The arrival of two of the Oracle's pegasi had not gone unnoticed in the palace or on the Floating Islands. As Juna and Jax approached, the great golden doors of the palace swung open. Sixteen armed sailors marched out and lined the marble steps. Behind them, on the top step, stood the sealord, resplendent in Barian Blue silk that rippled in the cold winter air. Several nobles, lords and ladies of the Floating Islands, gathered behind him.

Jax had been walking behind Juna, his head down with his memories. She stopped, and he stepped around her, raising his face to the sealord.

"Sweet goddess," Bryx murmured.

The other nobles gasped in shock. Even the sixteen sailor-guards gasped.

Ragged as he was in the dirty, rough spun clothes, there was no mistaking the half-islish prince. Even if someone had a doubt, it would have been quickly banished by the challenge in Jax's blue islish eyes and the wolfishness that hung around the corners of his small smile. This was clearly the son of Sealord Rax.

The small crowd watched in silence as the two brothers stared at each other. Then, slowly, Jax bowed, giving the one-handed Barian salute.

Sealord Bryx almost stumbled in his rush down the steps. He grabbed Jax by the shoulders and stared into his face. "By the holy mother." He grinned suddenly. "Sweet goddess!" He enveloped Jax in a huge hug.

The growing crowd cheered. Voices and hands reached out to touch the no-longer Lost Prince.

"A minute! A minute!" Bryx voice quelled the crowd. "Allow Prince Jax a minute to come inside and refresh himself. We'll have a banquet here in the Great Hall this night!" He nodded to his chamberlain then, arm around Jax, swooped him up the stairs and away to a large room overlooking the harbor.

The sealord turned to the nobles who had followed. "Leave us," he snapped, pushing the door. At the last moment he realized that an Oracular Priestess stood next to Jax. "Perhaps someone could get the priestess some tea and food." With that, he shut the door on the crowd and turned to look at the brother he hadn't seen in more than four years.

Jax was staring up at the huge portrait of a striking blond woman that hung above the roaring fire. A small, dark-haired boy leaned against the woman's silk skirts.

"That's my favorite picture of her," Bryx said softly.

"I've never seen it."

"Father hid it away when she died. I found it in a storage room."

Jax finally turned away from his mother's pale, Kordish eyes to look into those same eyes in the face of his brother. For a few long moments they stared at each other, both noting four years of changes.

At last Bryx spoke. "Where have you been, Jax? What happened to you?" He looked Jax up and down, noting the ragged clothing. "You are filthy." He sat and motioned Jax to do the same.

Jax had never required Bryx's permission to sit before, but now Bryx was more than his older brother: he was his sealord as well. So he began: "Your Majesty, I was abducted...."

Bryx listened, occasionally nodding. "So, you were the slave that Klaris saw."

"She told you?"

"Aye," Bryx nodded. "She sent me a letter. Magically."

"When?" Jax demanded. "When did she send this letter?" For so long he had believed that Klaris had done nothing but leave him enslaved to the trolls that he was suspicious of some other truth.

"When? Well, it must have been about a year ago. Yes, I remember the letter arrived in the midst of one of the fiercest storms of the Spring Rising. I went to the iron mines, when I could, a few months ago. The mine boss told me they sold their half-islish slave for bait. So, we assumed you were either dead, or not the same slave."

"You went to the iron mines this past winter?"

"Yes."

"I was there for three goddess-damned years, Bryx. It took you *seven* Risings before you could figure that out?" Speaking Islish, he lapsed into the islish way of counting the passage of time in Risings, rather than years.

Bryx stiffened, defensively. "We didn't think the slave could possibly have been you, Jax. Klaris said you weren't dead, and the poor slave who'd been sold for bait would have been slaughtered long before. The princess thought maybe you'd escaped somehow."

"I didn't escape, no thanks to her."

Bryx's pale eyes watched Jax carefully. "Well, you didn't end up as bait, evidently. Klaris was very concerned for you. In fact, I brought her here to see the Oracle."

"And they couldn't find me, either."

Bryx noted the bitterness in Jax's voice. "No one could find you, Jax. You are invisible to magic. The Oracle couldn't find you when you first disappeared seven Risings ago, and they couldn't find you for Klaris either."

"They got me in the end."

"Shouldn't you be glad they saved you from a traitor's death at Rippsgate?"

"Seems no more than a temporary stay of execution, provided I survive cross-magic on Sageham and then the Rising." Jax slumped, his elbows on his knees, his head in his hands, and closed his eyes as exhaustion overwhelmed him.

Bryx considered Jax's sun-bleached hair. Even matted and dirty, it was the unmistakable gift of their Kordish mother.

This thought shadowed Bryx's voice. "When you vanished and Kordon closed the Gates of Griffe to Barian shipping, we faced a crisis here. We still do. The fleet has been devastated and the Floating Islands are impoverished. I told Tallyn that if you turned up here, I would give you to the Kordish, provided they open the ports again."

Jax looked up. "That was nice of you."

Bryx rose and went to the window. In the blue twilight he could see people coming across the bridge towards the palace, coming to celebrate the return of the Lost Prince. Bryx felt the genuine warmth of his relief at finding Jax turning sour. He knew the Barians didn't love him, but he had no desire to be the lieutenant to his little brother as captain of Barian popularity. He turned back to the darkening room and considered the hardness in Jax's islish eyes.

"You were gone." His voice held a hardness of its own. "I didn't know where, or why, or how. The lords and ladies of the Floating Islands were all looking to me to do something, *anything*. We need the Kordish trade, Jax. All Baria needs it. I figured you'd have some good excuse that would save your skin. And you do."

Bryx crossed the room to a small table and poured two glasses of Farsouthian sherry. The candles in the wall sconces near the table flared to life. He looked up at them surprised then turned to bring a glass back to Jax. "I forgot you could do that."

Jax didn't answer, but the light revealed the white scars under the holes in his ripped shirt.

"Dragons," Bryx growled. "Who beat you?"

"Everyone. The trolls left the visible scars." He sipped the sherry and leaned his head against the back of the chair.

"Your Majesty!" A woman's voice carried over the sharp knocks on the door, startling both of them. "Your Majesty! A word, please."

Bryx frowned. "Come."

The Priestess Juna and Mother Ayslic, the Oracle's priestess to the Barian court, curtseyed deeply to the sealord.

"Mother, Priestess." Bryx acknowledged them. "What do you need?"

"I suppose they're here to make your decision for you," Jax said, placing his empty glass on a small table.

"My decision, *my lord?*"

"About what to do with me. *Sire.*"

"Your Majesty." Mother Ayslic gently inserted herself into their rancor. "The Oracle has placed a burden upon Prince Javix."

"He has told me, Mother," Bryx said in a voice that caused Jax to look up and raise one eyebrow. "But he has a duty to Baria."

"Your Majesty, with respect, the Oracle's mission is a higher call," Juna answered.

Bryx shook his head without looking at his brother. "But I have him now, and I'm not going to lose this chance to get the Kordish to open the ports."

"Sire—."

Bryx interrupted the priestess. "Listen, Priestesses. I know that there is no Weaver at the moment. There is no reason for Prince Jax to try to sail to Sageham on the eve of the Rising looking for something that isn't there yet. But he can go to Kree. A ship will leave on the next tide."

"You would send your brother to a traitor's death?" Mother Ayslic looked at Bryx, disappointment clear in her blue islish eyes.

"That's precisely what the Oracle proposes," Bryx snapped. "Only worse. Prince Jax can't stay on Sageham, not with Dragon force in his blood. If he follows the Oracle's plan, he'll be stuck somewhere in the Hantish wilds for the three weeks of Rising storms. And if he and the currently nonexistent Weaver survive that, then he's supposed to go to Kree to face the traitor's death. But if he doesn't survive the Rising, the cross-magic, the monsters and the trolls and never makes it back to Kree, then all of Baria will be forever locked out of Kordon, and *that*, my good mothers, is unacceptable!"

"But, Sire, if the Kordish execute him, all the Knownlands will be imperiled," Juna argued.

"Then perhaps you should go with Prince Jax and put in a good word on his behalf." Bryx sat down, with a smile that did not reach his eyes.

Juna shook her head slowly. "Sire, Prince Javix must go as the Oracle has decreed. The Weaver must be off Sageham before the Rising starts."

"But there is no Weaver."

"There will be."

Bryx stared stonily at the two priestesses. With a sudden sense of leaden foreboding, he realized that only one person could master the Mystic within the next week: Klaris de Farsouth. He turned, with horror, to look at his brother.

Sprawled in the chair, Jax had fallen sound asleep.

Mother Ayslic knelt in front of the sealord and put a hand on his knee. "Sire, the dragons are returning to the Knownlands. Your brother and the Weaver can stop them."

"How?"

It was Juna who answered. "That is for them to find out."

"Dragons," Bryx swore. He glanced again at his sleeping brother, dressed in rags and scars, and thought of the delicate bones in Klaris's face.

"Let him go, as the Oracle commands, Sire. It will be best for everyone, including Baria," Ayslic said softly.

"But not for me." Bryx felt the hideously familiar heartache that Jax always caused. "Whenever Jax is involved, it's not good for me."

Mother Ayslic took his hand. Juna had bent to wake Jax, who rubbed his face roughly. Musicians played snatches of discordant warm-up notes in the Great Hall below.

Jax sat up. "I need a bath."

Bryx pulled himself free from Ayslic's sympathy and rang for his page. "See to the prince. Get him cleaned up for the reception below. And send word to Master Illat that the *Drixa* will sail for Sageham on the morning tide."

"The *Drixa*?" Jax pushed himself up from the chair. "You're coming with me?"

"I am." The sealord's voice was decisive. "Your chances for survival are better in the flagship. Plus, I can then deliver you to Kordon, as I promised."

Jax pushed the haze of fatigue from his mind. "Sire, there's no place for the flagship to safely weather the Rising on the Krillian Coast."

"We'll have to make it to The Hant. We can bide the Rising there."

"The trolls will take us."

"No, they won't."

Jax stared at his brother for a moment. "They'll want islish slaves, Bryx. They'll know we're stuck there for the Rising, and they'll figure out a way to capture us."

"*Sire*, Jax," Bryx insisted between his teeth. "You've become paranoid. I was just there last winter with no problems. Besides, the Weaver can use the Mystic to defend us."

"No, your Majesty," Juna said firmly.

Jax looked at her sharply. He felt the Oracle's magic moving as she continued to speak.

"This quest belongs to the Paradox. To Javix alone. You, Sealord, will be needed here."

Bryx frowned at Juna. "Paradox?"

"Look at this." Jax pulled the scrap of prophecy from his pocket.

Bryx took it and frowned. "Is this Ancient? I don't read Ancient."

Jax took the paper from Bryx's hands. "The Oracle says it's a prophecy." He translated the two stanzas for his brother.

"I will not be brought to my knees," Bryx noted.

"We hope not," Juna said. "But you must let Prince Javix go."

Bryx turned to the waiting servant. "Get the prince cleaned up and send my compliments to Neben de Rillt. I will see him immediately."

"Neben?" Jax asked then remembered to add, "Sire."

"He has the best one-hand sloop in the fleet. Goddess knows you'll need it."

Jax considered the emptiness in his brother's pale eyes. "What happened to my frigate? Last I saw the *Shark Fin*, she was moored in Keffin Harbor."

The Sealord shrugged. "Ask Hix. I can't keep track of every boat on the water."

Jax hid his frown in his bow. Sleek and fast, the pride of Barian shipwrights, the *Shark Fin* wasn't just any boat. "Thank you. Your Majesty."

"I'll look for you in Kree after the Rising."

"Yes, Sire."

Scrubbed, shaved, and dressed again in the thick silks of royalty, Jax dove into the turbulent swirl of Barian politics in the Great Hall. After listening in horrified awe to his tales of enslavement and abuse, the nobles of Baria in turn regaled him with the hardships they suffered having lost the lucrative Kordish trade. Criticism of the new sealord and his handling of this crisis was widespread and often nearly treasonous.

After an hour or so, Jax began to fear he would collapse from sheer exhaustion. Unable to find the sealord, he decided he had to take matters into his own hands. He climbed up to musicians' dais and banged on one of their drums until the crowd fell silent.

"I thank you for welcoming me back to Haven," he began. The nobles cheered and he smiled. "It is so good to be home. To speak Islish again," his voice faltered with emotion and he took a deep gulp of wine. "But I cannot stay."

Jax had to bang the drum again to get the crowd to quiet again. He pulled the Oracle's golden chain from underneath his shirt. "I have been summoned by the Oracle and commanded to undertake a quest. I wish it weren't so, but I must leave tonight."

Again, the crowed irrupted in shouts of displeasure.

"Look for me in Kree after the Rising. Maybe I can get the Gates of Griffe open again. Maybe."

The crowd liked this idea and applauded and raised their mugs in a cacophony of loud toasts.

In the uproar, Jax slipped away and found Bryx at last, sitting alone sipping Nomad wine.

"You'll take credit for reopening the Kordish ports?"

"We can worry about who gets the credit when it's done."

"*Sire*. Damn your impudence, Jax."

"My apologies, my lord." Jax was too tired to fight. "I need to sleep. I'll go to the Cabyn and leave before the dawn."

Bryx stood up then. "You take care of gentle Klaris."

"*Gentle* Klaris?" Jax's memory of meeting Klaris nearly a year before was darkened by the haze of his own misery and the tension of his fears. But even then, he had noted the confident way Klaris wielded the Mystic. She had defied a very angry troll, three times her size. There were a lot of adjectives he might use to describe her, but *gentle* wasn't one of them.

Bryx's grip was bruising his arm. "You always have a lover. Shallyx here and Cheshir at Kree, and I'm sure you found solace during your long absence in a number of accommodating arms. But Klaris doesn't need someone like you."

"Someone like me? Sire." He pulled away from Bryx's hard fingers, his exhausted mind confused.

"You cannot honor your betrothal to Klaris de Farsouth. I forbid it."

"You and the goddess and everyone else in the Knownlands. I know that."

"You remember it too, when you're looking into her lovely green eyes. I won't have you toying with her."

"You do understand, my lord, that Klaris de Farsouth left me with the trolls?" Jax's voice was hard. "She knew who I was, and she didn't seem at all gentle or helpless. But she left me there in the iron mines to be sold for bait."

Bryx relaxed visibly. "I see. Go on to bed then, and goddess go with you tomorrow, Jax."

"I hope she does, for a change."

3

Jax stood in the corridor trying to figure out how to get out of Valla's Palace without going through the throng in the Great Hall below.

"Come this way, Your Highness." Bolo Powluna threw him a lifeline.

"You're saving me." Jax followed the gray-haired Barian who'd been his steward since he outgrew the nursery and left the care of Nanny Grosmith.

"Would that I could have saved ye seven Risings ago, my lord."

Bolo led him down a set of servants' stairs, through the bustling kitchen where Jax raised a hand to the cheer of the cooks and servants, then out into the fresh night air.

Neben caught them as they crossed the bridge to the Floating Islands. "I knew you wouldn't sleep on that damned rock."

Jax recognized the voice and stopped to embrace his old friend. "At this point I'd sleep just about anywhere."

"Not so particular these days?"

"My lords, we shouldn't tarry," Bolo insisted.

To Jax's surprise, several large figures stepped out from the shadows. "I've brought guards," Neben said, and fell into step next to his prince, the guards followed. "The streets are none too safe."

"Not safe?"

"Poverty leads to desperation," Neben answered bleakly.

"Is it that bad?"

"It can be."

Jax walked on wishing it were light so he could see the condition of the streets and buildings. "I hadn't realized we were so dependent upon the Kordish trade."

"No one had, until it wasn't there anymore," Neben answered then changed the subject: "I've put my best little yacht on your mooring. The sealord told me to provision it for a month and rough weather."

"Thanks."

"You know, Jax, Shallyx and I spent the time from Rax's death through three Risings combing every curve of coast from Blymouth to Tropix, looking for you. We never thought to look for you among the trolls."

Their footsteps echoed as they crossed the dark bridge from Jeff to Helm. "No one did." Jax answered.

But Neben wasn't ready to let it go. "We should have listened to the rumors. We'd heard of a half-islish slave on Hanter Lake, but no one could believe that could be you. You're a prince, you're—."

"A paradox."

"Well, that sums up how I feel right now: guilty we didn't find you, elated to have you back."

Jax laughed tiredly. "Guilty? You were the most unrepentant pirate among us."

He saw Neben's smile flash in the darkness. "Well, I haven't told you about Shallyx yet."

As Bryx had pointed out, Shallyx of Callisto and Jax had been lovers for years. "Ah? Has she shifted her alliance from Helm to Rillt?"

Neben cleared his throat. "Her alliance is still pretty clearly Callisto, but when you disappeared, she and I were both at such a loss; we couldn't figure out what had happened to you, or where you had gone. We gave each other solace and found something more."

Jax remembered Shallyx's saucy smile and her fearless love of rough seas and high winds. But he was too tired to hold onto that loss right now. "Good for you, Neben. Good for you both. But what shall I do, now that Bryx has forbidden me to honor my betrothal to Klaris de Farsouth?"

Neben dropped his voice. "Shallyx thinks Bryx wants her."

Jax rubbed his arm where Bryx's fingers had held him. "That would be a shame. The sealord can't handfast someone with that much magic any more than I can."

"Aye." Neben answered. "I wonder why Sealord Rax and Queen Jeress betrothed you two in the first place. I mean, you've always been in line to be lord admiral and she's been known to have spectacular magic since she was a baby."

Jax shrugged, glad to see the Cabyn coming into view. "I've always assumed it was father and Jeress flirting with each other."

"I wonder why everyone remembers it then?"

"Maybe Hix would know."

"Poor Hix is still serving as lord admiral."

"Dragons," Jax swore. "He must be, what, 160 Risings old?"

The lord admiral ran the Barian fleet. The position was the second most powerful role in Barian society, and it was customarily granted to the sealord's heir. Hix of Helm was Rax's second cousin and had been the lord admiral while Bryx and Jax were boys. Bryx had become lord admiral when he passed his captaincy trials, but since his heart wasn't in it, Hix had continued the day to day running of the fleet. Jax had passed his captaincy trials two years early and had been made vice admiral, but he had been considered too young to be given full authority of the fleet.

"We need you back, Jax." Neben said as they walked into the Cabyn. The servants stood lined up. As Jax entered, they cheered, gave the one-handed Barian salute and bowed in unison.

"Thank you," he said, smiling at the familiar faces. Goddess, it was good to be home. He turned to say goodbye to his friend. "I wish I didn't have to go."

"Come back, soon." Neben gripped his hand. "Your brother isn't the sealord that Rax was, or that you would be."

"Talk like that, and I won't be able to come back at all. Just because I've been accused of treason in Kordon doesn't mean that I'm actually willing to be a traitor."

Neben shook his head. "No, no, Jax. You know I didn't mean that. It's just that we all miss Rax."

Jax looked around the room. The servants had vanished to their chores. The room seemed empty, and he finally acknowledged the absence that loomed over every gathering and haunted every room. "I keep thinking he's here. That I'll see him in the next room. Or around that corner...."

Neben said nothing, but Jax read the sympathy in his friend's blue islish eyes.

"Thanks, Neben," he said at last. "Thanks for looking for me, and thanks for the boat.

"I figure we'll have to wait out the Rising on the Krillian coast somewhere. I don't dare go back among the trolls."

"The sloop is well provisioned," Neben said. "I can meet you in The Hant."

"No. Don't go near those damned trolls. I'm afraid they'll start taking islish folk as slaves."

"They never have before."

"They'd never had an islish slave before me," he explained. "Since I survived this fever that kills all their landish slaves, they said they wanted more islish. Or even half-islish like me. We're more durable apparently."

"That's awful."

"The danger is real. They take slaves from their borderlands with Ily, Ohe, and Norledge. They would have no qualms about stealing Barians off our ships."

"But the sealord was just there this past winter, to talk to the trolls at the iron mines." Neben paused and frowned. "Now that you mention it, the *Drixa* did lose a couple sailors. No one could find them, and it was thought they must have fallen overboard somehow."

"I hope that is what happened."

That answer chilled Neben's soul. He embraced his prince one last time. "Goddess go with you, my lord."

When Neben had gone, Jax stood for a moment looking at the familiar room, feeling the comfort of home. He closed his eyes and bowed his head. He was desperate for his bed but found that he couldn't yet go there. "Bolo!"

"Yes, my lord."

"I need to go to the sanctuary."

"Ah." Bolo nodded. "Of course, my lord."

Bolo led Jax through the dark streets to the white marble wall that gleamed in the moonlight. They slipped through a gate that opened into a courtyard garden. Small lamps gleamed in silent vigil for the Sharkin dead. In summer, Jax knew that fountains would sing into the flower-scented air. But tonight, the silence of winter and the cold salty sea breeze emphasized the absence Jax felt in his heart.

Mother Ayslic rose from a small stone bench when she saw Jax enter. "I have been expecting you, Your Highness," she said softly. "This way."

Bolo sat down on the same bench, wrapping his cloak around himself. Ayslic led Jax through a passage to another garden. In a corner, a small chair faced an altar where a lone lantern flickered above a frozen fountain. Two golden plaques gleamed side by side on the wall. He'd seen the one before, the one engraved, *Valla Stylla Estan Brondon of Kordon, Consort of Baria.* The second plaque was new. With grim finality, Jax read the words aloud. "Rax Jorvan Sharkin VII, Sealord."

He sank into the chair. The priestess retreated to the shadows.

For a few moments, he watched the light flicker off the gold and felt his own heart waver with the wind-tossed flame. Without a mother, Jax had clung the more fiercely to his father. His innate affinities for all things Barian and islish had strengthened the natural bond between father and son.

Now, Jax reached out for that bond and touched the cold hard metal.

He snatched his fingers away, curling them into the wound inside him.

"Goddess damn you," he whispered through clenched teeth. "How could you abandon me?" He thought suddenly of the lonely figure of his brother acting the role of sealord. "Abandon us."

Nothing answered him. He wrapped his own arms about his emptiness. There never was an answer. His whole life was one long tale of abandonment and grief, from the moment he had killed his mother by being born. This must be the price he would always have to pay for her life, and for his. This must be his penance for inflicting such grief on his own father, his brother, his grandmother: all those he needed to love, but who themselves had known and loved Valla.

He took a ragged breath and felt the Oracle's medallion against his chest. The weight of its obligation choked him.

"No!" He stood suddenly.

In the shadows, Mother Ayslic's eyes blinked.

"No," he repeated softly. It wasn't fair. These losses were his too. And he had paid for killing his mother with four humiliating, brutal years of slavery. As if that wasn't punishment enough, the Oracle was now demanding he give even more, maybe everything he had left.

He looked up again at the two plaques gleaming side by side. He remembered the silent melancholy that Rax had hidden with a broad smile, a sharp wit, and flirtations that went nowhere.

He wiped the cold tears off his face. Alright, he acquiesced silently. Alright. Dry eyed, he nodded to Mother Ayslic, woke Bolo, and silently returned through the shadows to the Cabyn. Thoroughly drained, Jax fell into his own bed for the first time in four years. Rocked by the gentle motion of the Floating Island, he dropped into a dreamless sleep.

Before dawn Juna shook him awake. "You must go, your Highness."

Every fiber of his body protested, but he sat up, turning his head away from the light she carried.

"I am so sorry, my lord."

He could not allow himself to soften into her sympathy. He needed every bit of resolve he possessed to push himself out of that bed.

"You are not at all sorry," he snapped. "You are as implacable as that damned Oracle."

Her answering smile was toothy. "Surely you, of all people, my lord, should understand that I could feel both the insistence of the goddess and grief for her instrument?"

"The paradox."

"Aye. The paradox."

"Don't grieve for me yet, Mother. Pray for me."

By the time the late winter sun touched the pine-covered peaks of Baria, Jax's tiny sail was just a distant dot on the northern horizon.

Klaris drained the ale from her mug and held it out to the lass for a refill. She gulped down half of it and let the warmth of it fuel the recklessness in her belly.

"Wish me luck," she murmured.

The lass watched the most powerful Mystic of this generation walk carefully across the great hall to where a group of Bricks and Mortar novices stood by the roaring fire. She noticed the sudden awkwardness as the others made room for Klaris among themselves.

Klaris noticed it too. It was always the same. Every time she joined a group of her fellow students, the laughter cooled, the smiles froze, the chatter that had been bubbling along as easily as water in a small stream suddenly became icy, erratic, and pooled to a stop.

Pretending that she did not notice, Klaris plunged into the silence. "The moon's full tonight. Is anyone trying an interesting scry?"

"I don't know that *you'd* call it interesting," Fortunato answered, his gray striped goatee bobbing. "I'm going to scry for my wife in Seare."

"Professor Essen is expecting all of us to try a distance scry tonight." Larrisa glanced across the room to where the professor, tutor to all the Bricks and Mortar novices, sat talking with the other faculty who taught the most powerful Mystics in the Knownlands. Larrisa turned her brown eyes back to Klaris and smiled, deepening the wrinkles on her face. "You know, Klaris, we're all still working to master the scry."

Klaris felt no contempt for the novices' lack of skill, but her stomach tightened at Larissa's defensive tone.

"It should be a good night for a scry," she said with encouragement. "No clouds to obscure the moon."

"That didn't help me last month," grumbled a gray-haired man whom Klaris didn't know.

She gulped more of her ale and turned to her purpose. Istov, a tall, fair-haired Norledgian looked down at her, his blue eyes kind. He was a good ten years younger than the other novices, but still probably ten years older than Klaris.

She let the ale give her courage. "And who will you scry for?" She laid a hand on Istov's arm.

"For my mother. In Grenze."

"I often scry for my mother," Klaris said helpfully.

"You must miss her." Xella smiled kindly at Klaris. "Being away from her so young."

Klaris unconsciously assumed her mother's regal poise. "I think I miss her now more than when I was younger."

"Younger!" Larrisa laughed. "You are but a child yet."

Klaris felt her face grow red. This was not at all the direction she wanted the conversation to go.

"Is it true, Klaris, that you came to study here when you were just thirteen?" the gray-haired man asked with a mixture of awe and skepticism.

"I was twelve, actually," Klaris answered rather grimly. "I'm not a child now."

Larrisa and Xella exchanged knowing glances.

"Of course not, my dear." Xella kept her face straight, but her eyes twinkled.

"Maybe I'll scry with you tonight." Klaris struggled to change the subject. The ale had gone to her head, as she hoped, but it just seemed to enhance her frustration.

"I would be honored to watch you scry," Fortunato said eagerly.

"I too," Istov's eyes lit with excitement, although not the kind of excitement she'd hoped for. Still, it was something.

"Let's do it then." Klaris smiled, her hopes rekindled.

A few minutes later, the group gathered in the scry room. Tall windows formed the walls on three sides letting in a silver flow of moonlight.

"Where's your bowl, Klaris?" Xella asked. "Do you want to use mine?"

"No, thank you." Klaris snapped her fingers and her own scry bowl appeared on the stone table in the center of the room. She took a deep breath and found the Mystic. The bowl filled with shimmering water.

"Oh, sweet goddess," said the gray-haired man, enraptured by the feel of Klaris's magic.

Professor Essen cleared his throat. Klaris had felt him enter the scry room, but evidently the novices had not.

"Professor!" Fortunato said abashed. "Klaris invited us to watch her weave."

Essen raised a hand. "Of course, it's fine. Fine. You are lucky to have the chance to watch someone with Klaris's skill. But remember it *is* acceptable to collect your bowl and water without magic."

Klaris had forgotten that most novices would have to fetch their implements without magic. She had not meant to show off. Taking another deep breath to steady herself and the Mystic, she looked at the faces around her. "Whom should I scry?"

"How about your sweetheart?" Larrisa suggested.

Just in time, Klaris tightened her weave and stopped Istov's face from appearing in the water. "How about my mother, after all," she said quickly.

The water in the bowl rippled, catching silver slivers of moonlight. Then the image appeared: a fire burning on a darkened beach. A priestess held an athame up to the full moon. A small group of people holding hands around the fire chanted the ritual in Islish, their colorful silks lifting in the ocean breeze.

The picture focused on the woman in the center of the group. Her gray-laced curls gleamed in the mixed light of fire and moon. Suddenly the green eyes lifted and looked directly at the watchers at Caledra. She smiled with such love that even the novices felt it.

"Goddess, she's beautiful," Istov said.

"Goddess, she's a *queen*," gulped the gray-haired man.

Klaris ignored this and let her own love float to her mother.

"Of course, she is, Mollen," Larrisa whispered. "Klaris is the Princess of Farsouth."

"Did she really know we could see her?" Fortunato asked, breathlessly.

"Yes, she did," Klaris answered, her eyes still on the water, now clear and void. "She passed the Corridor level here herself. She knows when I'm looking at her."

Professor Essen took the opportunity to educate his novices: "The house of Farsouth is the only royal family that has any significant magic. While this has seemed iniquitous to generations of Mystics, the Oracle has so far refused to remove the de Farsouths from the throne they've held for so long."

"The Mystic has proven quite tolerant of us, too." Klaris turned snapping green eyes on the professor.

He smiled gently. "The Mystic has yet to accept a royal Weaver, your *Highness*."

No one at Caledra ever used Klaris's Farsouthian titles.

"There have been three Weavers from Farsouth over the last 900 years," she protested. "And Farsouth does not have a large population."

"But none of those chosen were royal," Essen replied. "It would be unfair, don't you agree, to expect one person to have so much responsibility? It's a big enough job to hold all the threads of Mystic, to oversee the castle and the training of all the students and the care of the Sagehamites. It would not be right to expect the same person to also fulfill the duties of royalty to govern and secure the succession."

Klaris had heard these doubts and objections many times. In fact, she knew that most of the teaching staff had opposed her acceptance to study at Caledra. But other Farsouthian royals had been admitted in the past, most notably Klaris's own mother, and Weaver Bizzleworth had insisted that someone with the kind of power she held must get the formal training that was only available here at Castle Caledra. The Farsouthian government had also sent a firmly worded appeal.

This was the point that usually saved her. "Untrained power is a danger to both the user and the people at large," Klaris said, tired of having to defend her right to be where the Mystic so clearly required her to be.

"But as the Goddess' *Rote and Rede* notes, the concentration of too much power in one set of hands is also dangerous."

"Agreed." Klaris snapped, the vanished glow of ale and magic leaving her cold. She saw Istov drawing away to the edges of the room. "But I am not heir to Farsouth." Klaris's twin brother, older by five minutes, was Jeress's heir.

"One heartbeat away," Essen answered dismissively. "Now then," he turned to his novices. "Let's set up your own bowls and see if we can weave the Mystic."

Istov produced his silver bowl from a pocket and waited for Larrisa to pass him the water jug. Klaris moved to the back of the group, feeling superfluous.

A warm hand touched her shoulder. "Thank you for the demonstration, your Highness." The gray-haired Mollen smiled at her. "As you grow up, I trust that your hands will learn to hold all your powers with wisdom."

Klaris felt the unintended sting of his compliment. "My title is a liability here," she said sharply. "Please call me Klaris."

Mollen inclined his gray head. "Someday I hope to call you 'Weaver.'"

"Maybe then I can get laid."

Mollen laughed with the complacence of an adult considering a young person's passion. Annoyed by his condescension and the way the Mystic was seething as the novices tried to weave, Klaris fled.

Yes, she was young; yes, she had an unusually visceral relationship with the Mystic, but she was still a person. Why did so many of her colleagues treat her with such caution? Didn't they understand the soul-strength, the honesty, the maturity required to weave with such assurance? Didn't they appreciate the depth of scholarship it required? She knew that leadership was lonely, but she wasn't a leader yet.

In her own small chamber high in the round tower of the castle, she kicked wood into her fireplace and let it blaze. Pulling back the heavy curtains, she leaned against the casement and stared up at the moon. The snow slowly melting sent dark drops one by one off the tower roof into the slush far below.

She shivered. Equinox was coming and the Rising with it. The Farsouthian islish did not suffer Rising Fear with the visceral anxiety of the Barians, but all islish people, born and bred to life surrounded by the sea, shared an awareness of the incipient storms.

The moonlight bathed her as she thought again of Istov. She loved the height of him and his shy smile and his large hands. Closing her eyes, she could recapture the excitement of having those warm hands on her body at Solstice and again at Candlemas. He seemed happy enough to please her at the goddess' sabbats, but in between she couldn't seem to hold his attention.

She could sense the working of his magic in the room far below and turned away from the insistent call of the moonlight.

Sunlight poured golden and warm through the window next to the big fire. Professor Lellyn's quill scratched rhythmically across the page open on her lap. She did not look up as Klaris pulled up a stool.

"Let me finish the lines of this poem, my dear," the old woman murmured absently.

Klaris waited. Waited. Waited. Waited. The hard-won peace of her habitual morning sun salutations drained slowly away. Waiting was all she did these days.

Lellyn turned the page and continued to scratch her quill across the paper. One of the castle cats leapt onto Klaris's lap, kneaded her thick woolen dress for a moment, then sat down purring.

"You should learn to purr," Lellyn said, putting down her quill and bending to locate the stopper for the ink bottle.

"First I have to find contentment," Klaris growled, looking down at the cat.

"That comes with wisdom."

"I can think of one or two other ways."

Lellyn cackled but cut right to the heart of the issue. "Weaver Feilor waited two years for his Secret. Weaver Poppeffra waited five."

"It's not just that," Klaris said tightly. "I'm going home after the Rising."

"Really?" Lellyn sat up in surprise. "But I thought—."

"Yes, I know." Klaris interrupted. "A messenger will bring my Secret, and I assume he will bring it here."

"He?"

"I've gotten the Mystic to reveal that much."

Lellyn considered Klaris for a few moments. "What else have you gotten the Mystic to disclose?"

Klaris smiled, and Lellyn relaxed, relishing the return of the girl's habitual enthusiasm. "Tell me."

Klaris rose, dumping the cat to the floor. She walked to the window, turned her back to the light and sat on the sill. "I read through everything I could find about Axterre."

"As the Oracle suggested, yes."

"Then I questioned Simond Kashkavodian—you know, the Nomad fellow who's a Corridor Cadet?"

Again, Lellyn nodded.

Klaris continued: "Simond said Axterre was lost in a maze." She paused, lost for a moment in a labyrinth of her own thoughts.

The professor picked up the cat and settled it onto her own lap.

"Anyway," Klaris went on finally. "I read that the Oracles in Axterre practiced a meditation that allowed them to understand ... things. So, I tried it and found I could see Mystic in a different way. I could, in fact, see its Secrets."

Lellyn's mouth dropped open. The cat stared at Klaris with cogent amber eyes.

"Yes," Klaris admitted. "You know that I saw Emmil Rohan's Secret once he began his attempt to master the Mystic, but I think that was because I had worked within his weavings so often before." She stopped, and Lellyn heard the bitterness in her voice.

"His failure was not your fault, Klaris."

"There is a difference between what my mind and my heart will accept about that."

Lellyn moved the conversation away from painful memories. "These Secrets you've found, do you mean past Weavers' Secrets?"

"Past and future. And many that were unused but might have been. All of them but my own."

Lellyn gasped. A Weaver's Secret was the most private and personal of all spells. That Klaris should know them seemed almost a violation.

"You see," Klaris leaned forward, "you see why my Secret isn't here. The damned Mystic knew I could find it even if I wasn't ready."

"So, you must still wait for this messenger to bring it to you."

"Neat, isn't it?" Klaris asked, clearly frustrated.

Lellyn smiled, deeply relishing the convolutions that this revealed.

"And there's more," Klaris knew that Lellyn loved the mysteries of the Mystic. "When I scry for my messenger, the magic won't work."

"What?" Lellyn sat up, and the poor cat was once again displaced. "The magic won't work, for *you?*"

"No. It's as if I have no magic at all when I try."

Lellyn snapped her fingers, and a scry bowl filled with clear water appeared on the small table beside her chair. "Do it. Let me see."

Klaris breathed deeply. It wasn't easy to scry for someone unknown in the middle of a sunny morning, but it wasn't impossible either. She centered herself and pulled. Nothing. Trying a different approach, she withdrew into herself then opened her soul to the Mystic. It was there, but it would not obey her, would not form the weave.

Eyes closed, she felt Professor Lellyn pulling, tugging, pushing, trying all sorts of techniques to mold Mystic to her will. Nothing.

"Well now, that's something new." Lellyn said at last. "Not very pleasant either."

"No. It's almost like being without magic."

"I think that's what the Dark Fortnight would be like," Lellyn said, looking at Klaris with sharp brown eyes. "Both Bizzleworth and Feilor described it somewhat like that."

"I'll worry about the Dark Fortnight once I have a Secret of my own." Klaris moved her stool closer to the fire.

Professor Lellyn watched her. The old woman had lived at Castle Caledra for nearly fifty years. She'd been Tower Tutor for the last twenty-five. "What do you think the Mystic is trying to teach you, Klaris?" she asked quietly.

"Patience."

"Why?"

"Because I haven't any." Klaris stood up and returned to the window. "For goddess' sake, I watch the novices and acolytes struggle and practice to learn things that I could always do. Even complicated things like protect spells or invisible structures or Secret meditations don't take me long to understand."

"Are there other traits you might lack that you think the Mystic wants you to learn?"

Klaris smiled. "I haven't had enough patience to find out."

Lellyn laughed.

"But there's a strange contradiction here." Klaris went on more seriously. "A paradox, if you will. On the one hand there is an implicit urgency in gifting a magician as young as me with such power. Plus, there's the Oracle ruminating about dragons returning to the Knownlands. On the other hand, you have something holding back and something creating a...a wall to any more progress or any more understanding: I can't find my Secret. The Oracle can't remember their own prophecy.

"Why bring me so far at such a cost just to make me wait?"

"Cost?"

"I've given up my childhood. Emmil Rohan gave up his life."

Klaris stopped and glanced around the great hall. Other magicians were talking in small groups. Three Sagehamites mopped the far end of the room. Used to the arcane and sometimes explosive conversations between the professor and her few tower-tested students, the others tended to stay away.

"Is danger imminent or not?" Lellyn asked quietly.

"I don't know. But I'm tired of living with both possibilities."

"Maybe your Secret will resolve the paradox."

"I can only hope so. But I came to tell you that I'm not going to sit here like some helpless damsel waiting for her fairy prince."

"Helpless you're not."

"No. After the Rising I'll go to Farsouth for the spring."

"You wish to visit your mother?"

"I wish to be among people who don't view me as a child."

"Klaris—."

"Professor. I'm not new here. I realize most people have seen thirty summers before they're able to pass the Dock and Portal tests to become acolytes. When I came here, I *was* a child, and it doesn't help that I'm so short. But it's ten years now that I've been here. That's about the normal preparation for mastery, you know."

"I do know. And you're taller than I am."

Klaris rose to what height she could muster. "I'm going to enjoy some time on the beach at Farsouth. I'll be back by Dayfest."

"And if your messenger shows up with your Secret while you're gone?"

"Tell him to write it down for me."

N eben's sleek yacht cut cleanly through the cold waves and held tightly to the wind. A steady westerly blew off Jax's port beam across a sea that seemed to be resting before the Rising storms that would soon lash it into frothy mountains.

Jax went through the supplies. There was, as promised, plenty of ship-biscuit, fish jerky, dried berries, water, seaspirit in blue glass bottles and fresh water in a sturdy cask. He also found a scuttle full of black firerock for the stove, waterproof cloaks, and thick blankets, as well as the expected spare sails, lines, and other ship gear.

That evening as he watched stars winking in the violet sky, a shiver of Rising Fear tingled through his stomach, but the breeze remained steady, the swells gentle. He couldn't see any land, but he knew where he was.

Kordish nobles trained for knighthood; Barian aristocrats took what they called captaincy trials. Jax had struggled with the horsemanship and sword handling techniques required for Kordish knighthood, but he had proven adept and even gifted at the captaincy skills of sailing and navigation, often winning his class of the yacht regattas, and passing his captaincy when he was only thirty-two Risings old—four Risings (or two years) early.

One of the trials involved sailing solo from Baria up around Sageham Isle through the Barling Narrows and back again. Jax grinned into the night. His first Sageham Solo had actually been with Shallyx. A few Risings older than he and Neben, Shallyx brought an engineer's genius to the art of sailing, and both boys had been in awe of her. She'd smuggled Jax onto her solo sloop largely for her own pleasure during the four-day cruise. He had learned a great deal, some of it even involved sailing.

Jax had returned the favor when it came time for his solo. But the lord admiral had gotten wind of the plan and disqualified Jax's cruise because it wasn't a solo with Shallyx on board, even though she swore she hadn't helped sail. The lord admiral ordered Jax to make a second trip, alone this time. Without distraction, Jax completed the trip in near record-breaking time. Rax's obvious pride in Jax's achievement had overshadowed Bryx's knighthood that same summer. Kordish honors never carried the same weight with the sealord, and the fact that Bryx excelled at such things didn't make up for having failed captaincy several times before passing without distinction.

Overjoyed and a little relieved, Sealord Rax gave Jax the royal sapphire ring as a reward. The ring should, by rights, have been reserved for Bryx's eventual consort, but Rax knew the gift would force any skeptical Barians to acknowledge that at least one of their half-islish princes had inherited the legendary Sharkin understanding of seas and sails.

Jax watched the wind-ripples off to port for a few minutes then let the mainsail out a bit. He settled himself against the tiller and pulled his wooden dragonpipe from his pocket. He thought of Doc, who had given him the pipe, and that led to thoughts of Marith. Goddess, what would Earl Kora do with her and the nyad twins? He twirled the pipe between his fingers. Rippsmarch was an honorable man. He had promised to spare them in return for Jax's confession to treason.

So Jax confessed to spare their lives. Now he was not only a convicted traitor, but a confessed one as well. Midipex would make good use of that. In fact, he could probably justify killing Jax on sight. Goddess damn the xenophobic Kordish.

He sat up frowning. He'd tried to plant some small seeds of doubt about Midipex's integrity, but that hadn't helped him out of the Earl's dungeon. Foby had never even come to visit his cell.

Wrapping his Barian Blue cloak about him, he noted the smooth caress of the silk shirt underneath the heavy wool. He thought of Marith's compassionate eyes and the way she persisted in calling him son, and then of the woman who had died before she could ever do so. Alone in the night, he searched for resolve.

He pulled the Oracle's medallion from under his shirt and held it to the light of his small lantern. Three phases of the moon graced one side; on the other, strange runes spiraled inward to a pentagram.

The medallion was warm in his hand and the light bounced off it into the darkness. This quest the Oracle had given him ought to be impossible, and would certainly be dangerous, but if dragons really were coming back to the Knownlands, he, and every other noble worth his or her title, would have to step up to dangerous and difficult duties. Cross-magic and prejudice would be small troubles in comparison.

He tucked the pendant and chain under his shirt and remembered two gold plaques on the wall of the dark sanctuary. Javix Sharkin was the son of two of the oldest and most noble families in the Knownlands. He had been lord of the slaves in the iron mines. He had walked beside Mother Marith across half the Knownlands. He appreciated, maybe more than most, the privilege of silk shirts and warm cloaks. If he couldn't fulfill the Oracle's mission, who could?

Did his actions make him who he was, or did who he was determine his actions? He picked up his pipe and played into the night, leaving a trail of glowing phosphorescence and fading notes in his wake.

The next day Jax watched the blue sky film over with thin milky clouds. Shivers of Rising Fear ran through him intermittently, but the wind held, and he sailed on. He consciously refused to let his memories of the last Spring Rising panic him. By nightfall the clouds had thickened. Sea and sky were equally black until the moon rose and then everything was equally gray.

In the depth of that gray blend of sea and sky, Jax's yacht passed the mouth of Hanter Lake. Far to sea, he still caught the whiff of sulfur in the air, and the scent brought back the force of despair he'd faced a year ago and the terror of Oblek's dark pit. He'd tried to assert control over his fate, even if it meant nothing more than choosing the method of his own death. He'd sailed into that last spring Rising expecting to die and ready to. Here he was a year later, likely to sail into the impossible Rising storms, again likely to drown, but less willing. The revelation hurt.

The Island of Sageham loomed up from the sea as dawn turned the gray to pink. Jax frowned up at the mackerel-scale clouds. The west wind that had blown so steadily now became fitful, veering now north, now south, stopping all together, then roaring wildly again, slamming into his sails and forcing him to jibe or tack again and again, as the rigging banged and whistled.

The sea rose thick and heavy; the waves seemed unsure where they were supposed to be going and slewed through the sea without any rhythm. Rising Fear ran up and down Jax's spine. He stood at the tiller, willing the sails to stay full and taut. Off to his right, he could see the headland of the Krillian Coast as the sloop glided through the Barling Narrows.

The sun had been up for about an hour when he tied up at the wharf in the little Sageham harbor. He noticed that someone had already pulled all their boats far up on the beach in preparation for the Rising.

He dunked his head in the icy sea and dug a clean shirt out of the packs. Not wanting to waste any more time, he stepped onto the wharf.

The cross-magic struck him like a blow. He bent to retch into the water of the bay. When his belly was empty, he wiped his mouth and stood up again.

He could see the top of the castle walls on the cliff above the bay. He clenched his teeth against the cross-magic and forced himself to start along the path. Someone was coming down. His vision blurred, so he fixed his gaze on the trampled snow and continued walking.

After a moment he found himself face to face with one of the Sagehamites. Jax noted that the man's skin and hair were the same color as the gray walls of the castle above.

"Welcome!" The Sagehamite said in Landish. "We will shield you from the cross-magic."

"You will?" Jax had expected to be repulsed by the Mystic.

"We've been waiting for you."

"You have?"

"You are the Paradox Who Can't Be Found, yes?"

Jax grit his teeth as the words from the prophecy echoed through the fog around him. "Apparently. Yes."

The Sagehamite smiled. "Yes! Yes! Come!" He held out a gray hand to Jax, who took it. The moment he touched the Sagehamite, the nausea and fog of cross-magic vanished. Jax took a deep breath and stood straighter. Able to see more clearly now, he realized that the whole path was lined with Sagehamites.

"I'm Lad Yerran," the first one said, still grinning ear to ear. In fact, all of the Sagehamites were positively beaming.

"Lasses and lads, say a welcome!" Lad Yerran cried.

The Sagehamite lads and lasses cheered as Jax and Lad Yerran walked up the hill between them.

"So, you've been expecting me?" Jax asked, puzzled as he followed Lad Yerran up the hill.

"Sure."

"Do you know who I am?"

Lad Yerran crowed: "We know *what* you are."

"Aye, but do you know my name?"

The lad shook his head. "No, sir. We didn't expect you to be a Dragon either."

"But you knew I was coming—or someone was."

"Yes, sir. It's time. We've been waiting. We've been waiting a very, very long time."

Jax climbed the hill wondering if they would be so pleased with him when he snatched their new Weaver away into the Rising.

Klaris had been moving through her eighth sun salutation, her body warm, her breath steady, when she felt the Dragon force brush the Mystic. She focused her concentration for a moment: a sloop at the dock, a man, with Dragon? She opened herself to the fabric of Mystic that rippled around and through her. She felt the excitement and joy of the lads and lasses.

Her heart began to pound. Could it be? She had finally resigned herself to wait, and now? She continued to move rhythmically through pose and stretch. Briefly she opened her eyes, but the other magicians around her continued to flow through their movements. Every magician at the castle performed the daily sun salutations in order to restore their souls from the drain of working great magic.

All of the others seemed focused, still. She glanced at Professor Lellyn and saw an eyebrow quirk very briefly as the old woman bent toward her toes.

Klaris refocused her own breath: Inhale. Stretch. Exhale. Bend.

Finished, she lay flat on the warm stones, assimilating the silence and unity brought to her by the exercises.

Father Mallix rang a small clear bell to bring the magicians back to their bodies, back to the day.

Klaris sat up, eyes still closed, and bowed into her reverence. The Mystic hummed.

She opened her eyes and found herself face to face with one of the castle cats.

"The wait is over," said the cat.

Klaris stared open-mouthed. "Did you just speak?"

"Ummm." Purred the cat.

"Have you always been able to talk?"

"The time was not right."

"And it's right now?"

"It is time." The cat's eyes gleamed.

Klaris ignored the exclamations of the other Mystics who were backing away from the cat. She stood and ran up the stairs to her chamber in the highest turret. She thought she was ready for her weaving, but when Mystic could still surprise her, maybe she wasn't as ready as she thought. She couldn't afford surprises, not with what she was planning to do this day.

She stripped off the loose robe she wore for the sun salutations and ducked into one of the woolen dresses from her wardrobe. Without thinking, she used a bit of magic to do up the laces in back. From a gilt box she pulled a golden Farsouthian medallion on a long chain and looped it over her head. For a moment then, she paused. She took a deep breath, feeling the residual peace of the morning's salutations. Yes. She was ready. Damn ready.

All the residents of Caledra gathered in the Great Hall. Every one of them knew that Klaris had been waiting for a messenger to bring her the Secret of her mastery and knew that a stranger had arrived, but a Dragon? This was unprecedented.

The lads and lasses were convinced that this was the messenger, so the Mystics whispered among themselves about the discomfort of a Dragon here at the heart of Mystic and the weirdness of the talking cat.

Klaris made her way to the heavy wooden doors and threw them open just as Jax climbed to the last step.

"Sweet goddess," she gasped in Ancient.

"Princess Klaris." Jax answered in the same language. He bowed, averting his gaze from the disappointment on her face. He hadn't expected that.

For a moment no one spoke. Then an Ilyian woman stepped from behind Klaris. "You!" She said in Landish. "You were that slave on the Vrillbridge road."

"Indeed." Jax naturally switched to Landish. "I am Javix Sharkin and I've been sent here by the Oracle."

Speechless, Klaris reached out to touch him. He flinched away from her. Klaris struggled to overcome her profound disappointment. Javix Sharkin couldn't be her messenger. She mustered her Landish: "Your Highness, please come in. Have a seat by the fire, here."

He did not sit. She watched his sea blue eyes take in the majesty of the great hall and her own place at the center of Caledra's power. She noted the hard look when those eyes settled on her.

Confusion colored her disappointment, but she was glad he had gotten himself away from the trolls. "Pleased I am to see that you are well, and that you survived that troll."

Her broken landish was at odds with all the other forces she balanced. He bit back a sarcastic response. "We don't have time for pleasantries, my lady. I have been sent by the Oracle to take the Weaver to Kree. Before the Rising. That means we need to leave right now."

An old woman wrapped in layers of knitted scarves seated herself in a chair between Jax and Klaris and looked up at them. "There is no Weaver, my lord."

"Prince Javix, this is Professor Lellyn. She's the Tower Tutor." Klaris made the introduction.

"When will there be a Weaver?" Jax asked with growing impatience.

"When the Mystic is ready." Klaris remembered those golden whiskers on an emaciated slave.

Jax ran frustrated fingers through his hair.

"We've been waiting for a messenger, your Highness," Professor Lellyn said gently. "A messenger who will bring the next Weaver her Secret."

"What secret?"

"It's the key to the mastery," Klaris explained tersely.

"Are you our messenger, my lord?" The professor peered at him through narrowed brown eyes. "Are you the messenger we've been waiting for?"

Jax frowned. "What could I know about Mystic? I'm a Dragon."

"That would be a paradox, wouldn't it?" Klaris asked grimly.

Jax stiffened.

Klaris felt the magic wrap itself around him in that same odd way. When she spoke, it was almost as if she was talking only to herself, stumbling in Landish. "Even there on the Vrillbridge Road something about you that snagged the magic. And it swirls like that around the sealord too. Somehow you both impact the Weave."

"Then why did you leave me with the trolls, your Highness?"

Klaris frowned, stung by Jax's tone. "I was not permitted to help."

Jax raised a very skeptical eyebrow.

"It's true, my lord," Lellyn said. "Klaris was constrained under house arrest so that she could not get to you or anyone who could help you. We Mystics must live closely with the trolls, and we try very hard to be unobtrusive. Klaris wanted to find you and buy you away from the slave pens, but she wasn't given the freedom to do so."

Jax took a deep breath and felt the Rising Fear jangle along his nerves. He heard the linguistic struggle in Klaris's accent, so he spoke next in Islish. It was the language the Oracle had used with him. "The Oracle noted that none of us is free. Right now, for example, I have a very clear obligation to get the Weaver, or someone, off of this island before the Rising that is beginning to blow out there."

"Free?" Klaris breathed in fluent Farsouthian Islish. "What exactly did the Oracle say?"

Jax felt the Oracle's words come out of him of their own accord: "None of us is free, but we can be masters of our own destiny."

Klaris was still looking at him, but he could tell she was no longer seeing him. Slowly, a smile blossomed on her face, and she visibly relaxed.

"Of course," she whispered to herself. "Of course."

In that moment, with the magic flowing through her and the firelight glowing through her effusive hair, Jax thought she was every bit as beautiful as the fairy queen herself, and as powerful.

"Professor Lellyn," Klaris now spoke Ancient, "will you please help the lads and lasses shield Prince Javix?"

"Yes, Klaris. You go right ahead." Professor Lellyn reached a hand to Jax, her eyes sparkling with anticipation.

On the Vrillbridge Road, Klaris and her fellow magicians had woven a protect spell around him to shield him from their magic. This shimmering bubble was much thicker and stronger. He could see Klaris and the others around him, but it was as if he was under-water, looking out at people on the surface.

Klaris was going deep into the Mystic, that much he could tell. He didn't have the characteristic nausea or difficulty breathing usually associated with cross-magic, but he felt the pressure of her weave pushing against the shield. He sat down on the stone floor.

It seemed to take hours. The pressure grew; the shield shook and shimmered. Once it seemed almost to split and he felt the lads and lasses work to withstand the force of Klaris's weave and hold the bubble together.

Suddenly Klaris raised her arms. A bright orb of fire glowed between her hands. Slowly, she brought her hands together. The light shone through her skin, red and pulsing. She whispered something and the fire exploded. Rainbow sparkles filled the room and landed in glittering ashes.

It was over. Klaris collapsed to the floor. The magical shield fell away, and Jax felt cool ashes settle in his hair. Ecstatic Mystics cheered, danced, laughed, shouted, and swung each other off the floor with great whoops of joy. The Great Hall, in fact the entire building, was completely changed, rearranged by the powerful magic of a new Weaver.

He watched a tall lad lift the inert form of Princess Klaris off the floor and carry her away. Professor Lellyn wrapped Jax in a tangle of shawls that seemed to be a hug.

"Oh, she did it!" crowed the professor. "Did it like no one else could even have imagined!"

"So, it worked?"

"Worked? Worked! I'll say it worked. My lord, she increased the Mystic weave more than ten-fold!"

Jax wondered why no one seemed worried about Klaris. "She didn't look good when the lad carried her away."

"Well, I guess you've never seen this kind of thing, have you?"

"No. But I remember what happened when that mastery attempt failed last spring."

"Ah," Lellyn's eyes darkened. "Klaris will be fine. Once her Dark Fortnight is over, she'll have such power as no Weaver has ever known."

"Dark Fortnight?"

"She'll have no magic for the next fortnight. It's always the way after one masters the Mystic. It gives the new Weaver a time to rest and recover without magic. The mastery weave, as you probably noticed, is the most difficult weaving. It drains the soul, dangerously."

"Dark Fortnight," Jax repeated, realizing that Klaris would face a very long, cold and perilous journey without her magic. And so would he. He stood up and ignored the rumble of hunger in his stomach.

The lads and lasses were hauling out long tables and preparing a feast. The magicians had already opened casks of ale and wine and were celebrating.

Professor Lellyn poked a finger at him. "Interesting, that too."

"What?"

"You're not protected anymore, and yet there's no cross-magic, is there?"

"No. No cross-magic, but plenty of Rising Fear."

"Come eat, my lord. Let Klaris rest."

Jax grabbed some bread from a table but refused an offered stein of ale and went in search of Klaris.

He climbed stairs, peered into chambers, and noticed that the sun was already westering toward a purple bank of swirling clouds.

With growing desperation, he stopped one of the lasses in the hall and asked her to take him to Klaris.

At last, he found her, unconscious, on a bed in a room high in a tower turret. The tall lad stoked the fire.

"Will you please pack a bag for Princess Klaris?" Jax asked curtly. "She'll need warm clothes, good shoes, a cloak, and whatever else she might want from here. I don't think she'll be back soon."

The lad considered him carefully for a long minute then went to do as Jax asked.

"What are you doing here, my lord?" The same Ilyian woman from the Vrillbridge Road strode into the room.

"The Oracle ordered me to get the Weaver off Sageham before the Rising," Jax said. "That gives me about half an hour."

"You can't take her now. Not when she's so weak!"

"I don't have a choice."

"Lad Yob," the woman turned toward the lad, who had returned with a satchel of Klaris's things. "Please fetch Professor Lellyn and Father Mallix."

Jax slung the satchel over his shoulder and bent to pick Klaris up off the bed. He wrapped her in the thick down quilt and lifted her.

Feeling like a thief, Jax ignored the Ilyian Mystic's protests and carried Klaris out of the room and down the winding stairs. The other Mystics were reveling loudly in the great hall. At the bottom of the stairs, Jax paused. Corridors led right and left, while straight ahead more stairs descended to the noise of the celebration.

A gold and white cat sat looking at Jax.

"How do I get out of here?" he muttered to himself.

"Follow me," answered the cat.

"Sure. Why not?" Jax shook his head, but he followed the cat.

He had settled Klaris, still unconscious, into the cuddy of the sloop and was hoisting sails when the priest, Professor Lellyn, and several others arrived to stop him.

"Prince Jax! Please wait!" The priest, an old Barian, bent to hold the gunwale of the small boat. "The Weaver should not travel now."

"I agree with you, Father," Jax snapped.

"Then stay here. Bide the Rising with us and let Klaris recover."

Jax hauled on a line and a sail began to fill. "Listen to me, all of you. The Oracle commanded me to take the Weaver off Sageham before the Rising. It didn't seem concerned about anyone's comfort. We're so late now we may not make the Krillian coast at all. Give us a good hard push, Father. Now!"

Rising Fear boiling in his own Islish blood, Father Mallix understood the desperation in Jax's voice. He turned his grip and shoved the bow into the wind.

The sails snapped tight, and the little boat leapt away.

6

Jax re-fastened the hatch over the cuddy, buckled on his slicker, and squinted into the rain, trying to see what the wind was doing. Thick curtains of precipitation already obscured the distant line of the Krillian Coast, but he could still see the looming rock of Sageham behind him.

With a sudden bang, the wind shifted. The boom swung across the deck, and he came about into a dunking wave. Neben's boat was made to the highest of Baria's excellent standards. It bounced over or dove through the unpredictable waves, its tackle straining, but holding under the force of the wind. Jax removed his thoughts from his last experience sailing in a Spring Rising and concentrated on guiding the boat toward the land.

The day grew darker and the rain turned to ice, which froze along the sheets and weighted the sails. He came about again and again, trying to find the right wind to blow him ashore, straining his ears for the sound of waves crashing on the beach in the darkness. All he could hear was the scream of the rigging, so he hit the shoreline waves unexpectedly and sideways. He thrust the tiller around, hauled on the mainsheet, and held his breath.

The little sloop wallowed sideways on the crest of the wave, then turned its bow to shore and surfed down the incline toward the sandy beach.

Jax kicked loose the dagger board, released the sail and coasted to shore. Relief flooded through him at the crunch of sand under the hull. He splashed into the icy water and shoved the boat onto the beach.

He paused only a minute to catch his breath. Sleet blew sideways across the waves. He leapt over the gunwale, dropped and furled the mainsail then rigged the jib to catch the wind. He jumped back to the sand and went to the stern and began to push.

It was night before he got the sloop safely into the line of twisted trees that stood above the beach. He furled the jib and coiled the lines with numb fingers then slipped through the hatch into the cuddy.

Inside, it was pitch black.

"Weaver Klaris? My lady?"

When she didn't answer, he used his Dragon force to light a lantern. Klaris lay in the hammock where he had settled her. Her face was slack and for a moment, he wasn't sure she was breathing, but when he reached out to her, she flinched away from the touch of his cold fingers.

Jax finally realized how cold and hungry he was. He went back outside one more time to open the chimney flue then fastened the hatch against the sleet and snow. Inside, he lit a small fire in the galley, stripped off his wet clothes and found dry ones. He warmed water for tea and drank it as he ate some biscuit and dried fish, wondering why the tea he made never tasted right.

He settled himself in his own warm blankets in the second hammock and looked again at Klaris. Rising Fear still tingled on the tips of his fingers, but mostly he felt an overwhelming sense of relief. He snuffed the light and fell asleep.

A cold blast of snow and wind woke him with a start.

Klaris had opened the hatch, letting in dim sunlight and the blizzard. The wind slammed the hatch shut again. She turned back to her hammock, dug around the blankets until she found her green cloak and wrapped it around her shoulders.

Again, she pushed open the hatch and ducked her head into the blast.

"Here, my lady." Jax rose to help her hold the heavy wooden hatch cover so she could slip out into the gray morning. Snow blew everywhere.

Jax grabbed his own cloak, shoved his feet into his boots and followed her.

She climbed over the gunwale of the boat and jumped down to the snow-covered ground and began to walk away among the trees.

"Your highness?"

Klaris looked back at him a little confused. "I need...privacy, my lord." Her Landish was thick and awkward.

He answered her in Islish. "There's a head on the boat."

Klaris looked around her at the waving arms of the naked trees and the black waves on the heaving sea. Hard-blown snow stung her cheeks and clotted her eyelashes.

Jax swung himself out of the boat and took Klaris's arm. "Come, my lady."

Once back inside the cuddy, he pointed her to the head and relit the fire. After scooping fresh snow into the kettle, he latched the hatch.

Klaris returned and took a seat on a small bench near the galley stove. She looked out the porthole at the blowing snow. When she spoke, her voice was a small, shaky whisper. "I can't find the Mystic."

Jax nodded. "Is that the Dark Fortnight?"

"Yes." Klaris whispered. "I should be at home, at Caledra. Not out here. Wherever the dragons *here* is."

"The Krillian Coast."

"How did we get here?"

"This boat."

She shook her head as if to clear it. "Why?"

"Because the goddess-damned Oracle commanded me to get the Weaver off of Sageham before the Rising." He handed her a cup of tea and realized that no one had spoken to Klaris since she'd taken the weave. "Congratulations, Weaver."

Klaris responded with equal irony. "Thank you, Prince Javix."
He turned to poke at the fire.

Klaris watched him for a moment. "My lord, I am truly sorry that I was not able to get you away from that troll. I can't imagine what he must have done to you. But as Professor Lellyn explained, I was not permitted to do anything except write a letter."

"Right. Six or seven of the most powerful Mystics in the Knownlands were worried about one lunatic troll?" Jax didn't conceal his contempt.

Klaris shook her head. "No. It wasn't about the trolls at all. The issue was really that Emmil Rohan was mad at me. It was all politics. I'm sure you can understand that."

"Yeah. We're just pawns."

"Isn't that what the Oracle was trying to tell us?" she whispered, taking a sip of her tea. She coughed and looked critically into the thick brown brew. "Strong tea you brew, my lord."

Jax took a sip from his own mug and grimaced. "I never get it right. Here, have a biscuit, my lady."

A particularly savage gust of wind shook the boat; tea sloshed out of Klaris' mug onto her skirt. She shivered again. "I think we can let the honorific go. Don't you, Javix?"

Jax met her green eyes. Without her magic, she seemed so thin and frail, her black hair flying about in curly wisps. He thought about the trolls' dungeon where he spent the last Spring Rising, one year ago, aching from Oblek's nearly fatal beating. He remembered gritting his teeth against the pain and forcing himself to pace back and forth through the rotting straw, limping over the legs of his fellow slaves, striving to rebuild his strength. He'd worked so hard, nurturing the hope of freedom. But freedom hadn't come.

"Call me Jax," he said curtly.

Klaris frowned at the tone and braved another sip of the tea. After a while she spoke again. "Why did the Oracle want the Weaver off of Sageham before the Rising?"

"Dragons."

"Swearing isn't an answer."

"I'm not swearing. I'm taking about real dragons. They're coming back, apparently."

"Ah. The Oracle told me the same thing, but that doesn't explain why I had to leave Caledra before the Rising."

Jax set his empty mug on the floor and pulled his quilt around his shoulders. "They said the Millennial Cycle was coming due and it was time to remember."

"Remember what?"

"They did not tell me."

"Dragons," mused Klaris. "Maybe the answers are at Kree."

"Answers for you; a traitor's death for me."

Klaris frowned at him and declined the teapot he offered. "I heard you stole state secrets from the Kordish."

"I did not."

She smiled tightly. "Perhaps you are a pawn after all."

He admired the bravado in that answer, given her circumstances. "Here," he took the scrap of prophecy from his pocket and handed it to her. He could see the black ink of Lexyl's writing and the lines that Oracle had seared into the parchment.

Klaris read, frowned up at him, and read the words again. "That's you, Jax Sharkin. A paradox that can't be found. You don't know how many times I tried to scry for you after I had to leave you with the trolls, and then when I was looking for my messenger, not realizing that was you as well. But this still doesn't explain why we had to leave Caledra in such a rush, and it doesn't tell why we must go to Kree."

"Maybe there's more to the prophecy."

"You think?" She considered him. "You read Ancient?

Jax took the parchment back from her. "Yes. I like history and so much of it is written in Ancient. Also, Ancient was something I could study in both Kree and Baria. Growing up in both places I had to complete all the required courses in both but in only half the time: navigation, for example, on Baria and viniculture at Kree. But

Ancient was the same in both places, so I could just learn it at a regular pace."

"Not many nobles take the time to learn Ancient at all," she said. "My own brother doesn't know two words of it."

"Neither does mine. Let's see how you do with this." He pulled the Oracle's chain from his shirt and handed it to her. "The Oracle said this marked me as their special messenger. I can't read the runes."

She considered the three moons one side, then flipped it over. Silently she deciphered the twelve runes. "These are archaic. I wish I could feel the magic of this gold."

"Can you read it?"

She pointed to the first rune and read in order as they spiraled to the center. "*Earth, water, fire, air, magic, music, nyads, fae....*" She paused a moment. "This next one is tricky, but I think it's *mixed blood.* After that there's *megalith, dragon, and paradox.*"

"Paradox?" Jax nearly spat. "How is that helpful? It's supposed to tell people not to kill me!"

"Well, if it's any consolation there are probably only a handful of people who can actually read these runes." She handed it back to him. "I could, perhaps, translate it differently if necessary."

"That's a good idea." Jax ducked his head under the chain. "Perhaps in Landish it reads, treat the bearer with generosity, feed him well, and give him lots of fine wine."

She laughed, but shook her head. "I should have spent more time speaking Landish, probably. Most people who come to Caledra need the practice with Ancient, so speaking Landish, or Islish for that matter, is discouraged."

Her struggles with Landish felt suddenly overwhelming and merged with her general fatigue. She moved to get back into her hammock but struggled as it swung away from her.

Jax rose to hold the ropes and watched her pull the quilts up to her ears. A blast of wind shook the boat and he had to catch himself against the walls of the cuddy. He considered her green eyes, gleaming at him over the edge of the quilts.

"Can I get you anything?"

She didn't answer right away. He watched her blink and work to steady herself. "If you could find the Mystic, that would be nice. It's gone, and I can't sense anything."

She closed her eyes, and before Jax could come up with an answer, he realized she was asleep again. He added a lump of firerock to the stove and listened to the roar of the wind and the pounding of the surf. Whatever was coming, be it dragons, or the more immediate dangers of weather and monsters and trolls, he realized that Weaver Klaris was bound as tightly by the Oracle's chains as he was.

Long, snowy days and nights followed. Jax kept a tally of days so he would know when the Rising was over. He didn't want to be deceived by a temporary lull in the storms. He walked up and down the beach, usually at sunrise and sunset, when he could most clearly judge direction from the sun. He confirmed that they had landed somewhere on the Krillian coast, north of the great inlet called the Merg. Occasionally Barian whalers sailed these frigid seas, but usually they left these parts to the trolls and the monsters.

Mostly, Jax sat before the fire, played his dragonpipe, and thought about dragons. He reviewed history lessons learnt in both Baria and Kree about how dragons drenched cities in fire and death. The Barian islish had suffered in particular because they had all gathered for safety at Nec. When the dragons came and destroyed the city, most Barians had perished.

But the dragons hadn't gone everywhere. They'd ignored Farsouth and The Hantland. As he sat in the dark, wind-shivered boat, Jax began to strategize ways that Baria and Kordon might better survive a second dragon interregnum.

Klaris slept. After a few days she found her satchel and dug out a skein of yarn and some knitting needles. Wordlessly, she sat next to Jax by the stove and slowly began to knit.

"What are you making?" he asked.

"Strength."

"Looks like a scarf."

She smiled. "That, too."

On the fifth day, she attempted a few sun salutations while Jax went on his morning walk along the beach. He didn't stay out long. The wind was howling like a living beast and his breath froze on his whiskers. He returned to find her shaking with fatigue, trying to stoke the fire.

"Here. A little Dragon force will do it." He flicked his magic at the firerock, and flames leapt in the little stove.

A gust of wind shook the boat. "You're shivering," he noted.

"You have ice in your hair."

Jax pulled the quilts off the hammocks and wrapped them around them both. "We'll have to warm each other up."

He put the kettle on the stove then sat back on the bench with Klaris to wait for it to boil.

"You're dripping on me," she protested.

He used a blanket to towel off the wet tendrils of his hair. "We're melting the ice between us."

"Is there ice between us?"

Jax looked at her and her beautiful green islish eyes and remembered the devastation of finding himself still enslaved, as Doc drove him up to Hilsen Vale last spring.

The wind screamed. Finally, the kettle whistled, and he realized he didn't want there to be ice between him and Klaris.

"I've had enough tea," Klaris said cautiously, as Jax rose and set out the mugs.

"I was thinking of something more warming." He dug into the food locker and pulled out a blue glass bottle. "Have you ever had Barian seaspirit?"

"I don't think so." She watched him pour a dollop of the clear liquor into each mug then top it with boiling water.

"It's not considered genteel, so no self-respecting Barian would have offered it to a noble lady." He was digging in the food locker again and finally surfaced with a small brown nut and a little metal grater. He shaved some of the nut into each mug.

"Have I lost my status, or have you lost yours?" she asked.

"I've lost everything." He handed her a mug and sat back down, wrapping the blankets around them both again.

"I feel that way too, without the Mystic in me anymore." She sipped the hot drink. "Whew. That is rather nasty."

Jax looked at the light and shadows of the firelight on Klaris's skin. He listened to the roar of the wind and enjoyed feeling the warmth of her body next to him. He sipped his own seaspirit and felt its heat spread through him.

Klaris felt him relax. She snuggled a little closer to him and finished her drink.

Warm and soothed, Klaris's fatigue swamped her. She leaned against his chest and closed her eyes.

"Are we still betrothed?" he asked suddenly.

She didn't want to wake up. "Can't be."

"I know. But did our parents ever release us?"

She looked up at him. "I'm sure your father would have demanded my mother release you when I achieved the Tower level. I couldn't have hand-fasted with you after that."

"Tower level?"

"It's the highest level at Caledra. There are only four other Tower-tested Mystics living in all the Knownlands."

"When did you achieve that?"

"Midsummer, three years ago."

"My father was dead then."

"Oh."

"Bryx mentioned our betrothal. He told me I couldn't honor it."

"He's right." Klaris closed her eyes again.

Jax felt her breathing. He watched the firelight entwine itself around her curls and began to wonder how he would untangle this situation. Betrothal or no, they had at least another week stuck here and nothing to do but share each other's warmth.

The next morning Jax found monster tracks in the snow. The beasts had circled around the boat at a distance. He peered through the swirling blizzard, sure that the monsters must be watching him from somewhere among the bare, gray trees.

Back inside the cuddy, he found a boat hook and two long fish knives.

Klaris looked up from her knitting and frowned.

He met her gaze. "There've been monsters nearby."

She looked around at the stout beams of the boat. "Can they get in here?"

He shrugged, setting the knives by the hatchway. After a few moments, he rose again and began digging through the food boxes. Neben had provided enough for a month, and the Rising wouldn't last that long. He set out some packets of fish jerky and several Vitran limes.

Klaris watched as he went back outside to fill a pot with snow. He set it on the stove and when the water was warm, he added the jerky. While the dried fish softened fragrantly, he tied some spare cloth to a coupe extra spars and drizzled oil on it. He returned to the stove with more cloth and wrapped up balls of rehydrated fish, squirting lime juice all over them.

Klaris wrinkled her nose. "Do monsters like fish?"

He shrugged. "I don't know, but I bet they're hungry and the smell of this should interest them."

"It would interest me to have the smell elsewhere," she noted.

He grinned. "That's the idea. We'll toss these stinky packets out away from the boat. Then we'll wave these torches to drive the monsters away. I hope they'll take the food and leave us alone."

Crashing blows awoke them that night. Monster clubs thudded on the wood of the cuddy.

Klaris sat up in her hammock, shrinking away from the snarls and grunts of the monsters outside. Jax grasped one of the torches. When a monster club finally broke through the wood above the hatchway, Jax was waiting. A monster arm, hairy and grasping, snaked into the cuddy. Jax used his force to light the torch and shoved the burning thing at the monster's arm.

Singed fur sent a foul smoke through the cuddy. Jax shoved the hatch open. He lit a second torch and handed both to Klaris. "Wave these about."

Through the falling snow, Klaris saw torchlight reflected in six or seven sets of eyes. They stood back from the boat now, one of them licking his singed arm.

Jax took the smelly balls of fish and lime and threw them over the monsters' heads to the darkness beyond. The creatures seemed pleased to turn their backs on the fire and chased after the balls of food. Jax and Klaris stood in the wind and snow waving the torches until the monsters disappeared into the night.

"Are they gone?" Klaris's teeth were chattering.

"I think so." He doused the torches and stoked the stove. Closing the hatch, he surveyed the hole the monsters had made. With a small hammer and spare slats, he quickly repaired the break.

"Do you think they'll come back?" Klaris was burrowed deep into her quilts.

"Maybe. If they're hungry enough." He climbed back into his hammock.

"I feel so numb," she said.

"The stove will warm us up in a few minutes."

"It's not that kind of numb," she said. "Although, I am freezing. Without the Mystic I can't sense the world the way I'm used to. Some sensations are more intense, like smells. Your fish packets were awful. And I am constantly freezing. But nothing is as sharp or clear as it should be. I feel muted, muffled. It's terrifying."

Jax felt his own anxiety curl tightly in his gut. He rolled out of his hammock and took her, quilts and all, in his arms. "Yes. It's terrifying to be marooned like this." He felt her go limp. "You'll get the Mystic back."

"Sure. And I've supposedly learned to be patient."

He held her tighter. "Tomorrow, you're one day closer."

Klaris liked the warmth of his arms around her. She took deep breaths to steady and calm herself. Before long she fell asleep.

Jax sat holding her, staring into his own fears. Everyone knew monsters hated fire. He gulped down revulsion as he remembered the images of Axterre in flames that the Oracle's ghost had shown him. But what kept Jax awake that long night, was not the fear of monsters, but trolls.

The Spring Rising was hunting season. He knew that parties of trolls roamed the Forest Krill, seeking monsters. A troll could track a monster through new snow, old snow, no snow. The trolls could smell them, it seemed.

And now monster tracks led right to their boat.

7

Klaris awoke feeling warm and safe. With a start, she realized that this came from being securely held in Jax's arms. He was so different from Bryx, Jax was. She wondered for a few moments about this, finally noting to herself how different she was from her own twin. She slipped free to use the head and stoke the fire for tea. Jax sat amid her quilts, rubbing his face.

She glanced at him and frowned. "Did you sleep?"

He just shook his head.

In a few moments Klaris handed him a cup of perfectly brewed tea. "Are you afraid the monsters will return?"

"No. I'm afraid trolls will track the monsters to us."

"Trolls? But they don't want us." Klaris dug in her pack for her hairbrush. "Maybe they'd help us get to The Hant."

"Maybe." Jax watched the gray morning light lose itself in Klaris's dark curls. "Or maybe they'd take us for slaves. Me anyway. You they'd just kill."

"Why?" Klaris breathed.

"You have too much Mystic."

"But—." she stopped at the bleak look on Jax's face.

"We're not safe here anymore," he went on as if she hadn't spoken. "I'll rig a tent out of the spinnaker. It won't be as comfortable as the boat, but it will do until you can use the Mystic to build us a shelter."

"A tent...."

"We'll go a mile or so down the coast at low tide," Jax said, thinking aloud. "When the tide comes in, it will erase the signs of our passage so the trolls can't track us. We can move camp from time to time so we're not just sitting there like a beached whale. And when the Rising is over, we can come back and sail away."

Klaris looked out the porthole at the snow blowing in the stiff wind. "How long have we been here?"

Jax didn't have to look at his tally marks. "Seven days."

"Seven more days in my Dark Fortnight."

"The Rising will last a bit longer." He stood up and began digging in the lockers. "We'll have to carry as much food and firerock as possible. Let's eat a big breakfast then we'll go. The tide will be out by noon."

It took all the dark and windy afternoon to move. Jax returned two times to the sloop to bring out more supplies. On his final trip back to Klaris, he waded in the waves of the incoming tide to make sure the trolls couldn't trace his steps.

Jax had to fight the wind to arrange the spinnaker sail into a make-shift tent. Klaris provided engineering suggestions. Eventually with the support of a couple boathooks and a lot of rope, they had enough of a shelter to keep them out of the wind and snow. Jax didn't want to risk a fire, so they drank cold water instead of tea with their ship-biscuit and dried fish.

The stormy night howled around them. Without a fire, the inside of the tent was completely black and very cold.

Klaris sat wrapped in her blankets. "I am truly appreciating the Mystic right now."

"We trekked across half the Knownlands with no Mystic and used a tent," he said to encourage her. "It works."

"Who's we?"

"Mother Marith and two nyads. Marith's son bought me when... when you didn't."

Klaris lay down. The ground was as hard as Jax's tone. "Tell me what happened to you," she asked softly.

He lay among his own quilts and spoke to the darkness. He told her about the slave pens and the trip in Doc's bouncing buggy across the Hantish steppes, away from the sea and up to Hilsen Vale.

"Why didn't you tell them who you were?" she asked. "Surely they'd have freed you and helped you find your way home."

He sat up. He couldn't see her in the dark, but the memory of his humiliation and despair were vivid. "Sweet goddess, Klaris. I was so...lost. Marith said I was broken, and she wasn't just talking about bones."

Klaris remembered the look in his eyes as he asked for her help outside the iron mines. She had not helped. Now here he was endangering himself to care for her at the Oracle's command. "I didn't help you, did I?"

"No. But Marith did."

"Marith. The druid with the tent." Klaris heard him settle back into his quilts. The wind howled, straining the ropes and shaking the fabric.

Klaris spoke again. "I wonder if your Marith had some comforting words to help deal with the discomfort of sleeping on the hardness of the Holy Mother."

"Spoken like a true princess."

"Spoken like a true Mystic."

He laughed and thought of sleeping on, or next to, Klaris' soft body.

Warmed by his laughter, she closed her eyes and soon slept.

He woke in the night. The wind bent the tent almost sideways. He smelled smoke and heard distant shouting. Jumping out of his quilts, he groped in the dark for his cloak and boots then scrambled out of the shelter.

A red glow broiled in the distance where they had left the boat. He couldn't see more than that. Rough shouts and calls drifted to him on the smoke-filled wind. He knew that Neben's beautiful sloop would be no more than ashes by morning.

"What is it?" Klaris had quietly come to stand beside him.

"The boat. The trolls found it."

"Sweet goddess," Klaris breathed. "You were right to pack us out of there."

Jax didn't answer. Finally, thoroughly chilled by the icy wind and the reality of being marooned here on the Krillian Coast, he crawled back under the blowing fabric of the tent.

"I guess we'll have to walk to The Hant after all," Klaris said softly, rolling into her quilts.

In the morning, Jax used the sailcloth tent as a pack and loaded as much food and firerock as he could carry. Together they bundled Klaris's quilts into her satchel. Jax didn't think she would be able to handle more. She was still so frail and listless.

Overhead the clouds hung low and black. The wind still ripped across the waves and blew through the trees, but the snow held off. Jax paused for a moment, looking up and down the coast.

"Let's walk along the shore. There's no snow to wade through and the waves will erase our footprints." He hefted the awkward bundle onto his back.

"Wouldn't it be more direct to go overland?" Klaris looked behind her at the snow-covered hills that rolled off to the south.

"It would be." Jax nodded. "But it would also be easier for the trolls to track us."

"I see." Klaris's voice sounded very small in the blowing wind.

Jax walked down the beach to the hard wet sand right at the edge of the waves. The incoming tide would soon erase their footsteps.

The day brightened slowly, under the thick clouds. Walking in front, Jax's longer stride put him far ahead of the small woman. He stopped to wait, noting the exhaustion evident in Klaris's shuffling steps.

She gave him a brave smile when she caught up. "Your legs are longer than mine."

"And I've spent the last several months walking across the Knownlands, so I'm more used to this kind of thing than you are."

"Yes, your journey with Marith and the tent. Tell me about that," Klaris asked softly.

Knowing that conversation would help pass the miles, Jax fell into step on the seaward side of Klaris. As they walked, he told her about the long walk from Hilsen Vale to Dishroc.

"Are you sure they were the ruins of Axterre?" she demanded, as he got to that part of the story.

"I'm sure." He didn't elaborate, not wanting to remember the horror of the ghost Oracle. Snow began to thicken the wind.

Suddenly the ground under them lurched. Jax stumbled into a wave. Klaris fell to the wet sand. The earth heaved and rolled. There was no sound, just the wash of the waves.

"Dragons," Jax muttered when the rocking stopped. He reached a hand to help Klaris stand up.

"I think that was an earthquake," she said, brushing the damp sand off her mittens.

"I think you're right." Something made Jax turn to look back in the direction of Sageham. The island was hidden in the shroud of falling snow. He felt a lurch in his belly, a feeling similar to when the old Weaver had died. Quickly, he glanced at Klaris, but she didn't seem to feel anything. Her green eyes watched the Rising-tossed waves.

She frowned. "What's happening to the sea?"

The waves were pulling away from the coastline, revealing seaweed-covered rocks and flopping fish. "It looks as if someone has pulled the plug," she whispered.

"Oh no," Jax breathed. "Run!" He grabbed Klaris's hand and bounded up the beach towards higher ground inland. They made it to the trees, and Jax dragged Klaris bodily to the top of a small hill.

When the great wave crashed upon the Krillian coast, it swept up the ashes of Neben's boat and tore up thousands of trees. It swirled around the small hill, making it an island. The wave came again and then again, each time creeping a little higher up the slope, and sucking trees back out to sea when it left.

"Sweet goddess," Klaris sunk to her knees. "Monsters, storms, earthquakes, tidal waves. I'm afraid to imagine what's coming next."

Jax stood squinting into the snow at the black sea. "I'm afraid for wherever that wave hits next."

Klaris looked up at him then followed the direction of his gaze. Sharing his islish heritage, she knew that both Baria and Farsouth lay hunkered down for the Rising, vulnerable to the deep force that surged towards their unsuspecting shores.

"That's your prophecy too, isn't it?" she asked softly.

"I wish I could warn them."

Klaris rose to stand next to him. He felt her reach for the Mystic but find nothing.

"Can you use mine?"

She saw the grief and desperation in his eyes before he turned again to look away to the south.

"I'm always in the wrong place at the wrong time," he explained. "I'm never where Bryx needs me to be."

Klaris thought of her own family on Farsouth. She reached out to touch Jax's arm, searching for the small force of his magic: nothing.

"Call it," she ordered.

He pulled it, but with no focus, the power splintered and scattered into the windblown snow.

She felt it briefly, but only in an irritating, fleeting way like the snow that hit her skin then vanished.

Klaris set her teeth and pulled again on her own Mystic with the instinctive assurance of old habit. For a moment she felt a thread of power, then nothing. Again, she grasped for it and sensed something actively blocking her. Savagely, she pulled at Jax's magic. Something shifted, as if a curtain had slipped open then quickly pulled shut again.

"Damn!" she swore in frustration, opening her eyes to find Jax steadying her against the force of the wind. Below them, the corpses of the trees floated amid the jagged waves while thousands of snowflakes obliterated themselves in the black water.

Realizing that Klaris was spent, Jax set up the shelter, even though there were still several hours of daylight left. He didn't want to return to the beach until he was sure the waves were finished. Klaris went inside and fell into a heavy sleep.

Jax sat on his own quilts and repacked his bag to keep his mind occupied. When that was done, he tried to play his dragonpipe, but the music seemed stuck inside the instrument. Finally, he gave up and lay down to sleep.

Sageham Isle sat above the epicenter of the earthquake. The rocky island heaved and pitched like a boat in a storm. Lellyn stood in the great hall in a kind of ecstasy. She felt the Holy Mother's hand touch the fabric of Mystic and for one shining moment saw its purpose. Then the ancient tower of Caledra twisted loose from its foundation and crashed to earth, ending Lellyn's long life in an instant.

When the roiling stopped, the surviving magicians and the lads and lasses worked doggedly to pull the survivors and the dead from the wreckage. Amid screams of the wounded and moans of the grief-bound, Professor Essen and Larrisa pooled their aching magic to erect a very simple shelter from the rubble of the Great Hall. Father Mallix's tears fell on the lifeless form of Professor Lellyn and many others.

Across the Knownlands, a ripple coursed through the Mystic as so many powerful magicians died.

On Farsouth, Queen Jeress set her teacup down with a crack. She rose and went to the window to gaze out at the Rising rain that fell on the lush palace gardens.

Trajan looked up from his painting. "What is it?"

"Something's happened to the Mystic. Something bad."

"Klaris?" He put down his brush.

She shrugged. "I can't be sure." The Queen pulled a velvet ribbon which immediately brought a lady in waiting from the next room. "My scry bowl, please," the Queen said.

Trajan wiped his hands and watched as Jeress took deep, steadying breaths, then gathered her magic. The water in the bowl grew cloudy, gray, then inky black. Jeress frowned. What was this? She pushed the magic further, but the water remained opaque. She seemed to feel a cold wind on her cheek and caught the scent of pine, but that was it.

"I can't see her." Jeress waved a hand to end the spell. The water in the bowl became clear again. The Queen and her consort looked at each other for a few moments, sharing their silent anxiety.

"I'll try again tonight. Although there's no more than a quarter moon," Jeress said finally.

"When the Rising ends, we'll go to Sageham and find her." Trajan promised.

The tidal wave delayed them.

After it swept the Krillian Coast, the wave bulged through the sea speeding southward

It hit Haven, washing over the Floating Islands, slamming anchored boats into the rocky shore, and sweeping crates, people, everything out to sea. The great wave ripped free all but one of the thick cables that moored the Floating Islands in the harbor. Amid the heaving Rising seas, the Barians struggled to keep the Floating Islands secured to each other and to the anchors that kept them in the bay.

Neben and the other lords and ladies of the Floating Islands along with Lord Admiral Hix mustered their people and led them to face their Rising Fear, to leap into the surging seas to find cables and anchor lines, to row small craft through the driving sleet to reattach the ties that kept the islands from drifting out into the storm-wracked sea.

Sealord Bryx stood at a second story window in Valla's palace and watched. The wave had rushed across the shore, flooding the entire first floor of the palace and sweeping the royal stable off its foundation and into the sea, taking his beautiful horses with it.

Through the gray sleet, Bryx watched the Barians struggle to save their homes.

He did not go out to help. He believed that there was little for him to do. The nobles of the Floating Islands and Admiral Hix knew what had to be done, and the Barian people would follow them.

The sealord did not realize that his presence would have heartened his people, and his absence grieved them. As they counted their dead and missing, they began to feel that their land-loving sealord was somehow to blame.

On the southern end of the Barian Island the Oracle sat at the window that faced north.

They waved their wrinkled hand and a scry bowl appeared. The Oracle stared into the water but saw only a black swirl. Like Queen Jeress, the Oracle could sense a cold wind and the smell of pine, but they could see nothing.

"Sweet goddess," they grumbled. "Now neither of them can be seen." They drank the water from the bowl. "Oh, Holy Mother, did he get her out of that castle in time?"

A seagull that had perched upon the temple to escape the Rising wind suddenly found itself on nothing. The temple disappeared just as a vast gray wave washed across the Neck and Head of Baria. The seagull squawked and flapped away.

The wave spent the last of its fury on the north shore of Farsouth. It slurped two entire villages into the sea. Queen Jeress, Consort Trajan, and Crown Prince Joron, Klaris's twin brother, spent the next two weeks working to find survivors and bodies and restoring some form of shelter and community to the ravaged coastline.

The next day Jax and Klaris packed up again and continued their trek along the beach. Their progress slowed as they often had to crawl over the carcasses of huge trees that the waves had uprooted then abandoned on the shoreline.

Once in the early afternoon, Jax thought he heard rough shouts and monster screams, but the wind blowing off the sea snatched the sound away before he could be sure he had really heard anything at all.

Snow began falling with the dusk. Knowing how far it was to The Hant, Jax would have liked to go farther, but Klaris was clearly exhausted. She didn't say anything, but her green eyes were cloudy with fatigue.

He pitched the shelter well inland from the waves as the snow thickened. They ate ship biscuit and dried fish in the dark inside and lay down to sleep.

Exhausted from the tension of the day and from walking with the heavy pack, Jax was soon asleep. He was wakened by a sharp kick as Klaris shifted in her own quilts. Rolling over, he resumed his dreams. This time a knee dug into his back. He grunted and wiggled as far away from her as the small tent would allow. When her elbow hit him in the head he sat up.

"What is the matter?"

"I think there's a log under here."

He groped beneath her and, indeed, could feel some long hard object underneath the sailcloth. With resignation he pulled on his boots and stepped out. He reached under the fabric, found the branch, pulled it out and tossed it away into the night.

Once again wrapped in his own quilts he shuddered. "Damn cold out there," he muttered.

"Thank you."

He had fallen asleep again when yet another of Klaris's movements pulled the quilts off his shoulders.

"Damn it, Klaris. What is the matter?"

"What's the matter with *you?*"

"You've kicked me three times and now stolen my blanket."

"Oh. I'm sorry." She pushed the quilt back toward him. "I can't seem to sleep."

"I noticed."

She lay down and rolled away from him. He lay back and listened to her shift and sigh. Finally, he reached for her. "Come here."

"What are you doing?"

"I'm going to hold you, so you stop squirming. Close your eyes."

She was asleep in a moment. He settled his hips against her warm little bottom, felt the softness of her breasts under his arm, and returned to sunnier dreams.

Klaris awoke to the milky light that filtered through the snow-covered sail. She turned toward the warm body next to her and looked at him. Goddess, but he was beautiful with that straight profile and those islish eyebrows. Her fingers longed to touch his golden whiskers and slip down the sinews of his neck to the muscles under his shirt.

Happiness flooded through her, unexpected and surprising. She looked up at the roof of the shelter, bowed in by the weight of the snow and decided she rather liked Jax Sharkin.

But she did not like being without the Mystic. She remembered the strange shifts she'd felt in the swathing blankness around her after the tidal wave. Snug in the quilts, she explored the edges of her senses looking for those small cracks in the deadness around her.

After a while she realized that Jax's breathing had changed and she turned her head to find those sea blue eyes smiling at her. "Sleep well?"

She smiled back. "Eventually."

He lifted himself to a shoulder to see her better. "If you hadn't fallen asleep, I was prepared to offer other inducements."

"Such as?"

"You know sex is a soporific."

"Indeed?" She reached out to touch the muscles of his forearm. "But we haven't even shared a kiss." Green eyes rose to meet the blue ones.

He rolled onto her and remedied the lapse. His whiskers brushed her cheeks, and Klaris imagined how they would feel like on other parts of her body.

Jax loved the taste of her. He felt her heat and his own ripping response. She tasted so good, smelled so good. Joy bloomed in him as she responded.

He lifted his head and found those green eyes locked upon him was a power that had nothing to do with the Mystic.

"Sweet goddess," he choked, tearing his own gaze away, away from the face he'd dreamed of with such hope in the auction pens and such despair ever after.

Now here he was again, abandoned in a wilderness with precious few resources. Only this time, she was as stuck as he was.

He saw the confusion on her face and he bent to give her a more gentle kiss.

She took a deep, shaky breath. "Sweet goddess indeed." Turmoil ran through her: desire and fear all overlaid by the blanketing numbness of the Dark Fortnight. "You're not really a soporific, Jax."

He laughed and rolled away to find his boots and cloak and stepped out of the tent.

He welcomed the shocking cold. Goddess, but that was lovely. Everything about Klaris was lovely and brilliant. And she had left him with the trolls, no matter what flimsy excuses she offered.

He took another shaky breath to cool his blood and looked away towards the miles of snowy wasteland. It would be a very long walk to The Hant. Despite his fears, he found himself grinning again.

Back inside the tent, Klaris couldn't seem to stop smiling either. They ate biscuits and dried fruit then rolled up their quilts. Jax held the flap for Klaris to come out and saw her eyes widen at something behind him. He turned and found himself face to chest with an eight-foot troll.

"Looky here!" called the troll to his companions off in the trees. "I think I've found some islish folk. Come see."

Jax ducked away, pulled a fish knife free from his pack, and slashed the troll across the belly. Orange blood spurted on the white snow.

He saw Klaris lift the branch that had kept her awake half the night and position it between herself and a troll that came from her right. Jax turned to his left and stopped.

The troll facing him was Oblek.

Both of them gaped. Meanwhile, Klaris counted seven more trolls emerging from the bent and broken trees.

"FISHMAN!" Oblek spat. "It's the goddess-damned Fishman!"

Jax backed towards Klaris. "If you have any ideas, now would be a good time to share them."

"Ideas?"

Jax pulled on his force. He released it onto the trolls' clothes. Four of them caught fire, but trolls were smarter than monsters. Their friends grabbed them and rolled them in the snow, dousing the flames but not their tempers.

Oblek turned back to Jax with a roar of hatred. "I'm just going to kill you good and dead this time, Fishman. Good and dead!"

The troll swung hard with his mace. Jax ducked under the troll's arm and jammed his knife into Oblek's armpit. Oblek screamed, twisted, and dove towards him.

Jax lost his grip on his knife and fell backwards under the weight of the howling troll. He bumped into Klaris then the whole world tilted. He seemed to fall into a hole. Darkness swirled.

He landed with a thud and his head hit hard gravel. Gravel? The troll was on top of him, his thick fingers wrapped around Jax's neck. He kicked at the troll, groping for his lost knife and trying to roll free. The snow was gone, and the day was suddenly brighter.

Shouting voices rang in his ears, but still Oblek choked him.

Suddenly a face appeared beyond Oblek's shoulder. It was Captain Karric, King Kodill's Master of the Guard. Jax didn't understand how or why Karric should be here.

Sunlight flashed on bright metal and then Jax was awash in hot orange blood. It went up his nose and down his throat as the headless carcass of the troll slumped upon him.

Jax gagged and rolled away from Oblek's body, spitting blood and coughing. He rubbed his throat and sat up, looking around. This was Kree, the capital of Kordon. Somehow, he was sitting in the courtyard of the King's palace, covered in trollish blood.

"Dragons fry me," he choked.

Captain Karric wiped her sword with her cloak. A group of household guards stood around with swords drawn. More guards and now courtiers ran into the courtyard, shouting at one another.

Jax found Klaris lying in a crumple under her green cloak. He reached for her. "Klaris?"

She rolled on her back and looked up at him, her green eyes wide and shocked.

He helped her to sit. "How did you do that?"

She smiled slyly. "I found the crack in the shell."

This didn't make any sense to Jax. "I thought you couldn't use Mystic."

Klaris had closed her eyes and shook her head. Her breathing was shallow, clearly painful.

"Klaris? What is it?"

"Cross-magic." A convulsion knotted her, and she rolled into a ball.

"You cross-magicked yourself?"

Klaris coughed so violently blood trickled out of her mouth.

"Prince Jax, what is all this?" Captain Karric's clear voice cut through Jax's daze. He and Klaris had been speaking Islish. Now, he looked up at Captain Karric, cleared his sore throat, and spoke in Landish.

"This is Klaris de Farsouth, Captain. She's the new Weaver, and she needs a druid."

"I can see that, my lord." Karric noted. "But I'm rather sorry you've turned up here."

"Not as sorry as I am," he muttered, slowly climbing to his feet.

"What happened to her, your Highness?" Priestess Mollish had come running and now knelt next to Klaris.

"Cross-magic." Jax said, his voice hoarse, his eyes still on Klaris.

"I must arrest you, my lord," Karric said firmly. Firm hands pulled his arms behind his back.

Jax coughed again and spat, trying to get the taste of troll blood out of his mouth. He still couldn't quite believe that Klaris had managed to get them to Kree, and he was not prepared to face his political problems.

"We'll teach you to spit on Kordon, traitor!"

Ready or not, Jax turned towards the familiar, fluty voice of Thorag Addle, Duke of Midipex. Here was the source of so much grief, humiliation, heartbreak and betrayal.

Duke Thorag looked Jax up and down.

Jax cleared his throat again and spat onto the duke's shiny red shoe.

With one fluid motion the duke drew a thin knife from a sheath beneath his cloak and lunged.

Held by the guards, Jax could only twist aside so that the knife plunged into his shoulder rather than his heart. Startled, the guards dropped him as he gasped and fell to his knees.

"Your Grace!" Karric protested. "Your Grace, we have the prince in hand."

"You may think so, Captain," the duke said quietly. "But this half-isle is a slippery one. He will not escape this time, for I've just poisoned him."

Jax sat with a crunch on the gravel. The wound burned. He felt the poison start to crawl through his blood like spiders of fire. "Goddess damn you," he muttered to the duke.

Without thinking about it, he gathered his magic, pulling it together and wrapping its blanket around those fiery spiders the same way he'd use the Dragon force to snuff a flame.

He clenched his teeth and wrapped it tighter.

Someone in the crowd felt his work. "The prince is using Dragon force," she announced.

Jax heard nothing, just a mumble of voices behind the roar in his ears as he poured all he had into his raggedy effort. It held, and the spiders burned themselves out to cool puffs of nothing. The magic slipped and dissipated like smoke on a breeze.

He coughed again. Grasping the hilt of the knife, he wrenched it free. Blood flowed out, hot and throbbing onto his shirt.

Rising to his knees, Jax looked up into Midipex's pale blue eyes.

"The poison will kill you, even if the blade didn't," said the duke calmly.

"Why?" Jax breathed. "Why are you walking around the king's palace with a poisoned blade? Your Grace."

"To protect us all against wily traitors like you, Half-isle!"

"I have a name." Jax raised the knife dripping with his own blood. "I have a name that goes with this royal blood. Spill my blood and you've attacked Kordon itself."

The crowd watched in awe as the bloody prince rose unsteadily to his feet. "I am Javix Sharkin and you, my lord of Midipex, are a traitor."

"Karric should have let the troll finish his job," the duke lunged, wrapping his gloved hands around Jax's already bruised neck. Jax fell back and the duke followed him down. As they went down, the knife, still in Jax's hand, slipped into the duke's chest.

Jax felt the warm blood gushing over his hand. He watched the duke's eyes bulge in surprise. As the gloved fingers loosened their grip Jax asked the question that had stumped him for years: "Why? Why did you send me to the trolls?"

Blood dribbled from the duke's gaping mouth but no answers. Once again, Jax found himself pinned beneath a corpse.

He shoved the body away. Karric bent to check the fallen duke for a pulse. "You killed him, my lord."

Jax's sat up, head spinning and throat aching. He looked from the body of the duke to the sprawling corpse of the troll.

"He fell on his own knife," Jax choked.

At that moment Tallyn came running out of the palace followed by other members of the royal council.

"Sweet goddess!" shrieked the widow Duchess of Keffex. "Sweet goddess!"

"Midipex is dead, your Highness." Karric announced.

Jax heard the shocked voices. Blood still throbbed out of his shoulder. Darkness pushed at the edges of his vision, but he was remembering the tables of wergild he'd had to memorize and knew that the death of a duke, intended or not, would cost him all his manors at Norbay.

Gravel suddenly pushed against his cheek. He wanted to ask about Klaris; he wanted to see Tallyn, but something black was swallowing him. He felt himself lifted and carried away as rain began to fall. Each cold drop hitting him like an icy jewel bringing clarity only to his pain.

9

Four guards dragged Jax to the highest room in the ancient keep. They seemed determined to bind him with every chain in the castle. Iron fetters linked his hands and his ankles. More chains ran from these shackles to a great ring in the middle of the round room. Clanking, he hauled all this iron to the small cot and lay down on a moth-eaten blanket. He heard the lock click in the scarred darkwood door and the shuffle as a guard took up a position there.

Aching from the knife wound, the troll's abuse, and some residue of the poison, Jax drifted in and out of consciousness.

The sound of voices woke him. Gray afternoon light filled the round room from four small windows placed high on the walls. At least they hadn't locked him in some goddess forsaken dungeon. He shifted on the small cot, trying to get comfortable under the various tugs and weights of the fetters.

It took several tries to get sound out of his throat. "Hey!" he called. "Hey, could I get some water?"

"No, my lord."

He sat up noisily. His hair and shirt were stiff with dried blood: the troll's, the duke's and his own. "How about some of that famous Kordish wine, then?"

"No, my lord."

He lay back and let the strange sense of joy rise through his pains. Midipex was dead. Oblek was dead, too. He still faced a traitor's death, but he felt a deep relief that the authors of so much of his personal grief and agony were dead and gone. He felt almost giddy. Maybe this was an after-effect of the poison.

"I'm just going to check on the prisoner." A voice echoed up the stairs, jolting Jax out of his reverie. The guard mumbled some reply, but he couldn't make out the words.

"Don't be silly. I'm just an old druid. Do I look dangerous?"

A moment later, Marith ducked through the door into the round room. She pulled the threadbare chair over to the cot and sat down opening her black satchel. "Well, son, you're a mess."

He sat up slowly, staring in amazement. "I'm so happy to see you." The relief in his belly sent tears to his eyes. "How did you get to Kree, Mam? You should be half-way back to the Vale by now."

"They wouldn't let us go." Marith handed Jax a flask of water then began to wipe the blood off his face and neck with a damp cloth. "Borrel and Florin and I were brought here after you escaped from Earl Oklan's dungeon."

"Are they good to you? Ow."

Marith was pulling shreds of torn shirt away from Jax's wounded shoulder. "Yes, they've been very kind, but they're keeping an eye on us. I think they hoped you'd come back to Kordon in order to get us."

"Ow. Do you know what's become of Klaris?"

"She is in a very bad way. The priestess, Lady Mollish, is with her. Hold on a minute now, this antiseptic is going to sting."

"Sweet goddess, Mam." Jax wriggled and his chains clanked. "It's cross-magic," he said through clenched teeth.

"Why are you here, Jax?" Marith looked at him, her blue eyes wary. "We thought the Oracle got you away from the traitor's death. Why, by the goddess, have you come back?"

He shifted as she continued to poke at his wound. "I'm not sure the Oracle cares what happens to me. They commanded me to get the Weaver from Castle Caledra and bring her to Kree. If I had known that Klaris could get herself here, I'd have let her come without me."

Marith frowned at the wound. "I don't like the necrosis around the edge of this incision." She dabbed more of the stinging liquid around Jax's shoulder.

"The knife was poisoned," Jax breathed.

The guard put his head in the room. "Ye need to get on with this, Mother."

Marith ignored the guard. "You don't appear to be suffering from poison."

Jax shook his head. "I used magic and stopped it."

"But magic can't be used to heal."

"I didn't really heal myself. I just stopped the poison." He started to shrug, then stopped as this pulled painfully at the wound.

"I didn't think you had enough magic to do something like that."

"Neither did I, but after what Klaris did today, all kinds of things seem possible."

"What did she do?" Marith corked the bottle of antiseptic and pulled a wad of thick white bandages out of her bag.

Jax told her what he knew of the Dark Fortnight and how he and Klaris had ended up beached on the Krillian coast, fleeing monsters and trolls. "The last troll was my master from the iron mines, from the ferry. He wasn't going to let me get away again."

"No, he wasn't." Marith fingered the purple bruises on Jax's neck and remembered the haunted, broken creature Jax had been when he first came to the Vale. "So maybe it's a good thing the Weaver brought you with her."

"Maybe."

The guard entered the room. "Mother," he growled. "Your time is up. Leave now, please."

"Yes, yes." Marith packed up her satchel. "Oh wait. One more thing. Here, drink this. It's poppy extract to help you sleep."

Jax drank. He knew the poppy would dull the pain.

Marith kissed him quickly on the cheek and bustled out of the room.

The poppy worked. An hour later when Tallyn was finally able to slip away from the furious nobles of the royal council, she found Jax so heavily sedated that she could not rouse him.

"Damn," she swore quietly, raising her crystal lantern to look him over. The laces of his shirt had disappeared along with his boots. The guards were leaving him no options for flight. She noted the neat white bandage and assumed his druid friend must have seen to him. A golden gleam caught her attention. She bent and pulled gently on the chain to find the Oracle's medallion. She flipped it over then replaced it on his chest.

"What does the Oracle want with you?" A hundred more questions began to run through her thoughts as she considered various other people and powers that also seemed to want something from her bedraggled cousin here.

She turned to the guard. "I want to know when he awakes. Send for me day or night. Understand?"

"Yes, your Highness."

"Good."

She swept from the tower, the heels of her delicate shoes clicking rapidly down the stairs.

"Your Highness?"

Tallyn paused in her march across the great hall. Without a word, she took Cheshir's arm and swung the two of them into a small, private alcove.

"He's sedated," the princess said, answering Cheshir's unspoken question. "And rather filthy, covered in dried blood, but yes, he's as beautiful as ever. Maybe more so."

"Goddess, why is he here?"

Tallyn shrugged. "You aren't the only one asking that question."

"I must see him." Cheshir turned to look out the window. "I can't marry Frinz now...."

"Shirry," Tallyn stopped. Cheshir of Deepford was her oldest and best friend. The two had been foster sisters with Prince Jax and Lord

Foby, and the ties between the four of them were strong and deep. "Shirry, I don't know if we can save him."

Cheshir's dark-lashed blue eyes filled with tears. "I thought I was through crying for him."

"So, did I," Tallyn answered finally.

Trumpets rang through the rainy evening and echoed into the great hall.

"Dragons," Tallyn grumbled. "The dowager."

Cheshir blew her nose. "Are you sure?"

"Everyone else is already here." The princess gave Cheshir's hand one quick squeeze then strode toward the great doors. Captain Karric came in, water streaming off her cloak.

She bowed to Tallyn. "Your royal grandmother has arrived, your Highness."

"This is turning out to be a day of many surprises, Captain."

Karric smiled. "Yes, my lady. Have you seen Prince Jax?"

"I've seen him, and he's a dirty mess. But he was sedated so I couldn't talk to him." She looked the captain in the eye. "I would caution the guards to remember that Prince Jax is a Prince of the Blood and permit him some appropriate food and other comforts."

"Of course, my lady."

"And see if you can figure out what kind of poison the Duke of Midipex used on that knife.

"Yes, Ma'am."

In a gust of wet wind, the dowager queen slogged into the hall. Everyone, including Tallyn, swept into low bows.

"Ah, Tallyn." The dowager shrugged off a thick, fur-lined cloak, revealing her fine boned face, white hair, and icy blue eyes. "Is it true that Javix Sharkin has returned?"

"Yes, your Majesty."

"And he murdered Midipex?"

"Apparently the duke attempted to kill him, Ma'am."

The dowager cocked a fine eyebrow. "Thorag Addle had a bad habit of falling short."

Tallyn considered this assessment. As the Kordish lord chancellor, the duke of Midipex had seemed quite capable to her.

The dowager accepted a steaming mug of wine from a servant who took the old queen's cloak from Tallyn.

"Come, Tallyn," the dowager said. "Tell me what the council has been saying about all this."

Tallyn walked beside her grandmother through the halls of the palace toward the king's privy cabinet. "We know very little, Ma'am," the princess said. "The Weaver is unconscious from cross-magic. Jax is sedated but doesn't appear to be suffering from any poison. The troll who arrived with them is dead."

The members of the royal council rose to greet the dowager and the crown princess as they entered the privy cabinet.

"Hello, Mother." The king pecked a kiss on the dowager's powdered cheek.

"Well," the dowager sat down. "I suppose you plan to execute the half-isle as soon as possible."

"We were just discussing that, your Majesty," Earl Oklan Kora said cautiously.

"Discussing?" The dowager's voice was sharp. "What's to discuss? He's had his trial. And he confessed."

Tallyn spoke quietly. "Yes, Ma'am. But the confession was coerced."

"I believe there were a great number of witnesses when he murdered the Duke of Midipex."

Lord Elmore, Earl of Vobury, spoke carefully. "My lady, we were considering the unusual circumstances of Prince Jax's situation."

"I see." The dowager's voice was sarcastic. "The judgments of the royal council are only temporary."

Earla Stona of the Tarron March smiled. "That is my point, exactly, your Majesty. Either we adhere to our judgments, or we discredit ourselves as a decision-making body."

Frinz, the Duke of Aychex, frowned. "I'm afraid I agree," he said. Just a few years older than the princess, Frinz of Aychex had grown up with the same circle of young nobles. He had inherited his title from his father just two years ago. "You should not even see Jax Sharkin, your Highness. He's been tried and sentenced. He's a dead man."

Rippsmarch leaned forward. "I understand your desire to be consistent, Frinz, but it appears that we reached our decision without knowing all of the facts."

Several of the nobles shook their heads. Earla Stona snorted, but Lord Oklan continued. "My lords and ladies, I believe that the Oracle did snatch Prince Jax from my dungeon. Now he turns up with the Weaver. I think we must know more before we take any irrevocable steps."

"The Oracle? The Weaver?" The dowager sneered. "Such power doesn't need a murderous half-isle to further its policies."

Tallyn shrugged casually, "I noticed that he is wearing an Oracular medallion even now."

Patrice, Duchess of Chevvain, shifted in her chair. "My lords and ladies, while I agree that Prince Jax's activities have been questionable, suspect, and perhaps even treasonous, he has somehow managed to bring the new Weaver here, and I want to know why. Let's not forget that Klaris de Farsouth is the daughter of Queen Jeress."

King Kodill had been watching the raindrops chase each other down the window. He couldn't blame the Barian islish for hating the Risings. He longed to escape this tedious arguing by taking a long ride on his favorite stallion. But the Rising rain kept him cooped up here in this stuffy room. And now his mother was kicking his leg under the table and giving him that look that said *pay attention*.

"Enough." Kodill rose. The nobles fell silent and stood with him. "We will prepare to execute Jax in a week when this damn Rising is over. That will give Midipex's widow time to get here. In the meantime, all of you," he looked at Tallyn, "are forbidden to visit or speak to him. We will, however, question the Weaver when she recovers from the cross-magic. Then, if need be, we'll reconvene to beat this dead horse some more."

With that, the king strode from the room and went in search of a flagon of wine and a few imaginative lovers.

The next morning Marith found Jax sitting in the ratty armchair, his feet propped on the table, the chains dangling. He had been given some tea and porridge and was feeling well enough to worry about his future.

"The king has forbidden anyone to see you," Marith whispered, as she changed the bandage on his shoulder.

"Apparently the Royal Dragon and Priestess Mollish aren't anyone, then. They were already here for their own inquisition this morning."

"Well, you did apparently heal yourself." She dug a vial of ointment from her satchel and dabbed it on the wound.

"Mam, that stuff really stings."

"Stop squirming. The stinging tells you that it's working." She frowned, then shook her head. "A wound this deep really should have some stiches, but I don't want to trap any residual poison under the skin."

She paused and considered the color of his skin, which was difficult given the dried blood and whiskers. "Let me see your eyes." Gently, she spread his eyelids open and considered the white and blue of his eyes. "Toadfroth is nasty stuff. I want you drink about a gallon of water today to make sure it's all flushed from your body."

"Toadfroth?"

"Didn't Mollish or the Royal Dragon tell you? That was the poison the duke had put on the knife. Captain Karric found a paste of the stuff locked in his cabinet, along with some other very nasty mixtures."

"Is Klaris any better?"

"No. Priestess Mollish says she's never seen such a severe case of cross-magic."

Jax shrugged his filthy shirt back into place over the new bandage, stood and dragging his chains went to look out one of the high windows at the driving Rising rain and the beginnings of a construction project in the courtyard below.

He frowned, thinking about the pain in those green eyes as the druids had taken Klaris away. But when he turned to Marith he saw pain and worry in those eyes too.

"You shouldn't have come back here, Jax."

"It wasn't my choice."

"Well, I choose not to watch them execute you."

Jax sat back down abruptly as he simultaneously realized that the construction project was a scaffold for an execution and that the duke of Midipex must have had another target in mind for that deadly knife.

The chains clinked as he pulled the Oracle's medallion from under his shirt.

"I noticed that yesterday," Marith said.

The guard looked around the door. "Time's up, Mother."

"Yes, yes. I'm finished."

"Here," Jax flung the medallion and chain at the guard. The man stepped back and batted it to the ground.

"It won't hurt you," Jax said. "Will you take it to Captain Karric?"

"No." snapped the guard. "Mother, you must go."

"I'll take it for you." Marith picked the medallion off the floor.

Jax shook his head and took the golden chain from her hands. "You can't, Mam. You know already how dangerous it is to be my... friend."

Marith tried to hide her tears, making a big to-do about collecting her things. "Do you want some poppy tea?"

"Maybe in a week." He tried to joke.

"Mother, you are leaving now!" The guard grabbed Marith by the arm and pulled her from the round cell. Jax almost grinned as he heard her voice echoing up the spiral staircase. "You needn't be such a brute. I'm just an old woman...."

He looped the golden chain over his head and figured he would try with the next guard. But she also refused to touch the medallion, as did the people who brought him a bit of dinner.

Frustrated, Jax shrugged his shoulders under the golden chain and bitterly remembered the Oracle's words: *No one in the Knownlands will dare harm you.*

Right.

He ate the meager food then, restless, went to the window. Lights from the great hall below spilled into the courtyard and bathed the scaffold that stood in the dark rain. Jax stared at it, ice chasing the food through his gut. Slowly he smiled and gathered his Dragon force.

Tallyn leaned her forehead on the cold windowpane and watched the rain splash into the puddles far below. She wished she felt better. Her stomach turned again. All this Rising, she had felt sick and couldn't seem to shake it. Now, here Jax was back, the Duke of Midipex dead, the new Weaver dangerously and inexplicably cross-magicked, and all Tallyn wanted to do was go to bed. A long ride in the fresh air on the green downs might clear her head and settle her stomach, but there would be no riding until the Rising blew itself out. And then there would be an execution the likes of which had not been seen in Kree in over 400 years.

She turned away from the window and the rivulets of rain that barred her from escaping outside. The Weaver lay on the bed in the center of the room, as she had lain for a whole day now: her black skin stark against the white linen sheets.

Tallyn had watched Klaris's face for any sign of life almost all day. She had listened with increasing worry to the rattle of congestion in the Weaver's lungs.

Carte Serge, the Royal Mystic, sat knitting in a chair by the fire. "My presence is the best thing to combat the cross-magic," he had explained to Tallyn. "My Mystic will soothe hers."

"But I thought she didn't have any Mystic right now." The intricacies of magic had been of little interest to Tallyn, who had no magic at all.

"She can't access the Mystic," Serge had said. "But it's still there in her veins."

Priestess Mollish returned from an errand. She placed some more damp herbs on the fire, once again filling the room with thick, tangy steam.

Klaris coughed.

Tallyn thought she saw her eyelids flutter, but then decided it was just her imagination.

"So," Tallyn resumed her seat beside the bed as Mollish took up a small mortar and pestle and began grinding herbs into a paste. "So, I had never heard of this Dark Fortnight."

Carte Serge answered, his eyes still on his knitting. "It's not something that's widely known, my lady, outside of the most powerful magicians."

"Do Dragons go through the same time without magic when they become Highlords?"

He nodded. "They have a different system, but they also must bide a Dark Fortnight when they reach the highest status."

Tallyn signed. "You don't have any magic do you, Mollish?"

"No, my lady. But sometimes the Oracle shares their magic with their priests and priestesses."

"Being without magic is like being blind or deaf," Tallyn said. "Sometimes I feel as if everyone can see or hear something that I can't."

"That is exactly how I feel," a voice whispered in a thick Islish accent.

Tallyn jumped. Klaris was staring at her from eyes as green as spring leaves.

"Weaver Klaris," Mollish knelt beside the bed and took Klaris's hand. "Carefully now, my lady. Do not exert yourself. Can I get you something?"

Klaris coughed, heavy and wet. "Tea?"

"A tisane, yes." Mollish nodded and returned to the kettle at the hearth.

Tallyn leaned forward. "Weaver Klaris, I'm Tallyn of Kordon. Welcome to Kree."

"Thank you." The green eyes closed against the pain.

"Weaver!" Tallyn didn't want her slipping away again. "I'm sorry to trouble you, but we need to know why you are here."

"The Oracle...." She coughed.

Tallyn took a deep breath to contain herself. "The Oracle sent you? You and Prince Jax?"

Klaris nodded.

Mollish helped Klaris sit up on her pillows then handed her a mug of musky tisane, thick with honey. Klaris sipped it gratefully. "*Fellishous*," she thanked the priestess in Islish.

Tallyn tapped her toe and waited.

Klaris opened her eyes again. "Your Highness, where is Prince Jax? There was a troll...."

"The troll is dead. My cousin, Prince Jax, is imprisoned in the tower. He was convicted of treason, you know, and the royal council doesn't want to change its collective mind now. He is to be executed when the Rising ends."

Klaris coughed and sat up a bit more. "Don't you know what happened to him?"

"We have heard some stories, Weaver."

"The Oracle commanded him to bring me here."

"They did?"

Klaris took a sip of tea so she could keep talking. "Yes. Would you people execute an Oracular Messenger?"

"I wouldn't, no. But Prince Jax has already been convicted, and he confessed."

"Confessed?"

"Indeed."

Those green eyes flashed with concentration. "He must have lied."

"That won't help him."

A fit of coughing seized Klaris. Finally, Mollish, wiping blood from the Weaver's lips, looked up at Tallyn. "You must let the Weaver rest, my lady."

Tallyn rose. She leaned over the bed and squeezed Klaris's clammy hand. "Get better, Weaver Klaris."

Tallyn left the room and lifted her head as she heard a ruckus coming from the hall downstairs.

"Fire!" someone yelled. "Fire in the courtyard!"

10

Palm trees bent and whipped in the lashing rain, writhing in the black, tropical night. The Dragon Highlord ignored the wind and the wet. He did not need to see the sky to know that tonight the moon was new and most advantageous for his scry. Obviously, as the most powerful Dragon in the Knownlands, Raggar could perform a scry at any time, but the images the flames had shown him over the past several days had led him here, to this rainy night at the dark of the moon, to confirm the unbelievable.

Soaked to the skin, he called his magic. It came full and potent. Flame burst from the wet logs in the firepit before him and climbed the rain, sending great clouds of steam to dance among the waving trees.

Pictures formed in the wall of flame: A dark ruin on a snow-swept island. White waves wreathed the rocky cliffs in delicate lace. Pinpricks of light glowed among the ruins, and Raggar pushed his vision towards those flames. Gray people huddled towards the fleeting warmth. Beyond, in the shadows, rows of shrouded figures lay still as tombstones.

Raggar could feel the grief. Indeed, this vision was the same one he had already seen, but even more vivid. Where was that young Farsouthian? He had felt her achieve mastery, felt the balance of magic tilt as a result of the doors she'd opened. But then this destruction, this terrible loss.

The girl wasn't dead. He could still sense the weight of her power in the overall field of magic, even though it was muffled by her Dark

Fortnight. But where the dragons was she? And what by the goddess had happened to the Mystic?

A feline face appeared in the wall of flame, blocking Raggar's view of the ruins.

"Earthquake," said the cat.

"What?" Raggar asked, shocked.

The cat appeared to smile and purr. The image blurred, and with a sudden yowl the cat became a dragon, reaching its claws out of the flame: a dragon's claws.

Raggar slammed the spell shut, cutting off the flow of magic. The fire vanished. Blackened logs smoldered into the rain. He turned away from the smoking mess and strode back to his hut.

He threw his sodden clothes to a hook and took up a towel to dry his gray-streaked hair and beard.

Halla sat in a chair reading by the light of her magic. She looked up, her nyad brown eyes full of love and concern, and set her scroll aside.

"It's true," he said, grimly. "Castle Caledra has fallen. There's nothing but rubble there now."

"How?"

"An earthquake, apparently. At least that's what the *cat* said."

Halla's eyes narrowed, but she said nothing.

"Cat or dragon, I'm not sure which," he confided, pulling a loose linen kilt around his waist, and flopping into the chair opposite her. The hut shook as the Rising storm beat against the thatch. "I didn't see or sense the Weaver there anywhere. I know she's alive, but I don't think she's at Sageham."

"How could she be anywhere else?" Halla asked. "For goddess' sake, she has no Mystic right now...."

Raggar reached for a carafe of pale wine and poured a generous amount into a blue glass, then poured more for Halla. "I swear she's not on Sageham, but I can't tell you where she *is*."

"Where who is?" Blizzen stuck his head inside the hut. "May I join you, Highlord?"

"Of course, Blizzen. Come in out of the rain. Wine?"

"Thank you." He shed his dripping cloak by the door.

"We were talking of Klaris de Farsouth."

Blizzen sat with long familiarity in the third chair. "And she isn't where you think she should be?"

"She isn't on Sageham." Halla said.

"That does seem odd." Blizzen looked into his glass. "But why do we care?"

Raggar stretched his long legs out from the chair. "I was trying to figure out what happened to the magic, to Mystic."

"Ah." Like Halla and the Highlord, Blizzen had felt the magic shift when the new Weaver established herself just as the Rising began. But then about a week later something terrible had happened to the Mystic. All of them had felt it. To tell the truth, Blizzen was surprised at how concerned the Highlord had been, but then he himself was absorbed in the exciting new discoveries he'd been making in the last few weeks. This was what had brought him to the Highlord's hut in the middle of such a rainy night.

Born and raised in Kree, Blizzen had come to Dragonsholm years ago and risen to become the Orange Dragon, third in power, below only Halla the Red Dragon and the Highlord himself. He'd learned from long experience the value of waiting to share his ideas with the pair that had led Dragon force for the last sixteen years. "You have found some answers then, this evening?" he asked.

Raggar shrugged. "Perhaps, but they are unsettling."

"How so?"

"I know the prospect of returning dragons thrills you, Blizzen, but I am not so confident that it will be a wonderful event."

"Our force will increase, Highlord. Already it is increasing. Halla and I have seen evidence of this among all the students here at Dragonsholm, and even felt it ourselves. The power flows more fully, more freely."

"Yes," Halla said quietly. "And we felt it flow into the void left when all those Mystics died."

"Is that necessarily a bad thing?" Blizzen asked calmly. "I don't mean to condone the death of anyone, but the Mystic grew so much when the new Weaver ascended, now the balance seems more equal again."

Raggar sighed. "You are missing my point entirely, Blizzen. But it is not really a matter of concern for us right now. Did you come to see us for something?"

"Yes. Yes, Highlord." Invited at last to share his own enthusiasm, Blizzen leaned forward in his chair. "I have finally been able to see into a body! I figured how to channel the magic in such a way that it rolls over any old break or clot or hole and reveals it."

"I should think holes in someone's flesh would reveal themselves," Halla said kindly. She and the Highlord knew that Blizzen had been trying for years to devise a way to use magic for healing. Neither Mystic nor Dragon had ever been used this way, although many magicians of both Dragon and Mystic had tried. Blizzen lamented that Dragon force seemed rather useless, compared to Mystic, which built most of the houses, castles, shops, barns, and other structures people used across the Knownlands. He felt that if Dragons could become healers, they would bring a gift at least as important as shelter.

"Yes," he said now, his blue eyes shining. "Yes, the holes and leaks are usually pretty obvious. Halla, will you let me show the Highlord the technique I've now mastered by allowing us to scan your body?"

"What will your scan reveal?" Halla looked a little worried.

"Any old wounds or injuries and, I think, possibly areas of illness."

"Will it hurt?"

"Well...." Blizzen hesitated. "Well, it might just a bit. The magic burns the old injuries and tends to reopen them. I have to hold the flow quite tightly to make sure that it doesn't."

"Doesn't recreate the injury?" The Highlord poured more wine into his glass.

"I had a broken ankle once many years ago," Halla said. "I'm not interested in having that experience again."

"No, of course not. I had a little trouble with that at first, but I've got the problem solved now."

Raggar looked at Blizzen with increased attention. "How many people did you reinjure during your experiments?"

"A few."

Raggar's black eyes glared.

"Six, actually, Highlord, but I got the priestess to take care of all of them. It's the inner fire, you see, the spark of life that—."

"Dragons, Blizzen!" Halla interrupted. "You're experimenting with people's life force?"

"Well—. Highlord?" Blizzen stopped. Raggar had blanched and gasped.

Halla rose from her chair and knelt beside Raggar, staring up into his stricken face. The Highlord's dark eyes followed a small tabby cat that sauntered across the room, a dead mouse in its jaws. Instead of the cat, Raggar had seen a dragon slinking through the room.

"Raggar?" Halla touched his knee. "The cat?"

He blinked to clear his vision. "Yes, the cat." He drained his glass then poured another. He turned to Blizzen. "Look, I'm glad your work is bearing fruit, but you mustn't harm people. You know the *Rote and Rede* prohibits such a thing. And the Oracle will punish you if they discover you've already hurt people, even if your goal is laudable. Try your experiments on yourself, if you must, until you can be sure no one will be harmed."

"But I've already figured that out—."

"Good. I'm afraid you'll have to show me tomorrow. It's too late tonight."

"But—."

"Not now, Blizzen."

"Yes, Highlord." Blizzen rose, collected his cloak, and vanished into the wet night.

"Raggar?" Halla said softly. "What's wrong?"

He looked into her nyad brown eyes, eyes that had been supporting and loving him here at Dragonsholm for over twenty years. "It's too much magic. Too much power. I am drowning in the flow."

"What do you need?"

"I need the Weaver." He took her hands, his own sweating. "But I can't find her."

11

Foby Kora considered the food on his plate and sighed. State dinners at the Castle Kree were long, elaborate, and the food invariably arrived cold at the lower tables where he had to sit. Tonight's dinner was more inchoate than usual because the fire in the courtyard had disrupted the preparations. The scaffold was now a smoking ruin, and the Royal Dragon had been commanded to add a magician to Captain Karric's people guarding Prince Jax. Dinner was late.

Foby fed a soggy bit of liver paté to the dog under his chair and watched Tallyn at the head table with the king, the dowager, and the new ambassador from Dranstyl, who was the reason for tonight's feast. Tallyn had laughed herself silly over Jax's destruction of the scaffold, but she didn't look good now. He could tell she wasn't eating. Whatever it was that had been plaguing her since the start of this Rising, was still clearly bothering her.

Foby's sister, Thessaly, caught the direction of his gaze and put a hand on his arm. He glanced at her and shrugged. "I'm worried about her," he admitted.

"About who?" Florin asked from her seat across the table.

"The princess." Thessaly answered, thinking how everyone had almost gotten used to seeing such creatures admitted to the table at a Kordish state dinner since Tallyn had insisted that all of Jax's friends from his time in exile be included in the court's activities. The princess said this was to make it easier to watch them, but

Thessaly, informed by her brother's closer relationship with Tallyn, thought maybe she had another motive.

Borrel watched Tallyn for a minute. "Powerful." He named the word she embodied,

"Tallyn?" Thessaly asked looking into her brother's eyes. "Yes."

"Powerful," Florin echoed Borrel, still amazed at the company she now kept, or was kept by.

Marith, sitting between the two nyads, sighed as another dish of fowl in a congealing sauce was placed before her. "You folks create beautiful food, but I don't understand why you can't serve it hot."

A passing servant poured more golden wine into her crystal goblet. "At least you do make delicious wine."

"What's that?" Borrel sat up, looking around.

Foby raised his cup. "Westgrove from Darkwood. One of Kordon's finest."

"No, there was magic," Borrel clarified, as the dog under Foby's chair leapt to her feet and barked.

The double doors of the great hall flew open with a crash. Guards came running. Nobles and Knights of the Realm stood from their chairs.

Captain Karric's voice rang through the hall: "Mind the king!"

"Mind the king? Mind the king!" A resonate voice, neither male nor female, mimicked sarcastically. A small, gray-cloaked figure shuffled into the hall.

"Sweet goddess," murmured Thessaly. Marith, Thessaly, and Priestess Mollish rose from their seats.

"Mind the king, indeed! It's that impudent Weaver we've come to see."

King Kodill rose himself, his expression regal and angry. "Please state your name and your business here."

"Who is that?" Foby whispered.

The opalescent eyes looked directly at Foby. "The Oracle," they said then turned back to the king. "We are the Speaker for the

Goddess, your Majesty, and we have come to say some words to the Weaver."

Tallyn stepped down from her place at the head table. "I will show you the way, Your Eminence."

"Eminence," snorted the Oracle. "Call us Oracle. That's enough of a title."

"Yes, Oracle." Tallyn inclined her head and led the tiny figure through the palace and up the stairs to Klaris's room.

"The Weaver is improving," Tallyn explained as they walked. "But she isn't always conscious."

"She'll be conscious for us."

"I didn't realize you traveled," Tallyn said, noting that the Oracle was bounding up the stairs and down the corridors of the palace with more energy than she could muster herself.

"We haven't been away from our temple in a century. But the Weaver broke her Dark Fortnight, and goddess only knows what you've done with our Paradox."

At the doorway to Klaris's room, Tallyn stopped. "Your paradox?"

"He's *our* Paradox." The Oracle smiled. Tallyn felt filled with joy but couldn't say why. She pushed open the door.

Klaris turned listlessly toward them. Her eyes grew wide.

"Weaver Klaris, the Oracle is here to see you."

Klaris struggled to sit up. The Oracle walked into the room, pulling the door shut behind them.

"Sweet goddess," Klaris gasped in Islish, which came to her first.

"Sweet goddess is right," the Oracle snapped, using the same tongue. "How did you do that? How did you break your Dark Fortnight? And why?"

"I could feel the Mystic around the edges of the shell, the shell that blocked me. I pushed those cracks and found the weave there." Klaris coughed.

"Indeed, you did."

"Yes. But it hurts, and now there's another ache. I can't understand it, I just feel the pain."

"The pain, yes." The Oracle walked to the edge of the bed and sat down.

With the Oracle now close enough to touch, Klaris felt the emanation of its magic and she recognized it.

"It's you. It's your magic that imposes the Dark Fortnight," she wheezed. "Your magic that crossed mine."

"Aye, child. And it hurts, don't it."

"It hurts you, too?"

"Not exactly."

Klaris pulled herself together and sat up straighter. "A troll was about to kill Prince Jax. I couldn't let that happen. But I wouldn't have had to call the Mystic and break the Dark Fortnight if I'd been safe at Sageham. Why, by the sweet goddess, did you make Jax take me away from there?"

"Don't you know?"

She shook her head.

"You can't feel it?"

A shadow crossed Klaris's eyes. She did feel something else besides her own aching breath. There was that deeper ache somewhere in her heart. Fear tingled up and down her spine. "What is it?"

The Oracle took her hand. Their grip was cool and dry. "Caledra lies in ruins, Weaver Klaris. An earthquake shook it to bits. Many of your fellow Mystics were killed."

"No!" Klaris pulled her hand free and wrapped her arms around herself. "Professor Lellyn?"

The Oracle shook their head.

"Oh," Klaris breathed. "You knew. That's why you made Jax get me out of there."

"Yes. But why couldn't you abide your Fortnight, child? We thought you had finally learned patience."

"How can you know about unpredictable things like earthquakes but be unaware of entirely predictable Rising storms or the monsters and trolls of the Hantland?" Klaris was exasperated.

"Javix can't be seen, as you well know. It turns out that when you're with him, you can't be seen either."

Klaris cocked her head at this interesting fact. "Really? Well, a troll was about to kill him, and maybe me too. I wasn't sure I could get enough magic through those cracks to teleport two people. So, I pulled on everything I could get. I guess that was more than enough because I accidentally brought the troll through with us." She stopped to cough. "I knew I was breaking the Fortnight, but I would do it again."

"Despite the cost?"

Klaris waved a hand dismissively. Tears welled in her eyes. "Professor Lellyn," she whispered.

The Oracle stared at the young woman for a few minutes. Finally, they spoke without sympathy. "You need to get better, Weaver Klaris. Then you need to find the rest of that damned prophecy."

"What prophecy?"

"The one Jax has."

"Is it here?"

"It was."

"This is why you wanted Jax to bring me to Kree?"

"Partly, yes. Now, get well. Find the prophecy. Keep the Paradox close. You need him. Then learn to sing."

"Sing?" she coughed. "You do know they want to execute Jax."

"Of course they do. The Paradox Who Can't Be Found resolves the dichotomies, you see. That's problematic for those who are invested in such hierarchies."

Klaris was becoming lightheaded from hard coughing, and the Oracle's words spun away from her without making sense.

The gray figure stood up and walked towards the door. Again, Klaris coughed blood into her handkerchief. Gray eyes met green.

"Your Dark Fortnight ends tomorrow," the Oracle said.

"Good. I want my magic back."

The Oracle shook their head. "You have no idea what you've tapped into my child. When the magic comes back to you, well.... You're going to need everything you've got and then some."

To Klaris it seemed as if the Oracle just disappeared. She sank back into her pillows, her body and heart aching. What had happened to the Mystic? Who was still alive at Caledra, and who would care for them? Who would rebuild? How could she do that and find the Oracle's dragon-blasted prophecy at the same time?

The other members of the royal council had joined Tallyn in the hall outside the Weaver's chamber by the time the Oracle reemerged. The Oracle's gray eyes roamed across the ruling faces of Kordon. "Now then," they said in Landish. "What have you done with Javix Sharkin?"

"The traitor?" stammered Earla Stona.

"Our messenger."

"This way, Oracle." Tallyn again led the Oracle through corridors, downstairs, then back up the old, winding stairway to the tower. The nobles followed in silence.

"So, you're still imprisoning him," the Oracle noted.

"He has been convicted of treason," Tallyn replied.

"But none of you believes he's guilty."

The nobles glanced at each other.

At the door to the cell, the guard fumbled with his keys while the young Dragon magician gaped.

"Oh, for goddess sake," the Oracle grumbled, pushing at the door. The lock slid open. Five glowing bands of dragon force remained in place.

"Will you take that down, or do you want us to do it?" The Oracle transfixed the Dragon magician with a silver glare. The red bands splintered and disappeared into darkness.

Inside the room, Jax lay asleep on the cot. The Oracle created a light, and Jax rolled over, his chains clanking. He blinked and sat up slowly.

"Oracle?"

"Hello, Javix. Haven't you had a bath since the last time I saw you?"

Jax cleared his throat. "One. Surely, you didn't come here to discuss my hygiene."

"We came to see the Weaver and find out why she broke her Dark Fortnight."

"She wasn't so pleased to be whisked away from the safety of Caledra."

"It wasn't as safe as she thought," the Oracle said.

Jax frowned. "What happened?"

"You surely felt that earthquake. What do you think would happen to a building of ancient stones when shaken like that?"

"Ah." Jax nodded. "That's the ache in the magic."

"Aye, but it's odd you should feel it, since you have the dragons' force."

"Everything about me is odd."

"It's your burden, and your gift."

"You like those paradoxes, don't you?"

"You should learn to like them too. Resolving them is your destiny."

"My destiny?" He glanced at the faces crowded in the doorway. "The Kordish think my destiny is a scaffold."

"You took care of that already, didn't you."

Jax smirked. "A temporary measure, I fear."

The Oracle sighed. "I told you before, you can be master of your own destiny."

The chains rattled. "You know, Oracle, if the goddess wants us to understand what you are saying, you might try being a little less cryptic."

The Oracle made a strange dry noise, and at first Jax thought that the ancient creature might be having some kind of seizure. They doubled up, shaking and snorting.

"Less cryptic," the Oracle snorted. "Less cryptic!" Finally, the Oracle straightened, wiping tears from their eyes. "You're a treat, Javix Sharkin." They smiled. "We haven't laughed like that in centuries." Again, they bent over, making alarming noises.

"Ah, yes. Ahem." They fished among the folds of their robe and finally withdrew a very white handkerchief, blew their nose and laughed again. "You make us wish we were going with you and Klaris."

"Where are we going?"

"That's what Klaris is supposed to figure out."

"Does it have to do with the dragons coming back?"

"Probably."

"Dragons!" Jax swore. "Probably? Can't you just say yes or no? Think about what a return of the dragons would mean! I'm happy to help thwart them, or help the Weaver drive them away, but it would be nice if you could be a little clearer about what this involves."

The Oracle sighed. "Settle down, lad. Klaris is the Weaver, and you're the Paradox. The prophecy is coming due."

"The prophecy that *probably* has to do with dragons, or talking cats, maybe?"

"Talking cats? Where'd you hear that one?"

"I'll tell you, if you tell me."

The Oracle laughed again, but their eyes were steely. "You are irreverent. Stay with Klaris, Javix. Resolve the dichotomies." The Oracle turned to leave the room.

"Wait! Oracle, wait!" Jax whipped the chains, so they banged on the stone floor. "I am not free to resolve anything!"

The Oracle's gray eyes ran along the chains to the ring in the center of the room and back again to the fetters. "Didn't you show them the medallion I gave you?"

Jax pulled the golden chain with its dangling medallion over his head and threw it at the nobles gathered in the doorway. Chevvain bent to pick it up. "What is this?" she asked.

"It is the sign of the goddess," the Oracle snapped. "Obviously." With a great smooth wave of magic, the Oracle and their light disappeared.

"Dragons." Jax muttered, running his hands through his dirty hair. The fetters clanked. In the dim light of the guard's single torch he faced the ruling nobles of Kordon. They stared back at him.

"So, we must suffer a traitor to walk among us because the Oracle wishes it?" Earla Stona grumbled.

"I am not a traitor."

"Prove it. Your Highness."

Jax's sea blue eyes swept the nobles, without pausing as they crossed the face of the Dowager Stylla.

Many of the nobles recognized the smile that slowly grew on his face. "You'll just have to take me on faith."

The king was looking at the Oracle's medallion and remembering his dead sister and how she had loved Sealord Rax, who'd had that same grin. He tuned to bellow back down the stairway. "Captain Karric! Come up here and unlock these chains.

"I believe you, Jax." The king's pale blue eyes returned to his nephew. "I never thought you'd do anything to harm me or Tallyn, or Kordon."

Jax knelt at last, relieved that finally a Kordish face and pale Kordish eyes looked upon him with trust and kindness. "Thank you, your Majesty. Thank you."

12

The king bent and looped the Oracle's golden chain over Jax's bowed head. "Go get yourself cleaned up, my lord, then join us in the great hall. We're entertaining the Dranstyllian ambassador—though I can't understand half of what she says in that sloppy, sloshy accent of hers."

The king descended the stairs complaining to the sympathetic ears of his nobles about the way people in other landish nations butchered what he considered the "High Landish" of Kordon.

Jax rubbed his wrists where the fetters had chaffed him.

"Come with me, your Highness," Karric clapped Jax on the shoulder. "I'll take you to the chamberlain." She led him down an extra flight of stairs and through the back corridors in order to avoid the crowd in the great hall.

They stopped in the kitchen where the king's chef, an old ally from Jax's days as a hungry teenager, prepared him a plate of food and poured him a large glass of Chevvainian red, while the chamberlain and his staff rushed in and out organizing a bath, clothes, and a clean room for the restored prince.

In the end, Jax found himself in his old room, the Barian Suite, that he and Bryx had alternately used during their fostering. It was the same room Jax had been taken from by the Duke of Midipex all those years ago.

The chamberlain's staff had quickly dusted the unused furniture and changed the sheets. In a wardrobe, Jax found his own clothes and on the desk, his favorite silver dragonpipe, gleaming from some servant's recent efforts.

He sipped his wine and waited as the servants prepared the bath, surveying the familiar room.

His favorite books still stood on the bookshelf. A lute, its strings dangling, lay on a table. He picked up the dragonpipe.

Grief flooded him, more devastating now than when he'd first heard with disbelief that Rax was dead. Even the happy memories of this room only deepened his sense of loss. He could never regain the carefree days and nights laughing by that fire with his foster-mates, or in that bed with Cheshir.

He remembered hiding under that bed more than once, hoping that the dowager's minions wouldn't find him. They always did.

One of the servants refilled the silver goblet then set the bottle of Chevvainian red on a small table next to the bath. Jax shed the last of his dirty clothes and slipped into the water.

He closed his eyes and relaxed into the warmth. As a boy, Jax had learned to run from the dowager and make himself unobtrusive to avoid her humiliations. But as he'd grown fluent in sarcasm and adept at court politics, he'd unwisely lost his fear of her.

At this point, Jax conceded that this grandmother was well ahead in their game of hurt and humiliation. He was down by four gruesome years. The memory of her voice, *I don't want to see him again,* raised goose bumps on his arms even now. He took another sip of the rich wine and smiled. On the other hand, he had survived those years. Midipex had failed the dowager and she would have to see her despised grandson again and again.

When the door opened, he assumed it was someone come to help him shave and dress, and he closed his eyes for one last dunk in the water.

He yelped with surprise, toppling the silver goblet off the edge of the bath when he felt arms and legs joining him in the tub.

Lady Cheshir took his face in her hands and kissed him. Her naked body slid against his in the warm, scented water.

Sometime later, Cheshir ran her long fingers down the side of his face. "I believe you missed me."

He grinned. Indeed, she had felt so good, and loving her here in this room brought him back to the entitled man he used to be. Jax rose from the carpet where they'd landed and bent to fish his goblet out of the murky bathwater.

"Sweet goddess, Jax, those scars!"

He wiped the goblet dry and filled it. He handed it to Cheshir. "Slaves are beaten."

A brief knock preceded the perfunctory return of the chamberlain with a squire and three pages. Jax tossed a silken dressing gown from his wardrobe to Cheshir.

She belted it around her waist, her eyes never leaving Jax. "You're different," she said finally.

Swathed in towels, Jax leaned back in a chair as the squire prepared the shaving foam. He noted the way Cheshir stood, her blond hair disheveled, but still artful, her pale blue eyes thoughtful. He remembered a girl with a less sheltered heart; a girl with messy hair who hadn't fully learned the power of her beauty. He looked away, thinking of the lost years between them.

"Aye, Shirry. I suppose we all are."

The squire began to brush his chin with the foam, cutting off further conversation. Cheshir left, followed by a page carrying the frothy pile of her clothes.

"We can't very well argue with the Oracle." Earla Stona held her glass up to be refilled by a passing footman.

The Dranstyllian ambassador held out her own glass, her dark eyes on the group of nobles that had been crowded around this Prince Javix since he had entered the hall, his hair still damp, and interrupted her carefully crafted speech. A practiced diplomat, she let her frustration slip away as the rich wine caressed her tongue. "And the Oracle said he's not a traitor?"

"Not exactly," the earla grumbled. "They said none of us *believes* he's guilty."

"Forgive me, your Grace," the ambassador made a point of not looking at the earla's face. "But it seems to me that *you* think he's guilty."

Stona sipped her wine. "There's plenty of evidence. And he confessed."

Across the room, someone handed Jax another glass of wine. He held it for a few moments, but then it slipped from his hands and spilled across the table. The nobles yelled and laughed and teased him about being out of practice. Jax shrugged and took another glass from a tray carried by a passing footman.

"I want to hear more about fairies, my lord." Lady Raisha smiled up at him. "I thought they'd all disappeared from the Knownlands."

"I thought so, too," Jax answered. "Here, Florin, Borrel, you two know more about them than I do."

The nobles, distrusting the intelligence of any creature not Kordish, looked warily to the nyad twins.

"Tell them about the time the fairy queen kidnapped your trekking party." Jax encouraged Florin by grabbing a bottle of wine and filling Florin's cup and his own.

"They are beautiful, but dangerous," Florin began.

"Dangerous? Aren't they tiny?"

"Aye, but their magic isn't."

Jax turned away from this discussion to find Foby at his elbow. He raised his glass in mockery. "Cheers, brother."

Stung by Jax's tone, Foby protested: "I couldn't do anything for you. My father wouldn't listen to me."

"Didn't any other ideas occur to you? You could have sought a stay of execution, or even tried to break me free."

Foby flushed with shame and shook his head. "Then I'd be a traitor, too."

"You will remember that *I* never was a traitor. And *I* will remember that you dared not lift a finger to help me."

Tallyn finished the pink wine in her glass. Other young nobles were starting to pay attention to the conversation between her foster brothers. "Come with me, gentlemen."

Once the three were behind the closed doors of Tallyn's parlor, Foby raised a decanter filled with pale pink liquid. "More wine?"

Jax shook his head.

"I noticed you were very careful about what you drank this evening," Tallyn said, her own stomach roiling unpleasantly.

Jax toyed with his empty glass. "Midipex didn't act alone."

"Who helped him?" Foby replaced the decanter of Aychex rosé, untouched.

Jax glanced at Foby then turned his gaze to Tallyn. If Cheshir had grown up over the last four years, the princess had almost crystallized. Always a politician, there was a new hardness in Tallyn's colorless eyes, and her ability to answer unspoken questions now seemed dangerous, as if she knew more about others' thoughts than people wanted her to know.

As now, she read his silence. "Foby," she looked up at him. "My stomach is so queasy. Will you see if you can find me some bubbly water?"

"I'll ring for it."

"But they never bring it cold, and it's nasty when it's warm."

Foby frowned. "Fine. I'll go. But I want you to talk to Priestess Mollish about your stomach tomorrow. Please."

"Yes, I will. She's just been so busy with the Weaver."

Foby left the room, and Tallyn turned expectantly to Jax.

"What's the matter with your stomach?"

She shrugged. "I don't know. I haven't felt well this whole Rising. Rather as if I have a permanent hangover."

"I never knew you to have a hangover no matter how hard we tried to give ourselves one." He grinned.

"Tarron sweet wine, Jax. That stuff is deadly." She leaned toward him. "Now stop prevaricating. Foby will be back in a moment. Who helped Midipex abduct you?"

"Our noble grandmother."

Tallyn's gaze sharpened. "And you still fear her?"

"Damn right, I do."

The princess said nothing. Followed by two of his dogs, Foby returned to find the pair of them silent. He handed Tallyn a tall, cold glass. Bubbles rose from the bottom, twinkling in the candlelight.

"What did I miss?" Foby asked, sitting on the floor between his hounds.

Tallyn took a long drink and wrinkled her long nose. "Just more of Jax's improbable tales."

"I'll tell you what still troubles me," Jax said. "I don't know why Midipex abducted me. Why would he risk treason?"

"He must have felt fairly confident in his accomplices," Foby prompted. He watched Tallyn and Jax exchange a glance and remembered how often the two of them had seemed to be miles ahead of everyone else.

"But what were his motives, Foby?" Jax asked. "What would he gain by removing me from Kordon? I'm not important here."

"Why did he bother sending you to the trolls?" Tallyn drank more of her water. "We know he paid spies to watch for you. Wouldn't it have been easier just to kill you?"

"Probably. But that wasn't the point. The goal was suffering and humiliation. It's a kind of revenge."

"Why would Midipex want revenge from you?" Foby asked.

"Not the duke. His accomplice," Jax explained.

"You're not going to tell me who it is?"

"I don't trust you, Foby."

The young lord leapt to his feet. "You don't trust me because I didn't throw myself down into your pit of treachery?"

"I am not a traitor. But you left me in that dungeon for a week. You stood there and watched while your father threatened to execute innocent people. Where was your honor, Foby? Where was our brotherhood?"

Foby's dogs responded to the anger in Jax's voice and stood with raised hackles. "My honor?" Foby growled. "Where was yours? Did you lie to save your friends?"

"Yes, I did. I figured I was dead anyway, and I might as well save Mam Marith and the nyad twins if I could."

"Well, I couldn't do anything, Jax. I'm just a younger son. My only option was to wait until Tallyn came and hope we might be able to do something together to save you."

Jax watched Foby pet his dogs and calm them down.

"I sat in that dark, stinking dungeon. I waited for you. And you never came."

Foby rose and went to the window. Hail pelted the glass and thunder rumbled in the dark outside. "I am sorry, Jax. I was bound too. Bound by the law."

"The law wasn't going to kill you."

"That's not fair," Tallyn said softly. "Just because you make your own rules doesn't mean that others can."

Lightning cracked, and thunder boomed through the room. One of the dogs cowered into Foby's legs. "Wow," he said looking out the window. "I think that hit one of the trees in the sacred grove."

Jax put his elbows on his knees and his head in his hands. He didn't want to fight Foby.

Foby came from the window and put his hand on Jax's shoulder. "I couldn't have watched you be executed."

Jax looked up into the honesty in Foby's face. He took a deep breath. "Good."

"Why don't you try staying out of trouble for a while?" Foby wiped his damp eyes. Jax rose and embraced his foster brother.

"While the dowager lives, I'm always in trouble."

"Was it the dowager who helped Midipex?" Foby asked.

Neither Jax nor Tallyn answered. "I grew up here, too," Foby noted, exasperated. "I know the dowager hates you, Jax. She always has."

Jax pushed the conversation to different ground. "There's a greater danger facing the Knownlands than Midipex and his... friends."

"What's that?" The princess rubbed her forehead.

"The Oracle claims that the dragons are coming back."

"Sweet goddess," Foby breathed. "That would be a disaster."

"That's what I thought," Jax agreed. "But the Oracle hints that the Weaver and I can do something to avert such a catastrophe."

Tallyn looked at Jax sharply. "The Weaver and you?"

He pulled the medallion from under his shirt. "That's what this is all about. There's a prophecy, apparently."

"Dragons, Jax, you'll give us all nightmares." Foby placed his hands gently on Tallyn's shoulders. "Scheming royals and returning dragons. What next?"

"Next is bed," Tallyn answered. "If we're going to have nightmares, I want to close my eyes." She was not quite able to keep the fatigue and pain out of her voice.

Jax noticed the way Foby stood near Tallyn, making no move to leave the princess's room. He smiled and bowed. "Good night, your Highness."

Jax awoke at mid-morning to the sun shining in his face. He curled his fingers into the soft sheets and thought how far he'd traveled over the last two months. One month ago, he had been slogging through snowbound paths with Marith and the nyad twins, a slave collar around his neck. This morning, Prince Javix Sharkin stretched in the soft comforts of a noble bed, and the Rising was over.

His whole being felt lighter now that the oppressive Rising Fear and the threat of a traitor's death had evaporated like the clouds. He stretched again, scratched at the healing wound on his shoulder, and got out of bed. At the window he gazed at the familiar view of the town and the sparkling waters of Keffin Harbor.

An empty harbor. There should be a dozen Barian merchant ships moored out there. But today nothing but a few seagulls floated on the calm waters.

He turned away from the window and rang for squires to bring him breakfast and make him presentable. Goddess, how had the Floating Islands weathered that tidal wave? He pictured a black wave crashing over the buildings on Helm and foaming through the sacred gardens.

"Here is your tea, your Highness." The squire poured steaming liquid into a delicate china cup and pulled Jax's thoughts back to Kordon. "There's milk, but no sugar, of course."

His Highness sipped the plain, creamy tea.

The squire noted the predatory smile on milord's face and fled, glad he wasn't the one who had to shave the unusual prince.

Fed and tidied, Jax emerged from the Barian Suite to find the palace nearly deserted.

"Everyone's gone out riding," Marith told him when he finally found her reading in a sunny corner of the library.

"What about Borrel and Florin?" he asked, as she pulled aside his doublet and shirt to look at the wound in his shoulder.

"Florin's probably riding too. She made friends with one of the chief grooms. Seems he'd been to Stede to purchase horses for the royal stable, and so they had something in common." Marith resettled Jax's clothes. "And Borrel's usually with the Royal Dragon, both of them sheltering from the Weaver's magic."

Jax leaned his back against the sunny window, enjoying its warmth.

Marith looked up at him. The sunlight gilded his fair hair and gleamed on his regal silks. He was more relaxed and somehow more whole than she had ever seen him before. So, this is you at home, she thought with a pang of sadness.

"Have you seen Klaris?" he asked.

"Not today. I usually go in the afternoons to give Priestess Mollish a rest."

"Something's going on with the magic." Jax turned his head to look out the window. "I can feel a powerful vortex, like a Rising storm coupled with a hurricane."

Marith looked at his clean profile and heard his crisp accent now in context with who and what he was.

"Go see her," she said softly.

He smiled. "I think I will, Mam." He bent and kissed her cheek and was gone, leaving the old druid to ponder the tears that ran down her face in solitude.

Klaris lay in the large guest room at the end of the corridor beyond the Barian Suite, Tallyn's rooms, and the dowager's chamber. Tall windows let in bright sunshine that belied the tension in the room.

Mollish carefully tended her smudging steams to ease the Weaver's cross-magicked lungs. Carte Serge performed a number of small magical spells, building and rebuilding a corner of the wall. Assorted other druids and servants came and went.

Jax's entrance brought this controlled frenzy to a halt, as everyone stopped to stare at him.

He ignored them and sat on the edge of the big bed. Klaris did not appear to notice him, her green eyes glazed and fixed on nothing, her face slack.

"Sweet goddess," Jax frowned.

"The Mystic is coming back, your Highness," Serge explained.

Jax reached out for Klaris's hand. Her fingers were cold and limp.

"There's so much magic here," he said. He could feel it like a violent current of water or wind rushing around and through him.

"How can *you* sense it?" Serge faced the prince. "Why doesn't it cause you cross-magic?"

Jax heard the accusation in the magician's tone. He turned cold sea-blue eyes and a chilly smile upon the man. "It's a paradox, isn't it?"

A fat orange cat jumped onto the bed. Klaris's breathing caught and she coughed and shifted under the covers.

"This cat won't leave her alone," muttered one of the younger druids, reaching for the animal. It leapt away from her.

"Wait," Jax said. "Let it stay."

"Thank you," the cat said clearly.

"Sweet goddess!" shrieked the druid, backing away.

"Oh," Mollish breathed. "Oh, your Highness." Quietly she began to sing: *"The cats can talk. Unseen, one walks, through the light of day. The cycle turns. The Weaver learns to keep the beasts away."*

Jax shivered. "Where did you hear that?"

"It's an old fairy song, my lord. I learned it as a girl. Our lands are up at the edge of the Darkwood, you know."

"But there haven't been fairies in Kordon for centuries, if ever," scoffed Serge.

"Not since the dragon interregnum," Mollish agreed. "But the people of the forest still sing a number of such songs."

"What's it all about?" demanded the young druid.

"Dragons," hissed the cat.

The young druid fainted. Mollish and Serge and several attendants came to carry her away.

Jax found himself alone in the room with Klaris, the cat, and the ever-thickening magic, but what had been an inchoate storm now seemed to smooth and deepen in a quiet, steady flow. He felt Klaris's fingers tighten around his own and realized her eyes had closed.

He sat watching her. The sun streaming in warmed his bones and the late night, combined with the relief of being out from under the threat of execution and the Rising Fear created an inescapable lethargy.

Some time later Lady Mollish returned and paused at the threshold.

Klaris still lay breathing with difficulty, but her eyes were closed, and she seemed more settled and peaceful. Jax sat on the floor, bathed in sunshine, his head on the bed, sound asleep. He still held Klaris's hand.

The cat, curled tidily at the foot of the bed, watched Lady Mollish with clear green eyes. The priestess nodded reverently to the cat and left the room, shutting the door softly behind her.

13

She floated, weightless, disembodied. The raging storm of magic had finally ceased, the relentless pounding had stopped, and now she drifted, lost, whittled and hollow, sensing a bottomless abyss.

She tried to breathe, but her lungs were thick, and she could only catch half a breath at a time. Panic began to rise, and it focused her. Small breaths, then. Half breaths. And there, there was something different, a nugget of different magic, not her own, but familiar, prickly and sinewy. She reached for it and it steadied her the way a walking stick provides balance one already has.

That was good. For a while she rested this way, the half breaths enough.

Suddenly, the anchor was gone and her balance with it. She yawed through the waves of magic. Distantly she felt her stomach rebel, rise, and vomit. She heard voices, surprised, concerned, but she couldn't understand the words.

"Dragons!"

"Hold her hair back, Jax. Father, hand me those towels, please."

Again and again her stomach clenched and emptied. Her lungs strained to get enough air. But there! There was that little anchor again. With all the force she could muster, she grasped it desperately.

"Sweet goddess," someone choked. "What are you doing to me?"

Cool cloths wiped her face. Klaris opened her eyes. Afternoon light filled the room. She sucked in half a breath. An old druid with kind blue eyes smiled at her, while a princely looking man knelt over her, holding her head. The Mystic told her this was Jax, but she'd never seen him like this.

Her stomach rose again, but this time the druid was ready with a basin.

"Slow breaths, Weaver," the druid said gently. "Imagine you're just starting a sun salutation. Sit softly and relax."

Klaris closed her eyes again, not understanding the Landish. She held tightly to the rock of Jax's magic.

"Goddess, Mam, she's wrapped her magic around mine like she wants to pry it out of me." That was Jax's voice. What was he saying?

"Let go, then."

The anchor was gone. She moaned. Gasped. Gasped again. Suffocating, panic rose and vomit with it. No, she fought it. No! Which way was up? Damn it, she was vomiting again. Opening her eyes, she found Jax's worried face.

He sat on the edge of the bed again and took her hand.

She gripped him. Voices speaking incomprehensible Landish and the Mystic, deep and vast, swirled around her.

"I think she needs me, Mam," Jax said dryly.

"I think she needs to restore her soul," the druid said with equal dryness. "The mastery will have depleted her."

"How can she be depleted? She feels so full of magic right now."

"Come now, Jax. You know working magic depletes the soul."

"Aye." He did know. Mystics used daily sun salutations to replenish themselves after working their spells. Dragons used music to do the same.

"Well, how many sun salutations has Weaver Klaris managed since she mastered the Mystic?"

Klaris felt the anchor move, and she grasped it tighter than ever.

"Only a few," he choked.

"What is it, Jax?" Alarm rang though the druid's voice

"She's got a grip on my bit of Dragon. It's as if she's drowning and pulling me under with her."

"Do you have your dragonpipe? Play it. See if it strengthens you and her both."

Klaris let the unintelligible conversation drift around and through her with the magic. She felt Jax move, but he left his force there for her.

"That's the dragonpipe Doc gave you. How did you manage to hold on to that through the last month?"

"It's special."

Music began, soft and low. The simple tune grew, progressed, unraveled and remade itself. For the first time in her life, Klaris understood something about the way music worked. She felt Jax's magic center and solidify, and she pulled strength from this. The pipe squawked but then the tune resumed.

He played soft tunes and lively ones. Soft voices came and went. The steamy vapors that eased her lungs thickened.

Finally, the music stopped, and she heard his heartbeat under her ear and then a strange growl.

"I need a drink." His voice was hoarse.

"And food too, by the sound of your stomach," said the druid.

Klaris, calmer now, managed to open her eyes. Who was this old druid? Where were Priestess Mollish and Carte Serge? The druid handed Jax a cup and smiled at him in a familiar, maternal way.

"I am starving," he admitted, draining the cup.

The druid glanced at Klaris and smiled into her open eyes. "The Weaver looks more settled. They'll be serving tea now. Go eat."

"No," Klaris cried as Jax moved. "No!"

"Dragons, Klaris," he sucked in his breath as Klaris's Mystic once again clamped down on his own force.

"Breathe, Weaver." The druid ordered.

Disciplined by years of sun salutations, Klaris took slow, steady half-breaths. But her fingers clung to Jax's doublet. She heard his stomach grumble again and looked up at him. "I'm sorry," she said softly in Islish, her grip on his magic as implacable as ever.

"What is it?" he asked her, also in Islish.

"I can't find myself."

"You're in Kree, Weaver. Look. You've been here in this room for four days now."

"Not what I mean," she cleared her throat. "All I can feel is magic. I don't know where *I* am in all of this." She clutched at him again with both her hands and her magic.

She saw him blink and gasp as if something unseen had hurt him.

"I can feel you," she explained in a whisper, gripping his magic. "Only you. When you leave, I'm lost, completely gone."

"Alright then. I'll stay. But can you loosen your grip a little bit?"

She stared at him, uncomprehending.

"No?" His lips quirked. "Well, fine."

She watched him kick off his shoes and resettle himself on the pillows of her bed. She closed her eyes again, relieved, and leaned into him.

A bit later, voices and lovely smells intruded into her peace. She opened her eyes again.

Priestess Mollish hovered over her. "Drink some broth, my lady. You need to rebuild your physical strength so you can stand up to the Mystic."

Klaris sat up, coughing. She took the cup of broth and sipped.

"Don't bite my fingers," snapped the older druid as Jax quickly put the bread and meat she handed him into his mouth.

"You know," he swallowed, "I have had about two decent meals in the last two months."

"I know, son."

Klaris watched the druid look at him and saw the sorrow on her wrinkled face. She thought for a moment then spoke in Landish: "Who are you, Mother?"

Jax looked down at her in surprise. "This is Mother Marith."

"Oh. The druid with the tent."

"Yes." He smiled at her.

Klaris liked his smile. She swallowed more broth. Suddenly she was aware of that abyss again.

Jax felt Klaris's magic lurch and tear at him. He closed his eyes and endured.

"Breathe, Weaver," Marith said gently. "You'll find yourself again."

Klaris coughed but worked hard to take small, smooth breaths. Eventually she found she could ease her grip on Jax's magic just a bit.

"Thank you," he whispered and began eating again.

Priestess Mollish and Carte Serge stood at the foot of the bed, watching.

"I don't understand," Mollish said softly.

Mother Marith turned to them. "It's not a physical problem. It's a soul problem."

"Oh," Mollish breathed.

"It's the magic," Jax grumbled, his own breathing unsteady. "She's using my magic to anchor herself somehow."

"But why yours?" Serge demanded.

Jax offered a lascivious grin. "Why not mine."

Marith thought Jax's humor was pretty frayed around the edges. Whatever the Weaver was doing to anchor herself, it wasn't easy on him.

Once again, the bottom seemed to drop away from Klaris, and she closed her eyes to fight the nausea. Desperately she clutched Jax's magic. She didn't see him close his own eyes or bow his head.

Unable to move beyond Klaris's desperate grasp, Jax dozed, trying to ignore the feeling of something essential being ripped loose from the core of his being.

CRASH

"Serge!"

Jax opened his eyes. Priestess Mollish and Carte Serge were on their knees beside the fire wiping up some mess.

"What's the matter with you today?" Mollish asked, looking with concern into the Royal Magician's face.

Serge motioned toward the bed, saw the prince's islish eyes upon him, and closed his mouth into a grim line.

Jax stretched without releasing Klaris's hand. "What have I done this time?" He resettled himself on the pillows.

Serge busied himself with collecting pieces of broken crockery and didn't answer. As Royal Mystic, he had worked long hours alongside Captain Karric tutoring the young nobles of Kordon. Jax's love of history made him a voracious student of Old Landish and Ancient, and he had pushed Serge to the limits of his own scholarship. Discomforted by the prince's linguistic gymnastics and also his irritating bit of Dragon force, Serge had never been charmed by the lad's smart mouth or sweet face. Prince Jax flaunted rules, and Serge, as a powerful Mystic, had great respect for rules.

Now, to see this glib Jax Sharkin, a prince with Dragon force, sleeping with the Weaver wrapped in his arms, well it was wrong—wrong from many perspectives. A Dragon shouldn't be able to even touch the Weaver. And a prince shouldn't hold the Weaver, not like that.

Mollish's eyes had followed Serge, noting his refusal to answer Jax. "Does the prince's magic trouble you, Serge?"

"I can't even feel his magic."

"The Weaver has it," Jax noted.

"Goddess only knows why," Serge grumbled.

"Sitting here all day wasn't my idea."

Mollish heard the discomfort in the prince's voice and saw lines of strain around his eyes.

Serge sat down on his stool and explored the Mystic. Jax felt him intrude upon the force that floated all around Klaris. She gasped and clamped harder on Jax's fingers and upon the Dragon force within him.

"Can you stop that, Serge?" Jax asked tersely. "When you stir the Mystic, you seem to disturb the Weaver."

"How do *you* know? My lord."

Jax lifted his hand. Klaris's knuckles were white as she crushed his fingers together.

"Sweet goddess," Mollish bent to unwind Klaris's grip.

Klaris frowned. "No," she whispered, holding even tighter to Jax's hand.

Serge pulled back from the Mystic.

"It's alright, Priestess." Jax's voice was tight. "She'll loosen her grip in a minute."

Serge took up his knitting and the angry clack of his needles filled the room. Mollish tended her smudging steams. Eventually Klaris's grip eased. Jax looked out the window at the westering sun and thought of Baria.

"Serge, would you try a scry for me?"

Serge looked at him mulishly. "What do you want to see?"

"Baria. Haven."

"Why?"

"There was a tidal wave during the Rising."

"That's right," Mollish noted. "It damaged some farmlands up along the coast of Chevvain, I believe."

"If that wave hit Haven...." Jax began softly. He didn't finish, but both Mollish and Serge heard the worry in his voice.

Serge pursed his lips. He had come to hate scrying during the last four years as Princess Tallyn had demanded he search for the prince who now sat so inappropriately before him. But he had also learned to carry a small silver bowl with him at all times. Now he pulled it out and filled it with water. "You don't know how often I had to look for you, my lord, these past four years."

"I wasn't hiding."

"I'll watch the Weaver and let you know if the scry disturbs her," Mollish offered.

Serge glanced at her, but he couldn't refuse the prince. With a deep breath, he focused himself and began to weave the Mystic. It came, but not with the usual smooth lines. This was no clean weave, but a bundle of knots and wayward threads.

Klaris stirred and the Mystic moved, but Jax held her tighter, and she remained relaxed.

Serge held the bowl for Jax to see and watched with satisfaction the sorrow crossing the prince's face. Ruined buildings with broken windows bent over streets choked with trash and mud. Sunken boats lifted skeletal masts above dirty, rubbish-filled water. A few Barians worked amid the devastation, but most were gathered on the quays, staring out to sea.

"What are they looking at?" Jax asked.

Serge tried to ignore the ache in the prince's voice. He rewove the scry and shifted the view.

Four large ships lifted their sails to the evening breeze. A royal Barian pennant flew from the topmast of the largest ship.

"Sweet goddess. He's coming."

"Who's coming?" Serge closed the scry and the water cleared.

"The sealord." Jax remembered Bryx's promise to see him in Kree after the Rising. Did the sealord know he was here? Jax turned his gaze to the window and the coming night, wondering how Bryx could leave the Floating Islands in such a state.

"That didn't seem to bother the Weaver," Mollish said gently.

"She hasn't taken hold of the loom yet," Serge said.

Mollish resettled the blankets around the Weaver. "What do you mean?"

The Royal Mystic poured the scry water into a vase of flowers. "She has to grip the structure of the weave. It's the final step in mastering the Mystic, and some say the most delicate. Each new Weaver changes the weave, you see, opens new doors, new ways to work the Mystic. After resting for the Dark Fortnight, the new Weaver has to set the loom, establish it, so everyone else can use it."

"She hasn't done that yet?" Jax asked.

Serge shook his head. "Her Dark Fortnight wasn't very restful, was it my lord?"

"Is that my fault too?" Jax's eyes still gazed out the darkening window.

Mollish spoke before Serge could snap back. "Didn't you say, Serge, that Weaver Klaris accessed more magic than was there before?"

"Yes. The options she discovered and opened are almost limitless. But we can't realize that potential until she takes control."

"When will she do that?" Jax asked, flexing his cramped fingers.

"She should have done it as soon as the magic came back, my lord." Serge's pale eyes accused Jax. "Perhaps the presence of your Dragon force is thwarting her."

"I'll just go then." Jax moved away from Klaris, and immediately she began to writhe and choke.

"That's enough, both of you!" Mollish snapped. "My lord, give the Weaver your hand. Right now."

Jax did as he was told and submitted, once again, to the sense of being pulled apart. "Sweet goddess," he whispered.

Serge watched the prince's discomfort and frowned.

"Here you are!" Tallyn burst into the room followed by Lord Foby and Lady Cheshir. Cheshir waltzed around the bed and planted a slow kiss on Jax's lips. "What are you doing?"

"Enduring insults."

Serge snorted softly and avoided Tallyn's sharp gaze.

"How is the Weaver?" Foby asked, frowning at the sound of Klaris's shallow breathing.

"She appears to be drawing strength from Prince Jax," Mollish explained.

Cheshir's eyes grew wary. "What kind of strength?"

"Magical."

"You don't have any magic to speak of," Tallyn protested.

"Just enough to get me in trouble."

Mollish turned to the princess. "Are you feeling any better today, your Highness?"

Tallyn shrugged. "It was good to get out into the sunshine."

"But she was sick all afternoon," Foby revealed.

Mollish frowned. "Sit down, please, my lady." She began to examine the princess carefully.

Cheshir sat on the bed next to Jax. She noticed the way the Weaver gripped his hand. "How can the Weaver take strength from you? Shouldn't that be forbidden?"

"Indeed, it should, my lady," Serge agreed fervently.

"Dragons!" Jax swore. "What would you have me do?"

They stared at him with their light Kordish eyes. He felt Klaris tighten her grip on his fingers and looked down at her. Green eyes stared back at him.

"Weaver!" Lady Mollish pushed between Tallyn and Foby to offer Klaris a drink of water.

Slowly, Klaris took her clammy fingers from Jax's hand and sat up. She swallowed the water and breathed with discipline. Tangled curls drifted around her shoulders. Her green eyes seemed large and almost amphibious.

"Take the Mystic, Weaver," Serge begged softly. "It needs you."

Klaris blinked, slowly translating the magician's words. How could she possibly take hold of this amorphous force? She couldn't tell where it ended, and she began. Only the small rock of Jax's magic gave her any sense of stability.

Through the fog of the Mystic, she finally realized that it was Princess Tallyn, sitting on the foot of the bed. She watched Jax smile at the lovely blond woman next to him whose long fingers ran up his arm.

Half breaths weren't quite enough. Her head was light, and she couldn't find her Landish, so she asked her question in Islish. "Are they going to execute you?"

Jax answered in Islish. "The Oracle told them not to."

"Do they still think you're guilty?"

"They never actually thought I was guilty."

"But... you confessed."

"I lied. The confession is a standard pre-execution charade."

Klaris coughed, closed her eyes, and concentrated on breathing with a purpose.

"What's she saying, Jax?" Tallyn demanded.

"She wanted to know if you were going to execute me."

"I think Earla Stona still wants to," Tallyn smirked.

"And Frinz," Foby said pointedly.

Cheshir removed her fingers from the nape of Jax's neck.

Tallyn took hold of the conversation. "Jax, we wanted to have a private supper tonight, just the four of us." She gestured to Foby and Cheshir.

Foby grinned. "Like the old days, but without the homework."

Jax answered the warmth in his friend's smile. "We don't have to drink plum brandy, do we?"

They all laughed, remembering adolescent misadventures with the sticky drink.

"I can't even stand the smell of that stuff," Cheshir grimaced.

"I don't think Prince Jax can leave the Weaver right now," Mollish cautioned.

All eyes turned to Klaris. Their words had swirled past her, but she recognized that this must be friendship. Jax would have grown up with these people, and now they had him back. How lucky. She steadied herself and released his magic. Immediately vertigo swamped her. She set her cup down carefully and clutched at her quilts, focusing her gaze on one spot on the pink paisley print and breathing slowly.

"What's wrong with the Weaver?" Foby asked.

Jax had felt her release him. He watched her tremble and fight for control, steeling himself for the wrench that would come when she grasped his magic again. But she didn't.

"Goddess damn it," Serge swore. "Why can't she take control?"

"Don't you see what it will cost her?" Jax snapped. "You're the man with Mystic here. Surely you understand that wielding this power will imperil her soul."

Serge opened his mouth then shut it.

Jax bent to the Weaver and took her, again, in his arms. He spoke softly, in Islish. "Take it, Klaris."

She seized his magic with desperate force.

"What are you doing, Jax?" Cheshir whispered.

"Capitulating." Jax breathed, as Klaris somehow wrenched at his magic with sharp claws.

Cheshir stood, her eyes guarded.

Tallyn rose also. "We'll have that dinner another time. To tell you the truth, I'm not hungry."

Foby remained for a moment longer, watching Jax with the limp Weaver in his arms. "Why, Jax?"

He looked up, his islish eyes dark with a silent agony, but he had no answer.

14

Halla felt the magic flair through her veins and looked up from the matrix she was helping the novices build. A large black crane, its wings spread wide, circled down from the wind-rent clouds. It landed between palm trees and looked at her with cold, yellow eyes. Deftly she closed the matrix spell.

"We'll resume in an hour," she snapped to the startled novices.

Cautiously, Halla approached the bird. "I have your gift," she said softly, pulling the folded leaves from her pocket where they'd been waiting for the past week. She unwrapped the dried fish from the leaves and held it out to the bird. The eyes continued to stare at her, unblinking. With astounding quickness, the bird bent, the beak snapped, and the fish became lumps descending the sleek neck.

Halla dropped the empty leaves and knelt to the bird's long legs. She removed the scroll from its case. "Thank you," she whispered then strode for the Highlord's liana.

He sat in a high-backed wicker chair, picking out a complicated tune on a lute.

"Highlord!" Halla couldn't keep the excitement out of her voice. "Raggar, we've had an answer."

The Highlord lifted his head and looked at the nyad with eyes that were still focused on the geometry of his music. "An answer?"

"To one of the letters I sent asking about the Weaver. Since we can't find her in a scry I decided to contact all the Royal Dragons from The Hant to Dranstyl," she said gently, hearing more in the music than just the notes. "One of them replied."

The music stopped. "Good. Tell me."

"It's from the Barian Royal Magician." Halla unrolled the parchment and read: "*Greetings. Dragon Halla. We in Baria have suffered a grievous disaster. A vast tidal wave came out of the Rising. It destroyed much of our fleet and almost sank the Floating Islands.*"

"Sweet goddess," the Highlord frowned.

Halla continued to quote: "*The Weaver is not on Baria. But there is another person who cannot be found in a scry. You may know my lady, that Prince Javix, the younger son of our past Sealord Rax, disappeared from Kree some eight Risings ago. Naturally all of Baria spent many years looking for him. We discovered, to my chagrin, that the prince is somehow invisible to magic. The Royal Mystic couldn't find him either. This was so perplexing that the young Sealord Bryx went to the Oracle for answers. But found no satisfaction.*"

"What's the damned Oracle up to?" Raggar strummed a discordant note on his lute. His fingers had started trembling again.

"Listen," Halla continued. "*All Baria was overjoyed when Prince Javix returned to Haven just before this Spring Rising. Many people in Baria hoped he would stay here and help his brother as sealord, but the prince said that the Oracle had commanded him to fetch the Weaver off of Sageham. He sailed north a few days before the Rising started and hasn't been heard from since. I have attempted again to scry for the prince, but he remains invisible.*"

Raggar carefully set the lute on a table and folded his fingers to still them. "That means this Barian prince would have gotten to Sageham right when the Weaver mastered the Mystic."

"And taken her away into a Rising filled with tidal waves, if he fulfilled the Oracle's command," Halla agreed.

Raggar rose and poured himself a glass of palm wine. "Let's have Mother Willma in here to see if she can enlighten us about the Oracle's intentions." He offered a glass to Halla.

She frowned and shook her head. "It's too early in the day, Raggar."

"I fear it is very, very late."

An hour later, after listening to oblique explanations from Mother Willma and then receiving a clearer if not very soothing picture of the half-islish Prince Javix Sharkin from two Barian Dragons who were among the students at Dragonsholm, Halla decided that she would join Raggar in a tall glass of wine despite the fact that the sun had not yet reached its zenith.

Raggar ran a hand through his disheveled hair. Halla noted that the silver was overtaking the dark.

She gulped her wine. "How are we to face a return of the dragons without a coherent Oracle?"

Raggar tried to refill their glasses, but his hands were shaking so that Halla took the carafe and did it for him. The Highlord slumped back into his chair, mumbling. "The Weaver is supposed to do something. I think."

"Highlord! Dragon Halla!" Blizzen's voice carried on the gentle tropical air.

"We're here," Halla answered.

Blizzen joined them on the liana, holding out a scroll. "A crane came for you."

Halla ripped it open. "Kordon! It's from Dragon Cyril. You remember her. She studied with Blizzen. Now she's the Kordish Royal Dragon." Halla paraphrased Cyril's letter as she read rapidly. "The Weaver is in Kordon, Raggar! Cross-magicked, apparently."

"Cross-magicked? But—." The Highlord shook his head. "It's her Dark Fortnight. Besides, who would have enough magic to cross hers?"

Halla heard the flicker in the Highlord's voice that always surfaced when he mentioned the Dark Fortnight. She remembered the days he had spent without magic after he had achieved his Highlord status and knew the mixture of devastation and elation that time held for him.

She returned her gaze to the scroll. "Cyril says that the Weaver used magic to teleport herself and Prince Javix to Kree and somehow cross-magicked herself."

Raggar stared.

"Then, Cyril says, the Oracle actually visited Kree during the Rising and spoke to the Weaver. And, for goddess' sake, she says she's been working with a new pupil who's a nyad from up in the Hantland and is friends with this Prince Javix."

Raggar started violently as if something had hit him. His voice, when he spoke, sounded strangled. "I guess Prince Javix got the Weaver off of Sageham, then."

"Prince Javix?" Blizzen looked from one to the other.

"He's a Barian prince," Halla explained.

"He's a prince of Kordon, too," Blizzen offered, his pale blue Kordish eyes watching the other two closely. "But he committed some kind of treason and was condemned."

Halla heard the familiar disparagement in Blizzen's voice that often discolored his comments about the other races of the Knownlands like his disdain of palm wine or Nomad red, but right now she wasn't thinking about Blizzen and his Kordish prejudices. She considered his fair skin, peeling as usual from exposure to the tropical sun. "Prince Javix is Kordish and Barian?"

Blizzen sniffed in that maddening Kordish way. "His mother was Princess Valla of Kordon; his father was the sealord."

Halla turned back to the Highlord. "There is something here," she said, trying to place a finger on the memory that was pushing uneasily at the back of her mind. "Something from ancient nyad lore that I can't quite remember."

"There's all kinds of dragon-blasted confusion here," Raggar said softly.

"Maybe you should seek the Oracle again, Highlord," Blizzen suggested.

Raggar shook his head. "Can't." His glass fell to the floor as he began to shake uncontrollably.

Halla fell to her knees at Raggar's feet and took his hands in her own. "What is it?"

"I can't control the magic anymore," the Highlord's voice wrenched her heart. "I dare not use it."

Blizzen's face went white under its perpetual sunburn.

Halla stared into Raggar's face. "I will to go to the Verwood," she said with soft conviction. "There is something older than Dragon force here. I will go to the Nyad Magi and get some answers."

Raggar blinked. "I need the Weaver."

"I'll go to Kordon," Blizzen volunteered. "I'll get her to Paalm. You can meet us there."

"She may not come," Raggar said, his voice growing hoarse. "Caledra is in ruins. If I were her, I would want to go to my people, to the heart of my magic."

"Farsouth," Halla said, squeezing Raggar's sweaty hands. "She's Farsouthian, right? Tell her, the Highlord will meet her in Farsouth."

Blizzen frowned. "That's a lot of sailing."

"Deal with it," she snapped, her eyes never leaving the Highlord. Raggar shuddered.

Halla rose. "Come, Dragon Blizzen. I'll sail to Kordon with you and head to the Verwood from there."

Blizzen bowed his head. Like all landish folk, he hated boats, but spending time on them was the price every great magician paid to study, since both sanctuaries of magic sat on islands.

"I don't enjoy sailing either," Halla confided, her nyad eyes still on the shivering Highlord. "But we must get some answers."

The two walked away from the liana, the silent Highlord, and the spreading pool of spilled wine.

15

"**S**hall I bring you more wine, my lord?" The page carefully lifted the tray of empty plates off Jax's lap.

"No, but some tea would do." He sat forward, pulled the doublet over his head, and handed it to the waiting squire.

Carte Serge frowned but said nothing, for now, as the prince continued to address his squire.

"I'd like a lute if you can find me a small one."

The squire folded the velvet doublet over his arm. "Yes, my lord."

Jax shifted himself on the bed, plumping the pillows.

Klaris sighed, her eyes tightly closed.

Serge echoed the sigh and straightened himself in his chair by the fire.

The squire returned with a lute made of fine pale wood and a pot of tea. He poured some and bowed away. "You'll ring if you need me, my lord?"

"Aye, thank you."

Jax sipped the brightly flavored tea and fiddled with the lute, tuning the strings. After a few minutes he picked out the simple notes in the First Tune. As usual, his fingers began to amplify the notes into chords.

"What's that song called, my lord?" Serge asked.

"The First Tune."

"Because it's always played first?"

Jax nodded. "Anyone with Dragon force can play this tune on just about any instrument."

Serge watched the prince's fingers in the light of the single candle near the bed and the dim fire. The fair head bent over the lute, coaxing the melancholy tune from the instrument.

The Royal Mystic yawned, the stress of the past few days pushing him down into the deep chair and creating a profound longing for his own bed.

"Do you intend to chaperone us all night?" Jax asked, the tune never faltering.

Serge sat up a little straighter. "The Weaver is very vulnerable, my lord. I don't intend to leave her with the likes of you."

Jax's eyes remained on the strings of his lute. "The likes of me?"

"I know you fostered here in Kree, my lord, but you are a Dragon, and a foreigner."

"The Weaver is a foreigner, too."

Serge heard the accusation in the prince's soft voice and knew this prejudice seemed small-minded, but he also knew that the Weaver, bowled over by her new-found powers, would need a great deal of support and care, and he just didn't trust this wise-cracking rake with his hurtful spark of Dragon force to have the depth of soul to stick by her.

The music stopped and Serge realized the slanted, sea-blue eyes were focused upon him, waiting.

"I know you can sense her power, my lord," Serge said finally. "But I am not sure you appreciate the many ways she lacks strength and experience. She is very young to be Weaver."

Jax's fingers had started strumming again. "She is about my age."

"Exactly."

"Exactly what?"

"Ah, youth!" Serge said, exasperated. "So all-knowing while knowing nothing!"

The tune rose and fell, twisted back on itself and then danced with its own mirror image. In the silence when it ended, Jax spoke in a pensive voice:

"I find it so curious that you seem to see Klaris as some sort of fragile child. I don't understand why you fear I could, or would, harm her in any way."

"You've been in her bed all day," snapped Serge. "Surely you understand that's forbidden."

"It is the Weaver who holds me here. Not my own lascivious desire."

"So you admit—."

"I admit that I'm here because she has a grip on me that's merciless, for goddess' sake! I don't know why you fear my intentions when surely you can see that I'm giving the fey little Mystic a piece of my soul."

"Do you have a choice?"

Jax laughed and played a minor chord. "Is that the question? Could I stand up and walk out of here, leaving the Weaver to drown in the magic her own folly or hubris called forth?"

Another chord, a third, a fourth. "No. I am terrified of her. For her."

"Terrified?"

The minor chords progressed into another tune. Serge found it oddly beautiful and grumbled at the ache it raised in his heart. Exhausted as he was, he longed for dawn and the sun salutations that would soothe his own soul and bring some relief to the anxiety of the prince's presence and his unyielding position next to the Weaver.

Jax played on softly, not seeming to notice when Serge's eyes finally closed, and sleep took him and his censorious attitude.

He was still playing, the candle mostly gone, when Klaris stirred and opened her eyes.

"I've been hearing music in a whole new way," she said in Islish.

He kept playing. "Maybe you're hearing it as a Dragon now."

"Maybe. Why aren't you asleep?"

"I drowsed most of the day."

"Thank you, Jax. Thank you for staying and steadying me."

He turned his sea-blue eyes upon her, and she was suddenly conscious of her tangled hair and rumpled nightgown. But he didn't seem to notice. "You scare the dragons out of me, Klaris. I wish you'd figure out how to grasp the Mystic and let me go."

She sat up, pushing her wayward curls behind her ears, and reached for the water on her bedside table.

"Are you hungry?" he asked. "Can I ring for something?"

"Yes."

Quietly Jax's squire appeared, left and reappeared with some broth and bread. Serge continued to snore softly, his head thrown back in the deep armchair. Jax set his lute aside and accepted a crystal glass of brandy from the squire. He watched Klaris sip the broth.

"You're breathing seems easier," he said finally.

She nodded. "I feel better, but I still have no control over the magic."

"That is not reassuring."

Her lips twitched. "I can't find myself in the Mystic."

He watched her mouth for a moment then shifted to look her full in the face. "You've found me."

She took a deep breath. "Yes. Your magic is a rock, an anchor. It's all I'm holding on to."

"Why?"

Klaris sipped her broth before answering slowly. "That is the question no one ever asks."

"They're afraid of the answer, maybe."

"Are you?"

"I already admitted I am." He took a deep drink of the brandy. "Why are you lost in the magic?"

"I...." She finished the broth, set the mug aside, and started afresh. "When I went to the Oracle looking for you, it said that the dragons were returning to the Knownlands. From that moment forward, I started to prepare for such a disaster. I thought that if

I could increase the Mystic maybe I could thwart a second dragon interregnum."

"The dragons stayed away from Sageham last time?"

"Yes. And I read that a Weaver tried to face down the dragons, but they killed her."

Jax drank his brandy.

"I waited a long time for you to bring me the Secret of my mastery," Klaris continued. "During those months I read every ancient document in Caledra's library, some dating back to before the time of Axterre. I learned that the Weaver was stronger in the ancient past. During the time of the Axterran Oracles, the Mystic weave lost strength."

Jax grimaced, remembering his encounter with the ghost of an Axterran Oracle. "Axterre scares me even more than you do."

Again, her lips twitched, and again he found his attention captivated as she went on with her story. "Those Oracles learned how to know things. I studied their methods and found I could see all the other Mystic Secrets: past, future, some that had been used and some that no one had yet found. All the Secrets save my own. I decided that when it came time for my mastery, I would weave them all."

"And you did."

She nodded.

"So, you've accessed enough Mystic for what, a hundred Weavers?"

Again, she nodded, coughing gently.

"And you're lost in all of that magic now?"

She reached for her water and took a long drink. Jax poured himself another liberal glass of brandy. "Sweet goddess," he muttered. "Sweet goddess."

"Sweet goddess," she echoed. "Mystic is different from Dragon."

"Yes?"

"Dragon force flows like fire, like wind, like music, but Mystic is a weave, a foundation. It underlies everything." She tucked her hands beneath the blanket. "When I use magic, I rumple the fabric like this." She pushed a hand up under the quilt and a small mountain rose. "Each Weaver creates his or her own blanket with the mastery weave, but since I used so many Secrets, I've created a hundred blankets and they're all different. None is uniquely mine and yet they're all mine...." Her voice trailed off. "Goddess," she whispered. "I need Professor Lellyn."

"Serge would help you."

"He doesn't have the experience. I need to speak to someone who watched a Weaver set the loom."

Jax swirled the amber brandy and watched it glow in the candlelight. "Could the Dragon Highlord help you?"

"I wouldn't have thought so, but now that I have your bit of Dragon force so close to me, I think he might have wisdom to share."

"We might ask the Kordish Royal Dragon to send the Highlord a message."

Klaris coughed again and took a slow deep breath. She smiled into the comfort of enough air and in the ease of using her native language. Then she caught Jax's gaze on her mouth and found herself choking again.

"Want some brandy?" he offered, his own smile offering perhaps something more.

She shook her head and reached for her water.

"No, I need to keep my head."

Jax drained his glass. "One of us probably should."

Klaris warmed to this response. She pushed herself gingerly off the bed and went to the guardrobe. When she came back Jax had settled himself into the blankets, his eyes closed, but when she lay down next to him, he wrapped his arms around her and pulled her back against his chest.

She took a deep, slow breath and relaxed against him, resting on the little block of his magic and the muscles of his arms and belly.

The candle went out. Only the glow of the low embers reddened the three sleepers, each lost in uneasy dreams.

When she awoke the fire was out. Serge still slept in the chair, and pale gray light filled the room. Jax was solid and warm next to her. The Mystic undulated, limitless like a vast sea. She took a good, full breath and thought about Jax and his perspectives. Not many young noblemen would admit to fear while at the same time submitting to the grip she held on his force. But then Jax had been places most people hope never to go, noble or not. Despite these hardships, or maybe because of them, she had seen him exhibit a surprising generosity.

This train of thought led her to consider her own problem as maybe a matter of perspective and a problem of ownership. What if she expanded her idea of self? What if she broadened her outlook on the Mystic, where it was, and how it lay?

And then she got it. Standing, figuratively, on the rock of Jax's force, she lifted her magical vision beyond the immediate and found she could see in places and ways that had been hidden before. From this perspective she found her soul everywhere, as far and as wide, as deep and as high as the Mystic went. She was there and it was one.

Four steady breaths and she reached herself out into the one and grasped it.

The Mystic weave rippled across the Knownlands, shook, aligned and settled.

Jax came awake with an anguished gasp.

Serge leapt to his feet.

Far away, on Sageham, the lads and lasses whooped and hollered with joy, while the Mystics there and elsewhere in the Knownlands breathed sighs of relief as the fabric of their magic revealed itself again in a coherent weave, elegant and strong, bearing the imprint of the new Weaver herself.

The Oracle, breathing quietly in preparation for the sun salutations, began to laugh.

On Farsouth, Queen Jeress sat up in bed then relaxed back onto her pillows. "That's Klaris," she breathed. Her husband, magicless, slept undisturbed.

On Jezel, the Highlord Raggar dropped his protect spell because he wanted to fully feel the Mystic solidify into its new pattern. But the expected rasp of cross-magic never came. Somehow, incomprehensibly, he understood the Mystic weave in a way he had never expected or experienced before.

Klaris sank back into her pillows, smiling.

"Sweet, sweet goddess," Jax moaned, curled into himself.

Lady Mollish burst into the room. "What has happened?"

"She's set the loom, at last," Serge explained, clapping his hands.

Mollish looked into the green eyes and saw a vastness there she could not explain. She turned to Prince Jax, who writhed with some kind of pain. "What's the matter, your Highness?"

Jax didn't hear the priestess. He reached for the thin arms of the Weaver and shook her. "Give it back!"

Serge didn't need to understand the prince's Islish. He leapt upon Jax, pulling him off the Weaver. "Stop it, my lord! Stop!"

Klaris, freed, sat up slowly. Held fast by Carte Serge, Jax begged raggedly: "Give it back."

She frowned. "Did I hurt you?"

"Not at all." Jax's irony was completely defeated by the suffering evident on his face.

"It's here," she said.

He stared at her, the green eyes so promising. She reached out a hand to touch him, and her Mystic engulfed him. There, embedded deep in that thick supple fabric, was his own Dragon force, ripped free from his soul, existing somehow within hers.

"Use it," she said gently.

It took him a moment to pull himself together, to gather the force, to call it forth. The blackened logs in the fireplace exploded into flame.

"Dragons!" swore Serge.

Klaris hummed. "Oh. That feels good."

Jax shrugged free of Serge. "It's stronger," he said, "but it isn't within me anymore."

"It's in us," Klaris answered, smiling up at him.

Jax stared at her, still breathing roughly. That smile seemed to invite a way to refill the new emptiness in his soul. With a violence that surprised them both, he wrapped Klaris in a kiss as consuming and passionate as the Mystic around him. She gave it right back to him, oblivious to the laughter of the priestess and the angry sputtering of Carte Serge.

＃ 16

Lord Foby found a rumpled and disgruntled Jax staring out a window at the bright waters of Keffin Bay. "The Weaver turn you out?" he joked.

"Our esteemed Royal Mystic laid hands upon my person and threw me out." Jax's voice was uneven, and his sea blue eyes were wild.

"Why? What were you doing to the Weaver?"

"It's more what the Weaver was doing, has done, to me."

"What's that?" Foby asked.

"She took my magic, stole it, ripped it right out of me."

"Your little bit of Dragon force? Why? How?"

Jax ran a hand through his hair, struggling with the loss of his magic and the growing, visceral attachment he felt for Klairs. "Foby, she's beyond anything: audacious, courageous, merciless. Goddess damn me."

Foby put a hand to Jax's shoulder. "Everyone's talking about how she finally fixed the Mystic this morning."

"Fixed?" Jax laughed without humor.

"Come for a ride," Foby invited. "It'll clear your head."

"I'd rather swim."

"Of course, you would." Foby rolled his pale eyes. "But the royal council wants to see you before lunch."

"Dragons," Jax groaned, leaning his aching head against the window.

Foby clapped him on the shoulder. "You did kill a duke, my friend. The Oracle may have more or less exonerated you from the charges of treason, but Midipex was also the lord chancellor. While you've been tarrying in the Weaver's bed, Princess Tallyn and the rest of the king's council have been whispering, vying, and scheming to see who'll be the new chancellor."

Jax stood away from the window, his attention piqued. "Who does Tallyn favor?"

Foby smiled slyly. "That's what everyone wants to know, of course. Frinz thinks he should have the honor, but Tallyn thinks he's too young. Stona was too close to Midipex, and the Widow Keffex is only on the council for courtesy. My father doesn't want it. Nobody ever trusts Vobury, of course. Duke Von of Clairo is too old, according to Tallyn, but we think the king favors him."

"So," Jax ran a hand through his hair. "It'll be Chevvain then."

Foby laughed ruefully, remembering how Jax's mind worked. "That's what Tallyn thinks."

"And after all that they want to see me?"

"Of course."

"I am going for a swim. Thanks for the warning."

Jax strode to his rooms calling for his squires.

Tallyn took her seat between the king and the dowager, feeling only marginally better. Lady Mollish's peppermint and ginger concoction had helped her stomachache, but she still felt as if her brain was swathed in blankets.

The other magnates of the realm took their seats around the polished table, each troubled by the noticeable absence in Midipex's empty chair.

"Very well," King Kodill opened the meeting. "Today we must appoint a new lord chancellor. Thorag Addle, seventh Duke of Midipex, served us as lord chancellor for the past ten years." He paused and swept his pale blue eyes around the table. "We had thought Midipex to be a competent and loyal servant of the throne. Surely, he served well in many ways, but we have now heard very disturbing tales of treachery and treason that we shall investigate later today."

Tallyn kept her gaze fixed on her father, but all of her senses were engaged in following the reactions of the nobles gathered around the table. No surprises here: Earl Oklan bristling as the King praised Midipex, then Earla Stona frowning when the dead duke's loyalty was questioned.

Without conscious thought, Tallyn had known where lines would be drawn and pockets where power would coalesce. The wild card here was the dowager. The old woman's curious relationship with Midipex was well known for its very lack of predictability. In fact, one of the few ways the old queen was ever predictable was in her inveterate hatred for Javix Sharkin.

Would the dowager support Stona as the political heir to Midipex, or would she pull for old Duke Von, who had fostered with her nearly seventy years ago?

Either way, Tallyn knew that if she voiced her own preference for Chevvain the older members of the council would polarize themselves to the point of stalemate. So, she kept her face impassive, almost disinterested, and focused on ignoring her queasy stomach.

It took over an hour, mostly because no one expected Frinz to make such a compelling case for his own candidacy. In the end, as Tallyn (and Jax) had predicted, Aychex was considered too young and Duke Von sabotaged his own chances by consistently forgetting Frinz's name.

"For goddess' sake, Von, you're past it!" snapped the dowager finally. "Young Aychex is Frinz, not Foby. Foby is Rippsmarch's son, you know." She turned to the king. "Kodill, we have other affairs to consider today. I suggest you appoint Patrice of Chevvain, as Tallyn would like you to do, and get on with other things."

Tallyn, who had said nothing during the long hour of debate, smiled gently at her grandmother. The other nobles took note of the look that passed between the two and realized yet again that Tallyn would be a very different ruler than her father was.

Duly appointed, consecrated, and awarded the seals of the office, Duchess Patrice rose and curtseyed deeply to the nobles. "I shall do my best to serve, your Majesty." She then proceeded to seize her new position with both hands:

"Like all of you, I have been studying the laws surrounding treason and self-defense, with special attention to the considerations allotted to those of royal blood...."

Tallyn's head throbbed and she had to force herself to sip her tea calmly. Goddess, but she was tired of being sick. What the dragons could be wrong with her?

"...devastating loss of Duke Thorag." Patrice's voice, clear and concise, continued. "So, I propose we invite Captain Karric to give her eye-witness account then we'll have Prince Javix explain himself."

To Tallyn's surprise, the dowager made no comment to this suggestion, just pulled in her nostrils as if she sensed something foul-smelling.

With characteristic efficiency, Karric gave her report. "You are aware, my lords and ladies, that I have a bit of Mystic. On the day in question, I was on my way to the practice field during a lull in the Rising rain when I felt the magic shake. Suddenly there were people in the courtyard, people who came literally out of thin air. I knew one was a troll by the size of him. One was so small, I thought her a child. The third, I recognized as Prince Jax."

Earla Stona leaned forward. "Tell us, Captain, how you knew it was Prince Jax so quickly. He'd been gone for four years."

Karric's smile was a little superior. "The troll had been wounded by someone left-handed, your Grace. Goddess knows I spent many hours working to get him competent with his right hand, but it was always against his nature."

"His nature," the dowager repeated distinctly.

Karric continued. "The troll, propelled by whatever force brought them here, tackled the prince, and began to throttle him. Of course,

I knew that Prince Jax had been found guilty of treason, but he is a Prince of the Blood. I didn't think he should be strangulated by a troll. I beheaded the troll."

"You killed the troll?" Patrice clarified.

"Yes, your Grace. Then my guards took the prince into custody. He seemed as surprised to find himself at Castle Kree as we were to find him here. At that point, a number of nobles came out into the courtyard, drawn by the ruckus, I suppose. Duke Thorag marched forward and declared that Prince Jax was a traitor."

Karric paused and cleared her throat. "Prince Jax took some offense and spat on the duke's shoe. Midipex drew a knife and would have killed the prince then and there, but Jax ducked aside and the dagger only pierced his shoulder.

"Jax fell to the ground. I informed his Grace, the duke, that we had the prince in custody, but he laughed and said that the prince would die, as the dagger was poisoned."

"Apparently not," the dowager interrupted.

"We believe that the prince used his magic to stop the poison, your Majesty," Karric explained.

"How is that possible?" the king asked. "Jax hasn't any significant Dragon force and even if he did, we all know that magic can't be used to heal."

"More's the pity," the Widow Keffex said softly.

"I cannot explain that, your Majesty," Karric admitted. "But then the prince stood up. He took the duke's dagger from his shoulder and accused the duke of treason. Midipex then lunged at the prince and the two fell to the ground. The duke's dagger ended up in the duke's heart."

"That's an oblique way of putting it," young Aychex noted.

Karric nodded. "The prince was speaking to the duke. I don't believe he intended to kill him because the dagger was still in his right hand. If he'd been serious about defending himself or attacking the duke, he'd have used his left hand."

Earla Stona shook her head. "Figures, doesn't it? All those years he played right-handed so that we would grant him knighthood."

"And that brings us to the question of the day," Chevvain said in an implacable voice. "The Oracle implied that Prince Jax is not guilty of treason, but he did kill the Kordish Lord Chancellor. And he did confess to treason when Earl Oklan held him at Rippsgate."

"He didn't specifically admit to treason." Earl Oklan clarified. "And, even that statement was given for expedience."

"He lied?" Vobury asked provocatively.

Earl Oklan didn't answer.

"My ladies and lords." Karric lifted her chin. "I can't speak to what happened at Rippsgate, but I can attest that Prince Jax acted in self-defense in the courtyard that day. The duke stated he intended to kill the prince and admitted to using poison as well."

Earla Stona slapped her hands on the table. "If we accept our lying Prince Jax's improbable story, we would have to believe that Midipex stole the treasury documents. Why would Thorag do that?" She turned to the king. "He was lord chancellor, Majesty. He knew everything those documents contained. He had no need to steal them."

Silence fell around the table. The answer to this question was so appalling and so unlikely that no one would give it voice. Tallyn knew that everyone in the room recognized the threat to her own succession. She took another sip of tea. "Perhaps it is time for Prince Jax to explain himself," she suggested softly.

The king nodded to Captain Karric, who left the room. No one spoke. Several servants entered bringing more tea. Tallyn watched the steam dance off the liquid in her cup, forcing her stomach to calm by sheer willpower.

Karric's sharp militaristic knock preceded her return with four guards, swords drawn and Prince Jax.

Tallyn kept her face impassive as Jax bowed. She noted how he had changed. No longer did he appear insouciant or arrogant. He was as handsome as ever, maybe more so now that his muscles were harder and those fey, foreign eyes a little more distant. But there was also a depth there she didn't remember. She thought of the trolls she'd met in Hilsen Vale and the tales of brutality, and she considered the fact that he had given himself up to a traitor's death at Rippsgate to save Mother Marith and those nyad creatures.

"Thank you for coming, Prince Javix," the king began rather fatuously. "We have all heard that you believe Duke Thorag Addle guilty of treason for having abducted you."

"Yes, your Majesty."

Duchess Patrice tapped her be-ringed fingers on the polished table. "Who can corroborate your story, Prince Jax? Who beside the Hantish druid?"

"The Weaver."

"Not good enough, my lord." Aychex placed his cup in its saucer with a small clink of china. "It is accepted that the Weaver saw you as a slave, but she cannot give witness to how you got there in the first place."

"True," Jax admitted.

"True," Aychex repeated, looking into Jax's face. Frinz had fostered with Bryx Sharkin. Having spent his childhood playing, learning, working with the predictable Bryx, Frinz was often surprised by Jax. He knew this but pushed forward. "Yes, the truth is what we are seeking. Should we believe your confession at Rippsgate?"

Jax smiled. "Mother Marith saved me from the trolls. If you people can't see the value in anything or anyone not Kordish, then my Kordish blood isn't worth much. I'd give it and my Barian blood to set Marith free."

"That's queerly loyal of you."

"I've always been loyal."

The lady chancellor reigned in the point. "Why would the lord chancellor plot against you in the first place? It doesn't make any sense."

"I agree, my lady. I had asked him that very question when he tried to strangle me and fell on his own dagger."

"Fell on his own dagger?" Clairo sneered. "A dagger held in your hand!"

"I wanted answers," Jax snapped. "I spent four very long years wondering why the good duke would care enough about me to risk treason."

"His broken heart, perhaps?" mused the Duchess of Keffex, who had fostered with Thorag Addle.

Jax looked at her. "Broken heart?"

It was the dowager who answered. "For Valla, of course. They were betrothed and Thorag adored her. But then Valla met that rogue of a sealord, and we all know how that ended." No one spoke, so the old queen continued with venom thick in her quiet, cultured voice: "When you killed her."

Jax met the hatred in her gaze. "I'm sorry, your Majesty. But there is no wergild for a babe to pay to its mother."

"*You* pay?" the dowager spat. "*You* frivolous, wrong-handed, wise-cracking, *half-isle*. It is *I* who pay. *I* who will never see my beautiful daughter again."

Jax made a small gesture of denial, and the dowager choked to silence as she recognized the movement as one characteristic of that dead daughter.

Earla Stona leaned back in her chair, considering the half-islish prince. "I don't think that a thirty-year-old broken heart would have been sufficient to motivate Thorag to commit treason. I don't think he committed treason at all. But when you killed him, Jax, you killed the one witness who could exonerate you."

"Indeed, your Grace." He looked at her bleakly. "But only by inculpating himself in a far more serious crime."

The earla rose with her voice. "You're just trying to weasel yourself out of a traitor's death!"

"Enough!" Chevvain said firmly. She turned to Jax and regarded him thoughtfully. "I ask you again, my lord, are there others who could prove these allegations against Midipex?"

Tallyn held her breath. Jax's wolf grin answered her fears before his words: "I could give you a name, but you wouldn't believe me."

"Try us," Chevvain said, her voice hard.

Jax shook his head and the feral grin grew grim. "My lords and ladies, you all know my friendship to Princess Tallyn and to Kordon. You witnessed my oaths of loyalty to King Kodill. Surely, you know that I would never contemplate treason."

"We witnessed similar actions and oaths from Thorag Addle, and for longer than you've been alive, my lad," Vobury noted succinctly. "And you confessed."

Jax changed tacks. "I ask you this, your Majesties, my ladies and lords: Why was your lord chancellor walking the palace of Kree armed with a poisoned blade? He couldn't have known that I would appear by magic, and yet he had that blade ready."

The clear blue eyes of Kordon's greatest lords and ladies looked back at him. He waited just long enough before saying quietly. "He had another target in mind."

Tallyn took a deep breath as her stomach rolled again.

The door suddenly flew open. Captain Karric drew her sword.

"Mercy! Mercy!" cried the woman who entered. "Mercy, your Majesty!"

"Lady Estyl!" The king rose from his chair. "Mercy for what?"

Two of Karric's guards shoved Jax against the wall and held him there. The other two grasped the plump arms of Lady Estyl Addle, the widow of Thorag Addle. More guards pushed into the room, surrounding the men wearing Midipex's livery and holding yet another man bound with rope and wire. Tallyn remembered the man as one of Thorag Addle's lower staff.

"Your Majesty," Lady Estyl said in a voice wavering with fear. "I beg you, mercy. I am not, as you know, used to court circles. My family is not noble and maybe I was not suited to be the wife of a duke."

Estyl's groveling played to King Kodill's sense of royal magnanimity. "Duchess," he said gracefully. "You are ennobled by your own humility. Why are you pleading for mercy?"

Estyl sent a frightened glace around the room. Indeed, the eyes that met her were those of all the cold power of Kordon. She swallowed. "Majesty, I didn't know...."

"Didn't know *what*, Estyl?" the dowager snapped. "Get a hold of yourself."

Lady Estyl cringed then lifted her chin. "My lords and ladies, I fear that Thorag plotted against you." One of Lady Estyl's servants produced a lacquered ebony scroll case and held it out to Captain Karric, who handed it to the lady chancellor.

Earla Stona saw the seal on the case. "The treasury documents!" She reached across the table for them.

"There's more." Estyl said. "I believe that Thorag must have had the Duke of Keffex killed."

The Widow Keffex uttered a small cry.

"What makes you say this?" demanded the lady chancellor.

"Thorag was paying this wretched creature," she pointed to the man held by her guards, "to poison Princess Tallyn!"

Captain Karric pushed the Midipexian guards aside and put a knife to the small man's throat.

"Sweet goddess," Kodill covered his face with his hands.

Still held against the wall, Jax's voice cut through the exclamations of the other nobles. "Why, Lady Estyl? Why do you say this now?"

Estyl looked up at him and shuddered. "That man came to me for payment. *The job's half done*, says he. *Pay me the rest and I'll finish it.*"

Tallyn sat back in her chair. "Well, this explains my upset stomach."

"Send for Priestess Mollish," the dowager ordered. The old queen took Tallyn's chin in her bony fingers and pulled her face around. "Why would Thorag plot against me?" she asked softly, staring into her granddaughter's eyes.

"The throne," Tallyn answered. "With Keffex dead and the Barian princes gone, Midipex and his heirs stand behind me for the crown."

"Of course, he does, but he would never...." The dowager stopped.

For a few moments no one spoke. They had been circling this fact all morning.

"I remember him bragging once, long ago," Chevvain said softly. "He was so pleased that his children by Princess Valla would actually be able to claim more royal blood than a child of King Kodill and Queen Ansyn, more royal blood than Tallyn herself."

"But then he didn't end up with Valla," snapped the dowager, glaring at Jax. "All of this is the fault of those Barians!"

Jax shook his head. "No Ma'am. It is the fault of an ambitious duke."

"I didn't know," whimpered Estyl. "Please believe me. Thorag didn't come to Pexbury often. You know he preferred to be here in Kree, fulfilling his duties as lord chancellor. I always felt that I was a nuisance to him."

Rippsmarch found a handkerchief and handed it to Estyl.

Priestess Mollish came in running. "What is the poison?" she demanded.

"Tell us," Karric growled to the prisoner.

"No."

Jax pulled free of his guards. "The people were expecting a traitor's death," he said softly. "Do you know what that's like?"

The small man glared up at Jax, but he nodded.

The lady chancellor followed Jax's lead. "That can be your fate," she said. "Or name the poison and you can die quickly."

The man shivered at the implacable judgment on the faces that surrounded him. "Arconite," he mumbled.

"Damn," whispered Mollish. "Come with me, your Highness. This is going to be unpleasant."

"How did you get it to the princess?" Jax demanded.

"The wine," the little man muttered. "I put it in her decanter of pink wine."

"And the knife?" Earl Kora took up the questioning. "Do you know why the duke was carrying a poisoned knife?"

The little man shrugged miserably. Karric's own bright blade creased the flesh of his neck. "Answer the earl," she growled.

"I don't know. He said the arconite was taking a long time."

Tallyn stood, her head spinning. "One minute, Mollish. First, my lords and ladies, I move that we exonerate Prince Jax of all charges of treason and wrongdoing and return him to his full status as a Knight of Kordon and Prince of the Blood."

Silence.

"Oh, fine." Frinz placed both hands on the table and sent a sour glance at Jax. "Aye."

"Aye," the Earl of Rippsmarch seconded.

"Aye," old Duke Von and the Widow Keffex agreed more softly.

Vobury followed the wind, as usual: "Aye."

"Aye," Stona said grimly.

The dowager said nothing.

After a moment, the lady chancellor's clear, conclusive voice said, "aye."

"Very well," the king nodded. "Prince Javix, we expect you to resume your titles and duties to this realm."

Somewhat unsure of what titles he might have left, Jax knelt to his uncle. "Thank you, your Majesty."

The king smiled. "Now, Captain Karric, you will hold the prisoner until Princess Tallyn recovers."

"Yes, your Majesty."

With Priestess Mollish at her arm, Tallyn walked slowly around the table. When she got to Jax she hugged him. "If you hadn't killed Midipex, I might be dead myself by now. I'm very happy you've come back."

Jax, aware of coldness in other faces, bowed fluidly. "I am glad someone is."

17

Jax spent the next week besieged by bureaucracy. Since no one had broached the topic of paying a wergild for the duke's death, Jax decided not to bring it up. In addition to his manor lands at Norbay, a Prince of the Realm had lists of events to attend and obligations to fulfill. The young men and women who had served as his squires and pages four years ago had grown into their own positions. Even with the help of the chamberlain, it took several days for Jax to organize a staff to help him coordinate his duties, his wardrobe, and his schedule.

Lady Mollish had placed both Tallyn and Klaris on quarantine. Barred from personal visits, Jax received updates from Marith on their progress. It was all he had time for, as his days and nights were dedicated to reviewing accounts, listening to petitions, attending assizes, and of course drinking great quantities of fine Kordish wine while being readmitted to the highest court circles.

He laughed with Foby, enjoying his old friend even more after years of absence. He laughed at Carden Yemmel's cutting witticisms, wondering why a courtier so sly didn't see that Tallyn would never marry him. He laughed with Cheshir among the sheets of his bed but noted that each of them was more reserved than in the past.

Priestess Mollish tucked the thick quilts around the sleeping Weaver's thin shoulders against the spring chill. "The danger is well past, now," she said softly to the man by the fire.

"Yes." The contentment in Serge's voice soothed the priestess. With two important patients, Mollish had worked tirelessly for the past week, and she shared Serge's relief at the even sounds of the Weaver's smooth breathing. Now maybe Serge would see that the Weaver's association with Prince Jax had not harmed her, but had, in some way inexplicable to the traditions of magic and the goddess, secured her.

An hour later Mollish bent over Princess Tallyn's sleeping form. Someone had already pulled up the thick blankets.

"She seemed so cold," said a voice from the dark.

Exhausted, Mollish hadn't noticed the form, in glowing silk, seated in the shadows on the far side of the bed. "Lord Foby?"

"No. It's Jax."

"Your Highness! Who let you in here?"

"A druid you shouldn't trust."

Mollish agreed and resolved to settle the problem in the morning. "You are worried about her?"

"Midipex didn't act alone."

Mollish took her own stool by the fire, considering this uncomfortable information. Quiet filled the room. The priestess wrapped her cloak around herself, watching the princess's face, gleaming like an alabaster sarcophagus, still and cold.

Her lips tightened. The princess had stoically endured five days of ruthless purging and cleansing. Arconite was a deadly poison that lingered in the vital organs, slowly ruining them. The only known cure was to flush the patient with as much liquid as possible then encourage savage cathartics.

The door opened softly; Mollish raised her head.

"How does she fare?" The imperious whisper of the dowager queen hissed through the dark.

Lady Mollish stood, curtseyed then joined the old woman by the bed. "I dare not give her more purges, but the last ones seemed clear of the poison."

"Good."

With touching gentleness, the old queen bent to kiss the white brow. For a moment longer she considered her sleeping granddaughter. "Damn those Barians," she muttered gruffly, turned, and was gone.

Mollish lifted her dark-adjusted eyes to the shadow beyond the bed.

"I guess she doesn't want all her grandchildren dead," he said.

With a wry grin, he too slipped out of the room, leaving Mollish a knotty question to unpick during the long hours of the night.

Klaris awoke to a cool, rainy day. A druid bent over the fire, stoking it. "Good morning, Weaver!" he said cheerily, turning at Klaris's brief cough. "Shall I bring you a tisane?"

"I would prefer tea," she said softly.

"Ah, I am sure you would, my lady, but Priestess Mollish insists that the tisane is better for you, still."

Klaris accepted the musky drink with resignation.

"I'll fetch you some toast and custard," the druid winked. "You'll like that."

She considered his friendly face with cool green eyes. She wasn't sure what the word *custard* meant, and she was heartily sick of invalid food. As the druid left the room, Klaris ran her senses out along the long thick warp and weft of the Mystic and breathed a deep sigh of satisfaction. She sat up against her pillows and set her empty cup on the bedside table. It was time.

She dove into the Mystic and reveled in it with a power and clarity she had never known. Now she focused on the torn and frayed hole in the magic that represented Castle Caledra. Without a bowl, without water, without the light of a clear full moon, the Weaver saw, and the vision filled her soul with grief.

A small group of magicians, along with lads and lasses, huddled on the windswept headland. Klaris could smell the sea and the sage, and she could hear Father Mallix's prayers for the dead. She'd never gotten scent or sound from a scry before. She let her presence settle among them, comforted by Father Mallix and the ceremony.

The group of magicians looked up and around. They could feel her and knew she was watching them. Klaris realized that Professor Essen was the most powerful among them. He had entered the Tower to study but had not passed any of its tests. Sweet goddess, so much lost. So much learning, history, power, love. Gone.

"It's Klaris," someone said.

"Weaver!"

"Come home, Klaris!"

"Come home!"

Oh, how she wanted to. But even with all this power, and in part because of it, Klaris knew that her path lay elsewhere, despite the longing of her soul.

Father Mallix raised his hands. "No, no! Listen to me, people. Weaver Klaris can't come back to us now. She has the Oracle's work to do."

"But we need the Weaver to rebuild the castle."

"No, we do not." Lad Yerran stood with Father Mallix. "The lads and lasses built this castle long ago. We will build it again. We will build it for the Mystic. Weaver Klaris will return to empower it when she can."

The Mystics looked at each other.

Klaris knew that Lad Yerran and Father Mallix were right. Old scrolls in the castle vault had told the story of how the lads and lasses of Sageham had drawn the castle from the stones of the island. Over the centuries, as each Weaver seized the weave, the building changed, modified, and altered yet again when each Weaver died. With the enhanced insight of a Weaver, Klaris now recognized the rotten mortar, the fissured bricks, the fractured foundation that all these changes had left.

She could not speak across this link, but she could send reassurance. The Sagehamites would, and could, pull a new castle from the rock of the isle. Once raised, she and the other Mystics would imbue the stones with all the strength and power they could muster. She sent them hope, and strength, and a promise to return and felt their responses, their gratitude, and shared still their grief.

Pulling away, closing the spell, her vision snagged on the face of a gold and white cat. Its green eyes bore into hers.

"Weaver," said the cat.

A shiver ran down Klaris's spine. "Yes?" she whispered.

"Hurry."

"Hurry? To do what? Return to Sageham?"

"No." The cat's eyes did not blink. "They are coming. I can feel them."

"Who?" Klaris asked, fearing the answer.

"The beasts. You must prepare."

A fit of coughing shook Klaris and broke her free of the weave.

"Weaver! Easy, my lady." The druid, returning with the promised custard, slammed the tray down and wrapped his arms around her shoulders. "Here, Weaver, drink some water."

She drank then smiled. "Thank you."

The druid grinned back. This was the first time he had seen the Weaver smile, and it warmed his healer's heart. "That's better. The custard will soothe your throat."

It did indeed, and Klaris added another word to her growing Landish vocabulary. After finishing the custard and her toast, she sat back, sipping more tisane, and thought about the cat and dragons and again longed for Professor Lellyn. The wise old tutor would have known the answers, or at least would have had ideas of where to look for them.

And damn, if that cat hadn't sent words along a scry. She'd read something about that once, although it hadn't involved cats.

Even before the long months she'd spent waiting for her secret, Klaris had spent hours reading obscure texts from the castle vaults. Able to rapidly acquire the techniques and spells of the various levels of the Mystic weave, she'd always had extra time. Without friends her own age to share those empty hours, Klaris had read and reread, translated and deciphered almost every document within the library. Some of the spells she'd read about were only theoretically possible, others, like teleporting spells, had been done, but only by Weavers.

Mystics could speak into each other's minds using the Ancient when they were together, but only one or two had ever been able to speak across any distance. Klaris cleared her throat and gathered her magic once again.

Far away amid the ruins of a village washed to rubble by the tidal wave, Queen Jeress felt as if something hit her on the head.

"Mama?"

"Ouch! Klaris?"

"Yes. Does this hurt?"

"Not now. I just wasn't expecting it." As a powerful Mystic herself, Jeress was quite proficient in Ancient. Now she paused and addressed her husband in Islish: "No, Trajan, I'm talking to Klaris, apparently."

Klaris couldn't hear her father's words and realized that her mother must be speaking aloud. *"Just think the words, Mama. I'll hear you."*

"Are you alright? I feel an ache in the magic."

"Caledra was destroyed by an earthquake." Klaris took a breath to steady the spell.

"But you are alright?"

"I wasn't there."

"What? Where are you?"

Klaris was trembling now with the effort of the spell. *"Mama, come to Kree. I'll explain here."*

"I'll come."

Klaris dropped the magic and the link snapped. She collapsed in a coughing fit. The druid looked up from his book. "Weaver!" He poured more tisane. "Weaver, you must be gentle with yourself."

"Yes." Klaris whispered when the coughing finally subsided. "For now."

"It's killing Tallyn that Priestess Mollish won't let her be there today." Foby rubbed the ears of one of his dogs. Jax did his best to ignore the animal and continued writing.

"Just about killed me to get there," Jax grumbled absently. "Let me finish these notes, will you?"

"Don't you care to know why the council wants you this week?"

Jax signed his document with a flourish and pulled open a drawer, rummaging through its contents until he came up with an old stick of Barian Blue wax. He pulled instinctively on his Dragon force, but nothing happened. He took a deep breath, closed his eyes and reached out to the vast undulating sheet of Klaris's Mystic. He tugged on it and his stick of wax burst into flame. "Dragons," he muttered, moderating his grip on the power.

Hot wax dropped onto the parchment. He finally answered Foby. "I am afraid to speculate."

"No, you're not."

Jax's smile didn't reach his eyes, which remained on the dripping wax. He plunged his signet ring into the warm stuff and finally met Foby's gaze.

"I don't want it, you know." His voice was flat. "I never expected land in Kordon beyond the manors at Norbay."

"That was short-sighted of you." Foby's grin was friendly. "Surely you expected a seat on the royal council once Tallyn is queen."

Jax shrugged and shut the drawer. "Why? Just because we fostered together? I was, am, such a goddess-damned failure at all things Kordish that I never thought to help rule here. In Baria, on the other hand...."

"Ah," said Foby, remembering. "Right. You were the vice-captain, or whatever it's called."

"Vice admiral." Jax collected his papers and rang for his secretary. "I was vice admiral while Rax was alive, but now I should be the lord admiral. And that, my Kordish friend, is enough to keep me busy."

"Is it?"

Jax held his friend's gaze for a long moment. "I'd like to help," he admitted.

"Midipex made a play at you and lost. You know the cost his family will pay for that."

"Yes," Jax said quietly, handing his papers to his secretary. "Yes, I do."

Finding himself once again in the paneled cabinet where the king's royal council met, Jax took a seat along the wall. Lady Estyl entered the room and stood awkwardly, unable to decide if she should take Midipex's empty seat at the polished darkwood table or the chair next to the half-islish prince who had killed her husband.

The chamberlain saved the situation by bringing in another chair and setting it on the opposite side of the room from Jax.

Tallyn's place, to the right of the king, remained ominously empty.

Kodill swept into the room and took his seat. "Priestess Mollish tells me that Tallyn will recover," he began abruptly.

"Thank the goddess," the Duchess of Keffex breathed.

"We have questioned the would-be assassin about the death of Duke Kevlor Brondon," Chevvain said. "He claims that Midipex used someone else to administer poison, but the Priestess Mollish confirms that the symptoms of Keffex's last illness are consistent with arconite poisoning."

"It's a shame we promised him a quick death," Frinz said grimly. "I'd like to make him suffer as Keffex did, and Tallyn."

The king pursed his lips. "What else, my lady chancellor?"

Patrice shuffled her papers. "We must decide on the disposition of the Duchy of Midipex."

Lady Estyl fidgeted in her chair as the eyes of the royal council turned on her. "Mercy, your Majesty," she whimpered.

"Sweet goddess! Don't start that again," the dowager sneered. "Your husband abused our trust and murdered our cousin and very nearly our granddaughter."

"And grandson," Rippsmarch noted. The dowager tightened her lips.

"The threat has now been removed," the lady chancellor continued in her clipped voice. "The court is satisfied, Lady Estyl, that you and your young son did not know of Thorag Addle's perfidy, but we are not prepared to welcome Addle's line back to this table."

The king frowned at Estyl. "Who is your son, Lady Estyl? Why doesn't he foster here at Kree?"

"Our son Oran is fourteen, your Majesty," Estyl whispered.

"And he fosters at Chevvex," noted the lady chancellor. "Thorag told me he felt that he had so many responsibilities as lord chancellor that it would be a dangerous distraction to him to have the boy near."

Lady Estyl cleared her throat. "He shamed me, my lords and ladies. He said our son was not worthy of fostering at Kree, due to my own lowly birth."

"Nonsense," snapped Aychex. "He's heir to a dukedom!"

"Not anymore," the king growled.

"Excuse me, my ladies and lords," Jax interrupted. "Perhaps Midipex wanted to make sure his own child was well away from his treasonous activities here in Kree. The distance would protect his innocence."

"Indeed, indeed!" agreed Estyl. "We knew nothing!"

"We believe you, Lady Estyl." The king was growing impatient as the room became stuffy. "But the Addles will no longer be admitted to the royal council. Nor will I require Prince Jax to pay wergild."

"But the prince killed the duke, your Majesty!" Earla Stona protested.

"I will not have the traitor's family reimbursed for his loss." The king's words were final.

Estyl bowed her head.

"You cannot make that half-isle the Duke of Midipex," the dowager said, jumping ahead.

All eyes turned to her.

Into the silence, Jax spoke. "You are right, Ma'am. I have obligations on Baria that would make running a province as large and land locked as Midipex impossible."

The dowager frowned, clearly disliking the fact that Jax agreed with her on something.

Earla Stona had been watching Lady Estyl squirm and weep and remembering the long hours Thorag Addle had spent studying trade networks, tax structures, and transportation issues. "Majesty, I propose we split the dukedom." She rose and went to a large map of Kordon that hung on a wall. "Split Midipex in two. The Addles can keep the eastern reaches and their seat at Pexbury."

"But they can't be dukes," the King snapped. "I won't have them on my council, nor on Tallyn's."

"Understood, Sire," Chevvain rose to stand with the earla. "The Addles will become the Counts of Midipex, perhaps?"

"Barons," the King spat. "And after young Oran, the lands revert to the Crown."

"Very well." Chevvain motioned to a secretary who began scribbling. "Oran Addle will be Baron of Midipex, and the title dies with him." She paused for breath and her colorless Kordish eyes glanced off Prince Jax's quiet, sea-blue stare.

"Then, this half of the old duchy will be a new fief."

"A sweet one," Frinz noted bitterly. "With the Darkwood and all those fine vineyards."

"Call it Darkwood, then," suggested Vobury.

"Not quite large enough to be a duchy," the Widow Keffex said softly.

"A march?" offered Clairo.

"For goddess' sake, Von," the dowager grumbled. "You know that a march doesn't belong in the middle of a kingdom."

Kodill had been watching Lady Estyl dry her eyes and compose herself. He turned his gaze to his silent nephew. "Come here, Jax."

The prince rose and stood before the king. "I entitle you, Javix Sharkin, as the first Earl of Darkwood, with all of these lands and the rights and responsibilities thereto." He waved a hand. "You know the rest."

"Thank you, your Majesty."

The lady chancellor gestured to Midipex's empty place at the polished table. "Please join us, my lord Earl Javix Sharkin."

Noting the mixed feelings evident in the faces around the table, Jax took the vacant seat.

"Now then, Chevvain, what else?" asked the restive King.

Patrice was gathering her papers, listening to the whispers of her secretary, and it was Jax's voice that spoke. "Your Majesty, my ladies and lords. As my seat here today demonstrates, you now realize that neither myself, nor any other Barian, wished to harm Kordon."

"Right, so?" The distaste of prejudice tinged Chevvain's voice.

"So, your Majesty and my lady chancellor, I beg you to consider reopening the Gates of Griffe to Barian shipping."

The dowager shook her head slowly.

But the Widow Keffex sat up. "We could get Farsouthian sugar again."

Jax nodded. "And I'm sure Kordon would rather receive the customs duties that are now going to Ily and Vitrus."

"Fine." Kodill stood. "We will open the Gates. Aychex, Keffex, you will see to it."

"Yes, your Majesty."

Jax found himself walking down the corridor next to the dowager. "Earl of Darkwood," she muttered.

"Suits me, don't you think, Ma'am?"

"It's too civilized for you."

"What constitutes *civilized*, Ma'am? Fluency in language and art? Maybe a broad view of history and our place in it? It certainly should not be about exclusion or petty biases."

She stopped and pursed her lips. "You're rationalizing for your own benefit."

"Isn't that the civilized way?"

She considered the ruthlessness of his smile for a few moments then turned and walked away.

18

"Your Grace, the Royal Dragon begs an audience."

Jax looked up from his ledgers and over the heads of the three secretaries who were waiting to discuss various responsibilities with him. The squire shrugged. "She says it's of utmost importance, my lord."

After the Royal Dragon's interrogation upon his arrival in Kree followed by the discomfort of the magical imprisonment, Jax was disinclined to be amenable. "She can wait," he stated. "I'll see her in my salon when I'm done here. Bring her some wine or something. *I'll* want wine."

Jax's exasperation vanished when he walked into the room and found Borrel waiting with the Royal Dragon. He embraced the nyad with unabashed friendship. "Mam Marith told me you were working with Dragon Cyril."

The Royal Dragon considered the prince. He looked a lot better than when she'd last seen him, filthy and chained in the king's prison. He had not produced any viable explanations for how he'd managed to purge the Duke of Midipex's poison, and despite all Borrel had told her about the half-islish prince, his charm and his compassion, Cyril had put more faith in the reports left by the previous Royal Dragon. Younger than Carte Serge, her magical counterpart to the Court of Kordon, Cyril had still been training at Dragonsholm on Jezel while Prince Jax fostered at Kree. Her predecessor had faced the dubious pleasure of analyzing Prince Jax's magic and had kept notes detailing the lad's subversive wit and minimal Dragon force.

This assessment was reinforced when the prince used his magic to destroy the scaffold. Still smarting from that implied humiliation, Cyril weighed the consideration in the prince's sea-blue eyes and pondered the odd paradox of his empty magic that still somehow remained curiously potent.

"I've asked to see your Grace, because the Dragon Highlord very much wants to meet the new Weaver, and I understand you have a... relationship with her."

Jax laughed with little humor. "Relationship? I suppose you could call it that."

"Obviously, I cannot see her myself," Cyril said. "I was hoping you could speak to the Weaver on behalf of the Highlord."

"Will the Highlord come to Kree?"

"Apparently not, but the Red and Orange Dragons, our next most powerful magicians, are expected in a few weeks. We would like you to convey the Highlord's congratulations to the Weaver and let her know that the Red and Orange Dragons will wish to discuss other issues when they arrive."

Jax emptied his glass. "You do know that Priestess Mollish has prohibited visitors to Weaver Klaris until she recovers more of her strength. And I'm not sure Carte Serge will ever gladly see me with the Weaver again."

Cyril chose her words carefully. "I have heard that the Royal Mystic feels your relationship with the Weaver is inappropriate."

"And you?"

The Royal Dragon bristled at that sharp blue gaze. "The *Rote and Reed* is quite clear, my lord."

Jax took the opening her censure provided. "So clearly, you shouldn't ask a prince to convey the Highlord's congratulations."

Too late, Cyril realized the trap. She turned to the power of her position to break it: "As the ranking Dragon magician in Kree, I am responsible for all Dragons here, including you, Prince Javix. I'm not *asking* you."

Jax allowed his squire to pour more wine into his glass. "I'm not sure I am a Dragon anymore, but I will convey your message once I'm permitted to see the Weaver again."

"Very good, my lord." Cyril accepted more of the pale golden wine. "It is indeed strange that you don't suffer cross-magic from the Weaver."

"Indeed."

"Lexyl's magic didn't cross either of us." Borrel noted softly.

Jax watched the expression on Borrel's face for a few moments as he remembered the feel of Lexyl's magic. A slow grin grew in his eyes. "I think I have a better understanding of why you were so attracted to Lexyl now that I'm linked to Weaver Klaris."

"Linked?" Cyril asked.

"It is seductive," Borrel muttered.

Cyril set her glass carefully on a marble-topped table. "How are you linked to the Weaver?"

"She took my magic."

"Is that what happened?" Borrel asked. "You certainly don't have your force the way you used to."

"No."

"But you have considerable power," Cyril noted.

Jax felt her probe into him, searching for the magic that he no longer carried in his soul.

"Stop."

Startled by his anger, she pulled back.

"This sparring is unnecessary, Dragon Cyril. I will answer your inquisition as best I can, and I will speak to the Weaver on your behalf, but I prefer to be asked for answers or for services. Enough has already been taken."

Cyril was taken aback. "Forgive me, your Grace. I was just curious."

"You may assure yourself that I'm curious too. Somehow the Weaver ripped the magic clean out of me. I can use it and it is more powerful than it was, but it isn't the same."

"Does it hurt?" Borrel asked.

"Like grief." It was said so softly Cyril barely heard the words.

Finding her own compassion, she changed the subject. "Did you know, my lord, that some of the most powerful Dragons are hoping to use magic to heal?"

"I didn't know that was possible."

"It hasn't been, but you've done it."

Jax shook his head. "As I told you before, I merely suppressed the poison. I didn't cure myself the way a druid cures."

"Well," she smiled. "Dragon Blizzen, the Orange Dragon, is the leader among those hoping to use magic for healing. I know he will want to see you."

Jax rose. "Then I'd better get back to my accounts, so I'll be available when he arrives."

Cyril gathered her dress and stood as well, watching the prince turn to the nyad.

"I haven't seen Marith in days," he said.

"She's been helping Priestess Mollish."

"And Florin?"

Borrel shrugged. "Breaking Kordish hearts."

Jax laughed. "Do you want to go back to Hilsen Vale?"

The nyad glanced at Dragon Cyril. "I'm learning so much here."

"Should you go to Jezel, then?" Jax directed his question at Borrel, but he looked to the Royal Dragon for the answer.

"It would be possible," she answered. "With a bit more study."

Jax put a hand to his friend's shoulder. "Let's ask Mam what she wants to do, and when you decide where you want to go, let me know, and I will see that you have all you need."

"What I need. Where I want to go...." Borrel looked out the window. "No one is going there."

Dragon Cyril realized that the conversation had gone beyond her.

"Your Grace?" the squire's voice cut into the room. "Your Grace, Lord Maladour of Senner is here for you."

"I'm sorry, Borrel," Jax said softly then let himself be drawn back to his meetings and his papers.

Three days later, Jax awoke briefly to enjoy the pleasures of Cheshir's lips on certain sensitive parts of his body. Later, when she was satisfied, Cheshir sat up and rang for Jax's squire. The prince himself went back to sleep; Cheshir ate toast, sipped tea, and watched him sleep.

"Have you eaten all the toast?" Jax asked, his eyes still closed, his voice rough after last night's raucous celebration. It had taken a week for him and his staff, with the inspired support of the king's chamberlain, to prepare the feast to honor the new Earldom of Darkwood. The party had been a huge, rollicking event.

"Yes, I finished it. Shall I ring for more?"

He opened his eyes at last when the toast arrived, noting the wistful look on Cheshir's beautiful face. As he sat up and ate, she fiddled with a large aquamarine ring, the exact color of her eyes.

"I really have to stop this," she said.

"Breakfast?"

"No." She tossed a crumb at him. "Sleeping with you."

"There's not so much sleeping."

"But it's not going to break your heart to see me marry Frinz this summer, is it?"

Jax looked down at his tea. "My heart's already broken."

"So, are you giving it piece by piece to the Weaver?"

He sighed and looked at her. "She'll just take it if she wants it."

Cheshir frowned. "You can't take someone's heart if they doesn't want to give it. Believe me, I know."

"Shirry—."

"No, Jax." She stopped him with a lingering kiss, her open eyes pooling. "I'm not going to cry for you anymore." She slipped out of the bed and wrapped herself in Jax's robe.

He looked at her, not knowing what to say to the tracks of tears running down her creamy cheeks. She saw the pain in his eyes and fled.

Jax pushed aside his sheets and went to the window. The water of Keffin Harbor sparkled in the sun.

"Good morning, your Grace." His secretary entered with a load of scrolls under one arm and a fresh pot of tea in the other hand. "Everyone is raving about the success of your party last night. Today, of course, we have the execution at noon."

Jax extracted himself from the secretary's lists and duties long enough for a swim, but Cheshir's sadness lingered in his heart and grew as the grim hour of execution approached. A few minutes before noon, he joined the other members of the royal council on the steps of the palace. A cheer rose from the townspeople gathered in the courtyard as Princess Tallyn stepped into the windy sunshine.

He bowed to her, and she took his hand. "Are you feeling better?"

"Yes. I'd like to be up and about, but Mollish is still coddling me. How was your party?"

"Fine."

"Don't worry about Cheshir," she said softly. "She was very happy with Frinz until you reappeared. They suit each other."

"I'm glad to hear it." Jax was well aware that Cheshir would have gone running to their foster sister after leaving him that morning.

"And she's right about you and the Weaver, too."

Jax had no answer for that.

Lord Foby came slowly out of the palace, the petite Farsouthian on his arm. "My lords and ladies, may I present the Weaver, Klaris de Farsouth!"

Again, the crowd cheered.

Tallyn moved to stand closer to Foby, leaving Jax with Klaris.

"Hello, Weaver," he said in Islish.

"Good day, your Grace." Her voice was quiet and gently ironic.

"I trust you are feeling better?" he continued, aware of other eyes upon them.

"If I wasn't, Mollish and Mam Marith would have kept me in bed, I'm sure."

"I've felt you weave the Mystic."

Her smile was radiant. "Yes. And I've felt you use it, too."

There was something sensual in her voice, and he couldn't help his response. "Felt me?"

Klaris smiled but changed the subject. "Carte Serge has been helping me review documents from the library here."

"I suppose there's not much besides reading that the druids would let you do."

She had to look up at him this time to evaluate his multiple meanings.

"What are you reading?" he asked.

"Musty old things. There's a book on Axterran magic, but it seems highly imaginative."

"That's a strange choice."

"Not for me. Did you know that Oracle told me there's more to your prophecy, I guess it's our prophecy now, and that it's here in Kree?"

Jax fished the Oracle's medallion from underneath his shirt and looked at it in the sun. "The Oracle told me that you and I are going somewhere."

Klaris cocked her head to one side and considered him. "Where?"

"The Oracle didn't deign to tell me." He shook his head. "*Stay with Klaris and resolve the dichotomies.*" Jax mimicked the Oracle's voice.

Klaris laughed.

"Yes, the Oracle laughed at me, too," Jax said.

The king came out of the palace, followed by the dowager, who avoided Jax and looked down her fine nose at the small Farsouthian at his side. Suddenly the crowd roared. Royal guards were dragging the traitor from the barracks. The small man was screaming.

It was over in a moment of sudden silence. The traitor's body dangled limply from the rope and twirled in the cold spring wind.

A few people cheered half-heartedly.

Loud, clattering hoof beats broke into the grim mood. "Ships, Sire!" Shouted the rider. "Barian ships have entered the harbor!"

The king turned to Jax. "You'd better go greet them, your Grace."

Another rider pounded through the palace gates. "More ships!" She cried. "Farsouthians are coming!"

Everyone turned to Klaris, who smiled. "My mother."

19

Tallyn stood with Jax and Klaris at the end of the wharf. She watched the green water swell and ebb around the barnacle encrusted pilings and reached out a hand to Jax to steady herself. "I feel seasick just being on the wharf," she muttered.

"Look at the boats or the shore, not the water." Jax gripped her firmly. "Does the poison still affect you?"

"More likely it's Mollish's hideous cure still affecting me." Tallyn took a breath and looked out over the sparkling bay. A boat was being lowered from the giant Barian wingship. The Farsouthian ship was smaller and sleeker and still seemed to be doing something with its anchor.

Klaris looked up at Jax and caught a strange grimace on his face. "What's the matter?"

Jax answered in Islish. "It's customary for the sealord, or any captain for that matter, to stand in the launch."

The sealord, evident by the billowing Barian Blue cloak, sat huddled in the stern of his small boat as it splashed through the windy waves towards the dock.

Eventually the launch reached the wharf. Bryx grabbed hold of the ladder and climbed up. Tallyn, Jax, and Klaris all bowed.

"Hello Cousin Tallyn," Bryx said then turned to Klaris. "Weaver Klaris. I'm so pleased to see you here. Congratulations." He leaned forward to kiss her cheek. Klaris moved away before he could touch her, but Jax felt a rush of resentment towards his brother for the attempt.

Finally, Bryx looked to Jax. "I see they didn't execute you."

"No, your Majesty. They made me Earl of Darkwood instead."

"Sweet goddess, Jax. Only you could turn a death sentence into a seat on the royal council."

Again, Jax spoke in Islish. "You may have noticed, your Majesty, that the Gates of Griffe are open again."

Even without understanding Islish, Tallyn sensed the tension between the brothers. "Welcome, your Majesty, to Kordon." She took the sealord's arm. "The king will see you now, and we are planning a feast in honor of your return to Kordon."

Bryx looked up to the hills above the town and sighed. "I will attend, of course, Tallyn. But I want to sit next to Princess Klaris."

Tallyn stepped back as the sealord took the Weaver's hand.

"Look, Weaver Klaris," Jax intervened. "Here comes your mother." This gave Klaris the opportunity to pull away from the sealord.

Bryx turned back to look at the bay. "Ah yes, the lovely Queen Jeress. And it seems that Trajan is here, too."

Jax, Bryx, and Tallyn stepped back to give Klaris space to greet her parents. All three hugged together. Tears of joy ran down Queen Jeress's cheeks.

Tallyn sighed, missing her own mother, but she covered her feelings in a deep curtsey to the Farsouthian Queen. Next to her, Jax bowed; Bryx, equal in his own right, just nodded politely.

"Mother," said Klaris formally in Landish. "You remember Sealord Bryx and Crown Princess Tallyn of Kordon."

"Of course. And I remember Jax Sharkin too." Jeress spoke Landish with the same accent as her daughter. "Sealord Bryx, we hope Haven survived the tidal wave."

"The Floating Islands are badly damaged," he said. "But we'll repair them."

The queen nodded. "Now, Prince Jax. You must have quite a tale to tell."

"It was Jax who brought me the Secret for my mastery." Klaris cleared her throat. "And got me off Sageham before the earthquake."

Jeress looked from her daughter to Jax and smiled slowly and a little sadly. "Well, my lord, thank you." She took his arm. "Let's go see Kodill and then you can tell us all about this."

"I am honored, your Majesty." Jax smiled.

Jeress looked at him for a moment. "You remind me of Rax."

Tallyn saw Jax blink and Bryx sneer. She also noted the flash of annoyance in Klaris's green eyes as the sealord took the Weaver's arm to follow Jeress and Jax back to the palace.

"May I escort your Royal Highness?"

Tallyn smiled at Consort Trajan. They walked in silence behind the others, each watching the Barian brothers.

Bryx bent down to whisper something in Klaris's ear. Jax said something, and the Farsouthian Queen laughed.

Having spent a good hour that morning comforting a confused Lady Cheshir, Tallyn knew all about the interesting bond between her cousin Jax and the Weaver. To find Sealord Bryx inserting himself into that incomplete equation aroused all of Tallyn's considerable political instincts.

Sealord Bryx sat between Kodill and Klaris at the state dinner that night. He was pleased that Kodill spent so much time talking to Queen Jeress on his right, which gave Bryx the chance to share choice morsels of food and conversation with Klaris. He was waiting again for Klaris to finish something she was saying to her father, Consort Trajan, when he heard Jax and Jeress talking about slavery.

"Of course, everyone knows it's wrong," Jeress was saying. "But the *Rote and Rede* says we must let the various realms and peoples make their own decisions."

"That's just a comfortable way of rationalizing our complicit benefit from the practice, Ma'am," Jax answered.

Jeress cocked her head. Not many people would speak so frankly to a queen. "How do we benefit from slavery?"

"Do you use Hantish iron?"

"Some."

"Then slaves have served you. Besides, we all know it isn't right. If we sit back and ignore it, we are as much to blame as the trolls who actually wield the whips."

"What are you saying, Jax?" Bryx leaned forward to look around King Kodill and Queen Jeress at his brother.

"I'm saying that slavery is wrong, my lord, and that we shouldn't support it."

"But what can you do about it?" The dowager grumbled, displeased with her position next to Jax at the edge of the High Table. "They're trolls. They don't listen to civilized people."

"Maybe we civilized people haven't been using the right language."

Mother Marith, Borrel, and Florin sat far down the great hall at the state dinner that night. Marith watched the Farsouthian Queen speaking intently with Jax. She saw Klaris's polite but stiff nods to the sealord.

"I can't believe that the sealord is Jax's brother." Florin sipped her wine. "Look how different they are."

"Different inside and out," said an old Barian seated across the table.

With all the other chatter in the room and the music from the musicians, Marith couldn't hear what was said at the High Table, but she saw Queen Jeress laugh and watched Bryx grimace as Klaris raised a goblet to make some kind of toast to Jax.

Marith felt something release inside her. And it hurt.

The deep peace of the sun salutations lingered as Marith enjoyed a few extra breaths before she sat up for the reverence. As she opened her eyes on the gently rolling hills of Kordon, she thought about the distances she had covered over the last year. From her village high in the Ledden Rises, she, the two nyad twins, and her enigmatic slave had walked across much of the Knownlands. They'd met fairies, survived flood and drought, confronted hatred and met love. Finally, they'd solved the puzzle of Jax's imperious ways, his smart mouth, and his clipped accent that had made him such a troubling slave.

Marith stood, remembering the sight of him sitting on the floor of her burrow, bleeding from trollish abuse, but aching from a greater loss she had caused. She hadn't understood then what she had inadvertently taken from him. But during the long journey on the roads and paths of the Knownlands, she had watched him slowly rebuild his sense of self, only to offer himself up to a horrific traitor's death in order to save her life.

She took tea and fruit in the great hall and finally climbed the stairs to the Barian Suite.

Jax, his hair still damp from his morning swim, was already deep in a discussion about vineyard production with his agents from Twistford when his squire announced: "Mother Marith, your Grace."

"Mam!"

She answered the warmth of his smile with a hug. "May I have a moment, your Grace?"

He waved his staff and the agents out of the room. "Don't 'your Grace' me."

She pursed her lips. "You are picky. I can't call you son; I can't use your titles...."

He sighed. "Why can't you just call me Jax?"

"Because you aren't, just Jax, *son*."

"Sweet goddess!"

"Yes. The goddess blessed us all the day she led Doc into the slave auction."

"Aye."

"It's time for me to go home."

He turned away to pour more tea into his cup. "Want some? The Farsouthians brought sugar."

"No."

"I'm sure Doc and Adgar will be happy to have you back."

"Florin and Borrel say they'll go with me."

"I thought Borrel might go to Dragonsholm."

Marith covered his hand with her own. "He wants to go home too, but he's not sure it will be home."

Jax looked down and moved some papers on his desk. "I know that feeling."

Marith put a hand on his shoulder. "You know where I'll be, Jax."

He looked into her crinkle-lined eyes. "But I'll miss you."

The white coach rattled out of the palace courtyard on the start of its long journey back to Hilsen Vale. Among the trunks and boxes piled on the top were bags of fine herbs, rare crystals, and several crates of Kordon's finest Darkwood wines.

Klaris stood next to Jax, watching the coach go. His grief was palpable.

He ran a hand over his face. "I'm going for a sail," he said at last. "Want to come?"

She shook her head. "I told my mother I'd ride with her to the Dorphdown Henge."

He answered in a voice not quite steady. "Yes. Go with your mother."

A half hour later, Klaris slowed her horse from a canter to a walk. Jeress pulled alongside her. Behind them, several of the queen's Farsouthian courtiers chatted among themselves about the fine quality of Kordish horses and began to argue about whether or not Kordish men, fair-skinned and round eyed, were handsome.

"I can't decide who's more handsome," Jeress said slyly. "Prince Jax or the sealord."

"Jax, of course," Klaris answered absently. She'd been concentrating on the magic she felt emanating from the ancient stones of the henge. She did not notice her mother's sharp green gaze.

"Well," the queen said. "Bryx certainly finds you attractive."

This got Klaris's attention. "He shouldn't waste time with me."

The queen raised an eyebrow.

"He can't. We can't.... Besides. I don't want *him*."

"Whom do you want?"

Klaris thought of Jax and smiled but her answer was tinged with frustration. "Mother."

"Don't take that tone with me," Jeress said gently. "I am fully aware of all the difficulties involved in relationships even without the complications of magic and royalty."

Klaris slipped off her horse to wander amid the circle of tall stones. "Feel the old Mystic here?"

"Of course I do. Don't try to change the subject."

Klaris bent to pick a small yellow flower. "What would you like me to tell you?"

"What you feel. What you fear. What you intend to do."

"I don't know. I don't know, and I don't know."

Jeress smirked. "You'll have to figure it out, my sweet."

"Why did you betroth us, Jax and me?" Klaris demanded suddenly. "Surely you knew I'd have too much Mystic to marry a prince."

The queen cocked her head to one side. "That was mostly Rax and me flirting, and...."

"And?"

"Here, I'll show you." At the base of one large stone, a pool of clear water reflected the blue sky. Klaris smiled as her mother wove the Mystic and the water came alive with a memory.

Two black-skinned, green-eyed babies sat on a blanket. The boy with short curly hair clapped his hands. The other, a bald-headed girl, squealed with pleasure.

"That's Joron and me!" Klaris smiled.

A six-year old Bryx galloped around the babies on a hobby horse.

Sealord Rax, dark haired with gleaming sea-blue eyes, gave a familiar smile. "I don't know where Bryx picked up that gallop. We don't have horses here on Baria."

"On your travels to landish countries, maybe?" Jeress's voice replied. "Or Farsouth."

A white-haired boy toddled into the scene.

"Is that baby Jax?" Klaris asked.

"Yes."

Little Jax handed toy boats to both of the babies. The baby Joron began chewing on his, but Klaris made hers levitate and rock as if it was on the sea.

"Good!" Cried the little Jax. "Boat sail!"

"Well," said Sealord Rax. "I see your daughter inherited your talent with the Mystic."

"She has much deeper Mystic than I," Jeress replied, an unmistakable wariness in her voice.

"Come, Princess Klaris." Bryx batted the toy boat away. "Come ride with me."

Baby Klaris frowned, looking around for her boat. She began to fret. Suddenly the boat whizzed back into her baby hand.

"No, Princess. Stupid boat." Bryx again tried to take the toy from the baby.

This time she shrieked.

"Fine," pouted Bryx, pushing the baby away.

Jax was there to catch her as she toppled over backwards. He set her upright, put the toy boat back into her hands, and then gently patted her bald head.

He looked up at his father and Jeress, his islish eyes as blue as the summer sea. "I help her," he said clearly, his hand on her head. "My princess."

Jeress laughed. "Perhaps we should betroth them."

Rax's eyes flirted. "A lovely idea, my lady."

The image swirled and faded into a reflection of the cloudless spring sky.

Klaris leaned back against a stone, happiness bubbling in her stomach. "I remember that boat. I always thought it was special, but I never knew it came from Jax. I didn't know I'd even met him before."

Jeress spoke softly. "There was something about the two of you even then."

"He was a cute little toddler."

"And you were a beautiful baby."

"Beautiful? I was bald. And dangerous with that much Mystic. Why did you let me use it?"

Jeress paused before answering. "You are obviously much more dangerous now, Klaris."

The Weaver rested herself on the ancient magic of the stone circle.

The courtiers were quietly setting up a picnic under an ancient oak. Way off in the harbor, Klaris could see a small sailboat cruising among the larger Barian and Farsouthian ships. Her happiness shaded to fear. "I don't feel dangerous; I feel vulnerable."

Jeress saw the direction of her daughter's gaze and hugged her tightly. "After what you've put him through, I imagine he feels the same."

Klaris turned troubled eyes to her mother. "The Oracle told us to stay together, and goddess knows I want to. But the *Rote and Rede* says that I can't have someone like him, and he needs heirs. If I, if we…. It's going to break my heart."

Jeress squeezed her daughter again and smiled a little sadly. "Then let it break, my love."

20

Jax stomped through the streets of Kree towards the palace, oblivious to the polite 'milords.' Far from easing his heart, his sail had given him a new source of grief. The Barian ships riding the gentle harbor waves had been in a shocking state of disrepair. Worn ropes and patched sails rose above unpainted hulls sporting long growths of weed and barnacles. And these were the sealord's ships. They should have been the proudest, sharpest ships in all the fleet.

Lost in his thoughts of the fleet and its condition, Jax arrived at his suite of rooms to find two large trunks sitting in the corridor, surrounded by piles of loose documents, his squire and his secretaries standing against the wall in consternation.

"What is this?" he demanded.

"The sealord has requisitioned the Barian suite, your Grace." The squire shrugged as if this answered the question.

"The sealord?" Jax echoed, shoving into the room. A group of Barian servants was busy hanging clothes and rearranging the desk.

"Your Highness!" They said in Islish, giving Jax the one-handed Barian salute.

The sealord emerged from the bedchamber. "Hello, little brother."

Jax sketched the briefest of bows. "What are you doing, Bryx?"

"Don't 'Bryx' me. I've been on the *Drixa* far too long, and I'm sick of sleeping on that damn boat. I want a bed that doesn't move."

Jax noted the frowns on the faces of the Barian servants and answered in Landish, which most of the Barians wouldn't understand: "You shouldn't say things like that."

Bryx shrugged. "This is the Barian Suite. As sealord, I believe that I am *the* Barian."

"So, you've moved my things out."

The sealord nodded. "You can stay on the *Drixa*."

"In the harbor."

"In the goddess-damned harbor."

Jax ran a hand through his wind-blown hair. "Where am I supposed to meet with my Darkwood staff? I can't expect them to join me on a ship."

"Take a townhouse, my lord *earl*."

"Fine. Your Majesty." Jax replaced his hat. He motioned to the servants. "Please bring my things."

Jax marched out of the palace and back through the streets of Kree, giving terse orders to his staff to find him a house, and explaining that in the meanwhile he would stay on the sealord's flagship. At the wharf, Barian sailors lowered the trunks onto the longboat tied there. They rowed Jax out to the mighty wingship.

A hail of cheers from the crew greeted Jax as he climbed aboard. This response from the Barians soothed his chafed feelings. He arrived on the familiar deck, watching the captain straighten his jacket and give the one-handed salute. "Welcome, your Highness. Welcome aboard the *Drixa*."

Jax hid his surprise. Illat had served as fourth or fifth lieutenant on the *Drixa* for years under Sealord Rax, but never with distinction.

"Thank you, Captain Illat. I'll be staying on the *Drixa*, indefinitely."

"Wonderful, my lord. I'll prepare the lord admiral's cabin for you."

"I'm not the lord admiral," Jax protested.

Illat shrugged. "If Admiral Hix shows up, he'll be on the *Sharkin* and he can stay there."

Jax raised an eyebrow. Like all Barian nobles his age, Jax had been schooled for captaincy by Admiral Hix. He had tremendous respect for that old Barian. "It's your call, Captain, but I don't want Papa Bear angry with me."

Illat smiled at the nickname that a much younger Jax had first given the lord admiral. "Papa Bear never gets angry with you, my lord. Let me show you to the cabin."

As he followed Illat down the hatchway, a badly coiled line caught his eye.

One of the sailors noticed Jax's frown and jumped to tidy the coil.

Later, dressed in fresh clothes, Jax took a steaming cup of green seaweed tea up to the deck. Unlike his brother, he savored the feel of a ship rocking gently at anchor, the salty sea breeze in his face, and the tang of the tea.

A loose corner of a furled sail flapped in the wind. He frowned and walked to the pilot house. The sand in the hourglass had run out. No one had turned it. No bell rang. A sailor noticed the direction of Jax's gaze and shrugged.

"Cap'n Illat don't make us keep the bells when we're in port, my lord. He says the sealord don't like the clanging."

Jax hid his amazement. He returned to the quarterdeck and stood at the rail surveying the deck, the masts, the furled sails, anger growing slowly. There was more than money missing here.

He tossed down the last of his tea. "My compliments to the captain," he snapped to a midshipman. "I would like to see him at his earliest convenience."

Illat entered the Admiral's Cabin and found himself impaled by the prince's Barian eyes, so different from the Landish features of the current sealord.

"Can you tell me why the *Drixa* is so slovenly, Captain Illat?"

"The sealord has made no complaint, my lord." Illat protested.

"He shouldn't have to. This is the flagship of Baria, for goddess' sake. This ship is an example of what it means to be shipshape, to be well-sailed and well-captained."

"Aye, my lord. The sealord is in charge."

Jax shook his head. "You are the captain of the Barian Flagship, sir. I trust you can do a better job."

Illat opened his mouth then shut it.

Jax went on. "While the sealord is ashore, you will keep the hours and the watches. The decks will be maintained, the sails and sheets properly stowed, and the crew on a regime of repairs. And have the bowsprit repainted."

"Aye, aye, my lord."

"Thank you."

Jax fumed for another five minutes after Illat left. The *Drixa* had never been so neglected when his father was sealord. Finally, Jax left his cabin, called for the ship's small boat and spent the rest of the afternoon with his Kordish staff at a fashionable tavern near the palace.

He returned to the *Drixa* to dress for dinner. The crew lined up smartly to greet him as he climbed aboard. The swabbed deck gleamed in the afternoon sun.

"Thank you, Captain," Jax said to Illat, who stood at the head of his crew. "Tomorrow, please address these same concerns with your support cruisers."

"Aye, aye, my lord."

As the sun set beyond the Gates of Griffe at the western mouth of Keffin Harbor, Illat watched the longboat row Prince Jax back toward town. The prince stood in his place in the stern.

"We haven't seen a Sharkin hold his feet in the longboat recently," said Illat's first lieutenant.

"No."

"He stands like a sealord ought to."

"Yes, but he's not the sealord. Not even the lord admiral."

The lieutenant raised an eyebrow at the bitter twinge in Illat's voice. "But he will be," she predicted softly. "Old Hix can't do it forever. It's the prince's right to be lord admiral."

"I suppose." Illat listened to the ship's bell clang. "Then he can trouble the captain of the *Sharkin* and leave us alone."

"Good morning, Princess Klaris!" Bryx slipped out of his rooms, just as the Weaver was walking past.

"Good morning, your Majesty," she said, startled to see the sealord coming out of what had been Jax's suite. "Where's Prince Jax?"

The sealord shrugged. "On the *Drixa*, I suppose, or perhaps he slept in Lady Cheshir's bed." He took Klaris's arm. "What are your plans for this rainy morning?"

The Weaver removed her arm from the sealord's grip. "I'm going to see if I can decipher a text called the *Rimes of the Knownlands*." She quoted the title in Ancient.

"Say that again."

"Rimes of the Knownlands."

"I love to hear you speak Ancient."

Klaris frowned. "I doubt you'd enjoy my arguments with Carte Serge over the translations."

"How could anyone argue with your beauty?"

"It has nothing to do with beauty."

"You have everything to do with beauty."

"Stop, my lord. Your teasing is pointless."

"It's not pointless. Klaris, I—."

"No." She interrupted him. "Bryx, you and I have responsibilities that keep us apart."

"Yes. You are the Weaver and I am the sealord, and the goddess would prohibit a marriage between two such powerful people."

"Exactly."

"But what if we're just friends? Just pleasing each other?"

"Pleasing?"

"Sure, my beautiful princess. Put aside your scrolls and your studies for a little bit. Come ride with me this lovely morning."

"It's pouring rain."

Tallyn came trotting down the stone stairs, a large red cape billowing behind her. "The rain isn't stopping me," she said cheerily. "I'll ride with you, cousin. Leave poor Klaris alone to find answers to the Oracle's riddles. You and I can enjoy the fresh rain-washed morning."

Tallyn grabbed Bryx by the hand and hauled him down the great hall, calling for the grooms.

Relieved, Klaris once again admired the Kordish princess' political acumen.

Several hours later, she sat beside a roaring fire, rereading the latest transcripts that she and Carte Serge had settled upon. The lines of the ancient rime rolled around in her head: dragons and fairies and round towers. Absently, she rubbed the ears of the orange cat that purred loudly on her lap.

Tallyn blew into the room and came to the fire, holding her cold hands to its warmth.

"Thank you, your Highness." Klaris smiled at her.

"My pleasure, Weaver. It was a lovely ride, really."

Foby Kora and Carden Yemmel sauntered into the room. Foby bowed, and after a moment, so did Carden. The cat leapt off Klaris's lap and went to rub against Foby's legs.

"We need a third and a fourth for a game of cards," Carden grinned. "Would you ladies do us the honor?"

Klaris was ready to refuse when Bryx entered. Like Tallyn, his skin glowed from the ride in the rain, and his dark hair gleamed. Changing her mind, she agreed to play cards.

Bryx stood by watching.

"Where's our Prince Jax today?" Carden asked, waiting for Foby to make a move.

No one answered. Carden played a card and trumped Foby.

"Dragons," Foby muttered.

Klaris played next.

Carden looked at the sealord, who was watching the firelight glint off Klaris's wayward hair. "Did your Majesty kick Jax out of the palace?"

"I kicked him out of the Barian Suite."

"You did?" Tallyn turned in her chair to look at the sealord.

"I am *the* Barian, now."

At that moment, Jax pushed open the door.

"Well, here's the *other* Barian, then." Carden grinned at his cards.

Jax noted the tableau in the room. "The steward just told me that they're bringing lunch to you in here, your Highness." He bent to kiss Tallyn's hand. "Who's winning?"

"Bryx is," said Carden.

Jax laughed. "It's wise to let him."

"Wise-ass," Bryx grumbled.

"Where've you been this rainy morning?" Foby asked.

"Around town."

"Are you keeping secrets?" Bryx asked. "Or a mistress maybe?"

"Nothing so enjoyable," Jax removed Klaris's papers from the chair by the fire and sat down. "I was talking with the smiths."

"Goldsmiths?"

"Blacksmiths."

"Trump!" Tallyn crowed.

"You win every time," Carden snapped.

"I do." She smiled.

"She does," confirmed Foby.

"She always has," noted Jax.

Klaris folded up her losing cards and turned to Jax and mustered her Landish: "Why were you visiting the smithies?"

"To find out where they get their iron."

"From The Hant, no doubt," said Bryx.

Jax looked up at him with a speculative expression. "I wanted to know if there are other sources."

"Why?" Carden shuffled the deck.

"I have a bias against Hantish iron."

"It wasn't the iron that enslaved you," Carden said flippantly.

Jax got up and walked to the window. For a moment he looked out into the rainy garden. "Slavery is both an economic and a moral problem."

"Why don't you go find Lady Cheshir and let her take your mind off your problems," Bryx suggested waspishly.

The door opened, and the steward and his staff entered with trays of steaming soup and hot bread.

"Or let lunch take your mind off it," Carden offered cheerfully.

"Cheshir is going to marry Aychex," Tallyn said.

Jax pulled his chair next to Klaris. "She loves me not."

Klaris looked up at him, hearing a strange reserve in his voice. His hair was darkened from the rain and his eyes, too, seemed a darker, deeper blue. Desire ripped through her, hot and powerful. She turned away from him and buried her nose in her goblet of wine.

Bryx sat next to her on the other side, so she moved even closer to Jax. The sealord's pale eyes flashed over her curls to his brother. "Since when did you care about moral problems?"

"Since I found myself on the wrong side of some."

"I'm sure it was uncomfortable." Bryx complacently sipped his soup. "But when I went to the iron mines, I thought that the slaves seemed to be reasonably treated."

"Reasonably?" Jax's voice was hard. "Did you visit the caves where they sleep on the dirt like dogs? Did you see what they were fed? Did you watch them die their painful, lonely deaths, far from anyone who ever might have loved them?"

The sealord shrugged. "When was the last time you visited the bilge slums of Baria, Jax? It's not so different."

"Poor is not the same as enslaved."

"Isn't it?"

Klaris put down her spoon and spoke in careful Landish. "My lord, I do not believe the Barians could possibly treat their own people with the type of cruelty the trolls visit upon their slaves."

Bryx patted Klaris's shoulder and smiled. "I think you've led a very sheltered life, my lovely Klaris. What do you know about the world? You've lived in the finest palaces and been coddled and pampered by your royal birth and your great magic."

"Why do you assume that I am naïve?" Klaris asked, looking at the faces around her. With the exception of Jax's wary eyes, the others all regarded her with that same maddening sort of condescension she had so often received from the magicians at Sageham. "Is it because I am young? Or short? Or speak your Landish with difficulty?"

"No one thinks you are naïve, exactly," Bryx said gently. "But you've lived so much in books."

He stopped suddenly as a silver ball of smoke coalesced in the middle of the table. Among them all, only Jax had seen the Weaver mold the Mystic. All of them now watched in awe as images appeared on the swirling globe: *slaves dressed in rags, slaves crying out as whips slashed into their skin, a girl sobbing for her mother as she stood on an auction block; a pair of slaves struggling to pull a heavy cart through the muddy streets of The Hant while a troll beat them with a whistling crop; and finally a slave, muddy and shivering in the sleet at the end of a leash.*

"Why, that's Jax," said Carden, amazed.

"These images have not come from books," Klaris said.

The picture grew sharper: *Jax raggedly asking "help me" in Islish. Thick trollish fists grabbed his slave collar while others pinioned his arms and dragged him away through the black gates of the iron mines.*

Jax put a hand on Klaris's arm. She looked at him, closed her hands into fists, and cut the weave.

Carden reached for the decanter of wine and refilled his cup. He took a deep drink. "Game, set, and match to the Weaver."

21

Jax and Foby had ditched Carden and were heading off for a game of darts at their favorite tavern when Jax was corralled by the lady chancellor's first secretary. "We need you to translate again, your Grace," he explained while leading Jax away from a sad-faced Foby. "We're ready to finalize the trade agreements, and Queen Jeress asked specifically for your Grace."

With two royal embassies at Kree, the days and nights had assumed an increasingly frenetic air as the nobles of three kingdoms strove to entertain and impress each other with lavish clothes, food, music, and sport. Behind closed doors, their talks muffled by the music of revelry, ambassadors negotiated strategic trade deals. The Barians had the advantage in these discussions because the Sharkins were fluent in both Landish and Islish. This wasn't the first time Jax had been coerced into translating for the Kordish and the Farsouthians, which gave him and the Barians a further advantage.

"They will, of course, use the Barian merchant marine," Jax reported to Bryx that evening as the sealord was dressing for yet another state dinner. "We'll collect transit fees from both parties for each direction, but we'll have to refit some ships to handle the live-stock and the sugar in separate holds."

"Where's the money for that going to come from?" Bryx frowned at his reflection in the mirror as his squire fiddled with his waistcoat. "You may not be aware of it, but the Barian treasury nearly empty."

"Given the lack of paint and the sorry state of repairs on the *Drixa*, I can tell that you haven't been spending any money on your ships. But I was going to suggest that the Royal treasury could loan the money to the lords and ladies of the Floating Islands. They could make the retrofit. The Helm would charge a very small interest on the loan, but we'd take a cut of the transportation fees."

Bryx turned away from the mirror to consider his brother. "Perhaps we could make some loans."

"It is a bit dusty down here." The archivist lifted a lamp to illuminate this understatement. Long rows of shelves stacked with scroll cases, document boxes, and crumbling books sat under a heavy layer of dust.

Klaris raised a casual hand and a much brighter mage light appeared over their heads.

This revealed dark shapes scuttling away into the distant shadows and a few pairs of gleaming eyes.

"I'm not sure this place is improved by the light," grumbled Carte Serge.

"We've combed through everything in the library upstairs," Klaris reminded him. "If there's something here, I suppose this is where we must search."

"What exactly are you looking for, Weaver?" the archivist asked.

"We don't know." Klaris took a step deeper into the room, peering into the receding stacks. "A prophecy, we suppose. Something to do with dragons and Axterre, maybe."

"Well, mythology is usually kept back here...." The archivist shuffled through the dust to a shelf deeper in the cellar.

Klaris and Serge walked along the shelf, brushing dust from the labels on boxes, books, and scrolls in order to read the titles.

After a few minutes, Klaris stopped. "This could take months," she said. "I think there may be a better way."

Serge felt her gather the Mystic then extend it into the far corners of the cellar, tracing the ancient power that had created this part of the palace. It wasn't the building, though, that formed the purpose of her spell. One by one, each shelf became the focus of the weave.

Reveling in the elegant, clean power, Serge closed his eyes in ecstasy. As hard as they'd worked through the documents in the royal library above, translating ancient texts, searching, comparing, they'd found nothing that could fit with the two stanzas of this prophecy that she had received from Prince Jax.

At first Serge had been stunned and then rather frightened by the depth of the girl's scholarship.

"Well, how do you think I ended up as Weaver?" she demanded one afternoon when he had again expressed his amazement at her grasp of ancient languages and the scope of her reading.

"But you are so young—."

"For goddess' sake, Serge, I don't know what other people do with their time, but mine has largely been spent in this type of study. It's what I do, you see."

"Evidently, my lady. And to good purpose."

"To no purpose here," she had grumbled.

Now, Serge started as she abruptly closed her weave and cut short his reminiscence.

"There's nothing here." Frustration echoed in her voice. "Nothing but old accounts, some tales about fairies that shouldn't be classified as myths, and a whole lot of books with illustrations about someone named Mellanisha."

"Ah Mellanisha." The archivist smiled.

"She's rather a legend in Kordon," Serge explained as they climbed the stairs and emerged in a quiet salon off the main library.

"Legend for what?" Klaris asked.

Serge took a breath of sweet clean air and watched the archivist lock the door to the vault. He cleared his throat, but it was the archivist who answered with pride. "For sexual exploits, my lady."

The orange cat that followed Klaris everywhere sat on a brocade sofa licking a paw. "Sexual exploits," it said in a tone of withering condescension.

The archivist squawked. "It's true! The cats are talking to you!"

"Talking without saying anything useful," Klaris snapped.

She, Serge, and the cat watched the archivist flee the room.

"Not nonsense," the cat said. "Human sex is so bland it's a wonder you manage to enjoy it at all."

Serge again cleared his throat, uncomfortably.

Klaris ignored him and sat down next to the cat. "Do you know what I'm looking for?"

"Some of that bland sex," it answered smugly.

Klaris glanced at Serge. She was well aware of Carte Serge's opinions on what she considered her private longings. "I'm looking for the prophecy."

"Ah, that."

"Do you know where it is?" she prompted.

"I know where it isn't."

"Thank you very much, so do I."

The cat turned its green eyes full upon Klaris, whose greener eyes looked unflinchingly back. "You must find it, Weaver. The beasts are coming soon."

The cat stretched and its claws sank into the rich brocade. Then it dropped to the floor and sauntered away, its tail aloft like a flagpole.

"Sweet goddess," Serge breathed. "That's too fey."

Klaris sat where she was, her face frightened. For as the cat left the room, she'd seen it morph into a small, perfectly formed orange dragon.

Jax climbed on to the deck of the Farsouthian flagship and bowed to Queen Jeress.

"Thank you, Prince Jax, for all your help with our negotiations these past weeks." She spoke Islish as she led him to a comfortable collection of chairs in her bright cabin.

"It's my honor and my pleasure to be of assistance," he answered formally, accepting a glass of pink Farsouthian rum punch.

Jeress sat and he took a chair. At a nod, the queen's courtiers and stewards left the cabin.

"I also want to thank you for your help in Klaris's mastery of the Mystic, and afterward in the Hantland." The queen sipped her own punch.

Jax shrugged. "I don't deserve thanks for that. I was just following the Oracle's orders."

Jeress considered him for a moment. "Klaris was very upset last year when she couldn't get you away from those trolls."

"I was a little upset too," he admitted.

"That's understandable. But perhaps it was for the best."

Jax remembered the weeks in the auction pens and the humiliation of his months in Hilsen Vale. "That sounds like something Mother Marith would say."

Jeress smiled. "She and I talked about you."

Jax took a deep gulp of his punch, feeling like a little boy in trouble. He looked into the queen's leaf-green eyes. "I haven't done anything wrong, yet."

She laughed. "Not yet? Listen, Jax, we are leaving on the dawn tide. I want you to know that on Farsouth we will do what we can to prepare for a return of the dragons."

Jax and Klaris had told the assembled rulers of the Oracle's comments about returning dragons. Queen, king, and sealord took this information with characteristic differences. Jeress said very little but took a lot of notes. Kodill dismissed it as some kind of silliness or misunderstanding from his quirky nephew who had, perhaps, been somewhat damaged by his experiences in the slave pens. Bryx filed the information away. He had enough tangible troubles to face, without worrying about the ravings of the useless Oracle.

"Farsouth wasn't ravaged last time," Jeress explained. "We have records of what was done before."

"Would you share those with the sealord?"

"Of course."

Jax heard the hesitation in her tone and the silent criticism of the sealord behind it. He set down his glass. "Thank you."

"Baria needs you, Jax." She poured more punch from a pitcher into his glass.

"I know," he whispered. "But...."

"Yes. But." Jeress paused for a moment. "I am naturally pleased and proud that my Klaris has become the Weaver, but Jax, I am terrified for her. I do not know how the Oracle expects Klaris to face the return of the dragons, but I do know that a thousand years ago a Weaver died facing down the beasts at the beginning of the dragon interregnum."

"Dragons," he swore softly.

Jeress leaned over and lifted the Oracle's golden medallion from his chest. She considered it for a moment before looking up into his eyes. "You have a dangerous road before you, both of you. Be good to yourselves, to each other, because this task is going to be very hard on you."

He looked at her bleakly, wondering what exactly she was authorizing.

She stood with a wistful smile and ran a hand down the side of his face. "You've come a long way, Jax. Your father would be proud."

He kissed her hand to hide his troubled eyes. "Thank you, your Majesty."

"Yes. Rax and I did the right thing when we betrothed you two."

The sun rising across the bay shone into the squinting eyes of the crowd that had gathered to say farewell to Queen Jeress and the Farsouthians.

Klaris sighed heavily as the sails filled, and the elegant green and gold ship caught the morning breeze and heeled toward the Gates of Griffe.

"You miss her?" Bryx asked Klaris.

She nodded. "I've sailed away from her so many times, but I think this is the only time that I've been the one left ashore."

"You don't have to stay on land," Jax offered with a smile. "Come for a sail. This breeze is perfect."

"Or, you could ride with me," Bryx invited.

Klaris looked from one brother to the other. "I rode all the way to Griffguard and back yesterday," she said. "I think a sail sounds lovely."

Jax flourished a bow and gestured toward the end of the wharf where his launch bobbed. Before Bryx could summon a civil protest, Jax and Klaris were in the little boat heading for the *Drixa*.

"I'll ride with your Majesty." Lady Dayne had fostered with Bryx. He couldn't graciously reject her, and he ended up enjoying the morning spent galloping across the green hills recalling his foster years with deep nostalgia.

In the palace, Carte Serge sat at a window with a view of the harbor. He tried not to watch the little boat dart here and there across the blue water of the bay, but when it disappeared behind the bulk of Green Island, he rose with a muffled oath and went to find a bottle of wine.

Wrapped in a fleece-lined canvas against the spray and the cool spring breeze, Klaris let her melancholy go with the gentle motion of the boat. Her cheeks glowed and her eyes sparkled.

"I needed this," she smiled at Jax, who sat at the tiller, the mainsheet in his hand.

"Still no progress on finding more of our prophecy?"

"None. I don't know where else to look, so we keep digging out old texts, even when we're fairly sure they don't contain any relevant information about Axterre or dragons or the Oracle. I'm frustrated."

He didn't answer, but she sensed he wanted to say something, so she waited.

"Let's come about." He pushed the tiller over, and the boat swung around.

When she'd moved to sit on the other side of the boat and the sail had filled on the new tack, Jax spoke quietly. "I'm frustrated too, Klaris. I'm just hanging around Kree waiting for you to figure out what the Oracle needs from you and me, watching courtiers flirt and listening to Foby's fears that Tallyn will actually marry that idiot Carden. In the meantime, the Barian fleet seems to be falling apart and goddess knows what kind of mess Haven is in while the sealord chases after you."

"Don't blame me for that!"

His blue eyes swept slowly up her body. "I blame your brilliance, your power, your beautiful eyes, your—." Suddenly he dropped the sheet and the tiller and was kissing her, his hands running over her body. The little boat came up into the wind and slowed.

After a while, he pulled himself free.

"This is perhaps a frustration we share," she said, with a smirk.

Jax sat up and hauled on the lines and reset his course. "Yes," he said cautiously. "What are we going to do?"

"What do you want to do?"

"All the things that Carte Serge is afraid of." He grinned. "But there's more. I want to go to Twistford to see this new earldom of mine. I should meet the people, review the accounts. Midipex ran a tight ship there, but I need to know the people and the ground, see what kind of defenses we can manage if the dragons do return."

"How far is Twistford from Kree?"

"A long day's ride."

Klaris resettled her wrap, and Jax went on.

"I want to go back to Baria, too. I was raised to be the lord admiral when Bryx became sealord."

"I understand."

Jax looked into those fascinating eyes. For a moment he wasn't sure he was ready to give voice to the other plan he was forming. Something in Klaris's attitude compelled him.

"I keep thinking about the other slaves in the iron mines."

This caught Klaris by surprise. "You do? But it's been a year since you were there. Won't most of the people you knew be dead by now?"

"Maybe." He pulled on the mainsheet to adjust for the wind riffles he saw off the port beam. "But I owe them something."

"Why?"

"They looked to me. They relied on me. I can't forget they're still stuck in there."

"Oh." Klaris had been raised to understand the responsibilities of nobility. But she had rarely seen the theory put so dramatically into practice.

"I want to put an end to slavery in the Knownlands," he confessed softly.

Klaris sat back amazed. "You want to change the world."

"That part of it, anyway."

"Do you think you can?"

"If I can't, who can?"

She thought about that.

"If I don't, who will?" He spoke softly, letting the sail out as he turned downwind.

Klaris watched the sun sparkles on the water.

"But I'm not doing anything here now," Jax went on. "The Oracle's decree that I stay with you keeps me here in Kree unable to attend to any of my other responsibilities, or...."

"Or dreams," she finished quietly.

"I'm not blaming you, Klaris. You're caught more deeply in the Oracle's stupid prophecy than I am."

"I suppose so. I'd like to go back to Sageham. To help rebuild."

"But we're stuck here, apparently."

"Maybe not." Klaris looked at him. "I know the Oracle said we had to stay together, but it didn't say we had to stay in Kree. Books can travel. I could pack up whatever I'm studying and go with you to Twistford, even to Haven. And maybe we could visit Sageham."

Jax sat up. "You're brilliant, Klaris."

She shrugged. "I rather like the idea of changing the world."

<h1>22</h1>

"You dragon-blasted beast!" Jax swore, jumping up from the hard dirt where he'd landed. "Kormac! I will not ride this animal again."

"Yes, my lord." The groom leaned from his saddle and grabbed the reins of the horse.

So, his Highness Prince Javix, Earl of Darkwood, made his first entrance to his castle at Twistford on foot. The rest of his party from Kree, still mounted, followed slowly.

Arno Hyll, esquire, watched his new master stomp across the courtyard. Arno had been forewarned that the new earl was bringing half the power of the Knownlands for his first visit, but he didn't know how frustrated Jax had been as first Bryx, then Tallyn, then an assortment of courtiers invited themselves on what Jax had hoped would be a temporary escape from the dubious pleasures of court politics. Besides, Jax fully intended to work while he was here, and he wasn't interested in entertaining the court.

Sir Arno recognized the crown princess in red on a beautiful bay, and her betrothed, Carden of Traik, sitting on a magnificent white. Both of them had visited Twistford with the Duke of Midipex. Arno had also met Bryx Sharkin years ago and remembered his striking half-islish features: olive skin and dark hair that contrasted sharply with his pale Kordish eyes.

The sealord rode his gray stallion next to a tiny Black woman with the most amazing hair Arno had ever seen. It spiraled about her face and floated like a cloud in the afternoon air. Even though she was containing it, he felt the weight of her Mystic against his own bit of Dragon force and knew, young and small as she was, this woman wielded more power than anyone else in the Knownlands, save maybe the Oracle.

"You must be Sir Arno," the new earl was saying.

Arno bowed. "You honor me, your Grace."

"I hope you still feel that way after you've hosted all of us for a week," Jax muttered, turning to watch his companions dismount.

Arno studied him surreptitiously. He'd never met the younger Barian prince before, but he had heard all about him. Despite those tales of carousing with the princess's set and youthful mischief, Arno hadn't expected a half-isle to be so strikingly handsome. In fact, this prince didn't look anything like his brother. Arno had somehow expected him to speak with an accent as well, but Jax's Landish was as fluent and aristocratic as Princess Tallyn's.

"Come in, come in, my ladies and my lords," Arno bowed and smiled. "I have people to take you to your rooms and bring anything that you require. When you are ready, we have a small reception for your pleasure in the gardens."

Jax let the others go ahead of him and paused to look around the courtyard. Twistford Keep had been built centuries ago. For generations it, and its surrounding lands and manors, had been part of the Duchy of Midipex. Now these fertile fields of wheat and barley, the long rows of vineyards, the pastures of horses and cattle, and the timber industry that thrived along the edges of the vast Darkwood Forest were his.

For all its wealth, Twistford had never been the seat of Midipex and it showed. The keep was sturdy and clean, but its gray stones were utilitarian and unadorned. Jax finally entered the shadows of the hall, thinking that he'd ask Klaris to add some sculptures and fountains. He was a long way from the sea here, and he missed the sound of water.

An hour later, after washing off the dirt of the road, Jax stood on a patio surveying an astounding garden. Bright bursts of color flowed out to a vast tree-covered lawn that sloped down to the quiet

River Twist. Arno's wife, the architect of this splendor was showing Weaver Klaris around the flower beds.

"Prince Jax!" Klaris cried, delighted. "Come smell this amazing peony that Lady Hyll cut for me."

The flower's fuchsia petals glowed in the soft evening air. He bent and inhaled. "Almost as lovely as you, Weaver."

"Stop it," Klaris smacked him gently with the flower. "I get enough of that smarmy talk from your brother."

Jax grinned at the sparkle in Klaris's eyes. "Fine, lassie. Let's get a drink."

"Impudent!" she laughed.

Jax's stomach flipped at the sound. "Lady Hyll, I call you as my witness. She told me to stop being courtly, didn't she?"

Lady Hyll giggled. "Surely you know, my lord, that we must all pretend to despise flattery even when we love it."

"Flattery? You malign me. No compliment could possibly be adequate to Weaver Klaris's intellect and talent."

Klaris laughed again, and Jax's stomach responded warmly.

Arm in arm they followed Lady Hyll onto the lawn. Couches sat invitingly in the shade near tables of snacks. Three musicians played quietly.

Bryx rose from his chair and came to take Klaris.

"The host must not monopolize the best company," he said.

"I am not a commodity." Klaris turned away towards Tallyn.

"Your Grace!" Sir Arno arrived looking worried. "I was told that you have a bit of the Dragon in you, as do I, so I assumed you'd want music, but I do hope the players' magic doesn't bother the Weaver."

Jax glanced at Bryx. "She's quite capable of letting us know if something bothers her."

The next day was May Eve. The prospect of a Beltane celebration in the lovely garden on the lawns along the river sent the courtiers into a frenzy of anticipation. Sir Arno had arranged a lavish party and invited all the notable people from miles around. Jax spent the day meeting these people as they arrived, asking them about their homes, villages, crops and industries with an interest that astonished most of them.

Late in the day, Jax extracted himself from his guests and retreated to his own rooms. He had heard the musicians warming up, and the pulse of their music and the magic of spring filled him with anticipation.

He found Tallyn in his room, already dressed for the party in a flowing blend of red and pink silks.

"Ah, here you are." She poured a cold bottle of golden wine into a crystal pitcher then sprinkled in a handful of tiny white woodruff flowers. She swirled the flowers into the wine. "I was wondering if you'd have a drink with me."

Jax took the glass she offered and smiled at his cousin. "Always."

"To Beltane," she smiled.

"Beltane."

"You've gained some of the finest vintages in Kordon, you know," Tallyn said savoring the delicate flavor of the wine as a connoisseur.

Jax sipped his wine. It was true. In a country known for its fine wines, the vineyards around Twistford were renowned for their rich, creamy white wines and delicate floral reds. "Next time we come, we can bring Foby and go wine tasting," Jax suggested pointedly.

"Alright," Tallyn flounced to the window. "I know you don't think it's fair that I told Foby to stay home but let Carden come."

"I *like* Foby," Jax noted. "And it is Beltane."

Tallyn took a deep drink of her wine. "I needed some space. Space to think."

"About?"

"About getting married."

"Ah." Jax poured more wine into both their glasses.

"Midipex's attack on us has made me realize how important it is for me to have an heir, and I needed some time, some space, away from Foby's lovely eyes, lovely, well you know...."

"Then why is Carden here?"

"I don't care what Carden does. No one has seriously expected me to marry him for years. I wanted to know if Foby was the right one."

Jax watched and waited.

"I love Foby, of course," Tallyn said in a rush. "But I want to be in love, Jax. Swept away, passionate."

"And you don't feel that for Foby?"

"Actually, I do." Tallyn smiled. "But I needed a little space to see that. To be sure."

Jax sighed with relief. He knew that Foby was passionate about Tallyn. He always had been.

"And now you're sure, and it's Beltane, and Carden Yemmel, my Lord of Traik, is out there mooning for you."

Tallyn laughed. "Carden will find someone else. So will I tonight, for the goddess." She winked at Jax over the rim of her glass. "What about you?"

"What about me?"

"You've given Cheshir up to Frinz. I don't know if you've even noticed the play Lady Raisha has been making for you."

Jax watched the wine swirl in his glass. "I noticed."

"But you're interested in someone else."

"I'm confused…. You know she left me with the trolls."

"That's the past, Jax. That's over now."

"Tell that to my heart."

Tallyn stood up and finished her wine. "Scared?"

"Terrified."

Tallyn laughed and pulled him up from his chair. "Pour me another glass of your May wine and come dance."

The Beltane bonfires lit the spring night under the tall trees. Musicians played drums, fiddles, lutes, and pipes to spur the ceremonies. Golden May wine sparkled in crystal glasses.

Klaris chatted with a group of Kordish Mystics from the local manors. No matter how hard she tried to avoid him, Bryx hovered near all her chairs and on the fringes of all her conversations.

Finally, as the fires grew brighter, she found Jax. Or rather he found her. He appeared next to her, sweating and panting, having just finished a particularly fast and tricky dance. He tossed down a cold glass of wine.

"Come dance with me, lovely peony," his smile was reckless.

Klaris shook her head. Like most Mystics, she was musically hopeless. "I can't dance."

The drums and fiddle began a slow, stately song. Jax took her hand. "You can dance to this one."

"I believe she said no," Bryx snapped, having borne the brunt of many of Klaris's refusals that evening.

But encouraged by a flare of joy, Klaris gripped Jax's hand and followed him across the clearing and into the dance.

He faced her and pulled her close. "Now. One, two, three, four. Hear it?"

She listened. "No."

"Never mind, then. Just walk with me. Two steps this way. Two steps that way. Two steps here now, two steps back good! Two steps...."

Klaris was amazed. As a noble child, she'd been forced to spend hours trying to master the mixture of rhythm and movement that went into dancing, but never with any success. Now, a half-drunk Jax had her swinging and stepping, even spinning as naturally as if she had Dragon force, rather than Mystic in her veins.

The music finished. He didn't let her go. "See, you can dance."

"With you," she whispered.

Bryx arrived with a fresh glass of wine. "Here, Klaris. You must need a drink after that. They're about to do the Maypole. Come watch with me."

Klaris looked up at Jax, his tousled hair and cocky smirk. Goddess, how she wanted him.

"Come, Princess," Bryx insisted.

Afraid of her overwhelming desire, she let Bryx draw her away.

Jax watched them go. The band began another wild and sensuous tarantella. Lady Raisha swayed up to Jax. She didn't say anything; she just pulled him into the music.

The Maypole stood wrapped in colorful ribbons. Couples drifted into the darker shadows to answer the call of the goddess.

Klaris turned to face the longing in Bryx's eyes, realizing that she couldn't evade it anymore.

"Bryx, please leave me alone."

"I can't," he smiled charmingly. "You're the only woman I want. Come upstairs with me. Tell me what *you* want. Let me give it to you."

The pounding of the drums was echoed by something in Klaris's blood. "I don't want anything, Bryx. I don't want you."

"You want my brother," he growled.

Klaris opened her mouth to reply, and Bryx kissed her. She tried to pull away, but he held her too tightly. Furious, she wove the Mystic.

A flash of green lightning rent the gentle night air. Bryx found himself thrown back on the grass. The crack of Klaris's magic thudded into Jax. The music stopped with a squeal as the magicians reeled with a brief shock of cross-magic. Jax dropped Raisha's hand and turned to find Klaris marching across the lawn. Everyone made way for her.

"Weaver?" Jax asked.

She spoke to him in Islish so that the other guests would not understand. "Your damned brother just forced himself on me!"

"Sweet goddess," Jax frowned. "That's unacceptable."

"Indeed!" Klaris snapped.

Jax took a deep breath against a rush of desire. "I will ensure that everyone here respects your wishes."

"I can ensure that myself, thank you!" Aware of the staring crowd, Klaris fled the Beltane fires for her solitary room.

An hour later, Jax held his aching head and closed his eyes as Bryx repeated yet again his long list of grievances.

"Your feelings aren't the issue," Jax said for what seemed to be the fortieth time. "I know you're not used to refusals—."

"Speak for yourself!"

Jax started over again. "No one can control another's heart."

"*My* heart is breaking." Bryx launched again into his diatribe.

Jax stood up. "My lord," he interrupted. "My lord, I suggest you go ease your frustrations at the bonfires out there. Drink some May wine and please the goddess with a lovely courtier."

"Is that what you're going to do?"

"I am going to bed."

"Alone?"

"Dragons, what do you care?"

"I care about Klaris. And I know you want her too."

Jax rubbed his hands over his face. "Yes. I do."

Bryx's pale Kordish eyes narrowed. "If I can't have her, neither can you."

"She wouldn't appreciate being discussed as a possession."

"*I'm* possessed!" Bryx moaned.

Jax watched his brother slump into a low couch and bury his face in his hands. "It is a difficult situation, I know."

Bryx looked up, his face wet. "She's the only woman I've ever wanted. The only one."

"I remember a definite fascination you had for Lady Dayne," Jax smirked. "And the Dowager Countess of the Tarron March."

"Those were dalliances," Bryx grumbled. "Especially the countess."

Jax continued to remind Bryx of the other partners he'd enjoyed over the years and eventually, with the help of a valet and a steward, he got the sealord tucked into his bed. Jax stayed until his brother finally fell asleep, wrestling with a growing sense of guilt at the fact that while neither he nor Bryx could ever handfast the Weaver, at least she didn't spurn his kisses.

Finally, he left the sealord and walked softly through the dark corridor. He paused outside the door to Klaris's room. Should he check on her? He remembered the feel of her body during the dance and the delicious taste of her lips. How easy it would be to slip into her room, maybe even into her bed and blame it all on Beltane.

He reached for the door handle and paused. Dylith's face and violet eyes floated in his mind's eye. The thoughtful barmaid from Hilsen Vale had helped him put together the broken puzzle of his heart. She had found him watching the Beltane fires that cold May Eve, one year ago and had taken him off into the forest. He remembered the frosty mountain air filled with the clean scent of pine and Dylith's deep warmth.

Her kindness and generosity over the summer healed some of the internal scars left by the slave pens, but it hadn't been easy on Dylith. He wondered where she was this Beltane. Who would hold her under the towering pines tonight?

Jax let his hand fall away from the door latch and bowed his head. Whatever was or might be between him and the Weaver would be far more potent and complicated. He wasn't sure he was ready to risk his battered heart on Klaris de Farsouth, never mind what the goddess might have to say about it. He turned away and found his own room.

He didn't need a light to throw off his clothes and fall exhausted into bed.

"Here you are at last," Raisha's warm hands reached out for him.

"Raisha," he sighed. "I don't think...."

"It's Beltane, your Grace."

"Yes, but—."

"You can't have the Weaver, my lord, but you can have me."

Raisha's mouth moved down his neck whispering. "One last time, Jax. For the May moon. For me."

The loud clatter of hooves in the courtyard woke Jax at first light. At least three horses thundered across the cobbles. Someone shouted at the gate then the hooves pounded onto the road and rumbled away into the morning.

"Who's up so early on this morning?" Raisha mumbled.

"Sealord, probably." He rolled over and went back to sleep.

The sun rose above the leafy green of the Darkwood Forest and poured its golden light onto the litter across the lawns: overturned chairs, scattered wine cups and bits of clothing lay abandoned under the lazy veil of smoke from the embers of the bonfires.

Klaris padded through the dew-damp grass to the little grove for the morning sun salutations. She expected to be alone as most everyone else would be sleeping off the various excesses of last night's celebration, so she was surprised to find Princess Tallyn already there, sinking into her meditative breathing.

No druid came to lead the exercises, so Tallyn and Klaris moved through the poses and stretches each to the rhythm of her own breathing.

After the final rest and reverence, they stood together. Tallyn smiled. "Did you enjoy the party?"

"Part of it."

Tallyn stretched sensuously. "I always enjoy Beltane: the fires, the sweet spring grass, and pure requited lust."

"No requital for me," Klaris mumbled.

"Why not? You've got both the Sharkin brothers longing for you."

Klaris looked up at the tall Kordish princess. This type of conversation was new for her. With no one her age to experiment with or discuss these things with, she'd had to find her way with ideas gleaned from her books or the advice of much older people.

"I can't have either of them."

Tallyn took Klaris's arm and slowly walked back to the gray bulk of the keep. "Why not?"

"Well, I don't want the sealord."

Tallyn smiled conspiratorially. "But Jax?"

"But what? The goddess, the Barians, the people here, Lady Raisha. Everyone wants a piece of him."

"Of course: bright, charming, sexy: he is delicious, our Jax."

Klaris laughed, despite herself.

"Great love always faces impediments."

"You're quoting Mayle Featherfletch," Klaris noted.

"I am, but she's right."

Klaris stopped walking. "No, my lady. I just can't see how it will work. Jax needs to be here and on Baria. I need to be on Sageham. And he needs heirs."

"You are getting ahead of yourself, my friend. Right now, the Oracle wants the two of you to stay together, right?"

"So they said."

"And if the dragons do come back, all other bets are off."

"They *are* coming."

Tallyn heard the conviction in the Weaver's voice and answered with fervor of her own. "All the more reason to seize the opportunities of today."

Klaris could see some logic in this.

"As I am," Tallyn continued. "You see, I've decided to marry Lord Foby of Rippfell this summer. The Beltane fires confirmed it."

"Really?" The question escaped Klaris before she had the chance to consider if her curiosity would damage this new intimacy with Tallyn. "A crown princess marrying for love?"

"That's right." Tallyn's voice was firm. "Foby brings out the best in me. I'll be a better queen with him as my consort."

"Blessings to you both, then." Klaris smiled. "Many blessings."

As she climbed the stairs to her room, Klaris caught a glimpse of Lady Raisha slipping down the corridor dressed in a man's shirt. This dampened the pleasant glow of Klaris's new-found friendship with Tallyn. She turned away from her lonely room and retreated to the keep's small library, hoping she might find some solace in the poems of Mayle Featherfletch.

One of Jax's sleepy squires pushed open the bedroom door and mumbled: "Lord Carden Yemmel, your Grace."

Carden, looking thoroughly rumpled, slumped into the room and sat on the edge of the bed.

Jax sat up wondering what good it was to have a squire who couldn't keep visitors away at unsociable hours. "Hey!" he called to the departing boy. "Some tea, please!"

"You'll be lucky to get it," Carden grumbled. "Everyone's still sleeping off the party."

"Why aren't you?"

Carden looked pointedly at Raisha. She took the hint, stretched luxuriously, and slipped out of bed. She pulled Jax's discarded shirt over her head and bent to gather up the silken pool of her dress. "I can't get into this thing without three maids to help me." She smiled, beautiful in the morning light.

"I don't know why women waste time with complicated clothing," Carden said sourly as the door closed behind her.

"What's the matter, Carden?" Jax yawned. His head hurt and he wanted his tea.

"Tallyn is going to marry Foby."

"Don't tell me you're surprised."

Carden shrugged. "I *am* her betrothed. I'd hoped she'd marry me, since I'd bring a bigger and better manor to the crown than Foby's little wasteland out along the border."

"She doesn't care about the lands."

The young nobleman frowned and looked out the window.

"You don't love Tallyn," Jax rubbed his sleepy eyes. "Not the way Foby does."

"Love, love, love. We're nobles. We have to make political marriages. We can always have lovers on the side."

Jax shook his head, comparing the willful blindness of both Bryx and Carden when it came to matters of the heart. "You should know Tallyn better than that."

"I know she's the most acute politician of our generation."

"And a romantic, at heart."

Carden snorted. "I'd have made a good king consort."

Jax grinned. "You'd have been the wise-ass scourge of Kree."

"Exactly."

Neither spoke for a few moments. Jax understood that Carden's horizons would be much narrower as merely the Lord of Traik.

Carden stood up. "I came to thank Your Grace for the party and let you know that I'll be leaving as soon as my people can find someone to feed us and saddle our horses."

Jax realized that as the earl in his seat, the others had to pay these respects to him. "Of course, Carden. When you find someone, tell them I want tea too."

He settled himself back into his sheets and dozed. After a while his door opened again. The steward appeared with a pot of tea, fresh bread, and Princess Tallyn.

The Princess was bright-eyed and buttoned into her red riding habit, her blond hair wrapped in an elaborate series of braids.

She dug in Jax's wardrobe and tossed him a robe as the steward poured tea for both of them.

"You're quite fresh this morning," Jax mumbled as she settled herself next to Jax on the bed.

"I've been to the sun salutations with our lovely Klaris."

Jax sipped his tea and sighed.

"Bryx is already gone," she said slyly.

"I heard."

"You've got a nice little love triangle there, don't you?" She took a sip of tea.

"It's a pointless triangle. Neither of us can...."

"Have her?"

"Bryx says he's already possessed."

"That's a pity."

"Indeed."

"Because he has no chance."

"Neither do I."

Tallyn reached for the teapot and refilled their cups. "Actually, there is something about you and Klaris together."

"Frustration."

She laughed. "When you danced with her last night, Jax, there was a rightness to it. To everything."

"You're sounding like one of those romantic ballads you love," Jax grumbled, but her words lifted something in his chest.

"Well, the Oracle told you to stay with her."

"Goddess damn them. Damn me."

"No one's going to be surprised when you sort it out."

"*I* will be. Look, Tallyn, if people like Klaris and me don't uphold the goddess' *Rote and Rede*, then who will?"

"Very noble of you, my lord, but I think that somehow, for some reason, you and our Weaver Klaris are going to change that law."

Jax finished his tea, and Tallyn pushed her point. "You always have changed the laws, Jax. You're not like me. I'm just a crown princess."

"Just."

"Yes. My role is fixed, predictable, bound by countless traditions. But as the Oracle said, you are a paradox in so many ways. Your life isn't and never has been normal or fixed: not for a Barian, not for a Kord. Not for a peasant, not for a lord."

"Put it to music," Jax said. But he thought about her point as he ate a bite of bread. She was right, as usual. His unique heritage and combination of positions had often allowed him or forced him to find his own rules. He remembered the Oracle's words that he would resolve dichotomies. But what about the conflicts in his heart?

"Even if I get around the goddess' rules and the sealord's jealousy, I'm not sure I can risk it," he said finally.

"Coward."

"You haven't had your heart broken."

"No. But I watched Cheshir's break."

Jax sighed.

Tallyn went on. "But she'll be fine. She's learned to love Frinz."

"It's not about learning to love. It about what I can give."

"What do you think Klaris needs?"

He shook his head. "What do I have left?"

Tallyn considered him for a few moments. The Jax she had known as a child would never have questioned his own value. For the first time, she began to appreciate what survival had cost him. "Maybe you should think about what Klaris can give you."

Jax ran his hands through his rumpled hair, disheveling it further.

The princess rose from his bed. "I'm leaving today."

"You are?"

"I have a wedding to organize." Her creamy skin glowed, and her clear blue eyes sparkled.

"Foby is a fortunate man," Jax observed.

"I'll take Raisha with me." Tallyn went to the door. "She and Carden can console one another."

Jax stretched and smiled. "So, Bryx is gone, Carden's gone, you and Raisha are gone: that leaves me here with Klaris."

Tallyn answered his grin. "A blessed Beltane to you, Jax."

Hot sun gilded the dust of the road a golden bronze as the nobles cantered their horses away from Twistford Keep that afternoon. Klaris, hidden in the library, found refuge from her emotions in the beautiful poems of Mayle Featherfletch. She was still mad at Bryx, but she was furious with herself for using magic to repel him when a simple *no* would probably have sufficed. She'd gone to the sun salutations this morning in search of peace for her soul. Instead, her conversation with Tallyn just seemed to inflame her. Or maybe it was the poetry.

"Here you are, Weaver!" Priestess Mollish slipped into the library. "Princess Tallyn asked me to give you this." She handed Klaris a small, silk bag.

Klaris untied its strings and pulled it open to find a collection of pretty sex toys and implements to enhance and extend pleasure. She started to laugh and then found herself crying.

"My dear!" Mollish laid a gentle hand on Klaris's shoulder. "What's the matter?"

Klaris wiped her face and laughed again. It took her a moment to find the words she wanted in Landish. "Tallyn is promoting mischief. Or heartbreak."

"Or love." Mollish rose and slipped away.

Klaris sat reviewing the toys and vials. After a few moments she closed up the silken bag and decided to take a walk along the river.

A maid accompanied her, following discreetly in case the Weaver should want anything, or get lost.

Klaris enjoyed the peace of the tall trees and the calm swish of the river. When she came to a large, deep green pool, the river seemed to speak its invitation to her. She called to the maid: "I'm going to swim here."

Shocked, the maid wasn't sure she'd heard correctly. "You are going in, Weaver? No! Please. The river is very dangerous."

Klaris turned to the sparkling water. "I'll be fine. Please go find me a towel."

The horrified maid ran back to the castle.

Klaris pulled off her dress and slipped into the water. It was cold and invigorating.

"My lord! My lord!" The maid ran screaming into the court-yard, where Jax stood sweating in the dust, reviewing plans for a larger wine cellar with Sir Arno. "My lords! Weaver Klaris is going to drown herself!"

Jax remembered the fire in Klaris's eyes when he'd seen her last, stomping across the lawn under the May Eve lanterns. "Drown herself?"

"She's going into the river!"

"Oh, no," said Arno. He turned to call the people in the stables and the bakery, "Men! Men!"

"No, Arno. Stop." Jax put a hand on Arno's shoulder.

"What, exactly, did the Weaver say?" he asked the maid.

"I don't always understand her accent, your Grace. But I know she intended to go into the river."

"That is a splendid idea on a hot day like this."

"My lord," Arno frowned. "The Twist is very dangerous."

"Well then, I'd better go make sure the Weaver is safe," Jax grinned. "Someone bring us a few towels."

Within a few minutes, Jax stood on the shore, squinting out onto the bright water.

"Oh, she's gone!" wailed the maid. "Here are her clothes."

"I'll send people down to the ford, my lord." Arno's voice was heavy. "Bodies usually wash up there."

"She's right there." As Jax pointed, Klaris took a breath and dove under again. Jax wanted to tear off his own clothes and join her in the smooth, green water.

"Did you bring a towel?" Klaris called as she swam toward the riverbank.

Flummoxed, the maid stepped cautiously toward the water, holding out the towel. Klaris emerged, her dark skin shining. Water drops sparkled in her hair as she wrapped the towel around her body.

"Thank the goddess, you're safe, Weaver," breathed the maid.

Klaris looked at Jax in confusion. "Safe? Is there danger?"

"The river, my lady," Arno said slowly and sternly as if addressing a child. "The river is very dangerous."

"As am I." Klaris skewered Arno with a frown.

"But you must be careful, my lady."

Jax watched Klaris look from one befuddled Kordish face to another. He felt her summoning the Mystic again. Since Klaris had taken his own force, he was somehow part of all the spells she wove. Now, he sensed her weaving protect spells so she wouldn't cross-magic any of the other Dragons, like Arno, as she prepared for something much more demanding.

"Look," Klaris gestured towards the river. The water in the broad stream stopped running. It stood perfectly still, silent.

"Dragons!" swore one of the men.

"No. Not *dragons*," Klaris snapped. "Mystic." She snapped her fingers and the river ran once more. She stood there, much smaller than any of them, wet, and wrapped in only a towel. "I appreciate your concern, but I am not exactly helpless."

"I am," mumbled Jax. He cleared his throat. "I think a swim is a lovely idea."

"Not you too, my lord!"

"Arno, islish folk can swim. Please have some lunch sent down for the Weaver and me. And more towels."

"Very well, my lord," Arno grumbled.

Jax winked at Klaris, pulled off his clothes and splashed into the clear green water. The cold of it shocked the breath from his lungs.

He turned back to shore. Klaris stood watching.

"Come back in?" he invited.

She dropped the towel and dove.

"Let's swim out to that boulder," she suggested.

They pulled themselves out onto the sun-warmed rock. It had been worn smooth from years of floodwaters. Klaris turned to the shore, wriggled her cold fingers, and the fresh towels and picnic basket floated across the water to the rock.

She wrapped herself in a towel, rubbing at the goose bumps on her arms.

To distract himself, Jax delved into the basket. He flinched as Klaris's cold finger touched a scar on his back.

"Is this what the trolls did to you when I left you there?"

"No. Those scars are older."

Her fingers tickled a line around his body as he turned back to look into her troubled eyes. On this beautiful day alone with this amazing woman, he didn't want to remember the annihilation he felt at being left to the brutal humiliations of slavery. He didn't want to think of the heavy stink of rotting human flesh or the long, dark days of pain.

He let her cold fingers rest against his belly and fetched up a smile. "We don't have a bottle opener."

Klaris seemed to recognize his forgiveness. Her magic flared, and the cork popped free.

"That's helpful." He poured the wine into two glasses.

Klaris pulled her eyes from his body and took a deep drink of the wine.

He watched her, wanting her, yet fearing what she would do to his heart.

She took a bite of bread and cheese. "All my life I've wanted one thing, Jax, worked for one thing, poured my whole essence into this one thing."

"Mastering the Mystic."

She nodded. "Yes. And now I have it, but don't feel like a master of anything. Caledra lies in ruins. All the best teachers are dead. Where am I? What am I doing? Reading irrelevant ancient poetry, running afoul of the sealord, being scolded by minor Kordish nobles, and lusting after you."

"Lusting?" He couldn't help his lazy smile.

"Yes."

He carefully put down his glass, pushed her back on the rock and kissed her, tasting the wine and the river on her mouth. The towels were pushed back. Klaris's glass fell aside and rolled into the water.

She sat up to watch it sink. "I don't want to fall in love," she whispered.

Turning back to him, she saw wariness in his eyes.

"What can I do?" she asked. "I'm over my head."

He stood and gathered her into his arms. "We both are." With a wicked grin he plunged them both into the deep icy water.

24

Highlord Raggar heard the rumbling again and finally looked up from the crumbling parchment.

"Will you not eat, Highlord?" One of the acolytes stood with a tray of food.

Raggar finally realized the noise he'd been ignoring was the growl of his own stomach. He took a bit of sweet yellow fruit and sucked it thoughtfully, thinking over what he'd just read: The sad chronicle of Sawn the First.

Sawn had been a sickly child. His twin brother had shown a remarkable fluency for the Mystic weave and eventually became the Weaver some nine hundred years ago.

But Sawn, uncomfortable and misunderstood, had finally been diagnosed by the Oracle themselves as the first person in the Knownlands ever born with the dragon's magic in their blood.

This was, of course, only a few years after the great beasts had gone and people still lived who had known the devastation, the loss, the fear of the terrible dragon interregnum.

Hounded by cross-magic and hatred, Sawn had fled the land of his birth and sought refuge in the remote jungles of Island Jezel. Here, where the dragons had their rookery, their magic ran deep, and Sawn recovered from his cross-magic. As others were born like him, with Dragon force, they came to him for solace and understanding. Thus, Dragonsholm was founded.

As years passed and memory faded, people began to accept those born with Dragon force. They were valued for their musical abilities and the light they could make, along with the other services that made life with magic just a little easier.

But Dragon force had never attained the usefulness of Mystic. Still, Raggar knew that even as more and more people were born with the gift of Dragon force, fewer were born with Mystic, and of those, fewer had the great power of the ancient days.

That was the topic of this crumbling text. A complaint it was, really. That Mystic had been weakening, diminishing since the days of Axterre.

Raggar licked his fingers and took another piece of fruit.

Axterre. The Oracle told him and Klaris to study Axterre, but most of what he could find had referred to the fallen empire only in passing, other than the famous poem that the better educated nobles and scholars were forced to memorize about the fiery demise of the ancient city.

They'd had some kind of magic, those ancient Axterrans, but it couldn't save them. Raggar didn't know either the source of their strange magic or what had happened to it.

He finished the fruit and took a long drink of coconut milk.

A cat slid in the open door and sat looking at him.

"Stay a cat, will you?" Raggar begged softly.

The cat licked a paw.

Raggar picked up the bowl of ceviche and ate it, eyeing the cat warily. Goddess but he missed Halla. Even Blizzen would be a comfort now.

The cat jumped onto his lap and stuck its nose into the bowl of cured fish.

"Here." Raggar set the bowl on the floor. The cat gracefully dropped to the ground and began to eat.

Raggar's vision flickered. The cat became a small black dragon.

"No," whispered the Highlord. "No."

The dragon resumed its cat form. It looked up at him with sympathetic eyes.

"Sweet goddess," Raggar ran a hand over his face.

"No," said the cat.

"What?"

"Not the goddess. You need the cat god."

Raggar's heart squirmed inside his chest.

"Find the cat god," insisted the cat.

"Where?"

"Axterre."

The novices, acolytes, and senior dragons on Jezel spoke together in knots of worry.

"Blizzen went to bring the Weaver to Farsouth," one said.

"But now the Highlord is talking of going east."

"Farsouth is to the west."

"There he goes again. Sweet goddess, do you feel his power billow like wind-blown flames?"

Indeed, the Highlord stood in his liana with every map at Dragonsholm and some borrowed from the Jezellian folk at Tropix spread on the tables and chairs. The Dragons watched him mutter to himself and pace through the night and they wished their Red and Orange Dragons hadn't rowed away to find the Weaver.

When the Highlord stepped into the Jezellian canoe a few days later, the Dragons begged him to stay.

"I cannot stay here," he explained to them, as the dark-skinned Jezellian rowers held the boat in the warm, clear waves. "I must find the cat god."

"Where, Highlord? Where are you going?"

"To Axterre."

"There's no such place!"

"There was once."

Halla's eyes resumed their focus and she looked away from the campfire to the crumbling ruins of Fleet above the beach where they were camped.

"What did you see?" Blizzen asked, settling his rug around his shoulders.

"The Highlord is on the sea." Her nyad brown eyes were full of grief. "But he's not going to Farsouth."

"But he's supposed to meet me and the Weaver there!"

Halla shook her head. "I don't suppose you need bother."

"Well, where's the Highlord going then?"

"I don't know, but he headed east. He's making for Dranstyl."

"Goddess damn it!" Blizzen swore. "What are we going to do in Kree then? What am I supposed to say to the Weaver?"

Halla rose and went to her bags. She returned with a map, which she unrolled and held to see by the light of the campfire.

"We're here." She pointed to the Toe of Darcan. "We should be in Whicksmouth in a week."

"If there are no more blasted storms."

"I don't like to travel in Kordon," Halla went on. "But I'll get a horse there at Whicksmouth and ride for the Verwood. Goddess, I won't be there before Lugnasade."

Blizzen stared at her. "What's the matter with traveling in Kordon?"

She laughed mirthlessly. "Your fellow Kords do not see nyads, Blizzen. It's impossible for me to get a bed or a meal anywhere in the whole blessed realm."

"Oh." Blizzen shrugged. "But the wine is good."

"I wouldn't know."

He didn't answer as she rolled up her map and replaced it in her pack.

"What should I do?" he asked.

"Go back to Dragonsholm. I'm sure the Dragons there could use some comforting."

He shook his head. "By the time we make Whicksmouth, I will have been aboard this boat for a month. I'm not going to just turn around and spend another month going straight back to Jezel." He paused to look to the other campfire where the Jezellian rowers were roasting fish and chanting in Islish to the rhythm of the pounding of the waves.

"I'll go to Kree, as planned," he decided. "I'll visit the Weaver myself and see what she thinks about dragons returning to the Knownlands."

25

Abstinence was not a familiar concept in the Knownlands, where all acts of love and pleasure were considered rituals to the goddess. Nobles, especially, were expected to enthusiastically seek the blessings of the goddess from the time they were sixteen. Most found bedmates as often as they desired. Klaris, isolated by her youth among the others at Castle Caledra, was perhaps the one exception. Jax was no exception at all.

Despite everyone's fervent devotion to the goddess and her many pleasurable rituals meant to stimulate the fertility of flocks and fields, babies were rare in the Knownlands and almost never born to unwed couples. Even those who were married often had no more than one child, or no child at all. A couple with two children was considered particularly favored, and people like the Dowager Queen of Kordon who had three babes were widely sought to bless parents-to-be and parents-who-would-be.

All babies were precious and seen as a blessing of the goddess, even those like Jax, who had cost his mother her life.

The new Earl of Darkwood had little predisposition to follow the rules of people or trolls, but he had a profound respect for the laws of the goddess. He found himself now torn between the goddess' prohibitions and the Oracle's commandment. He found a copy of the *Rote and Rede* and confirmed what he already knew about the prohibitions against two powerful people hand-fasting. Grumpily, he re-rolled the old scroll and shoved it back into its case. How could he expect his people to follow the law if he himself did not?

His confusion was exacerbated by his undeniable desire for Klaris and his fear for his heart. She'd left him to a hideous fate at the hands of the trolls. He'd survived that, no thanks to her, but then she'd stripped him of his magic. If she took his foolish, broken heart what would be left?

Abstinence seemed the safest path through these dilemmas. But it wasn't easy.

He diligently distracted himself for a week by reviewing accounts and records for the new Earldom of Twistford. Each day he rode to a different manor or village, studying the local industries and asking questions about houses and roads, the availability of local druids, and charming everyone he met.

Arno had never known a noble to understand so intimately the concerns of village life.

"Most lords turn up their noses at the local ale," Arno said, as they rode a carriage through the late afternoon shadows back towards Twistford.

Jax shrugged, thinking of the many pints of black Vale Ale that he'd drunk while living with the druids in Hilsen Vale. Just a year ago he'd probably have been sitting at Aric's pub on an evening like this. He wondered if his friends Borrel, Florin, and Doc were there now. And Marith. He looked out the window, missing Mother Marith's acerbic care. "Most nobles haven't lived among the people as I have."

"When you were... away?"

"Yes."

"In the Hantland, my lord? But wasn't it trolls who enslaved you?"

"Mostly. But for the last year, I lived with a family of druids and worked for them."

Arno sat back in the carriage, the ale they'd both drunk loosened his tongue and emboldened him to voice the questions he'd been yearning to ask. "You *worked* for people, common people? Didn't they see you have a birthright sigil?"

"The sigil was forcibly removed."

Arno gasped. Removing a birthright sigil was treason.

"Besides," the earl continued, "no one in the Hantland would have recognized a sigil for what it is."

"It seems incredible." Arno murmured. He didn't need to see a tattoo to recognize that Jax was a prince from head to toe. His status was evident in his speech, the way he walked, the way he greeted the world.

Jax fixed Arno with his sea blue gaze. "Just what do you think a prince does every day, sir? We're supposed to work for the people, the *common* people."

Arno stared, his mouth open, as he thought about this.

Jax changed the subject. "I'm going to send a crew of Barians to build a dock down below the ford."

"A dock? For boats?"

"Barges, actually." Jax nodded. "I believe that the river is navigable all the way up from Keffin Harbor."

"Navigable?"

"Think about it, Arno. We can ship Darkwood wines directly from Twistford Town all across the Knownlands. No more bottles broken by jolting across rough roads to Kree or Rippsgate—and no more duties or carting charges."

Arno quickly saw the financial advantages of the earl's plan. "But boats, my lord, or barges?"

Jax waved his hand. "Barians will handle them. You can bet they'll come once they realize they too can avoid the merchants in Kree."

"The king will still demand a duty."

Jax grinned. "Probably, but not until he figures out we haven't been paying it."

"That'll take a year, at least."

"Let's hope so."

Each evening after his day's journeys, Jax dined with a different group of merchants, manor lords, or guild masters. Klaris joined these small banquets, along with a handful of staff. Priestess Mollish had remained with the party, enjoying the chance to visit with her Darkwood family. She sat through these dinners trying to ease Carte Serge's continued concerns.

On the surface, nothing was amiss. The earl spoke to his guests, asked questions, and actually listened to the answers. The Weaver said little, but her green eyes darted around the tables. From time to time the Weaver and the earl spoke briefly in Islish to each other. They apologized to the others, saying that this was to help Klaris understand some nuance that she couldn't comprehend with her broken Landish, but Serge's fears grew.

He found Klaris one afternoon in the entry court to the keep, drawn by the feel of her Mystic at work. The plain, unadorned walls and window embrasures writhed and twisted. Klaris stood in the courtyard, one hand raised, directing the stones.

Serge smiled. As always, he relished the smooth and elegant weaving of her Mystic. She created a design as balanced and graceful as her power but infused with themes from the new Earl of Darkwood's life. Serge watched as a wave motif rolled above the windows and doors. Thick tree trunks, like those that grew within the Darkwood Forest, swathed the columns.

Finally, pulling from a subterranean branch of the river, Klaris created a fountain in the middle of the courtyard, so that the sound of water would reach into the residential windows above.

Klaris dropped her hand and looked over her shoulder at Serge. She took a deep breath and surveyed the work of her magic. "Do you think he'll like it?" she asked quietly.

The old magician was well aware of the emotions that infused Klaris's magical redecoration. "You're flirting with blasphemy, Weaver," he answered quietly.

"Flirting, anyway. Come Serge, Priestess Mollish has brought an old druid who knows the fairy songs from the Darkwood. Maybe we'll find some clues there."

He followed her into the keep, surprised by the glimpse of fear he'd seen in those green eyes.

Klaris fixed a friendly smile on her face and kept her voice polite as she thanked the old druid for coming. Having listened to two hours of the raspy old voice singing tunes mostly invented for children had left Klaris's tolerance paper thin. Sure, a few songs mentioned dragons and cats, but for goddess' sake, the puerile lyrics told her nothing.

Carte Serge stood up and stretched. "*...the magic dragon lived by the sea,*" he crooned off key.

"Show me a dragon that isn't magic!" snapped Klaris.

"Would you care for some tea?" Lady Mollish pulled the cord to summon servants.

"I'd like a glass of that lovely forest wine that we had at dinner last night," Klaris answered.

"I will bring some, my lady," replied the maid who had entered just in time to hear Klaris's words.

Whether it was the irritation of the old druid's singing, the joy of working her magic on Jax's castle, or just having started drinking early, the wine went right to Klaris's head that evening. Or maybe it was the swift, warm kiss Jax gave her when he thanked her for embellishing the courtyard. She made it through dinner but couldn't follow Jax's conversation with a delegation of wine merchants who brought their bubbly vintage, which tickled Klaris's nose. She would have preferred the forest wine, but it wasn't offered.

She whispered her excuses and left the hall soon after dessert.

Unlike Klaris, Mollish and Serge both loved the crisp bubbly wine. Serge watched Klaris leave the hall and saw Jax's gaze follow her. The magician grabbed another bottle from a passing servant and poured more of the shimmering liquid into their glasses.

Mollish raised her glass. "Here's to springtime."

Serge clanged his glass against hers. "You are no help."

Mollish smiled slyly. "It's the goddess' way, Carte."

The smell of rotten eggs filled her nose, and she choked. A hot dry wind blew back her hair. She reeled from the sulfurous stink and realized she stood on a rocky mountain top. Above her in the pale sky something writhed, something sinuous and reeking. Then she felt a wall of Dragon force crash into her and she had to raise every defense she had to withstand the cross-magic.

The First Tune warbled out of a dragonpipe. Next to her, his blue eyes fixed on the thing in the sky, Jax played ferociously.

From somewhere behind him a baby gurgled.

Jax turned towards her, still wailing away on that pipe, his eyes pleading with her.

"What?" she gasped. What was she supposed to do?

His lips to the pipe, he couldn't answer her, but he kept playing that familiar tune.

The thing in the sky was almost upon them. Swirls of orange, red, green, and black resolved themselves into a great flock of dragons. Giant wings blocked the sun, flapping loudly.

A great orange beast raised its massive head. Fangs flashed.

The dragonpipe rose to a scream.

Flames engulfed them.

She rolled in the fire, wrapping herself around Jax. The flames evaporated their clothing and she suddenly burned with a different kind of fire. She found Jax's lips, then his throat. His dragonpipe was gone, but his hands were everywhere and his mouth.

Again, distinctly, she heard the sound of a happy baby behind her then a lush voice saying, "it's about time!"

Klaris woke with a start, gasping at the intensity of her lust. Rolling over she blinked into the darkness of her room. The dream had been so vivid, the smell, her terror, the dragons, and Jax. Jax.

She slid out of bed, created a small ball of mage fire, and left her room. The castle slept in silence. She lifted the latch and slipped into Jax's room. The mage fire dimmed as she pushed aside the bed curtains.

The sheet down around his waist, Jax lay dreaming. His bare chest rose and fell with shallow, rapid breaths. The fire of her own dream flared again, and unable to bear the heat, she ripped off her shift. Naked, she straddled his body and bent to kiss him.

He pulled her down to him. After a while his eyes opened slowly. "I thought I was dreaming." His voice was rough with sleep.

"This isn't a dream," she said.

He pushed the hair back from her face. "Are you sure?"

"I'm awake."

"Yes, but are you sure you want to do this?"

"Are you?"

"I definitely want you, my princess."

Klaris gasped and let herself go into him.

Hot and desperate they finished quickly. The second time was slower and deeper. Afterwards he wrapped her in his arms, and she closed her eyes, relishing a warm glow of satisfaction and the feel of his body alongside hers.

"You make my dreams come true," he murmured into her hair.

"Mine too."

After a few moments he spoke a little more clearly. "But there were dragons in my dream."

"What?"

"I was dreaming of dragons. We were on a mountaintop, you and I. And there was a baby there and dragons."

Klaris sat up. "That was *my* dream."

Jax pulled through the Mystic and lit a candle so he could see her face. "You had the same dream? Dragons and then flames and then you and I...?"

"Yes. You and I." She licked her lips.

He couldn't resist that. After a long kiss he spoke again. "There was a baby making baby noises. Also, a voice saying that it was about time."

"I heard that too!" Klaris's thoughts were spinning. How could they have shared the same dream?

They looked at each other in the dim light. Finally, Jax flopped back down and pulled her with him. "The dragons aren't here yet. I imagine we'll have a much more human problem to deal with in the morning."

She tried to rise. "I'll go back to my room."

"No. Stay with me."

She looked down at him, his blue eyes inviting but cautious.

"Stay with me," he repeated. "Always."

Something blossomed in her heart, and she lay back down, settling herself against his chest. "I will."

Towards morning she awoke again with a rush of joy and desire. She roused him with a distinct purpose. As they fell asleep again, he spoke softly into her hair. "It was the fairy queen."

"Who?"

"The voice in the dream. It was the fairy queen."

Klaris fell asleep wondering what the fairy queen had to do with dragons, babies, and her own passion for Jax Sharkin.

Morning light streamed through the windows as Jax awoke in the shadows of the bed.

"I have your tea, your Grace," a page was saying as he set a tray down on the table.

"Thank you," Jax mumbled. "I will ring when I'm ready for you."

The page shot a puzzled glance at the bed and noticed the night-shift on the floor. He flashed a grin and bowed out. "Yes, my lord."

Jax sat up and turned to look at Klaris. Her hair fanned out on her pillow and over her shoulders, caressing her fine black skin. He thought he could actually see the blood pulse through a vein in her throat. He decided he should kiss that throbbing pulse.

Carte Serge sat slumped over his untouched breakfast in the sunny parlor.

"Carte." Priestess Mollish put a gentle hand on the magician's hunched shoulder.

He shook his head as Mollish sat down next to him, stirring honey into her tea.

"The whole keep is buzzing with it," Serge grumbled. "The Weaver missed the sun salutations and turns up in bed with the earl. It'll be all across the Knownlands by Dayfest."

"Probably sooner." Mollish smiled.

"How can you be so complaisant about this?" Serge snapped. "You're a priestess of the Oracle. You should be the one lecturing those two to keep their unholy desires in check!"

"Unholy?"

Serge sputtered. "Of course! The goddess clearly prohibits this, this—."

"Love?"

"Love," he scoffed. "Lust, more like it."

Mollish sipped her tea. "That's unworthy of you, Carte. You know them both better than that."

Serge rubbed his hands across his face. "I do know them, and I like them. Well, I like *her*," he admitted. "That's why I'm so concerned for them. Young Klaris has been cloistered and protected all her life. Now she has this assignment from the Oracle. She has no idea what it's really going to take for her to be the *master* of the Mystic weave. She doesn't have time to play the *mistress*."

"Do you think that's all Jax is offering?"

"What else can he give her? He needs heirs; he can't be hand-fasted to the Weaver."

"He will give her his life," Mollish said softly.

26

Princess Tallyn recognized the tiny, dark Weaver among the group of riders cantering across the green hills and pulled her own horse to a stop. A meadowlark sang in the sunshine as the thunder of hooves grew louder and closer.

"Hello, your Highness!" Klaris glowed, exhilarated by her ride across the Kordish countryside and from the pleasant joys of the last few days in Twistford.

"Welcome back, Weaver." Tallyn answered Klaris's smile. "Where's Prince Jax?"

"He's coming in a carriage."

Tallyn laughed gently. "I don't blame him."

Klaris gazed back the way they'd come. "Aye, but it is a shame to be jostled and bounced inside a coach on such a lovely day as this."

"We had heard that he wasn't able to keep himself away from the lovely Weaver." Tallyn watched Klaris's cat-like smile.

"He wouldn't ride with me today."

"Not on horseback, at least."

Klaris laughed. They rode side by side for a few minutes. Tallyn waited.

"We have been lectured about the goddess' rules by Carte Serge and various others," Klaris said finally. "But it appears to me that the Oracle, and therefore the goddess, has other ideas for the two of us."

Tallyn noticed that while Klaris still spoke Landish with a definite Islish accent, her grasp of the language had clearly improved.

"I'm afraid you'll probably face a few more lectures once you get to Kree, but I hope you enjoyed the little gift I left you."

Klaris's smile was radiant. "Oh, yes."

They crested the last hill. In the distance the white walls and towers of Kree shone against the blue of the sky and the azure bay. Several ships, including the *Drixa*, rocked gently on the glittering ripples.

"I see the sealord is still here," Klaris said, now understanding what Tallyn had been saying.

"He's been absolutely unbearable," Tallyn stated. "I fear you broke his heart, Weaver."

"Broke his heart?" Klaris wondered if she understood correctly.

"He's decided to establish a residence here," Tallyn went on. "He bought a tract of land just beyond the town green. I believe he hopes your Mystic will help him build it."

Klaris cocked her head. "Why doesn't he go back to Baria?"

"He says that the Kordish market is so important that he needs to have a base here."

Klaris rode along, feeling the joy of the day draining away.

Jax was indeed jostled and bounced inside the coach, but he preferred this to being thrown off his horse three or four times during the long ride back to Kree. He used the time to draw up lists of supplies he wanted to lay by and various warehouses and depots across the fief. If dragons ravaged one portion of his lands, he wanted multiple resources available to sustain the survivors.

He had been more than pleased with the lands and the people of Darkwood. Frinz was right: he'd gotten a peach of a fief. His only difficulty had been his decree that the smiths stop using Hantish iron. He'd called a meeting of all the blacksmiths and iron merchants, tinkers, and such who sold iron wares in the Darkwood.

"We will use iron ore from Vitrus and Dranstyl," he told them.

"How will we get it here, my lord?" protested a tall blacksmith.

"I'll have Barians deliver it. We're going to build a dock here, just below the ford."

"But surely it will be more expensive than Hantish ore," complained a merchant.

"There's a cost in Hantish ore that I won't pay." He paused and watched them a moment then continued: "Hantish ore is mined by slaves. Men and women forced from their families; children ripped away from their mothers. The trolls use them like beasts. Slaves are worked, beaten, and starved until they die. The trolls make themselves fat and rich off of the blood and heartbreak of people like you and me." He looked into their colorless Kordish eyes. "Do you want to be a part of that?"

Heads shook.

"Good. We shall use other sources of iron."

In the bouncing coach Jax closed his notebook and put away his pencil. He looked out the window at the rolling green hills of Kordon. Hedgerows stretched away from the road making a quilt in spring greens and yellows. The coach followed a bend in the road and the quilt turned blue as Keffin Harbor came into view.

Jax sighed and ran his hands through his hair. Even at this distance he recognized the *Drixa*. He had hoped Bryx would be gone by now. The sealord was not going to be happy with him.

He stuck his head out the window and called to the driver. "Take me straight to the dock."

"Yes, milord."

At least the *Drixa* and her complement of smaller cruisers still looked shipshape.

"Has the sealord been aboard?" he asked Mr. Illat.

"No, my lord. He's been busy with a project ashore."

Jax frowned at something in Illat's tone. "Project?"

"Aye, sir. They say he's building a royal residence here."

Jax turned away so that Illat couldn't see his anger. Did Bryx think this would endear him to the Weaver? Didn't he realize that the Barians needed their sealord?

"I'll have to go up to the palace," Jax said grimly, handing Illat his hat. "But first I'm going for a swim."

Jax waited on the king in a small antechamber. From the window he could see beyond the edge of Kree to a brown patch on the otherwise green slopes above the harbor. Workers pounded stakes in the green sod, while others unloaded wagons of yellow marble that shone in the sun, even at this distance.

"I heard you threw a lovely Beltane Gala, your Grace," the king said jovially. "Maybe next year we'll all come."

Jax bowed. "It would be my honor to host you at Twistford, your Majesty."

"Now, Jax," Kodill leaned forward sternly. "What do you think you're doing carrying on with the Weaver?"

"Following the Oracle's command, Sire."

The king snorted. "Nonsense. You're just indulging yourself because she's young, and charming with that throaty way she speaks Landish. You can satisfy yourself with any number of lovely women, but the Weaver is off limits to someone like you, and you know it. The *Rote and Rede* doesn't have many rules, but you know this is one of them."

"Sire, the Oracle decreed that we should be together."

"Can't you be together without blasphemy?"

"*Is* it blasphemy?"

The king's face reddened. "I will not have you bringing the wrath of the goddess down upon Kordon. Don't let me catch you fooling around with the Weaver here in Kree. Do you understand, my lord?"

"Sire, if the Oracle—."

"Damn the Oracle," the King interrupted, standing up. "I don't trust that crazy old gray thing. The *Rote and Rede* is clear, and we will not argue with it. Come along now. Tallyn is holding a prenuptial tea. I know she'll be happy to see you. Raisha will be too, surely."

Indeed, Tallyn shimmered in a gown the same pale blue as her eyes. The "tea," held on the lawn near the fragrant spring gardens, involved a great deal of champagne.

"Hello, your Grace!" Tallyn swirled up to Jax, followed by Foby and Bryx.

"Good evening, your Highness." Jax kissed her cheek.

She grinned and twirled so that the gossamer folds of her dress shimmered like fairy dust in the late afternoon light.

"I heard you rode back to Kree in a coach." Bryx's sneering voice cut through the tinkling tea party.

Jax gave his sealord the one-handed Barian salute. "Majesty."

"That's disgraceful," Bryx snapped.

Jax downed his champagne. "I figured there are only so many falls I can walk away from, my lord."

Bryx snorted. "A Kordish noble should ride, not get carted along like a hog to slaughter."

Jax retorted in Islish. "And a sealord should stay on his ship and not ignore his fleet."

Tallyn took Foby's arm. "Let's leave these two to their brotherly love." She glided away toward the music.

"It's none of your business what I do, Jax." Bryx continued to argue in Islish.

"It is my business if you wreck the Sharkin name."

"Wreck the Sharkin name? What do you think you're doing carrying on with the Weaver?"

"Let's leave her out of this. Why are you building a palace here? Why are you ignoring Baria?"

"I'm the sealord," Bryx sneered. "I can do what I want."

Jax stared. "You sound like a spoiled toddler, not a ruler. Father would be appalled."

Bryx's fist caught Jax on the chin. He staggered back and tripped over a lawn chair. He scrambled back up and launched himself at Bryx, but Klaris was there between them.

"Gentlemen," she said firmly. "I am probably the only one here who can understand an argument in Islish, but everyone will know what a fistfight means."

"It means my brother is a traitor," Bryx growled.

"The traitor is the one who harms the country," Jax snapped.

"We have a traitor's death on Baria, too. Keep up these insults, little brother, and I'll arrange for you to meet it."

"Stop this," Klaris hissed. "Take this stupid conversation somewhere private, if you must."

Bryx finally looked at the Weaver, her green eyes highlighted by a pale pink shimmer of a dress. He gulped. "How could you betray me, Klaris? Betray me with my own goddess-damn *brother?*"

"My lord," Klaris said softly, but firmly. "There is no betrayal. I have nothing for you."

The sealord ran his hands over his face. "I would do anything for you, Klaris. Anything." He turned and marched away.

"Ask him to go back to Baria and do his job." Jax righted the lawn chair and sat down, rubbing his chin.

She crossed her arms. "Have the two of you always fought so much?"

"We weren't together very often." Jax waved to a servant who brought more champagne. He tried to find a memory where he wasn't at odds with Bryx but came up as empty as his glass. The servant handed him a full one.

"But I do pity his broken heart." Jax looked up into Klaris's face. "Everything I do hurts him."

"You don't intend to hurt him."

"Do you think that matters?"

"It matters to me." She sat on the arm of his chair and bent to kiss him.

He pulled away. "We can't do that here."

"What?"

"The king forbade me from 'fooling around' with you here in Kree."

Klaris frowned. "It's none of his concern."

"He called it blasphemy."

"Well, he's wrong."

"He is my liege lord. I can't disobey him."

"Does a Weaver outrank a king?"

"I stood on a scaffold once, Klaris. I don't want to go there again." Jax finished the champagne in his glass and grabbed a full bottle from a passing steward. He offered some to Klaris, who refused, before refilling his own glass.

"Not even for me?" Klaris smiled.

"Not here. Not in goddess-damned Kordon."

"It's a good thing we're speaking Islish if you're going to talk like that."

He looked at her with such a strange intensity that she turned her gaze back to the party. "Isn't that the dowager coming our way?"

Jax followed Klaris's eyes. "Aye."

Klaris frowned at his grim tone. "You don't have great relationships with your family, do you?"

"The Dowager Queen of Kordon conspired with the Duke of Midipex to send me to the trolls."

Klaris was horrified. "Why?"

"She blames me for killing my mother, who was her youngest daughter."

"I think Mollish tried to tell me that, but I thought I didn't understand the Landish. It's so ridiculous."

"Bryx blames me, too."

By now the dowager had crossed the lawn and stood facing them. Jax rose from the lawn chair and bowed. Klaris made a graceful curtsey.

"Good evening, Princess Klaris." Dowager Stylla's lips were so tight, her words came out sounding pinched. "I heard that you and Javix enjoyed a pleasant stay at Twistford."

"Yes, your Majesty. Thank you."

"But I must tell you, Weaver, that you should not trust this half-isle."

"The Oracle trusts him," Klaris answered.

"He is like his father," hissed the dowager. "Charming, even handsome in a foreign kind of way. Of course, you're islish too, aren't you Princess, so you might be more used to those pointy ears and whatnot."

"Perhaps." Klaris pointedly tucked a lock of black curls behind her own islish ear.

Jax took a sip of champagne to hide his grin.

The dowager eyed him, sensing his smile, even if she didn't see it. "Walk with me a moment, Princess." She tucked her arm in Klaris's and led her off under a grove of trees on the edge of the lawn. Jax watched them go, wondering what poison the dowager would pour into Klaris's pointed ears.

"You must be wise beyond your years," the dowager was saying in a confiding voice, "to have mastered the Mystic at your age. You are obviously intelligent and disciplined."

Klaris said nothing, wondering if this were flattery. The dowager had never spoken directly to her before.

After a moment, the old lady continued. "I, my dear, have seen the death and devastation these Sharkin men bring with them. The Sealord Rax was bad, but Javix is worse. He kills everything he touches. Perhaps he doesn't always mean to, but the result is still death."

Klaris didn't answer right away. She thought about what it might feel like to lose a child. Dowager Stylla had lost both of her daughters, one to childbirth, and another to a riding accident. She realized that the bountiful blessings the goddess had bestowed upon the dowager had become a source of unending pain: another paradox with Jax at its heart.

"With the destruction at Sageham," the dowager went on, "the Knownlands can't afford to lose you, too."

"I am not without resources to defend myself," Klaris said quietly.

"Ah," the dowager patted her arm gently. "Weaver Klaris, your resources are of magic and intellect. Can they protect your young heart?"

This was an apt blow and the dowager, noting the set of the princess's mouth, pressed her advantage. "I watched my daughter Valla fall in love with Rax, watched her give up her family, her home, and even her life to bring forth Rax's babies. Bearing Bryx nearly killed her, then of course Javix did." She spit the name.

"You can't blame the babe for that."

"Can't I? I see Valla's poise in the way he holds his head; I hear Valla's happiness in his laughter. But he killed her. He shouldn't be here."

Klaris stopped walking and looked into the old queen's pale blue eyes. "Do you have any idea of what the trolls did to him, Ma'am?"

"Not enough."

"You mean they didn't kill him."

Dowager Stylla shrugged. "I don't want him dead."

"You just want him to suffer."

"What do you know about suffering, young lady? Whom have you lost? How many scars ache with each beat of your heart?"

"Don't you think all those deaths, those losses, hurt Jax too?"

The dowager's nostrils pinched together.

"Think about it, Ma'am. At least you knew Valla. He never got to know her. Her death cost him his brother's love, and yours too, apparently."

"Indeed," snapped the dowager. "Stay away from Javix Sharkin. There's nothing but pain for those around him."

Klaris looked across the lawn in the deepening twilight, remembering the wariness that lingered in Jax's sea-blue eyes and the way he understood both sides of an issue. Under twinkling lights Tallyn and Foby led the court in a seductive dance. She couldn't see Jax.

"Thank you for your concern, Ma'am." Klaris disengaged herself from the dowager's claw-like grip, turned and strode across the lawn, searching for Jax. Instead, she found Bryx.

He appeared out of the shadows and wrapped his arms around her shoulders. "I hope my lady grandmother didn't bore you," he said, smiling ruefully. "She bears a hatred for Jax and me, you understand."

"Let me go, Bryx."

He removed his arm. "I intend to build the most beautiful palace in the world here. I was hoping your Mystic would be a part of it."

"I am not available for such projects," she said stiffly.

"I need you."

She looked up at his dark face and his pale Kordish eyes, trying to find the sympathy Jax had shown, but she came up only with frustration. "My lord, I have other responsibilities. And so do you. Go back to Baria."

She whirled away and sought refuge in the library and a highly explicit novel about a traveler who had fallen in with the fairy queen.

Caught in the intricacies of the dance, Jax missed Klaris's flight across the lawn. Later when he couldn't find her at the party, he climbed the stairs to her room. He found Captain Karric sitting on a small chair at the top landing.

"Good evening, your Grace," she drawled.

"Hello, Captain," he moved to pass her, but she stuck her sword in his path and shook her head.

"Oh, for goddess' sake," he muttered.

"King's orders, milord. They do have something to do with the goddess, actually."

"Dragons," he swore. "When did everyone become so pious?"

"You were gone a long time, my lord. Maybe you forgot the *Rote and Rede* while you were surviving the slave pens. Although you memorized it pretty quickly as a lad, I recall."

Jax sat down on the floor next to Captain Karric's chair and put his head in his hands. The long day in the coach and the champagne were catching up with him. *"Once each month when the moon blooms full...."* Jax closed his eyes and quoted the first sixteen lines of the *Rote and Rede.*

Karric listened, remembering that Jax had been a dismal student when it came to swordplay and anything having to do with a horse, mostly because he was left-handed and horses hated him, but despite this, she had always liked him. On the training ground he never gave up, but would work doggedly with intelligence to master something, despite his handicaps. He had always had a smart mouth and a sly sense of humor, often directed at himself. And he was damned good-looking. She'd forgotten that.

She considered the changes in him, noting the leaner muscles underneath the silk of his shirt, and harder lines in his face under that sun-bleached hair, but the eyes, that's where the difference was. Gone was the insouciant impudence of a young, favored noble. Now she saw a burden of grief and responsibility.

"I'd sail for Baria if I could," he whispered, "but the damned Oracle told me to stay with her, Karric. And then...."

"And then." Captain Karric's stoic heart softened. She stood up and stretched. "Come on, milord. You're not the first lovelorn noble I've ever known. I'll take you to the Sword and Scabbard and help you drown your frustrations."

27

Klaris woke before the dawn. She stretched in her cool sheets. It felt good to sleep for a change. She had not slept much during those last nights at Twistford, aflame in the dark hours with Jax.

She sat up and pulled aside the bed curtains. Outside, night was giving way to the deep blue before dawn. Three soft chimes rang harmoniously from the garden below her window as a palace priest or druid quietly announced the morning sun salutations.

Klaris hopped out of bed and shrugged quickly into her exercise robe, grabbed a silken jacket and headed to the grove.

She took a spot on the dewy grass, next to Carte Serge and two other Mystics. Several bleary-eyed nobles and Mollish's assistant druids filled out the group. Priestess Mollish rang her chime one final time then raised her arms to begin.

Inhaling and exhaling, Klaris felt the familiar release and openness of the ritual. She followed Mollish through the routine of stretches and poses as the sun brought clarity to the garden, the palace, and the view of the blue waters of Keffin Harbor. Absently, Klaris noticed a Barian wing-ship gliding smoothly into the harbor, its sails rosy in the dawn.

Thoughts and images rose to the surface of her mind: the looping scar below Jax's collarbone, Tallyn's gossamer dress, the dowager's ice-blue eyes, Bryx's boxy figure, and the sharp edges of love. She exhaled each thought free and sent it floating away in the morning, like a child's iridescent bubble, until her mind was filled only with breath and morning light.

At the end of the ritual, she sat with the others in a circle, eyes closed, and bowed towards the center. "Blessed be." Her voice blended with the others.

Into the stillness of her mind, the Oracle's voice said clearly: *Find the prophecy. Keep the Paradox close. You need him. Then learn to sing.*

Klaris's eyes popped open in surprise. She looked around, wondering if anyone else had heard the voice. The others were slowly getting to their feet, greeting each other softly.

She remained sitting, stunned. She hadn't been thinking about the Oracle, and their intrusion brought back the heavy frustration of her weeks of fruitless wading through difficult ancient texts without finding anything that seemed to match the two stanzas she already had.

"Find the prophecy," Klaris repeated aloud, remembering the weight of cross-magic in her chest, the pain of each breath, and the numbness of being without magic when the Oracle had spoken to her that evening almost two months ago.

Slowly she got to her feet. The Oracle's words swirled and echoed in her mind. Hearing the words now, her breathing clear, her magic strong and focused, she wondered why she had assumed the prophecy would be found in the palace. She slipped her shoes on, wrapped herself in the green silk jacket, and headed out of the palace gate and down into the cobbled streets of the town.

Kree was just waking up. Vendors called from pushcarts laden with strawberries and apricots, and the warm smell of fresh bread drifted through the alleys. In a square lit by the fresh spring morning and scented with the sweet aromas from a nearby teashop, Klaris paused to look at a sparkling fountain. She turned towards the delightful smells of the teashop, but never saw it. A small purple door opened across the square. Out stepped a very thin white-haired man, his face a wad of wrinkles, his eyes the clear blue of the tropical lagoon that surrounded Farsouth.

"Weaver!" He bowed, bending himself double. "Weaver, I have something for you."

The Mystic flushed through Klaris. She followed the man into the shadows of his cottage.

Bookshelves lined the walls and made a maze of the shadowy room. Books, scrolls, and sheaves of loose papers covered every surface and spilled into disorganized piles on the floor.

"Here it is! Here! Here!"

The Mystic throbbing, Klaris followed the sound of his voice around a bookshelf and came face to face with a leather-bound book. The man held it to her nose, as if she were nearsighted.

"I heard you are searching the Kordish archives. This is what you want!"

Klaris frowned, her nose tickling with the dust streaming off the ancient book. The leather cover was lined with wrinkles, much like the bookseller's face. She looked up into his bright eyes. "I don't even know what I'm looking for. Why do you think this is it?"

"I awoke this morning, thinking about this old thing. Then I look out the window and whom should I see strolling in the square? You! I don't have enough magic to flip a coin, but I know the Weaver when I see her."

Klaris glanced down at the simple robes she was wearing. She could tell that the man had no magic. She cocked her head to one side. "You recognized me?"

The man shrugged his sharp shoulders and smiled gently. "There's only one Farsouthian in Kree, and I read a great deal."

Klaris took the volume and nearly dropped it. The book bore down upon her with a twisted, black magic. She gasped and set the thing down on the floor. "You read a great deal of what, friend?"

The old man shrugged. "No one has read that, Weaver. But we brought it to Kree thirty-two generations ago. See?" He pointed to a large genealogy on the wall. At the base, Klaris read the first name listed, written in the Ancient script *Bladdanvor, Book Guardian.*

She poked the book with the tip of her shoe and again felt its weird magic, layered like the many veils of one of Tallyn's skirts until what was underneath was completely obscured.

"Where did Bladdanvor, Book Guardian, find this thing?"

"I don't know the answer to that, Weaver. But family legend says that we had been the Book Guardian for centuries even before the Oracle told Bladdanvor to bring it to Kree and wait."

"Wait for what?"

"For you, of course. For this morning."

Klaris looked down at the ancient book. She didn't want to touch it. Something unwholesome lingered about it.

"Take it, Weaver," his voice was gentle.

She pulled the Mystic and wove a cocoon around the old book to block the black magic that rose from it like a fetid odor. Then she lifted it and turned to the bookseller. "What do I owe you?"

A cat jumped onto a pile of books and looked up at Klaris. "You will pay enough for it, Weaver."

"Dragons!" yelped the bookseller.

Klaris considered the cat for a long moment, the book's black magic seeping like fine dust through her blanketing spell.

The cat spoke again. "You will need the Paradox."

Battling the dark magic, Klaris's patience for mystery snapped. "Tell that to the king, would you?"

She hurried through the streets of Kree back towards the palace, the dust of the ancient book smearing unnoticed across her clothes and face. Once back in her room, she set the book on her desk and rang for breakfast. She ate and considered the thing. Despite the blanket of her own magic, the book continued to give off an unhealthy miasma.

Finally, sipping her second cup of tea, Klaris dared to wipe the dust off the cover. No writing adorned the ancient leather. One symbol, the gilt long gone, had been embossed into the cover. It looked like a tower, a round tower.

This was odd. Like all Mystics, architecture was important to her. It wasn't easy to build round towers, with or without magic. In fact, she could name the ten of them that existed in all the Knownlands. Make that nine, now that Caledra had fallen.

She peered closer. There was a river or something like that running beside the tower. Klaris took another sip of tea. She wondered if she should call Serge. He had dedicated so many fruitless hours to her quest already. She thought about his grim censure and his distrust of anything "foreign," and knew that he would voice plenty of objections to this book.

She didn't care much for the thing either, but clearly this was what the Oracle had wanted her to find. Klaris took a deep breath.

In his own rooms, Carte Serge looked up from his tea and wondered what the Weaver was doing to be pulling on so much Mystic, so early in the day.

"Come, ma'am," the sailor on watch called softly to the *Drixa's* first lieutenant. "There's a wing-ship sailing through the Gates of Griffe."

"At this hour?" Ryxa rose from her inspection of the watch log and followed the sailor out of the pilot house.

The first light of dawn turned the warm spring morning a gentle dove gray. The lieutenant trained her spyglass on the mouth of Keffin Harbor, where two massive cliffs formed a narrow passage between the bay and the open ocean. Many a ship had run aground on the submerged boulders that lurked under the surging tide.

Through her glass, Ryxa watched a massive Barian wing-ship slip smoothly through the strait. The sails, perfectly calculated to catch the light morning breeze, billowed tight and the great ship glided gracefully into the harbor.

"It's Papa Bear," she said, almost to herself.

"The lord admiral?" asked the sailor, squinting into the distance. "Can you see his pennant in this light?"

"I don't need to see his pennant. No one else can sail a wing-ship with such grace." The lieutenant collapsed her spyglass and tucked it away in her pocket. She and the sailor watched the lord admiral's flagship slip silently through the growing light.

"Admiral Hix ain't been off Baria since the tidal wave last Rising," the sailor mumbled. Ryxa sighed. She and her family had served the Sharkin Sealords aboard the *Drixa* for generations, but like so many of her fellow Barians, the lieutenant struggled to respect the current sealord. His seamanship was notoriously poor, but it was his actions since the last Spring Rising that rankled even the most loyal of his subjects.

The *Drixa* had, of course, been at Haven when the huge black waves came out of the north and swept across the Floating Islands. The lieutenant shuddered at the memory of swimming through the unpredictable Rising waves to get back to the *Drixa*, where she had been on duty. Seventeen other crew members had not made it back. The ship strained at its anchor, and only her quick thinking to let out all the line had saved it from tearing a huge hole in the hull. She knew that at least three other wing-ships had not survived. Their wooden hulls either ripped open or upended by the wave. Hundreds of Barians had been killed, sunk within their ships, or swept away into the stormy sea.

But the sealord, warm and dry up in his land-built palace, seemed indifferent to the needs of his people. As soon as the Rising ended, he took his flagship, the *Drixa*, and the handful of small cruisers still fit to sail and made for Kree. And he'd been here ever since.

Lord Admiral Hix had not left Baria. In the absence of the sealord, Hix had overseen the repairs to the fleets, the Floating Islands, and the land-based 'hard ports' of Bran, Roust, and Port Jorel, along the Barian shore. Hix had organized the rescues and the repairs. Hix had inspected the dark, flooded holds of the Floating Islands and reviewed the long accounts of losses. Hix had met with Mystics, nobles, and grief-stricken common people to help Baria rebuild.

Now, as midsummer approached and with it the annual Gather of the Barian fleet, Hix had finally sailed away from Baria to find his errant sealord.

On the deck of the *Drixa*, the sailor and the lieutenant watched the lord admiral's flagship cross the glassy waters of the harbor like a majestic swan.

"Shall I wake Captain Illat?" the sailor asked finally.

"Aye. Do so."

The sailor stepped to obey, and then turned back. "What about the prince? Should we wake him, too?"

"He was singing sweet songs to the stars when he came aboard late in the middle watch." Ryxa shrugged with a grin. "Let Illat decide."

Captain Illat, accustomed to the sealord's preferences, decided to let the old lord admiral wake the Sharkin Prince if he wanted to.

Illat splashed water on his sleepy face and dressed quickly. He arrived on deck just as the lord admiral's launch pulled alongside the *Drixa*.

Hix Sharkin had been lord admiral for fifty-five Risings under Sealord Rax.

The lord admiral not only oversaw all the workings of the Barian Fleets but was also responsible for the nautical education of most Barian nobles, taking them around the Knownlands from the time they were sixteen Risings old. Hix had trained Bryx to be lord admiral under Rax, and then trained Jax to be lord admiral when Bryx became Sealord. When Prince Bryx finally became competent enough to take on the job, Hix had happily retired.

When Bryx inherited the Helm, Jax disappeared, so Hix had come out of retirement to manage the Barian Fleets once again, and he'd been doing it against a prevailing current of indifference from his sealord ever since.

Captain Illat glared at the line of his silent crew somewhat relieved to see them looking smarter than usual and felt a sullen sort of gratitude that the damned prince had chivvied the crew into better shape. He straightened to attention as the old Barian admiral hitched himself over the rail with a grunt.

"Good morning, Captain Illat!" Hix boomed, used to making himself heard over the scream of wind and roar of waves. "Sealord not up yet?"

"The sealord is ashore, Admiral."

"What's that? Speak up, man!"

Illat cleared his throat. "The sealord is ashore, my lord."

"Dragons," growled the admiral, heading down the hatchway. "I'll have tea in my cabin here then before I go up and find him. Bring me your logbook."

"Sir!" Illat trotted after the old Barian. "Sir! Not your cabin just now—"

"What's that?" Hix turned, frowning. He glared for a moment at Illat, who couldn't find his voice. The old Barian turned and pushed open the door to the admiral's cabin. "Damn you, Illat, who have you got sleeping in my—?"

He stared, open-mouthed. "Goldilocks!"

Jax rolled over and opened his eyes. "Papa Bear."

"That explains why this ship looks decent for a change." Hix announced, the pride evident in his voice.

Jax closed his eyes again.

Hix ripped the curtains back from the big stern windows, letting sunlight strike Jax full in the face. "Stop laying there like a lazy Landish lord."

"I am a lazy Landish lord, who was up 'til the middle watch last night." Jax rolled away from the sunlight and got out of bed.

Hix saw the scars on Jax's back. "Sweet goddess," he whispered reaching out to touch the spider web of lines. "Sweet goddess, lad. Is this what the trolls did to you?"

Jax, now washing his face, mumbled something incoherent into a towel.

"I'll kill them," Hix vowed. "How dare they!"

The steward tossed a white linen shirt over Jax's head then handed him a supple leather belt for his trousers. Still barefoot, Jax slumped into a high-backed chair and accepted a cup of tea.

Hix took his own tea and sat in a facing chair. It didn't seem that long ago that he'd taken the oddly fair-haired boy aboard the *Sharkin* to begin his training. Hix remembered fearing that the child would prove as awkward as Bryx. The lad stood out so, among the dark Barian children.

"My Lord Goldilocks," Hix had sneered with a mock bow to the young prince at his first line up as a midshipman.

"Admiral Papa Bear," Jax had answered saucily.

"A smart mouth will land you in the brig, son."

"As will disrespect. My lord."

Hix remembered pausing, recognizing the boy's smile. It was Sealord Rax's own wolf grin, crafty, mocking and weighted with generations of political entitlement.

Hix had turned away, more worried than ever, but young Jax's extraordinary abilities for all things having to do with boats, oceanography, navigation, and Barian, quickly dispelled Hix's fears. While the admiral continued to think of Jax fondly as 'Goldilocks,' the prince's sarcastic retorts had quickly stopped anyone else from taking it up. But 'Papa Bear' had stuck to Hix, and he knew it. Only Jax would still say it to his face, but across the fleet everyone from captains to cabin kids knew the lord admiral as Papa Bear.

Over tea and biscuits with fish bacon and fruit, Hix finally got Jax to tell him about the years of exile. As the tale went on, Hix slumped farther down in his chair.

"We tried to find you, lad," he muttered when Jax was finally done. "Goddess knows we did. I can't believe we missed you on Hanter Lake."

Jax shrugged and looked out the window. "It's history. I'm more worried about the future now."

Hix frowned. "You're back. What are you worried about?"

"Dragons, blasphemy, and keeping the Sharkins at the helm of Baria."

Hix's sea blue eyes narrowed. "Which Sharkin?"

"The rightful one, of course."

"He doesn't deserve to hold the Helm."

"It's not about deserving."

The lord admiral shook his head. "I can tell you: I am tired of serving as both lord admiral and sealord."

"You should tell Bryx."

Hix thumped his mug down on the table. "Yes, I should. That's why I came here. Let's go find that brother of yours and make him step up to his duties."

28

Jax followed Admiral Hix slowly up the palace stairs toward the Barian Suite. At a landing the old Barian stopped, huffing loudly.

"Stairs," he grumbled in Islish. "These landish folk just love to pile their rooms one atop another."

"We're almost there," Jax encouraged, alarmed at the old isle's fatigue.

They found Bryx still in his dressing gown, sipping tea and peering at architectural drawings.

"Hello, Hix. I saw the *Sharkin* had come to port."

"I came to discuss the fleet, your Majesty, and to report on the conditions in Haven."

Bryx sighed and looked back at his drawings. "You can go, Jax."

Neither the sealord nor the lord admiral looked at him as he left the room. He glanced down the hall. He could feel Klaris weaving in her own chamber. With a grimace, Jax sat in the chair that Karric had been using last night. He pulled his old wooden dragonpipe from a pocket and played the First Tune. He let the music expand, upended the chords, took the melody apart then put it back together, all variations on the same theme.

Klaris opened the book.

She stood back from the wraith that rose like smoke from the page. She watched it carefully and felt it dissipate. Quickly she opened all of her windows, letting in the fresh spring breeze. Rarely had she come across any magic this old. It had been as powerful as any she had ever encountered, but now, its sources long crumbled, it was a shadow of itself, a very dark shadow.

She turned the page. Blocky purple script covered the parchment. She knew the letters, but they did not form any words that she recognized. Carefully, she flipped more pages. More unintelligible words; more gray ghosts drifted free and blew away in the sunlight.

Outside in the corridor someone began playing the First Tune on a dragonpipe. She recognized the caress of Jax's disembodied force within her own weave. Klaris stood up and was about to go out to him when the tune snagged in the words in the book. She felt the book's magic flare and pop.

"Jax!" She called, dashing to her door. "Jax! Come look at this."

He rose, his eyes guarded.

"I've found it," Klaris said insistently.

"The prophecy?" He had to follow her into the room to hear what she was saying. Pointedly, he left the door wide open.

"I don't know if it's the prophecy." She pushed the curls back from her face, smearing dust across her forehead. "But this is clearly what the Oracle meant me to find."

Jax looked at the book and stepped away. Its magic pushed against him. "Sweet goddess," he whispered. "That's Axterran."

"How do you know that?"

"The ruins reek and ache. Just like this."

Klaris cocked her head to one side, considering the book in the light of this information. "I'll shield you. Now can you read it?"

Jax gathered himself and took a step closer to the book. Despite the shield, he felt the residue of hatred and old nausea. Klaris ran her fingers along a line of the symbols.

Something about the placement of the sigils, the repetition of them made Jax think of music. "It's a cipher," he whispered. "A code. Is there a key anywhere in the book?"

Klaris flipped pages. "Maybe. There is one page where someone wrote a line in the margin. Here."

The script in green ink curled and cued above a line of the blocky symbols.

"*Opposites must now....?* I don't recognize the last word there." Jax pointed.

"*Adhere.*"

"*Opposites must now adhere.*" Jax read the completed phrase.

Klaris stared at the book; Jax stared at her, longing to touch her.

The orange cat came in through the open door. It looked up at Jax. "Paradox," it purred. "Play."

"Yes," Klaris urged. "When you were playing in the corridor a minute ago, I almost saw through the code."

Jax backed out of the room and pulled his chair up outside the door. "I'll sit out here and see if I can keep everyone happy—including the cats." He launched again into the First Tune.

Klaris felt his magic flow within her own. She stared at the book. The symbols wavered and flared and suddenly the code broke wide open: she read *Oracle speak the Mother's truth....*

Klaris jumped back as if she'd been struck.

Jax's tune wavered as he felt her recoil, but he knew instinctively that she needed him to continue. So, he got behind the chorus and played for all he was worth.

"Steady, Weaver," said the orange cat at her elbow.

"Goddess," Klaris breathed. "You're not reassuring. The last time I saw you, you were a dragon."

"You are seeing all things more clearly now."

She turned back to the book and read on. Jax's music, progressing through the familiar chords, wove with the Mystic. Unconsciously, she began to hum along as she read the tale of magic denied and power seized. Focused on the horror of the story and on holding the shadow of Axterran magic at bay, she didn't notice when Jax stopped playing. Humming to herself, she kept reading, oblivious to the Landish voices in the hall.

"Are you serenading your lover?" Tallyn put her hand on Jax's shoulder.

"I'm awaiting my fate."

She laughed. "And who'll decide it?"

"Not I."

Tallyn cocked an eyebrow.

Jax explained: "The sealord is visiting with the lord admiral of Baria, and Klaris thinks she finally found what the Oracle wanted her to see."

Tallyn peered into Klaris's open door and saw her head bent intently over a dusty book. "That doesn't look very interesting. Tell me about the lord admiral."

"As heir to the sealord, I should be the lord admiral."

"Earl of Darkwood isn't enough for you?"

Jax pocketed his dragonpipe. "No. I want to be the lord admiral. I was raised to it."

"What, exactly, *is* the lord admiral?"

"The lord or lady admiral runs the Barian Fleets."

"Is that all?"

Jax laughed. "It should be all, but old Hix has also had to take charge of rebuilding Haven and basically run the country while Bryx dallies here and pursues this folly—."

Bryx's door opened suddenly and Hix strode out. He did not seem to see Tallyn at all, but the look of devastation and betrayal in his sea-blue eyes cut into Jax's heart.

He jumped to his feet. "Admiral?"

Hix held up a hand, turned his back, and strode away.

Jax's shoulders slumped.

"Javix!" Bryx's voiced reached them in the corridor.

Tallyn watched him straighten. She met the cold anger in his eyes for a moment then Jax went to his sealord.

Bryx strode across the room and shoved Jax into a wall. "You goddess-damned usurper!"

Jax resisted the urge to fight back. Bryx was the taller and heavier of the two, but Jax's years of hard physical labor made him stronger. This fight, however, wouldn't be won with his fists.

He held his arms out to his side. "I'm not usurping anything. You are abdicating."

Bryx slammed him again into the wall.

"You damned prig! Don't play innocent and superior. You and everyone else in Baria think you'd be a better sealord."

"I would be."

Bryx's fist slammed into Jax's jaw. He stumbled away, wiping blood from his lip.

"Don't be an idiot, Bryx. You don't like Barian ways, Barian food, or Barian ships. And I do. You know that. It's always been that way."

Bryx charged Jax again, and again slammed him against the wall. "I'll kill you!"

"That would be stupid," Jax gasped. "Stop pounding me into the paneling and listen for a minute."

Bryx gave him one more shove then stood back.

Jax straightened himself, walked to the table and poured a cup of tea. He handed it to his brother. "Sit down."

"You can't order—."

"*Please*, sit down, *your Majesty*."

"Damn you," Bryx said again, but he took the cup and slumped into an overstuffed chair.

Jax poured tea for himself, took a sip to wash the blood out of his mouth and sat opposite his brother.

"Look, Bryx, it's quite clear to everyone that you don't want to be sealord."

"What I want isn't important. I *am* the sealord."

"Exactly. None of us has a choice about who we are, but we can choose how we want to be what we are."

Bryx sneered and sipped his tea. "You want me to choose to make you sealord?"

"No. Be quiet for a minute and listen to me." Jax paused and held his brother's eyes. "I want to keep the Helm of Baria in Sharkin hands. Our family has ruled Baria long and well, and I don't intend to let you undo the sacrifice and hard work of our ancestors."

He held up a hand to stop the words he could see climbing up Bryx's tongue. "I do not want to be sealord, Bryx, but I do want to be lord admiral. Think about it. As lord admiral, I'm no threat to you. I can take over from Hix, who is getting too damned old, and I can ensure that the fleet supports the sealord—You."

Bryx took a deep breath. "You claim you don't want to be sealord, but you're asking for all the power of the fleet."

"You need to give me that power. You clearly don't want to manage the fleet or the Floating Islands yourself. And if you don't let me do it, then you're going to endanger the Sharkin legacy that you've been given, and that's my legacy too."

"So, it is about you. Your power."

"Our power. Our jobs, for goddess' sake, Bryx. It's not just about new palaces and pretty women."

"You should talk!"

Jax sipped his tea. "Yes, I should talk. Make me lord admiral. Before you have a mutiny to put down."

"Mutiny! The only reason they'd mutiny is if you lead them to it."

"You're almost right." Jax nodded. "They think they want me to be sealord. I would be a sealord like they're used to. But it's not an elected position. You can't give it up, and I can't have it."

"No, you can't have it."

"And I don't want it."

"Because then you can't have Klaris."

"According to a number of people, including the king, I can't have Klaris anyway."

"I should kill you, then I could have her." Bryx's voice became a growl.

"No, you couldn't."

The sealord stared at him with a look of such loathing that Jax had to suppress a shiver.

"She doesn't want you."

"She might if you weren't here to distract her."

Jax shook his head.

"How can you possibly think I'll make you lord admiral after all you've taken from me?"

"You don't have a choice. And neither do I."

"You can choose to stay out of her bed!" Bryx snapped.

Jax rose and poured them both more tea. He spoke softly. "The Oracle gave me no choice at all, and whatever becomes of Klaris and me is not the point of this discussion. Someone needs to pay attention to Baria, and if you aren't going to do it, then I will."

Bryx stood up and went to the window. "You have such a charming way of asking for a favor."

Jax watched his brother. "I don't see being lord admiral as some kind of favor. I see it as a necessary and critical component of keeping the Helm of Baria in our family."

"*My* family," snapped Bryx. "It will be my child, not yours who is the next sealord or seaqueen."

"I hope so. The goddess wouldn't give me heirs with the Weaver." He watched the blow go home and regretted it.

Bryx turned from the window. "I will give you this, Jax, but on one condition." He paused and Jax saw his calculating smile. "You will give up Klaris de Farsouth. You will not touch her, you will not kiss her, you will not sleep with her."

Jax dropped his head.

Bryx continued: "I want you to know what it's like to lose what you want most, what you love most."

Jax looked up then. "What do you think four years of slavery was like?"

Bryx shrugged. "It doesn't really get any easier over time, does it?"

Jax turned away from the pain in his brother's eyes. He thought about Klaris's delicious skin, the taste of her, the smell of her and the caress of the Mystic when he was with her. But against all that stood the ruined fleet of Baria and all he had been raised to do, to be.

"Tough choice?" Bryx sneered.

"Dragons fry you."

29

Humming, Klaris read, pausing only to pull out paper and quill to make some notes.

The maid who came to offer her mid-morning tea found her, smeared with dust, distracted, and still in her exercise robes.

"Would you like to dress, my lady?"

"Not now." Klaris waved her away.

Serge knocked on her door at lunch time. "Are you humming, Weaver?"

She looked up; her green eyes clouded with the Mystic. "I found it, Serge. I found it this morning in the bookseller's shop down in Kree."

"What is it?" He leaned over her shoulder to look at the page. "What language is that?"

"It's in cipher. It was written by a Mystic from Axterre."

"Axterre!" He stepped back, frowning. "There's something very black about this, Klaris."

"Indeed. I've had to keep a barrier up, which makes it hard to crack the code. It was Jax's music that showed me how to read it. Now if I hum the First Tune, I can see it, but if I don't...." She gestured back to the book. "It's nonsense."

"*You*, hum?"

"If Jax would come play his dragonpipe, I believe this would be easier." She blinked up at him, her eyes imploring. "This is what the Oracle meant. I need the Paradox!"

"The king has forbidden it."

"It's just his music I want. This morning."

Serge raised an eyebrow, but he spoke gently. "I am sorry, Klaris. Here, I will hum."

With the awkwardness of the musically inept, Serge began to hum the First Tune. He didn't hit all the right notes, and he skipped several bars in the middle.

Klaris turned back to the book. She began to hum along and soon enough, the words again made sense and she continued to read.

The sun was bowing towards the Gates of Griffe when Serge summoned Klaris's maid and sent for wine. Both of their throats were dry, and their souls baffled. Serge poured wine into two glasses. Klaris slammed the book shut, releasing a cloud of dust. She picked up the paper bearing her own clear writing and considered again the expanded prophecy that had slowly emerged from the narrative of the book.

> *Oracle, speak the Mother's truth:*
> *Dragons come with claw and tooth.*
> *Your purpose for one thousand years:*
> *Is to remember fire and tears.*
>
> *A Paradox who can't be found.*
> *The Mother stirs and shakes the ground.*
> *Oceans rise to touch the trees,*
> *And bring a ruler to his knees.*
>
> *The opposites must now adhere,*
> *And blood must mix while frontiers clear.*
> *Align the magic, love and fae,*
> *To turn the dragon threat away.*

Serge drained his glass, the blood having drained from his face.

The orange cat that had slept all day while they worked rose and stretched. "Why are you so surprised?" it asked. "We've been telling you the dragons are coming back."

Klaris refilled their glasses. "I'm not surprised," she snapped.

"You're not?" Serge sat down heavily and frowned at the cat, who now jumped into his lap.

"No." Klaris took a deep drink from her glass. "The cat's right. We know the dragons are coming back. We don't know when or where or what anyone is supposed to do about it. And we still don't know."

Serge marveled at the snap in her voice. There was no way he would be anything but reverent about a document so ancient and malevolent.

Klaris looked at the paper again. "It's incomplete."

"What?"

"Well look at it! It doesn't tell us what do to!"

"I guess not."

Klaris rounded on him. "I guess not. Goddess-damned Oracle."

"Weaver!"

"Look. We are supposed to do something, clearly, but we are not given the information necessary. And you and the king aren't help-ing by keeping Jax Sharkin away from me. He's supposed to help me with this!"

Klaris grabbed the paper and strode from the room.

A collection of Tallyn's courtiers lounged in a bright parlor while the princess considered large swaths of cloth, trying to decide which to use for a wedding gown.

Lady Raisha leaned out the open window, relishing the after-noon sun on her creamy skin. "What's going on down on those boats?" She stared across the rooftops of Kree at the harbor beyond.

Tallyn came to join her. A small crowd of boats gathered around the two big wing-ships at anchor in the blue bay. Even at this dis-tance, the women could see a throng of Barians gathered on the deck. Colorful pennants streamed on the breeze.

"There's Prince Jax." Raisha pointed. "You can tell him by his hair."

"Where's Jax?" Klaris stuck her head into the room. Her cheeks were flushed, and her green eyes snapped. "Excuse me, your Highness. I don't mean to interrupt."

Tallyn smiled. "Come see."

Klaris joined them at the window. "I am looking for the Prince Jax," she said, her long day and the wine thickening her Landish. Then she saw the commotion on the ships. "What are they doing?"

"We were wondering the same thing."

The three women watched Jax kneel on the deck. The sealord, evident by his billowing Barian Blue cloak raised a sword that flashed in the sunlight. The sword descended once, twice then Jax rose and the roar of the cheering Barians floated up to them on the breeze.

"I think," Tallyn said thoughtfully, "that we've just witnessed the result of a conversation that Prince Jax had with the sealord this morning."

"What do you mean, Ma'am?" Raisha asked.

Tallyn turned away from the window and went back to her fabrics. "I believe that the sealord just made Prince Javix the lord admiral of Baria."

Raisha eyed the little Weaver with her fly-away hair and grimy exercise robe critically. "An earl might lie with a Weaver, but an earl who is also the lord admiral of Baria would have too much responsibility for such a dalliance."

Klaris smiled at Raisha. "Ah, but what is a dalliance? Nothing to fret about, surely."

Tallyn laughed quietly, and Klaris pretended not to see the sour look on Raisha's face. She turned back to the view of the ships in the harbor, wondering how she was going to pull Jax away from the festivities. She needed him, wanted him with a desperation she had never known before.

Something tickled against her magic. Something comforting and familiar. Then she saw it.

"Oh, look," she whispered. A small gray boat emerged from the shadows of the Barian ships.

"Look at what?" Raisha snapped.

"It's a lad!" Klaris almost jumped with excitement. "It's a laddie from Sageham!"

She dashed out of the room.

"You'll have to leave him to her," Tallyn said gently to Raisha.

"The king's forbidden them." Raisha smiled tightly. "Dalliance or no."

The Barian revelry lasted well into the night. The town guard tried twice to quiet the music and shouting coming from the ships, but it wasn't until Captain Karric herself came down from Castle Kree that the fireworks stopped and things settled down enough for the townsfolk to sleep.

Klaris hadn't noticed the noise. She had met the small gray boat as it pulled up to the dock. She embraced Lad Yob with tears streaming down her face. Back in her rooms, she had listened for hours as he described the devastation at Sageham and the subsequent efforts to rebuild.

"I can return to Sageham soon, I think." Klaris leaned forward to take the lad's dry hands. "Do you know that the dragons are coming back, Laddie?"

He nodded. "Talking cats are an omen, a harbinger."

Klaris stood up and walked to the window. In the distance the sparkle of the Barian fireworks gleamed on the water. "Do you know what I'm supposed to do?"

The lad shook his head. "No. It has been a long time." He smiled, sadly. "The Axterran Oracles dealt with the dragons for several millennia, but...." His voice trailed off.

"Yes. I've just read all about that. Look at this." She picked up the book and handed it to him. "What do you make of this magic?"

"Ouch!" He dropped the book, which fell with a bang to the floor. "Weaver, that is Axterran magic!"

Klaris considered him, wondering yet again about the lads and lasses of Sageham and what they knew. "I've disarmed most of its dark magic, but it's still pretty ugly, isn't it?"

Lad Yob just shuddered. "You touched that thing?"

"I had to. It's where the Oracle hid our prophecy. Part of it anyway."

"Part of it?"

"The prophecy here is incomplete."

The orange cat walked into the room. It looked at the lad then shimmered and became a small dragon.

"Sweet goddess," the lad breathed.

"Not just the goddess," said the dragon-cat. "There's a cat god too, you know."

"Cat god?" Klaris demanded.

The creature blew smoke out of its nostrils. "Isn't that fun? Can't do that when I'm a cat."

"I read about a cat god once," Klaris mused. "At Caledra...." She frowned at her memory. "I'd found an old scroll and half of it had been defaced, as if someone had taken water to the ink." She stared at the small dragon. "I remember the line that so confused me: '*The Cat God helped to fuse the magics....*' No one, not Weaver Feilor nor Professor Lellyn could help me understand. What magics could fuse? And how? And why?"

"To banish the dragons," the dragon-cat said.

"How!" Klaris shouted. "HOW!"

The small dragon recoiled at Klaris's raised voice.

A fist pounded on her door and the dragon scuttled under the bed.

The lad rose to answer and found himself facing an empurpled sealord.

Bryx ignored the thin gray Sagehamite. "What is the problem, Weaver? Do you need assistance?"

Klaris felt Bryx's intrusion like snow down the back of her jacket. She rose. "It is not your concern, your Majesty."

"It *is* my concern, Klaris. Don't you understand? Everything you do, or don't do—sweet goddess, what is that under your bed?"

The dragon-cat slowly came out from under the long quilts.

"Sweet goddess," the sealord repeated.

"How about sweet *cat god*?" suggested the dragon-cat, rather proudly.

Bryx took a step back and made an incoherent noise.

Klaris controlled her voice. "I am meeting with Lad Yob, my lord. And discussing the Oracle's prophecy. Good night." She shut the door firmly and turned to the dragon-cat. "You are no help."

The dragon-cat blew more smoke rings from its nostrils. "What do you want?"

"Answers." Klaris poured the last of the wine into her glass and drained it. "I think it's time for another visit to the Oracle."

The dragon-cat leapt to the window ledge. It turned luminescent green eyes on Klaris. "The fairies don't like dragons either, you know." With that, it spread its orange wings and jumped into the night.

30

Lieutenant Warrix rubbed his red eyes and squinted into the flashing sparkles of the harbor as the sun rose behind him. Silently he cursed his luck at being assigned the watch on this particular morning.

"I'd have thought all Barians would still be sleeping off the celebration," a sailor mused, following the direction of the lieutenant's gaze.

"I wish I was," grumbled Warrix. He had perhaps been unwise to throw himself into the festivities with such gusto, but he had been in Jax's captaincy class and was especially excited to have the Sharkin prince assuming his rightful place as lord admiral. He was a little surprised at the grimness in Jax's smile and the joyless way he had downed glass after glass of seaspirit. As a lad, the prince had been full of mischief and laughter. But then, four years of slavery was likely to change a man.

He pulled out his spyglass and focused it slowly. The small rowboat bobbed through the bay, oars splashing. He handed the spyglass to the sailor at his elbow. "It's two people."

The sailor squinted through the glass. "It's the Weaver, sir. I got a bit of Mystic in me, and I can feel it's her."

"Dragons!" The lieutenant snatched the eyeglass away from the sailor. "Dragons!" he swore again. News that that the Farsouthian Weaver had been sleeping with Prince Jax here in Kordon had swept from the *Drixa's* crew to the *Sharkin's* faster than flames through sailcloth. Like everyone else in the Knownlands, Warrix knew that such a liaison was forbidden by the goddess, and he'd been quietly relieved that the Weaver hadn't shown up to celebrate the new lord admiral last night.

But apparently, she was on her way now. He turned to survey the deck. The crew of his watch was slowly swabbing the deck, their own hangovers probably as severe as his own. Hix would have his commission for the sorry shape of the ship, and he was sure that the new lord admiral wasn't likely to be any more lenient—even if everyone was so slow due to his own celebration.

"Go wake the lord admiral," Warrix ordered. "Tell him the Weaver will be on board in five minutes."

"Aye, sir."

As the sailor hurried down the companion way, the lieutenant slapped the bosun on the back. "Call the watch to action. The admiral will be on deck in a moment."

"Aw, dragons!" The bosun pulled his pipe from his pocket and tweeted orders. The startled crew leapt to action.

"My lord. My lord, wake up!"

"No."

"My lord, the Weaver is here."

Jax rolled over. "Klaris?"

"Aye, my lord. She'll be here in a few minutes."

"Dragons." Jax swore roughly, his head spinning and his stomach lurching. He hadn't had more than an hour or two of sleep. His steward shuffled in with a basin of water and a clean shirt. Jax rinsed his face and shoved wet fingers through his rumpled hair. He wasn't ready for this confrontation. By now he could feel Klaris's Mystic and knew she was close. With lead in his belly, he climbed up onto the sunny deck.

Lieutenant Warrix noted the way the new lord admiral's gaze swept the deck and cringed, wishing he'd spurred the crew to action earlier.

"This is unacceptable," the admiral said, rubbing his hand over the stubble on his chin.

"Yes, my lord."

Jax considered the lieutenant. He appreciated that the man made no excuses.

"I'll entertain the Weaver in my cabin so you can get this ship in shape." Jax said as he heard the gentle thump as the small boat came alongside the *Sharkin*.

"Aye, my lord."

"Have the steward send us tea. And breakfast."

"Yes, sir."

The bosun's pipe was singing. The morning sun glowed through Klaris's curls as she climbed the ladder up to the deck. Jax realized how desperately he had missed her these last two nights. He steeled himself: "Welcome, Weaver," he said finally, formally.

Klaris's green eyes swept him. With his tousled hair and sleepy eyes, she found him irresistible.

Jax recognized the longing in her look. He couldn't move as she sauntered up to him, stood on tiptoe and kissed him.

He gave her a stiff smile and pulled away, slightly, watching the frown slip into her eyes.

She spoke softly. "Congratulations, my lord admiral."

"You may take that back when you know what I did to get it."

The frown in the green eyes deepened and she turned away to gesture to the gray Sagehamite who had followed her onto the deck. "You remember Lad Yob?"

"Of course," Jax said, clearing his throat. He didn't really remember meeting the lad, but the knowing look on his face seemed familiar. "Let's go below, Weaver. I can offer you tea and breakfast."

Tea and a Barian breakfast of smoked fish and biscuits steadied Jax's hangover, so that he could focus on the parchment that Klaris was waving in his face when all his thoughts and senses seemed consumed with the soft floral scent of her, with the way her body moved beneath the silk of her dress, with the tendril of hair that curled against the skin of her neck.

Lad Yob ate nothing, but he sipped a little tea, watching the Weaver explain her translations. The laddie hid a grin behind his teacup as he watched the lord admiral try to concentrate. Yob remembered this same prince, mud-splattered and shivering, on the Vrillbridge road and his own surprise that Klaris would be interested in what had seemed to be a doomed slave with a bit of Dragon force in his veins.

But Mystic is a wily weave, and Klaris had sensed what the lads and lassies had remembered at last. It had been so long since the fate of the world relied on the Paradox and the Weaver that even the oldest of them had almost forgotten how the forces had to align.

All those millennia when the Oracles in Axterre solved the dragon problem had let us forget, Lad Yob thought to himself. But the Mystic doesn't forget.

Klaris's point finally penetrated the heavy foreboding clouding Jax's thoughts. He propped his elbows on the table and pushed back his hair with both hands. "I suppose my blood is mixed."

"Yes." She leaned towards him. "And what do you think this line means?" She pointed: *Align the magic, love and fae.*

"I don't know."

She smiled at him, that seductive look back. "I have an idea...." He wouldn't meet her eyes. She stood up, her head cocked to one side. After a moment she went on. "I think the prophecy is really more of an instruction. But it's incomplete. We still don't have it all."

"Where's the rest of it?"

"That's what I intend to ask the Oracle."

"So, you want to go to Baria."

She nodded.

He rubbed his hands over his face. Klaris watched him, something cold rising within her. She put a hand on his shoulder, and he flinched as if stung.

"Jax? What's wrong?"

He looked up at her finally. "You know that Baria is a mess."

"Yes."

"You know that the economy was wrecked due to four years without the Kordish markets. That's my fault."

"Not really."

"It is. And then the tidal wave killed hundreds, and more have died from illness and starvation."

"You're not going to take the blame for that too."

His eyes were merciless. "It is in that prophecy."

She picked up the paper and looked at it without seeing.

His voice continued. "Baria needs a Sharkin hand at the Helm. Now maybe more than ever since we returned from the Wider Seas. Baria needs its lord admiral."

She looked at him.

"It's my responsibility."

Klaris bent to kiss the despair away from his face.

"No," he breathed. "Don't."

She grew very still, her face inches from his.

"Bryx made me lord admiral on the condition that I would give you up."

"Give me up?"

His eyes pleaded for understanding. "I can take you to the Oracle. I can play music for you, but I can't, we can't...."

Klaris moved away slowly. "*Stay with me?*" she quoted him softly. "*Stay with me, always?* Is 'always' about a week for you?"

He met her eyes but made no defense.

"Never mind then. I'll ask the Sealord to take me to the Oracle."

"Klaris...."

She saw something in those blue eyes that wrenched her heart, but her very soul was bleeding. Blindly she ran from the cabin.

Lad Yob rose, gently returning his teacup to its saucer. He left the cabin to the crash of smashing china as the lord admiral upended the table and kicked it across the room.

31

"Blizzen! Oh, Blizzy!" The plump woman dropped the towel she'd been folding and dashed to embrace the son who had appeared unexpectedly out of the sunny morning.

"Hey, Ma." He hugged her back.

"Son?" Blizzen's father came in from the back garden where he'd been pulling weeds. "Son!"

Blizzen enjoyed hugs all around. "We decided to leave Dragonsholm in such a rush that I figured I would get here in person as fast as any letter."

"It is so good to see you." His mother still held his hand. "Come sit outside. Would you have some tea?"

"Or ale?" asked the father.

"Ale, yes. I rode all the way in from Limmold this morning."

"That's a ride to give a man a thirst this time of year.'

"Yes, it was dusty." Blizzen sat in the peaceful garden and enjoyed the fuss his parents made over him. It didn't matter that he had counted more than forty birthdays. Here in this sunny pocket of green, he was a lad again, cherished by his parents.

"You've come back to talk to the Weaver?" his father asked, after Blizzen had told about his long journey from Jezel. "But won't your magics cross?"

"She and I can shield ourselves for the length of a conversation."

His mother rubbed her chin in a gesture so familiar it almost brought tears to his eyes. "You know, Blizzy, I'm thinking the

Weaver might have left when all them Barian big boats sailed away t'other day."

"You might be right," mumbled the father.

"I hope not!" Blizzen snapped. "It's a horrible journey between Jezel and Kree. I pray it hasn't been in vain."

"You get to see us, at least," said the father.

The mother poured more pale golden ale into their mugs. "Maimy Bellgory's daughter works up t'castle, you know. She said that Prince Javix—him that was thought to be traitor but weren't— he went with the Barians. And of course, everyone knows that the little Weaver is a-lustin' for him. Maimy's girl says everyone vies for his favors, he's so fetching."

"Ma." Blizzen tried to focus her rambling gossip.

"Maimy's girl says that the king warned Prince Javix away from the Weaver, but that the Weaver don't hold herself accountable to the king."

"She doesn't?" Blizzen thought about this. "But the king's right. A Weaver can't have a prince. Besides, isn't he the one with a bit of Dragon force?"

"Yep," answered the father. "A bit. Have you ever seen him, son?"

Blizzen shook his head. "I've seen the older one, the one that's sealord now."

"Prince Javix don't look nothing like the sealord," Ma said.

"And he ain't just a prince no more," the father noted. "King made him Earl of Darkwood and gave him the best part of Midipex."

"Why?"

The father explained. The mother inserted a variety of colorful tidbits of gossip into the narrative.

"So is the Weaver here or not?" Blizzen asked with some exasperation.

His mother, well past sixty herself, smiled rather wistfully. "Were't me, I'd risk boarding one o'them boats for a bit of time with that sweet face."

"Dragon Blizzen! I am honored. Come in, come in!"

"Hello Cyril. You are looking very well. Clearly you're flourishing as the Kordish Royal Dragon."

Cyril smiled broadly. "It is rewarding work."

"Good." Blizzen settled into the chair she offered and pulled his cloak around his shoulders.

"Are you cold? Would you prefer to have tea?" Cyril held out a glass of peony-pink wine.

Blizzen took the glass shaking his head. "It's always so hot on Jezel; I think my blood's grown thin." He sipped the wine. "What vintage is this?"

"Aychex Florarose. The new duke has been making it and Princess Tallyn is a fan, so it's all the rage. Very hard to get, actually."

Blizzen took another sip, savoring the complex flavors. "Tell me about the new Weaver. Why has she gone off with the Barian prince?"

Two hours and two bottles of Florarose later, Blizzen headed down the stairs. A small page was coming up, his view obscured by a pile of glittering fabric. Blizzen moved aside, but he wobbled with the effects of the wine and knocked the bundle. This threw the page off balance and the lad stumbled then fell backward down the stairway, his screech echoing through the palace.

Blizzen got to the child first. Excited to finally have the opportunity to use his power for healing, he lifted the child and carried him gently to a nearby couch.

"Ow ow ow ow ow! I want Nanny! I want Nanny!"

"Hush, tell me your name." Blizzen soothed, as other servants and even a druid appeared to crowd around them.

"Fontick of Volake," said the child. "My arm hurts. It really hurts."

"Let me see it." Blizzen gently pushed back the sleeve.

"Here, sir, I'm the Priestess. Shall I take him?"

"Ah, Mother." Blizzen smiled, recognizing the robes of a priestess. "At Dragonsholm we've been developing a way to use magic to heal."

"This is Dragon Blizzen, Priestess Mollish," Cyril explained from the edge of the crowd. "He's the Orange Dragon, third highest Dragon in the Knownlands."

"I see."

"Watch." Blizzen turned to young Fontick. "Now, take a deep breath, lad." Blizzen called his force and scanned the arm quickly, knowing this would cause the boy more pain.

The boy's screams echoed horribly off the stone walls.

"Hush, lad. Deep breath. I will make it all better in a moment."

Those with magic in the crowd felt Blizzen's power rise like a wave. Carte Serge, in the palace garden, sensed it too and shuddered, shielding himself from cross-magic.

Fontick felt the bones in his arm snap and burn. He screamed again: a scream to freeze the blood and break the heart.

"Here, now!" Mollish put a hand on Blizzen's shoulder.

The scream choked off. Fontick sobbed once then looked up. "It doesn't hurt anymore."

"That's because I fixed it for you."

The boy sat up, wiping his eyes. He held out his arm, flexed his fingers and bent his wrist.

"Let me see, Fontick." Mollish took the little arm in her cool, competent hands.

"Remarkable," she breathed, looking up at Blizzen. "Truly remarkable."

As word spread through Kree and then throughout Kordon that a Dragon could heal all kinds of breaks and wounds, people flocked to the little house on the edge of town.

Blizzen was not surprised to find Dragon Cyril at the door late one afternoon. "Show me how to do it," she begged with a smile. "It is so wonderful, so useful."

For the next week Blizzen shared his magic with Cyril, letting her into his spells, into the flow of his force, but she could never quite master the knack of healing.

"Maybe I don't have enough magic," she conceded finally, as she and Blizzen were sharing a bottle of Florarose in the twilit garden behind the small house.

"I don't think that's it," Blizzen said softly.

Cyril didn't answer at first. "No. You are right. I don't have the emotional strength."

"It isn't easy to inflict pain," Blizzen said. "Even when we know it will stop shortly, and it serves a purpose."

Conflicted, Cyril sought the Priestess Mollish.

"Yes," Mollish admitted. "All healers sometimes have to cause pain or discomfort in order to heal."

"But *such* pain," Cyril shuddered, remembering the screams as Blizzen had healed a woman's burns.

"Perhaps I should go see."

Mollish was glad she had spent time watching Blizzen's methods when she was summoned by the dowager a week later and asked to look at a painful tooth.

"It will feel better if I pull it, your Majesty."

The dowager frowned. "But that will hurt?"

"Yes."

"What about this Dragon healer? Can he fix it?"

Mollish nodded. "I believe he can, but that will hurt too."

"Bring him to me, Priestess. I want to see him."

"Yes, Majesty."

"Yes, your Majesty, I can heal your tooth, but you will feel an increase in pain, first."

"Why?"

"Two reasons. First the magic runs like a flame through your body. It snags on any old wounds or scars and wants to reopen them.

That causes those old injuries to burn and even bleed. Then, we tap into the spark of life within you. This burns too, but it is your own fire that sears and heals. Once the wound or illness is gone, there is no more pain, no slow recovery, no lingering ache."

The dowager considered Blizzen with ice-pale eyes. "Very well. Let's have you fix this tooth."

Older servants in Castle Kree remembered the screams and howls from the dowager's three births. She was not a woman to mute her feelings. But even those legendary bellows were eclipsed by the horrible screeching and wailing when Blizzen cured her abscessed tooth. Even Lady Mollish had to leave the room.

When it was over, the dowager reclined against her pillows, her face still pale from the experience but the pain completely gone.

"That was something unbelievable." Her pale eyes skewered the Dragon.

Blizzen suppressed a squirm. "I apologize, your Majesty. We wouldn't do it at all, if the end result was anything less than total recovery."

The dowager took a deep drink of her favorite clear cocktail. "If this is what you do to people you are trying to help, I pity your enemies."

Blizzen laughed shakily. "We have no enemies, Ma'am."

The dowager sipped again. "Don't you? Isn't the Weaver trying to thwart the return of the dragons?"

"No one wants another dragon interregnum."

"No. No, we don't." She smiled, her tongue testing the new painless strength of her old tooth. "No, but she is committing some kind of blasphemy with Javix Sharkin."

"The prince?"

She drank again. "Aye. Tell me again why the body scan is so painful."

He answered slowly, thoughtfully. "It's the fire of the magic, which is a concentration of our life force, you see. It burns. Then there are the old wounds, old injuries. The magic explodes them. I have to work very hard to stop that."

"And if you don't?"

Blizzen cleared his throat. "The wounds rip open again. The bones shatter again."

"But you can stop that from happening."

"I can, Ma'am. I have had to learn how, but I can stop it."

"What if you didn't?"

Blizzen stared at her with horror. "I could kill someone."

The dowager smiled into her empty glass. "And it would hurt, wouldn't it?"

Halla walked slowly through the streets of Rippsgate, her skin crawling. For nearly a month she'd hiked across Kordon, the land green and fertile, the people cold and unseeing. No one would sell her a horse, and she'd found it nearly impossible to get anyone to sell her food. She'd started singing to herself for company and checking for her own shadow to be sure she wasn't invisible.

But Rippsgate was different. No one spoke to her, but they clearly saw her, and saw her with suspicion. She had thought to spend the night here, sheltering in some stable or barn out of the spring rain, as there would be no more chance of a roof until she reached Bly, another fortnight to the north. But the dark looks from the people in the street changed her mind.

She headed towards the bridge, deciding to risk the rain on the Ilyian side of the river.

"Hoy there! Stop!" Two guards came out of the small gatehouse at the end of the bridge. "State yer name and business."

Halla hid her surprise. "I am Halla Felstar. I am headed north."

The guards walked around her, frowning. "Yer a nyad, ain't ye?"

"I am."

"You alone?"

"I am."

"D'ye know the Prince Javix?"

"The prince...? No."

The guard glowered. "He was here with two nyads a few months back and caught and held for a traitor."

Halla considered this. "I don't know them."

"Ye best not."

"Wasn't the prince exonerated?" she asked carefully.

"What's that mean?"

"I had heard he was not guilty of treason."

"Yeah. So they say. You going north, then?"

"Yes."

"Go then. Be off with ye."

Halla didn't need to be asked twice. She walked briskly across bridge and didn't stop until the moon was halfway across the cloud-clotted night sky. She pitched her tent when the rain came and didn't mind it. As she fell asleep, she wondered what had happened to Prince Javix's nyad companions.

32

J ax stood next to Hix on the *Sharkin's* quarterdeck and kept his face impassive. One hundred yards off their starboard bow, the *Drixa* ploughed a white wake through the heaving blue sea. He could see the broad bulk of the sealord on his own quarterdeck and the smaller, green-cloaked figure of the Weaver. Even at this distance, he could read the reserve in Klaris's stance as the sealord bent to say something to her.

Jax hoped she was regretting her decision to spend the week-long voyage in Bryx's company.

"We're still gaining on them, Captain Blanx," Jax noted.

"Indeed, we are, my lord." The *Sharkin's* captain gave a series of orders to spill wind from the sails and slow the massive wingship so it would keep its precise position off the *Drixa's* stern.

"Shame to waste such a lovely breeze." Hix grumbled.

"Why is Illat captain of the *Drixa?*" Jax asked.

Hix heard the wealth of criticism in the question. "The sealord went through four captains before settling on Illat."

"But Ryxa, the first lieutenant, is far more competent. She used to beat us all in the regattas."

"That's why she's there," Hix said softly. "She saved that ship when the tidal wave hit. If there is ever a true emergency, she'll do what needs to be done. And Illat and the sealord will let her."

Jax glared at the *Drixa*, frustrated and amazed at the continued luffing of its sails. He took a deep breath. "We need to go slower yet, Captain."

"Aye, my lord." Blanx gave another series of orders.

Hix watched the crew leap to the orders and felt the ship slow. "I left the fleet counts and the Gather schedule down on your desk."

"The Gather," Jax repeated thoughtfully.

Each year the great lords and ladies of Baria took their combined fleets to a prearranged location in the ocean for a grand review, meeting, and party. Here the latest candidates for captaincy took their final trials. Here the nobles confirmed their marriages, negotiated trade agreements, and schemed and vied for royal favor. Here the best Barian sailors challenged each other in the largest regattas of the season. The sealord would be there, Jax assumed, but as the new lord admiral, he knew all those islish eyes would be on him.

"Where is the Gather this year?" he asked.

"Back of Baria."

"I like those Back of Baria Gathers."

Hix noted Jax's grin and remembered with a teacher's pride the lad's successes in the annual yacht races. The prince had consistently won those competitions when the Gathers were held in the bigger seas and higher winds that characterized the ocean on the western side of Baria.

But the old admiral also saw the lines of fatigue on the prince's face. "Why can't you sleep?"

Jax shrugged. There was little privacy on a ship.

Hix pursued him. "What is haunting you, lad? What makes you wake up screaming every night?"

Dragon fangs, the smell of sulfur, blood, screams, then sex, always sex, sensual, hot.... Jax shook his head.

"You need to be rested for the Gather," Hix said.

"I'll be fine."

"Good, because I won't be there."

"What?" Jax turned to Hix, wrenching his mind away from the nightmare visions. "You're not going?"

"That's right."

"That *is* a nightmare. You can't miss the Gather! I'll need you."

Hix laughed. "No. I'll just be in your way."

"How so?"

"I've been lord admiral for so long people are going to look to me when they should be looking to you."

"But I haven't been lord admiral for a week! *I'll* be looking to you." Jax did not relish the idea of facing the combined fleets at the Gather without Hix to help him navigate the complicated political winds and currents he would find there.

"Hix smiled. "You're new to the title, Jax, but you were bred for this. You know I've been preparing you for this your whole life. Besides, my absence will be seen as a vote of confidence."

"Or not." Jax did not like this at all. "Some will see it as a lack of confidence; a lack of endorsement."

"No. The crew here on the *Sharkin* knows the truth. It will spread from them to all the other ships at the Gather."

"Damn," Jax said softly, looking out to the easy blue sea.

"Besides," Hix said brightly, "I have something else I want to do."

"What?" Jax snapped sourly.

"Revenge."

"Revenge for what?"

"For those scars on your back."

"My scars?"

"When those trolls beat you, lad, they beat all of Baria. You're our prince, for goddess sake. No one, no creature in the Knownlands, can treat us that way."

"The trolls didn't have anything in particular against Barians," Jax noted dryly. "They beat everyone."

"Well it's not right, and I'm going to make them pay."

"How?"

"I'm not sure yet. I thought I'd sail the *Eagle* up to Hanter Lake and see what opportunities present themselves."

"Opportunities for revenge?"

"Aye, lad. Revenge."

Jax considered the old admiral for a few minutes. Slowly he grinned. "I don't want revenge, Hix."

"But—."

Jax interrupted, "I want slavery to stop. I want to close the Hanter Iron Mines, or at least stop them from using slave labor."

"But—."

"And I have an idea."

Now it was Hix who grinned. Captain Blanx, standing on the other side of the quarterdeck discreetly watching, thought that the two of them, the old admiral and the young one, shared that same Sharkin wolf grin.

Hix remained on deck long after Jax had gone below to review his papers. The old Barian watched the night creep up from behind the two ships. Lantern light spilled out from the admiral's cabin below and streamed out onto the dark sea.

"Back off a bit," Hix ordered the lieutenant. "The *Drixa* hasn't put her lanterns out yet, and we don't want to bump her in the dark."

"Aye, sir."

Belatedly, when full dark had settled around the ships, the *Drixa's* lanterns winked to life. Even then, Hix stood on the quarterdeck, as he had for so many voyages. He knew this was likely to be his last sail with the *Sharkin* and while he was damn glad to be done with the day-to-day business of running the fleet, he would miss this beautiful, sweet-sailing ship that had taken him all across the Knownseas.

The moon had risen, and the watch changed again before Hix slowly descended the companionway to the admiral's cabin. He motioned the sentry for silence and slipped in.

The lantern light gleamed upon the fair head that rested on the piles of papers on the desk. He walked to the desk and gently pushed the hair away from the sleeping face.

"Jax," he shook the lad's shoulder. "Go to your bunk, son."

Jax awoke with a start. He blinked and wiped his mouth. "I just want some tea."

"Tea!" Hix bellowed. "You want your bed."

"I do not want my bed," Jax snapped.

"The nightmares are in your head not your bed."

"That has occurred to me."

Hix snorted. "You could share a bunk with that sweet lass from Jeff, or Mella the Bosun."

"Shut up, Hix."

"No lad, you listen, and listen good. I know what you gave up to be lord admiral, and I appreciate how dedicated you've been to reviewing the manifests, accounts, and reports of the fleet this past week, but you can't do your duty if you're exhausted. And if you can't do your duty then your sacrifice is worthless."

Jax put his elbows on his desk and tangled his fingers roughly in his hair.

"Steward!" Hix called. "Seaspirit and lemon!"

"No," Jax protested.

"Yes. My lord." Hix poured two glasses full of the clear liquor and added a dollop of lemon juice to cloud the mixture. "Drink your medicine, Jax."

An hour later the grumbling steward poured both admirals into their separate berths. "I hope this works," he said to no one in particular.

Flames exploded from the burrows lining Hilsen High Street. People ran screaming. Mother Marith, with terror in her eyes, herded a group of crying children. In the middle of the street, Borrel stood straight and pulled on his magic but he suddenly burst into flame, his face melting, his skin crackling. A vast black dragon swept from the sky. From out of the smoke, drums began to beat, echoing the rhythm of Jax's blood. A pipe and a fiddle entwined themselves around a melody. Dancing girls naked, their nipples

taut, swayed toward him tongues licking their red lips. Then it was Klaris on top of him, her breasts warm against his palms, her hands clasping him.

He awoke throbbing, panting with a strangled groan.

"Goddess," he pleaded to the dark. A few moments later, he pushed himself out of his tangled sheets and sought relief up on the deck.

The sentry watched him climb the companion way. Every night it was like this. She knew he'd spend an hour or so up in the dark wind then come down again, his hair windblown, his breath steady, but the despair of the nightmare still shadowing his eyes.

Then he'd light a lantern and spend the rest of the night reading through the piles of ledgers and ships' logs. It was a shame really, the sentry thought. Despite, or maybe because of, his mixed heritage, the admiral was strikingly beautiful, and there were plenty of sailors amid the crew, herself included, who'd be happy to distract him from whatever it was that stole his sleep.

Screams shattered the night. Over and over the wrenching scream of a mother watching her child die. Klaris ached with it, tears poured from her eyes. She rolled away into warm hands. Hands rubbing her bare skin, massaging, brushing, smoothing, preparing her body for pleasure. There was Jax, his eyes desperate, his lips on her breasts, and goddess she was ready. She spread her legs.

"Weaver!"

Klaris woke, choking on her own desire. The sealord bent over her, his hands on her arms.

Her chest heaved and she squirmed. "No! NO!" She turned her face away from him.

"It's another nightmare, Klaris," Bryx said gently. "You woke me, again."

Klaris sat up, pulling the blanket up to her chin. "Get away from me."

He pulled back, the hurt evident in his face. "I just want to help."

"Get away!"

Lad Yob entered the cabin, without waiting for his knock to be answered. "Weaver?"

Klaris shook her head, her breath still uneven.

The sealord moved further from the bed. "She's had the nightmare again," he explained.

Lad Yob sat on the edge of the bed and peered into Klaris's eyes. "You know that it won't go away until you resolve its source."

"I know its source." Klaris had gotten a hold of her breath now. She looked into Lad Yob's calm grey eyes. "It's the dragons. The destruction, the death, goddess, the *grief*...."

"Weaver," Lad Yob's voice ached.

"I'm supposed to stop them." She looked beyond the lad to the sealord in the shadows against the wall. "Jax and I are supposed to stop them."

"Well," Bryx shrugged. "He chose Baria."

Visions of flame seared the back of her eyes, the screams echoed again inside her ears. "Goddess damn him." She closed her eyes and put her hands over her ears, but this did not block the horrors within her memory.

Bryx answered with a smirk. "I hope she does."

"What's he doing now?" Captain Blanx stared at the *Drixa*, which was awkwardly turning into the wind. Then he understood.

"Hove to!" Blanx shouted. "Drop sail!" The bosun's whistle chirped briskly and the *Sharkin* smoothly rounded to a stop, rocking on the gentle waves.

"Deck!" The masthead lookout called from a perch in the rigging. "She's putting down a boat, sir!"

"Goddess," Hix grumbled as the *Drixa's* jolly boat dropped unevenly into the sea and a sailor, tangled in a rope splashed in beside it.

Standing on the quarterdeck next to Hix and Blanx, Jax marveled that the flagship's crew couldn't even manage this simple task without bungling it.

Eventually the *Drixa's* crew fished the sailor out of the water. Three others dropped deftly into the jolly boat, followed by the thin gray figure of Lad Yob and the Weaver.

"Where's she going?"

Jax glanced to the west, where the top peaks of the spine of Baria poked above the horizon like hard nipples—sweet goddess, deprivation was warping his mind. He took a deep breath. "She's going to the Oracle," he said, his voice hard. "It's more direct to go from here and make one leg of the triangle rather than two."

"Ah. Yes." Hix nodded.

They watched as the jolly boat lifted its small sails, caught the steady breeze and pulled away from the giant wing-ships. Jax's eyes couldn't seem to release their gaze on her hair that streamed like a flag from the stern of the little boat.

Hix, however, had turned his own sea-blue eyes on the *Drixa*. After a moment he swore. "Dragons, I can't watch any more. Let's go review your plan for piracy on Hanter Lake."

Jax grinned, despite the hurt in his chest. "I wouldn't call it piracy."

"The trolls will."

33

The sun was just dropping behind the bulk of Baria as Jax stood with Hix on the *Sharkin*'s quarterdeck. The anchor cable smoked out of the hawse hole and plunged into the blue water of Drix Harbor. Both admirals had turned away from the spectacle of the *Drixa*'s crew attempting with little success and less care to straighten her spars. Instead, they surveyed the wreckage of the port.

"Sweet goddess," Jax breathed. "It must have been horrible." The images he had glimpsed in Carte Serge's scry were just a small picture of the true devastation of the Barian capitol. Two months after the tidal waves, flotsam still clotted the harbor. The masts of several sunken ships rose out of the water, trailing tattered wisps of sail like flags of surrender into the shrouding twilight.

Once upon the dock of Helm, the Sharkin's Floating Island, Jax could no longer mask his horror and dismay. Rubble and waste still clogged the avenues and alleys. Tree stumps thrust to the sky like broken bones. Windows gaped into blackness, and beggars in rags sat dejectedly in the shadows.

He turned to the sealord. "Your Majesty. This is unbelievable."

Bryx stopped outside the bronze doors of the Sharkin Cabyn. "Good thing you're here now to take care of it, my lord admiral." He strode off toward the bridges to Valla's Palace, leaving Jax in stunned silence.

He'd heard plenty about the sealord's indifference, noted evidence of it in the poor way he allowed the *Drixa* to sail, but to see it, here, amid the ruin of their home, stunned and shamed him.

Inside the Cabyn the lords and ladies of the Floating Islands cheered their new lord admiral, but he greeted them with grim eyes.

"This is disgraceful! Can no one even pick up the trash? Why are there beggars in the streets?"

"We're all poor, my lord," grumbled Janil of Phlyx. "Since we lost the Kordish markets, we barely have the funds to equip our ships."

Jax's eyes swept up Janil's rich silken robes. "I see. If the nobles of the Floating Islands are unable to care for their own, I suppose the Helm will have to do it."

"The Helm?" asked Lady Villar of Ayx with a sneer in her voice. "The sealord hasn't done a thing."

"That's not true, Villar, and you know it!" shouted Hix. "Why, the Helm and its fleet have worked here tirelessly for the past two months, while all the rest of you dashed off to resume trading with the Kordish!"

"Because we need to reestablish the markets!"

"Enough!" Jax snapped. "If you want the Helm to continue to clean up this mess, we shall do so, but we'll have to increase our tax levy."

The assembled lords and ladies considered the smile on the face of the new lord admiral and remembered Sealord Rax.

"I will look into what will be necessary," he said. "And I'll see you all at dinner with the sealord at Valla's Palace in two days."

The nobles grumbled and bowed away.

If Jax had expected to sleep better in the Cabyn, he was disappointed. His nightmares were worse as the dragon-borne destruction was now focused on his beloved Haven and the familiar comfort of his own bed evoked even more wanton activities.

Bolo Powluna, his steward, thought to find the prince still sleeping when he brought him green seaweed tea and smoked fish for breakfast early the next morning. Instead, he found Jax had been up, had a swim, a bath, and was deep into Helm's logbook.

"I'm going to review the Islands today," he told Bolo.

"Ah. Of course, my lord."

Jax looked up at the reservation in Bolo's tone.

"It's just that the streets aren't safe, sir."

"That's what you and Neben said when I was here before the Rising."

"It's gotten worse, since the Great Wave."

"I can see that." Jax closed the logbook.

"Misery breeds foolishness, my lord."

"Are you suggesting I'd be in danger?"

"You're the sealord's brother. A number of people think he's more to blame than the lords and ladies of the Floating Islands."

"Is he?"

Bolo shrugged.

Jax had earned his devotion from the Barians. In other parts of the Knownlands, he had been subject to prejudice and cruelty, but here he had always been able to prove his competence for Barian ways and gain acceptance, despite his mixed heritage. It hurt to imagine that the Barians would have forgotten how very proudly Barian he was.

He didn't like the message that taking guards along on his tour would send to the people, but he finally agreed to let a secretary accompany him. Bolo feared that this wasn't enough, so he went along too.

As the day spread from morning to afternoon, Jax looked with increasing anger into ruined houses, looted stores, and shuttered workshops. He began to see what Hix and Bolo had been trying to tell him. People gathered around him, occasionally cheering, but more often he felt the heavy accusation of their silence.

One voice wasn't silent. He never caught a glimpse of the speaker, but time and again Jax's comments to a crowd were scorned by a low voice speaking Bilge Islish.

"We should shut that one up, my lord," Bolo growled.

But Jax had noticed that the crowd didn't like the insults. They might be angry with their poverty, but they weren't quite ready to disrespect their nobles. Still, no one dared to expose the nasty-voiced speaker. Jax remembered the slave pens and his own caustic insubordination. He knew this game. "We can't shut him up," Jax answered his steward. "He'd become a martyr."

They came at last to a small square on the Island of Ayx. A crowd spilled from a bodega, to look at him.

"I want you to know I see your problems," he said to group.

"Ye see naught but the very tip o'the wave, you!" the nasty voice called from the edge of the crowd. "Ye ain't seen the depths o'the trough."

Jax felt the malevolence of the people and the fear of his staff, but his own anger rose to meet them. He had used insolence to rally the morale of his fellows in the slave pens, and he didn't like being on the other side of that knife. He was supposed to be a ruler here, and rulers couldn't answer this with force.

"He's just like the sealord! He don't care 'bout us!"

Jax realized then what he could do and took a step towards the filthy ally.

"My lord, no!" Bolo put a restraining hand on his arm. "They're dangerous."

"Aye. The situation needs a sacrifice." His patience shortened by the grimness of the day, the black memories of the slave pens, and the ongoing, convoluted frustrations surrounding Klaris, Jax knew that if he didn't step into the role, the wrong person might.

Bolo saw the calculation in the prince's eye, the challenge in the smile, and dropped his hand.

The angry voice was calling again. "Lookit him hide there with his fancy servants."

Fully aware of what was about to happen, Jax laughed and walked away from his two men and into the shadows of the alley.

"Dragons," Bolo swore to the secretary. "Run back to the Cabyn and get reinforcements. Send someone to the far end of the alley, and fetch Hix, too.

A narrow door opened off the alley and gave onto a small dim room. A rough crowd sat on barrels, drinking straight Barian seaspirit from dented tin cups. The people from the square crowded behind Jax, darkening the room.

"Oy! T'is the prince hisself!" squealed a woman from the shadows.

"Yes, it's the prince himself," Jax stated, looking around the crowd with hard eyes. "Tell me what you need, and I'll see what I can do for you."

"What I need, you can't give me," mumbled a grey woman at Jax's elbow.

He saw the grief in the woman's islish eyes. "No. I can't bring back the dead or restore all the lost. But I have gotten the Gates of Griffe reopened for the Kordish trade."

"That just helps you damn blue bloods."

Jax peered into the gloom, trying to find the source of that angry voice. "If the fleets make money, we can pay for repairs at home."

"It was you caused the Kordish to shut us out in the first place, weren't it?"

"Come out from behind your friends and speak to my face," Jax demanded.

A bald, gap-toothed isle with keen eyes walked up to Jax. "I'll talk to yer pale Kordish face, milord, but not here where ye can twist my words and shame me afore me mates. Come into the back room. Jest you and me."

Here it came. With a shrug Jax followed the man into a back room. Two others slipped in behind him. When the door was shut, the gap-toothed one turned with a big smile full of blackness.

"Yer pretty stupid, ain't ye?"

"Maybe. But not as stupid as you," Jax said. Then his world went dark.

Lad Yob kept his gray eyes fixed on the long blowing grasses, which was all that was visible on the Head of Baria. He did not need to look at Klaris. Attuned as he was to the magic and its Weaver, he felt her fatigue and her frayed patience almost as if it were his own.

For most of the day he had sat beside her on the hard plank of a seat as the *Drixa's* little jolly boat splashed up and over the waves. Klaris had dozed against him for a couple hours before the nightmare woke her. Then she had sat, with glassy green eyes unseeing as the Oracle's white temple came slowly closer.

He had glanced at her when the temple winked out of existence as the boat approached the beach. The smirk on her face then shocked him.

The Barians jumped into the waves and towed the boat onto the shingle. Klaris leapt to the shore and without a word or a backward glance began to climb the path to the empty headland above.

Lad Yob followed her. At the top, she stood in the spring wind, her hair and cloak streaming behind her.

"Patient I am not!" she was saying in Ancient to the wind. "And frankly, I didn't think you had the time for these games either."

Lad Yob began to frame a puzzled answer, thinking she must be speaking to him.

But Klaris continued apparently talking to no one. "Next time I'll just teleport into your parlor like the Highlord did."

The Sagehamite felt the Oracle's magic as a wave engulfing him. He fell gasping to his knees, but Klaris remained defiant, standing now nose to nose with a wizened creature about her own height. The white temple gleamed behind them.

"Really, I don't mind talking to the wind," Klaris growled.

The Oracle turned abruptly and strode into the temple. Klaris followed them, while two gray-clad priests helped Lad Yob to his feet.

In the round room with the wide windows showing the white-capped sea and the windblown headland, the Oracle rounded on Klaris.

"Why are you *here?*"

"The prophecy you left me is incomplete."

"Incomplete? Did the Book Guardians damage it?"

Klaris opened her small pack and removed the ancient book. "See for yourself."

The Oracle made a gagging noise. "Axterran magic."

She thrust the book toward them. "I know. It's nasty, isn't it?"

The Oracle's fingers wove a complicated dance in the air and the book flew from Klaris's hand to land on a lectern. The cover opened and the pages turned, as if blown by the wind.

"Yuck," the Oracle said inelegantly.

"Indeed. And I already banished most of the ghosts."

The Oracle leaned over the book without touching it. The pages fluttered forward and back. Finally, they spoke, their voice ringing with magic:

> *"Oracle, speak the Mother's truth:*
> *Dragons come with claw and tooth.*
> *Your purpose for one thousand years:*
> *Is to remember fire and tears.*
>
> *A Paradox who can't be found.*
> *The Mother stirs and shakes the ground.*
> *Oceans rise to touch the trees,*
> *And bring a ruler to his knees.*
>
> *The opposites must now adhere,*
> *And blood must mix while frontiers clear.*
> *Align the magic, love and fae,*
> *To turn the dragon threat away."*

Klaris waited.

The Oracle's gray eyes turned toward her. "Sit down, Weaver. We will have tea and a story."

The tea appeared, steaming in cups next to the deep red velvet chairs. Klaris sat and schooled herself to listen. But for several long moments the Oracle said nothing. They stared into the steam rising from its tea. As Klaris watched, the steam coalesced into dragons, wings beating, smoke belching from sharp-fanged mouths.

"*...remember the fire and tears.* Little chance anyone could forget." They paused and closed their eyes. Then they began to speak in Ancient.

"There was a small boy. His mother is pulling him by the hand, and they run, run away from their home, their village burning behind them. They flee into the trees, but the forest is burning too.

"All the Verwood burned. The Nyad homeland was left a smoldering wasteland. But the boy escaped. His mother was not a nyad. She knew other ways and other routes.

"A boat she had, it carried them away on a pounding river, away from the red sky. Ashes fell upon them, silently as snow. The mother held the child and her tears mixed with the ashes on her face and on his.

"The rivers of the Verwood are turbulent and full of cataracts. Eventually they plunge out of the Barthrobar Mountains over great falls and into the flat lands of Ohe.

"The mother knew she wouldn't survive the falls, but still she held him tightly...."

Tears pooled in Klaris's eyes, but she said nothing.

The Oracle, their head bent, continued. "When the boy woke, he was with the fairy queen. He never saw his mother again. Nor his father. Nor anyone he had known before.... The fairy queen fluttered around him. Her people brought him food and she herself held him when he cried for his mother. After a few days the queen took him to a sunlit meadow. Autumn leaves glowed brilliant yellow in the sun, as if giving back all the sunlight of summer.

"The fairy queen spoke to the boy there. *You must banish the dragons,* she told him. *You are the Knownlands' only hope.*

"The little boy didn't understand what she meant.

"Years have passed since you flew to us with your mother's love, the queen said. *You will not be a child when I return you to the world above."*

"Frightened and confused, the child said nothing. The fairy queen reached out her hand and touched him." The Oracle's wrinkled hand rose to touch their faded cheek. When they spoke again, Klaris could hear the voice of the fairy queen:

"You are the babe. The mixed-blood babe. The others who should have been here to help you perished years ago. Now the dragons grow restless. They've been here one hundred years. If you play the tune, they will go. They must go. She put a little pipe into his hands and then she held him and hummed. All around them, as the golden leaves fluttered to the ground, the fairies gathered and sang along. There were no words, just a tune to break your heart.

"The boy fell asleep, and when he woke he was a man, grown. He sat alone on the rocky top of a mountain that rose by itself into the sky. He still held the little pipe, and the echo of the song still played in his head.

"He started to blow into the instrument and music came out, but not the fairy's song. All kinds of other tunes came out. At first, he thought this was the fairy's magic, but then he realized it was a power all his own. He could touch the flow of magic that linked rock and tree, wind and stream. It wasn't Mystic. It wasn't fae. It was a power deeper, broader, older than these. And he could turn that power into sound, into music.

"It seems he sat there through seasons and maybe years. He felt no cold, no hunger. The magic fed him. And then one day they came.

"At first, he thought they were birds. But when he felt their force, he understood—he remembered. Even as a child he had felt the dragons' force as he and his mother fled the burning Verwood.

"So, they came and circled the mountain. He used the power he had and made a shield for himself. They blew their fire at him, but it would not harm him.

"The dragons didn't leave. They settled on the mountain top, encircling the man, snarling, growling, but curious, perhaps. Or waiting. One or two of them would fly away and return with deer or other animals and the flock would feast. One evening the hunters returned with something that glowed and sparkled.

"It was a fairy. You wouldn't think such a tiny creature could feed so many great beasts. But they pulled that fairy apart and each dragon ate just a tiny morsel. Clearly this invigorated them like no other food. The beasts jumped and belched fire and roared and pranced.

"The man watched in horror."

The Oracle paused and gulped their cold tea. "It took that fairy a long time to die. Just before he did, he looked at the man out of violet eyes. *What are you waiting for?* The dying fairy gasped. *Play! Play and banish these beasts before they kill us all.* Then a dragon snapped off his head."

Klaris shuddered.

"The man picked up the pipe and played. He played a song for the trees and the wind and rock. The dragons listened; they seemed to enjoy it. Most of them settled down and slept."

The Oracle took a deep slow breath. "He played for days and nights and months. The dragons gathered. They continued to hunt and feed, and he watched more fairies die, and others too: people, nyads, animals, even a sprite.

"And one evening the largest of the dragons appeared with the fairy queen herself impaled upon its razor claws. She bled sparkles.

"The dragons were ecstatic. They flapped and roared. This was a prize unlike any other for them. It took the man a long time to realize that the Queen, amid her torment, was trying to speak to him.

"*Banish them!* She begged him. *Play the song we taught you!*

"Then she looked right at him. *Don't waste my sacrifice.*"

Klaris leaned forward, intent.

"He played, of course. Played with all his magic and all his soul. The fairy queen died. The dragons danced. But they were not banished."

The Oracle shook their head, their gray eyes distant. "He stopped the music then. The fairy queen had let herself be captured and eaten alive so that she could speak to him. But his playing did not work. It wasn't enough to banish the beasts. He felt inadequate and guilty in the face of the queen's bravery and sacrifice.

"That night the moon rose full. It was winter solstice and the veils between the worlds were thin. The man could feel the grief of the fairy folk in the flat color of the moonlit mountain. Something as essential as sunlight was gone from the Knownlands.

"In his grief he took up the pipe. He remembered how the queen had held him. How his mother had held him. He heard the love, the longing, behind the fairy queen's song. He let down the magical shield and he played to the dragons.

"They'd been snoring, resting after the orgy of their feast on the queen. When the shield dropped their great glowing eyes popped open, but he played on.

"He played for the green shadows of the Verwood of his childhood. He played for the souls of the dragons' victims. He played for the moon, full and white. He played for love and loss.

"The dragons rose up. A great stinking flock. The power of their wings beating all together blew sand and rock into him, his hair, his nose. He closed his eyes and played.

"The dragons began to scream.

"Then the long night ended. The sun cracked the darkness of the horizon. The greatest dragon—a vast golden creature—raised her head and blasted the man with her fire. The others joined their tongues of flame to hers.

"Goddess, it burned," the Oracle's voice cracked. "But he thought of the fairy queen and his mother, and he played on.

"The dragons roared, so loudly the man couldn't even hear the music of his own pipe.

"And they flew away. A great screaming flock of beating wings and sulfuric flames. The man's vision expanded, and he could see other dragons joining them. Dragons from Jezel and Nec and the Verwood. Together they flew west with the sun.

"He played all that day until the sun set, taking the dragons with it away beyond the Wider Seas.

"Silence fell. But we heard. We heard the Darkfest songs from all across the Knownlands. We felt each Darkfest fire and each prayer.

"Took us a long time to get used to that. We roamed the Knownlands seeking understanding. The dragon fire had scarred us, made us what we are now, but no one ever ran from us or feared us.

"We found Sawn the First when he was ill from cross-magic and shunned. We learned that the dragon's force had seeped into the blood of Knownlands folk. We tried to go to Axterre, but the pollution and grief was so toxic it sickened us. We found that old laws, old dichotomies held no power any longer, but new divisions did. The Mystic weave was now balanced by Dragon force. In the absence of the old empires of Nec and Axterre the collection of smaller nations grew across the Knownlands and the goddess was pleased to keep power divided among many hands. Eventually we came here to speak for the goddess, for the new ways."

"We?" asked Klaris, breaking her long silence.

The Oracle looked at her with iridescent eyes.

"Did you find it?" she asked softly.

"Find what?"

"Understanding."

"You have so many questions, Klaris."

"And you have precious few answers."

"That's because truth generally has more than one answer." The Oracle refilled the tea cups. "We learned that long ago the folk of the Knownlands, nyads, fairies, and islish had worked together to banish the dragons when they returned in their millennial migrations. The nyads, with their long tree memories, knew that the Oracle was to remember something, but not exactly what. The fairies, as one would expect, knew that a bond of pleasure and music were integral parts of the banishment. And the goddess revealed to us that all truth involves a paradox.

"Of course, we had thought the Book Guardian preserved all of the parts to the Prophecy of Banishment."

Klaris shook her head. She stood and, looking out the window, realized that the spring day had drawn its long purple evening cloak down from the mountains and across the sea. "Stay this night, Weaver." The Oracle's voice was wan. "In the morning you can go."

"Go where?" she whispered.

The pipe wailed, dipped, its song soared with desperation and fell. Dragons dove towards her, their flames engulfing. She screamed as her skin burned, melted, crackled.

Hands cool, firm, insistent held her. Her heart pounded and his did too. She clung to the familiar hard shoulders and felt a different heat consuming her.

Something shook her lose. She opened her eyes to the Oracle's lined face.

"Sweet goddess, child," they said gently. "Does this happen to you every night?"

Klaris sat up. "It happens every time I sleep."

The Oracle sat on the edge of the bed. "Can't be pleasant for anyone trying to sleep with you."

"No one is sleeping with me."

"We shouldn't think so, with all that screaming."

Klaris drew a shaky breath and pushed the hair out of her face. She stared at the wizened creature for a moment before daring to give voice to her fears. "The fairy queen called you the mixed blood babe."

"Aye, she did."

"Jax's blood is mixed, too." She couldn't voice her fears of what this might imply. The Oracle pulled a thin golden pipe from the shadows of its robes. "We don't know how the banishment originally worked. You must adhere, Klaris, align the magic, love and fae. The dichotomies must dissolve." They thrust the instrument at her. "Give this to the Paradox."

She took the pipe. It tingled in her grasp the way Jax's magic used to. "He has chosen a different duty."

"He doesn't get to choose." The Oracle's voice was hard now. "Not about this."

"Tell that to the sealord."

"No." The Oracle's smile flashed in the dark. "You tell him."

"Me."

"You don't get to choose either."

She flung herself out of the bed and faced the Oracle. "I am not a pawn."

"Certainly not. You are the master, Weaver."

34

Klaris stared at the sealord in disbelief. "But he is somewhere on the Floating Islands, right?"

Bryx got up from his desk and took Klaris in his arms. She was so delicate, so fine. Like a porcelain figurine. He wanted to protect her. "I'm sure he'll turn up pretty soon. The Barian people have always loved him. He probably just got drunk with some good-ol' sailors and passed out with them."

Klaris shrugged away from the sealord and moved to the window. Evening sun shone golden down on the roofs and masts of Drix Harbor. She considered the sealord's calm excuses for his missing brother, which were at odds with the frantic faces of the other Barian nobles she'd encountered after her visit with the Oracle.

Where he'd gone after he disappeared into the scruffy bodega on Ayx and what had become of him were still a mystery.

Her heart throbbed with fear, forcing her to acknowledge that what she felt for Jax Sharkin was more than simple lust. And denying it hadn't made it go away.

Suddenly the magic hummed. It was Jax, pulling on the bit of Dragon that now nestled in the great heart of Mystic. She focused: where was he? Could she follow the magic? As quickly as it had started, it was gone again.

"Damn!" She swore. "I just felt a flare of Jax's magic. He must have lit a candle or something."

"Have a glass of sherry, Klaris," Bryx said gently bringing a lovely crystal glass filled with glowing amber liquid to where she stood by the window. "He'll turn up. He always does."

Something foul plugged his mouth. His arms were bound tightly behind him so he couldn't pull the thing off his face.

Without opening his eyes, he took a calming breath through his nose, smelling bilge water and mildew.

"Ye ought to have hired a scribe," a voice said in Bilge-Islish.

"Yeah, and let all of Ayx and the rest of the Port know we got the prince."

Jax recognized the voice of the gap-toothed man.

A woman spoke timidly. "Ye could ask Doc Vixy to write it. He can keep his mouth shut, and I know the losses have been hard on him."

"Lost his two little daughters."

"That's what I mean."

Jax wondered why he hadn't been rescued yet. Surely Bolo knew where he'd gone. He had to get out of here before these poor folks hurt him, thereby committing treason. He decided to open his eyes. A small boy was peering at him, not three inches from his nose. Both of them jumped, each startled.

"Oy!" screamed the child. "'E's waked up!"

Jax coughed around the gag in his mouth and struggled to sit up. The three adults huddled at a wobbly table. Above them a cracked lantern flickered, giving off more smoke than light. He could hear the slap and splash of water and knew he was in one of the small compartments deep in the holds of the Floating Islands.

The woman pulled the child away, but he continued to stare at Jax from around her legs.

The gap-toothed man stood up and looked down at his prince. "We believe you want to help us, milord, and now you will."

Jax leaned back against the cold metal of the hull. It felt good on his sore head.

Gap-tooth frowned. "We're gonna ransom ye back to yer brother. We'll use the money to clean up this mess of a Floating Island and buy some vittles for us n'our mates."

Jax shook his head. A warm trickle of blood oozed down the back of his neck.

"Yes, we will," Gap-tooth argued.

The second man had remained seated at the table. Now he stood and held an irregular scrap of parchment for Jax to see. "'Ere, milord. Ye can read yer own ransom note."

A thin, badly lettered scrawl crept across the parchment. *Giv us 1,000 golden drixas or Prince Javyx die.*

"No." Jax grunted around the gag. The misspellings were the least of his concerns.

"Ye don't like it, do ye?" Gap-tooth snapped. "Yer like Lady Villar and all the rest. Ye ain't never been hungry. Ye ain't never watched a baby die. So fine. Ye nobles can sail off to yer merry fetes, and we'll care for our own. But yer gonna pay for it."

Jax pulled on Klaris's magic and the scrap of parchment burst into flame.

"Ow! Damn!" The man dropped the burning scrap.

"Cut it out!" Gap-tooth roared. He kicked Jax hard. Jax kicked back, catching the man on his knee, but bound as he was, he got the worst of it.

"Dragons blast you, bloody toff!" The gap-toothed man seized a large knife off the table and limped toward where Jax lay struggling for breath around the gag.

The small boy, oblivious, pushed between the adults' legs and pointed. "Look, Da! His blood's still red. Not any blue a'tall."

Mystic, thick and raw, hung around the boy like a cloak.

The boy poked a finger in the blood streaming from Jax's nose. "Da says yer a damned blue blood, but yer blood ain't blue. Yer hair sure is funny."

Jax choked, suffocating against the gag and the blood in his nose.

The gap-toothed man picked the boy up by his shirt and threw him across the room. The child hit the wall with a thump and crumpled silently to the floor. "Keep the brat quiet, can't ye, Thyl."

He turned to the other man. "Get the others, Logil. It's time to take our token then."

Logil ducked out the hatchway. Gap-tooth let the knife tickle Jax's cheek.

Jax held the man's eyes with his own. Goddess, but he hated bullies. This one was going to get his mates killed.

"Ye ain't too smart are ye, *milord?*" The knife ran under his chin.

"Say, Dury." The woman, Thyl, was gently rubbing the child who curled on the floor where he'd landed. "Dury, ye could take a lock of milord's queer hair. T'wouldn't be such harm in that. And the sealord would surely recognize it."

The knife rose to scratch a hot line through Jax's hair. Warm blood ran down his face, into his ear.

"Why ain't it blue?" the boy whispered.

The hatch door creaked open. Logil returned with the two burly men who'd followed Jax into the back room.

"Alright," Dury shifted his grip on the knife. "Ye two lads hold his shoulders and legs. Logil hold down his arm, 'ere."

Jax fought. He kicked and rolled and again reached for the magic.

"He's a-gonna burn somefing again!" the boy shouted.

Sure enough, Dury's shirt took fire.

"Dragon blasted—." The rest of Dury's curse was muffled by the blanket Thyl threw around him to smother the flames.

By this point, the other three isles had Jax pinned. Consciousness receded. He couldn't get enough air, and one of the men was kneeling on his chest.

Dury unwrapped himself from Thyl. He peeled off his blackened shirt, revealing a few hot pink burns on his chest.

"Ye ruined me shirt, milord. Ye'll have to replace it."

Dury's knife sliced through the silken laces of Jax's shirt, and with the help of his mates, he soon had the garment off Jax and on over his own head.

"Ooh." He flexed his shoulders. "T'is soft." He picked his knife up again and approached Jax, who lay pinned to the floor by the three other men. The knife dipped towards the Oracle's medallion on Jax's chest. "Might take this little bobble too. That'd buy a lot of seaspirit, eh mates?"

"That's a magic thing," the boy piped.

One of the other men picked the medallion up and peered at it. "T'is the sign of the Oracle, Dury. My auntie's a druid, an' she's got this type of stuff all over her cabin."

Jax pulled an arm free and plunged his fist into someone's stomach.

"Let's get this over with," Logil grunted as Jax managed to kick him in the kidneys.

"Hold still, ye coward," Dury snapped. "Or I'll take yer whole hand!" With the help of the other men, Dury finally got Jax immobilized. Someone's knee pinned Jax's right wrist to the metal floor and Dury pushed Jax's fingers into a fist, allowing only the fourth to lie flat.

Thunk.

Jax convulsed as searing pain shot up his arm. He closed his eyes, thinking of music, hearing notes he couldn't play without that finger: unfinished chords, truncated progressions.

"Did we give the prince an owie?"

The men laughed awkwardly at Dury's joke.

Jax watched them pick up his finger and the signet ring that he had worn there.

"This way yer sealord will know we're serious."

The tragedy of the situation gnawed at Jax. Bryx couldn't ransom him, and he knew by the way the others treated him that Dury and his plot had little support. But now, having spilled his goddess-damned royal blood, these men had crossed the line into unpardonable treason. They'd all end up dead while the poor of Ayx and the rest of Haven would be no better off than before.

He was mad at the sealord, but furious with himself for trusting Bryx to rescue him and wondered why he'd had such faith in his brother in the first place. Seven Risings in the slave pens should have taught him something about Bryx's interest in saving him.

But he could say nothing. He could barely breathe.

"I wish ye'd let someone else deliver yer note, Dury," Thyl said softly. "Someone who ain't got the responsibility of a family."

Dury sneered. "It's a-cause of you and the lad that I'm doing this." He turned to Jax. "See, milord. See how responsibility works?"

The irony of this was not lost on Jax.

Logil sat at the table rewriting his ransom note. The other men retied Jax's hands behind his back. Dury folded Jax's finger and signet ring in a scrap of cloth torn from the scorched shirt.

"Done." Logil rose.

"Right, then." Dury slammed the point of the knife into the table so it stood quivering, still dripping with the prince's prosaically red blood. "Let's make our delivery, mates."

The four men left the room.

Jax shivered, the metal floor of the hull cold against his bare skin. His head and his hand throbbed, and he still couldn't get enough breath.

Thyl came silently across the room. She wiped his face and cleared his nose. "Now ye can breathe a bit, sir. Let me bind this up too." Gently, she pushed Jax over to his side and quickly bound his bleeding hand with pieces of Dury's old shirt.

Suddenly a hurricane of Mystic swept the Floating Island. It shimmered and ripped through the small hold.

"Oy! D'ye feel that, Mama?" The boy sat up.

"Feel what?"

Jax caught the boy's eye and nodded.

"T'was the weave a-shakin', Mama. The whole Mystic a-shakin.'"

Klaris. Looking for him. Jax watched the rapture erase the tear tracks on the boy's thin cheeks. Klaris would know that a scry wouldn't find him, so she was trying something else. He didn't know exactly what her weave was supposed to achieve, but the sheer power of it was stunning.

The woman had set about cooking on a small brazier. The smoke floated hazily against the ceiling, only gradually finding its way out the narrow flue in the corner.

"Ye dinna feel it, Mama?"

"No, lad. Ye know I have no Mystic."

"Milord felt it, though. Dinna ye?"

Jax nodded.

"See, Mama! 'E says 'e felt it too."

Thyl stood for a moment, considering the prince where he sat on the floor. His odd fair skin and hair were clotted with dried blood. None of it, as her son noted, was blue. But his eyes were. As sea-blue and islish as her own and her son's, those eyes watched her. She couldn't quite read the expression in them. Surely it wasn't pity. After all she'd heard from Dury and his mates complaining about Barian blue bloods, it wouldn't be pity the prince would feel for her. And surely not after the way Dury had cut him. She glanced at him again. But he'd closed his eyes now and leaned his head back against the wall.

Thyl and the boy shared a fishbone broth. Jax listened to the slap of water on the other side of the cold bulkhead, and he finally dozed off.

He snapped awake as the gag slipped from his mouth.

"'Ave a bit of broth, milord," Thyl said softly. "But make no sound. Dury's mates is just outside, and I'll be in trouble if they know I'm givin' ye anything."

Jax sipped the thin broth. Its heat made him realize how cold he was. He drank half the bowl. "Thank you."

The little boy shoved himself between the woman and Jax. "The Mystic was lookin' fer ye, warn't it?"

Jax nodded. "You have a deep Mystic, lad."

"I do. But ye haven't got any magic, you. Yet ye use it. And ye feel it. Hows come?"

"I'm...lucky."

"I don't know about that," Thyl said softly, raising the foul gag back to his mouth. She secured it firmly, but it wasn't quite as tight as before.

"My lady, the Weaver has asked you attend her."

Wexalay Milram put aside the letter she'd been re-reading and rose to follow the page through the dark streets of Jeff to the Cabyn on Helm. She strode the streets without fear. The robes of her office as Royal Barian Mystic would keep her safe from anyone looking for mischief.

But there was plenty of mischief afoot, if she were to believe all she'd read in Carte Serge's letter. Poor Serge! As she read, she recalled the lanky young Kord trying to come to terms with his prejudices while they studied together at Caledra, some fifteen years ago.

It was no surprise that both of them had ended up as Royal Mystics in their home countries. Neither was Tower-Tested, but both had mastered the Corridor level, which was no small achievement. Indeed, two of their fellow Corridor Cadets were now Royal Mystics as well, one in Ily and one in Thequis.

Wexalay hadn't seen Serge since he left Sageham, maybe ten years ago, but they had written each other regularly, until the Kordish closed the Gates of Griffe to Barian ships. Eagerly she had read this letter, the first in eight Risings, her fears growing with each page.

Serge, knowing that Weaver Klaris was headed for Baria, informed Wexalay all about the search for the Oracle's prophecy, the eeriness of the talking cats, and finally the blasphemous liaison between the Weaver and Prince Jax.

Wexalay remembered Serge writing years ago about his skepticism that the teenaged Prince Javix really wanted to learn Ancient. In truth, such scholarship was unusual among the great aristocrats. But young Jax had also asked Wexalay for help, and as she had tutored him through the finer points of Ancient grammar and pronunciation, she'd realized that his curiosity was driven by his passion to understand history as it had been written by those who lived it.

She'd been pleasantly surprised by his increasing fluency, and supposed that having already mastered two languages, the third was no great challenge. Indeed, few things on Baria seemed to truly challenge Prince Jax. He was a crafty sailor, deft with the mathematics, and charmingly witty with the court.

But Wexalay also remembered a slim, lonely fourteen-year-old girl, with wild hair and a glorious way of weaving the Mystic. As she climbed the steps and entered the Cabyn, the Royal Mystic worried that Serge might be right. Young Weaver Klaris would have few defenses against Prince Jax's good looks and easy charm.

"Thank you for coming," Klaris said as Wexalay entered the small salon. "You remember Lad Yob?"

Wexalay smiled. The Lad had not changed in the eight years since she'd left Sageham, but Klaris certainly had. The girl wasn't much taller, but her grasp on the Mystic was fearless and her eyes were not those of a child.

"I am trying to find Prince Jax," Klaris explained. She spoke in Ancient, comfortably slipping into the language used among the great Mystics at Caledra.

Wexalay smiled and answered in the same. "But he won't appear in a scry—."

"As I am well aware." Impatience crackled in Klaris's voice. "I'm going to do a sweep, the way one might sweep a text, looking for certain content."

Wexalay raised her eyebrows. "But here you'll be looking for the prince."

"Exactly. And I won't be sweeping texts, either." She cast a sharp glance at the lad and continued. "But I don't know the layout of the Floating Islands well enough to search them. Will you weave the sweep with me and direct the search?"

The Barian opened her mouth but found no answer. This is what Serge had meant when he wrote about the Weaver's audacity.

"What will you be searching, then?" Wexalay asked, afraid of the answer.

"Thoughts."

"But that's invasive! And not permitted."

Surprisingly, Lad Yob came to Klaris's defense. "The Weaver isn't mind-reading," he said, his voice slightly resigned, as if he had lost this argument himself. "She'll just be looking for anyone who has some vision of the prince in his or her mind."

Wexalay frowned. "Can you do that?"

"Maybe. If you help me."

Wexalay took a long, deep breath.

"We fear the prince may be in grave danger," Klaris said, controlling her irritation with the delay. "The sealord has had search parties out all afternoon and evening to no avail."

Wexalay saw the longing in Klaris's green eyes, and with the characteristic honesty required by powerful magic, she admitted to herself that she would give almost anything to weave the Mystic with Klaris.

"Yes. Tell me what you'd like me to do."

Nothing had prepared the Barian Mystic for the maelstrom that opened as Klaris built her weave. Wexalay was awed and terrified, but no less power would have been able to focus this type of search with any clarity. Street by street, building by building, hold by hold, the Mystic swept through the people's minds. Most of them never felt a thing. The Dragons among them, might have experienced a slight moment of headache; the Mystics might have recognized a brush of the Weaver's power.

In fact, many people did have thoughts of the once-again Lost Prince. Klaris saw him from their perspective: a distant figure in Barian Blue.

Then at last they found something more. Wexalay had directed the search down and down again deep into the dark hold of Ayx. There, Klaris's weave snagged on a potent well of Mystic. It was unformed, the power of a child. Still, it recognized the Weaver immediately and understood that her Mystic wanted, needed the prince.

Klaris pushed the weave to a great storm, but that was all she could learn. Nothing more.

She closed the weave so abruptly that Wexalay fell to her knees.

"That child is with Jax," Klaris announced.

With Lad Yob's help, Wexalay subsided into a chair. "I need a drink," she murmured.

"We should all eat," Lad Yob suggested.

"A fine idea." The sealord swept into the room. "I have already ordered our supper sent here." He smiled at Klaris. "I gather you didn't find our lost Jax?"

"Not exactly." Klaris did not want to eat, and certainly not with the sealord, but the food smelled heavenly.

"Starving yourself won't help him," Bryx said, offering Klaris a succulent slice of poached white fish.

Klaris took a bite.

Bryx spoke through most of the meal. Wexalay was exhausted, and Klaris was distracted with formulating her next plan. Lad Yob watched her and ate a great deal.

"Your Majesty! Your Majesty!" The Cabyn's chief steward crashed into the room, his face stricken.

"Your Majesty! Someone just dumped this outside the kitchen. We searched but found no one."

Bryx took the bloody scrap of fabric from the steward's trembling hands. A ring and some thin, waxy thing fell to the table.

Wexalay leaned forward for a better view and gagged.

Bryx poked at it with his dessert spoon. "That's unwelcome on a dinner table. Let's see what the note says."

Klaris rose to peer at the thing on the table. "Is that a finger?"

"Jax's apparently." Bryx looked at her. "His captors are asking 1,000 drixas. Do you notice that he keeps getting more and more expensive?"

"Are you joking, my lord?"

"No, of course not." The sealord turned away from Klaris and went to a small writing table. He dipped a pen and wrote briefly. When the ink was dry, he folded the scarred parchment and sealed it with Barian Blue wax and his own signet ring.

He handed it back to the waiting steward. "Put this in the kitchen yard where you found it in the first place and leave it. Unwatched. I want the miscreants to come back for it."

"But if we watch, we can—."

"They'll know if we're watching." Bryx resumed his seat, picked up a clean spoon, and pointed to the finger: "Take that thing to the priestess. Maybe she has some way to preserve it so it can be reattached." He bent to take a bite of his melting sorbet.

Klaris, still standing, watched him. "What did you write?"

Bryx took another bite and swallowed slowly. "Not much. You know I can't pay the ransom, Klaris. No noble would ever be safe again."

35

Thyl put the boy to bed and sang him a lullaby. Jax dropped his head to his knees and let the old, familiar tune wash over him. The song reminded him of Nanny Grosmith. How he had loved her, and how he had tried to hide his tears when she died when he had twenty-seven risings. Thirteen and too big to cry. Stupid. Dury was right, he thought grouchily, slipping into sleep.

He couldn't breathe. The cold pressed all around him, locking him in the suffocating darkness. Elsewhere he heard screams and cries, but he was held tightly and could not move, could not get a breath. He tried to yell...

"Shut up, milord." Dury's boot knocked him out of the nightmare and onto the reality of the cold metal floor. He heard Thyl sob softly and understood the nasty reality behind the cries he'd been hearing in his dream.

Dury reeked of cheap seaspirit and sex. He stumbled, swearing across the dark room until Jax relit the lantern with Klaris's magic.

Dury scowled and blew out the lamp. "Folks like us don't waste a light when we don't need it. I can find me bed in the dark."

"Ow!" squealed the boy. "Ye stepped on me!"

Jax heard the thump of a fist hitting flesh. "I'll stomp on ye, little pest!"

"'Ere, Dury," Thyl said in a quaking voice. "'Ere's yer bed, love."

"Yeah, love."

Again, the sound of fist against flesh. And again.

Jax at last managed to roll the gag out of his mouth. "Dury! You're not allowed on ships, are you?"

"Who untied ye?"

"Captains can't have bullies aboard. Your attitude makes you unfit to crew. You're clearly unfit for a lot of things."

Dury thumped across the darkened room and stumbled into Jax.

"Bully am I? It's the damn blue bloods like you who bully the lot o' us." Dury's hands reached for Jax's throat, but the prince's long years in the slave pens had hardened him against bigger threats than this. He kicked hard, catching the gap-toothed isle in the groin.

Dury bellowed.

Jax rolled to his feet in the dark and took Dury in the chest with his shoulder. The Barian's head cracked against the wall and he went limp.

Jax relit the lantern and stood panting.

"Sweet goddess," whispered Thyl.

Logil and another man burst into the room. Together they took Jax down.

Thyl dragged Dury onto the bed and applied a cloth to his head. Logil and the other retied the gag and this time, bound Jax's ankles together.

"I told him the prince'd be dangerous," Logil muttered, as he looked down at Dury's still form.

The little boy sat up suddenly. Jax felt another great rush of the Mystic weave. The boy, his movements stiff and awkward, rose from the rags of his bed and came to peer closer into Jax's face. When he spoke, it was Klaris's aristocratic Farsouthian Islish that came out of the boy's mouth. "Sweet goddess, you're all bloody. Where are you?"

Gagged, Jax couldn't answer.

"What's got into the bairn?" Logil asked, backing away from the child.

The boy's eyes moved slowly around the room. "What is this place?"

"T'is yer home, son." Thyl left Dury and took the boy by the shoulders. She recognized a foreign force behind her child's sweet eyes. "Let him be!" She shook the boy's shoulders. "Let him go!"

"I will. I suggest you do the same with Prince Javix."

The boy slumped as the outside animating force suddenly withdrew.

"What was that?" Logil demanded again.

The boy sat up straighter and turned a wide grin on the adults. "That's the loveliest Mystic ever, Mama. So lovely. I'd like to have it back again."

"But who was it!" Logil growled, his fear apparent.

"The Weaver, o' course," the boy said, as if this should be obvious to everyone.

Logil and Thyl looked at each other over the boy's tousled head. "The Master of Mystic? *That* Weaver?"

"Course," repeated the boy. "She wants milord. The Mystic does. Hey. D'ye think maybe *her* blood is blue?"

"Hush up, you. Get back to bed." Thyl pulled the rags over the boy's shoulders.

"But it was lovely, Mama. Lovelier than anything."

Logil slumped into the chair by the table. Thyl moved to sit on the edge of the bed. She pushed the hair back from Dury's slack face.

"You shouldn't stay here," Logil told her softly. "Take the lad and go."

"Go where?"

"Doesn't matter. Ye don't want to be here if the nobles come down."

Thyl glanced at the prince. Again, there was that strange expression in his eyes. Thyl shook her head. "I can't leave Dury."

Logil bit his lip, considering the unconscious figure on the bed. He turned to find the prince watching him with clear eyes. "Goddess," Logil whispered. "Goddess, Thyl, we're all gonna die."

Silent behind his gag, Jax agreed.

Exhausted, Wexalay sat stiffly and watched the Weaver's eyes regain their usual sharp clarity.

"I found him," she said.

"Found Jax or this boy with Mystic?" asked the sealord, who stood next to the dark window.

"Both." Klaris took a deep steadying breath.

"Where?" The sealord stepped closer and put his large hand on Klaris' shoulder. She looked up at him, and he moved away.

"It was Ayx, right?" She looked to Wexalay, who nodded briefly. "A very small room, with little furniture. And it smelled of mildew."

"The bilge slums," Bryx muttered.

Klaris rose and faced the sealord. "There was a man and a woman there along with the boy and Jax. They had him gagged. He was alert but covered in blood."

"Well, he was warned," Bryx noted.

Klaris stared at him. The sealord cleared his throat. "But, yes. I'll alert the search parties." He turned and left the room and the Weaver's accusing stare.

"Weaver," Lad Yob quietly stepped from the shadows of a corner. "Shall we do the moon salutations?"

Klaris turned to look out the window at the lights of Helm dancing on the dark waters of the harbor. It was very late. It seemed like days since she'd left the Oracle, rather than just this morning. "Yes."

Wexalay sighed audibly, and Klaris sent her an exasperated glance.

"I know, it wasn't quite ethical," she said to the censure in the Royal Mystic's eyes. "But look what they've done to him." She pointed to the waxy stub of Jax's finger, where it lay in a bowl of clear potion meant to preserve it so it could be reattached—*if* they could find the rest of him. Again, her heart clenched in fear as she remembered the view of Jax in that dingy little room, bound and bloodied. "And I did no harm to the boy."

"May I share the moon salutations with you, Weaver?" Wexalay asked. "I feel that I too need to restore my soul."

"You may," Klaris snapped. "If you stop being such a prig about this."

Wexalay bowed in a somewhat reserved acquiescence and followed the Weaver and the Sagehamite down the hall to a wide saloon with a view of the dark bay. Lad Yob began the chant that would lead them through the rigorous exercises.

Wexalay tried to calm herself and let the poses do their work. She knew that finding the lord admiral was a matter of national security, but to infiltrate someone's mind without permission was not right. Of course, what the bilge rats were doing to the prince wasn't right either.

But this unlikely attachment, this link between the Weaver and the lord admiral, was clearly prohibited. Still, she could not deny that the Mystic demanded Prince Jax in a way that should not have been possible. She remembered the bright, irreverent boy he had been and ached for the man she'd seen tonight in that dark bilge.

Wexalay tried to let these thoughts go to the moon through the exercise, but her mind would not find quiet. She stretched and held a difficult balancing pose. There was indeed something about Jax and Klaris that formed a powerful equipoise. Having shared the weave with Klaris this evening, she had felt the curious spark of Jax's Dragon force within the Mystic. And of course, many people were quite aware of the many additional attractions of Javix Sharkin.

Suddenly she wobbled, lost her balance and tumbled sideways out of the pose.

She steadied herself and focused her breath then moved to a headstand. She closed her eyes against her view of the room, upside down. Love respected no law, but the Knownlands could not afford to have someone as powerful as the Weaver wiggling with ethics.

In the Cabyn's great hall, the sealord reviewed the information coming in from the various groups searching the Floating Islands for his lost brother. He listened attentively and thanked the many searchers and well-wishers, sharing everyone's outrage that some bilge rats would dare to kidnap the lord admiral and then have the audacity to demand a ransom. Lady Villar of Ayx wasn't there, so he didn't mention Klaris's conviction that Jax was being held in her bilge.

"Your Majesty," the chief steward pushed through a crowd of nobles. "The burghmasters of Helm and Rillt have requested an audience."

Bryx considered this for a second. The burghmasters were not nobles, but as the chief merchants for their Floating Islands, they were both influential and rich.

"I'll receive them in the Privy Cabinet." The sealord moved away from the crowd. He entered the small, ornately paneled room and squared his shoulders. He always felt the presence of his dead father here, and therefore he felt inadequate.

"You're gone," he said softly to the emptiness. "You left me with this dragon-blasted mess. Now you can watch me put it back together my way."

"Your Majesty." The two burghmasters bowed deeply. "Your Majesty, the people of Rillt and Helm are deeply ashamed that anyone would raise a hand against the Sharkins. We heard that there has been a demand for ransom." The Rilltian held out a heavy leather bag. The Helmsan pulled a similar bag from his own robes and continued. "The people collected this money to free Prince Jax."

They set the two clinking bags down on Rax's mahogany desk.

"Your loyalty, the loyalty of Helm and Rillt is commendable," Bryx said steadily. "But we cannot pay a ransom."

"We know the treasury has been hard hit with the loss of the Kordish market and then the great wave," the Rilltian said. "We thought 2,000 drixas might contribute to the ransom."

Bryx blinked at their misunderstanding. He opened his mouth to explain that it wasn't a matter of money but of principal, but then realized how far $2,000 drixas would go in repairing damage to Helm, to the *Drixa*, and to the stables up at Valla's palace. "Your donation will be put to good use, Burghmasters." He smiled confidentially. "But you must understand that some of the nobles don't wish to pay the ransom. They fear others will emulate these traitors and no noble will be safe on the streets again."

"But the prince can't be left with those bilge rats!"

"Agreed. Agreed." The sealord soothed. "We'll get the prince back, but do not expect to hear that any ransom was paid. That must be our secret."

The burghmasters exchanged glances, clearly honored to be in on the sealord's strategy. "Yes, Sire." They bowed.

Bryx rang for his steward. "I am ready to return to the palace. Tell the Weaver I want her to come ashore with me."

The Weaver refused to leave her unfinished moon salutations but agreed to come to Valla's Palace to sleep. The sealord, not as disgruntled as he might have been, marched through the streets of the Floating Islands, the burghmasters' gift of support heavy in his pouch. Numerous torches lit up the dark streets, despite the late hour.

"Lots of people still out and about," Bryx noted, with some surprise.

"They're looking for the prince, my lord," said a young page. "No full-blooded Barian will sleep well tonight."

"He's been found," Bryx said, forgetting that he hadn't shared Klaris's information.

36

Dragons screamed. Smoke filled the air, clogging his lungs.

"Dragons! Can't ye make the tea wiffout suffocating us?"

Dury's grumble pulled Jax from his dream. Indeed, a heavy haze of sulfuric smoke filled the small room.

"The flue's got plugged again," Thyl said gently. "Run up and see what's blocking it this day." She nodded to the boy.

"Watch this!" The boy grinned at Jax. "Poof!" he shouted.

Jax felt the wild outpouring of untrained Mystic whipping through the room and writhing up the chimney. The boy was too young to know how to manage such power, and Jax knew that this was too much. The old soot-encrusted pipe would burst, exploding into whatever rooms or shops or homes lay above. Instinctively Jax reached out to the boy's weave and gathered it tight, so that it stayed within the flue until it reached the stack of old bags that had blown across the upper opening.

Two women scurrying by in the early morning light saw the burlap bags blow off the chimney where the wind had left them, but busy gossiping about the now double-lost prince, neither paid this a second thought.

"How'd ye do that?" the boy pouted to Jax. "Ye ain't even got magic, but ye can grip a-holt a mine."

Gagged, Jax could only shrug. Even if had the ability to speak, he wasn't sure he could explain.

The sensuous interlacing of Jax's curious use of magic blended well with the erotic pleasures of Klaris's dream. Suddenly she woke, realizing that the interweaving wasn't a dream.

She ran her own powers along the gently undulating weave, trying to trace what she'd felt. Like a tear in a fabric that had been sewn up with mismatched thread, she could see where Jax had done something to contain that little boy's unschooled power. She couldn't help but smile. Goddess, but she loved the feel of him weaving within the Mystic.

But what had caused him to do that, and what the child had been doing eluded her. She pushed the Mystic and was rewarded with smells: the rotten egg smell of firerock fuel dissipating on a sea breeze, and toast.

Toast.

"Dragons!" She fell back among her pillows. How had Jax done that? And why? She jumped out of the bed calling for her maid.

"Have they brought Prince Jax back yet?" She asked the Barian servant who came in.

The woman looked at her as if she was a fretful child. "No, My lady. He hasn't been found."

"Why not?" Klaris stared.

"The people have been searching all night."

"How big is Ayx? How many bilge slums are there?"

The maid, clearly perplexed, shrugged. "Shall I bring you your tea, my lady?"

"No." Klaris went to the window, pulled back the rich brocade curtain and grit her teeth. The window looked inland, up to the dark pine forests that cloaked the Barian mountains. The sun was aflame in the very topmost trees. She turned away and went with some desperation to join the sun salutations.

"T'is a bluff, I'm tellin' ye!" Dury shouted. "A bluff!"

"Tain't." Logil sighed. His shoulders slumped as he followed Dury back into the little room.

"Did ye get an answer then?" Thyl asked nervously.

Dury threw the scrap of parchment at her. She unfolded it carefully. "What's it say?"

"Show it to his lordship."

She held it out to Jax. It was Logil's badly written note. Two words, written in thick Royal Barian Blue ink, flowed across the black scrawl: *Kill him.*

Jax laughed. He laughed until tears spilled from his eyes and he choked on the gag. Bryx's response was absolutely brilliant.

"What's it say?" Thyl shouted, alarmed by the prince's reaction.

"Take off the gag, afore he kills hisself with laughing at us." Dury snapped. "He'll tell ye."

Jax cleared his throat, laughter still spilling out of him. "I would have told you I was a worthless hostage."

"Worthless is right." Dury growled.

"We're gonna die fer yer worthless head," Logil snapped.

"Not for my head, but for my finger." Jax sat up a little straighter.

Dury walked meditatively to the table and pulled the knife free. He approached Jax waving the blade slowly side to side.

"I am worthless to you as a hostage, but not as lord admiral," Jax said, knowing he couldn't escape through movement.

"I ain't gonna feed the shark for just snippin' off yer toff little finger, milord. I'm gonna die fer killin' ye."

"Wait!" Logil stepped between Dury and Jax.

"He's got a point, the prince has." Logil glanced down at the messy figure on the floor. "If we kill him, the blue bloods is gonna come down even harder on us. They'll be reprises."

"Reprisals," Jax corrected quietly. "Dreadful reprisals, I'm afraid. And you'll be blamed for them."

"Move aside, Logil. Don't make me cut ye to get him."

"But if you spare me, you'll be heroes down here."

"Ye don't know nothin' about what goes on down here!" Dury spat.

"Don't spit on me. I'm trying to help you," Jax snapped. "You are a dead man, Dury. But you can die a hero for your cause. You can be the martyr who dared to tell the sealord the truth of life in the holds; or you can become the villain who called down the wrath of the sealord and every Barian noble upon the poor in the bilge slums."

"And the Weaver too, Da!" piped the boy. "The Weaver wants the prince back, too."

Dury yelled incoherently and swung about, sweeping the knife in a broad circle around himself. Logil jumped back in time, but the boy didn't. The blade sliced into the soft, thin cheek. Thyl screamed.

Logil lunged at Dury, who stood looking with horror at the blood drenching mother and son. The blade clattered as he threw it vehemently across the room.

"Go get a druid," Jax ordered.

Dury wiped his hands over his face and stomped out of the room.

Logil fetched the blade and faced the prince.

Fear quivered in Jax's stomach and he strove to hide it.

Logil moved and the knife flashed, slicing through the ropes that tied him.

"Get outta here, milord, afore Dury gets back."

Jax pushed himself up with the wall to his back to steady his tingling legs. "I didn't mean for this to go so far," Jax admitted.

"Dury ain't never been one to cross," Logil grumbled.

"Nor is the sealord." Jax moved slowly across the room and bent over the bleeding boy. "You come see the Royal Mystic, lad, when your face heals. We'll make something of your magic."

He pulled all the coins he had from his pocket and dropped them on Thyl's lap. "This is to pay the druid. And to help you move on when Dury's gone." Thyl just stared at him, her sea blue eyes wide with confusion.

Jax moved to the door. "I won't be able to save you, Logil, but I can see to it that it's quick."

"Jest go, milord. Go, but don't forget what ye saw down here in the bilge slums."

A dark hatchway disgorged Jax into an alley clogged with rubbish and reeking from the empty casks of ale and seaspirit. He climbed over the trash and walked into the small lane. Three or four people were busy sweeping and opening small shops for the morning.

They glanced at the dirty, shirtless fellow who stumbled into the street. Goddess, he must've gotten into some kind of brawl. That weird hair was spiky with dried blood.

"Sweet goddess." A shopkeeper dropped his broom.

"Milord?" A woman in a clean white apron came toward him. "Ye must be Prince Jax."

"Aye."

"Oy, what did they do to you, sir?"

"Exercised their frustrations."

"What's that? Here, Stavy, come help milord! We'll get ye home, sir. What's wrong with yer hand?"

"Majesty! Your Majesty!" The Cabyn's steward burst into the sunny parlor interrupting the sealord's quiet breakfast with Klaris.

"Your Majesty, the lord admiral has returned."

Klaris jumped to her feet.

"He's home now, Sire. At the Cabyn, I mean."

"Is he alright?" Klaris demanded.

The steward shrugged. "I was told to fetch Mother Ayslic after I found you, Sire."

"Yes." Bryx set his teacup down, surprised at the depth of his own disappointment at this good news.

Klaris was already out of the room. Bryx followed more sedately.

In minutes they arrived at the Cabyn. Jax sat in a parlor, as disheveled as he'd arrived, while druids poked at the wound on the back of his head and unwrapped his right hand to look at the place where his finger should be.

Klaris, breathless from rushing through the streets, drew up short when he raised those cautious blue eyes to her.

"You're alright?"

"Sure."

Bryx entered, followed by Mother Ayslic and the steward with the jar containing Jax's finger.

"Good morning, your Majesty." Ayslic gave Bryx the one-handed Barian salute then turned her eyes to Jax. "Let me see your hand, your Highness."

Jax held it out to her. Klaris cringed at the sight. It was crusted with dried blood. The absence of the fourth finger was eerie.

"That's going to make it hard to play a dragonpipe," Bryx said casually.

Klaris's head snapped up. She hadn't thought about that.

"I know," Jax said, his eyes still on Klaris.

"That's a problem," she said sharply.

"Why?" Bryx asked.

"Because we need his music. I need it. We all need it."

"Why?" Bryx asked again.

Klaris pulled the Oracle's golden instrument from the pocket of her dress and tossed it to Jax. He caught it left-handed. Its magic stung him.

"Ouch. Whose is this?"

"The Oracle's or maybe the fairy queen's." Her voice was grim. "Tell me you can play it without your finger?"

He looked at the small holes on the pipe and set it on the table, shaking his head.

Mother Ayslic was wiping his hand with stinging disinfectant. Klaris knelt and put her hand on Jax's knee. He took a sharp breath.

"What were you thinking?" Klaris asked, staring up into his face. "What were you thinking to risk yourself when you know, you *know*, the prophecy involves you?"

"He wasn't thinking," Bryx snapped. "He was acting as he always does, without any regard to propriety, or duty, or the feelings of others."

"Don't talk to me about duty," Jax said tersely. Aware of the other people in the room, he wouldn't castigate the sealord now. In any case, the painful things Ayslic was doing to his hand pulled his thoughts away. "Could I have some poppy extract, Mother?"

"Not for something like this," the priestess answered shortly. "I think we can reattach the finger, but I'm not sure it will function as it used to. The process will be somewhat painful, and if it goes septic, it could kill you."

She looked at Jax, her blue islish eyes steady. "Or we can leave it as it is. Many people live without fingers. It's your choice, my lord."

Klaris rose and looked at the hand, then back into Jax's face. "But without the finger you can't play."

Jax gazed at her for a long moment. Goddess, how he wanted to lie with her and let her skin, her hair, her lovely soft parts soothe his pains. He turned instead to the priestess. "Reattach it, Mother."

It was, as promised, a slow and painful process. Jax, wondering why Ayslic refused him the refuge of the pain-numbing poppy, sat with his left hand over his eyes while the priestess and two other druids slowly stitched the finger back to the hand.

Klaris's remorse warred with her resolve as she watched over the priestess' shoulder. She knew the Oracle's prophecy required Jax's participation and she knew she needed his partnership. But as she watched him endure the priestess's needles, she realized how much more she wanted from him: more than duty, more than mere partnership.

Mother Ayslic had turned the hand over and was nearly done stitching. Klaris focused her Mystic and sensed the mess underneath the closed skin the same way she could sense veins of rock and pools of water beneath the surface of the land.

"What about the vessels and the bone?" she asked. "You can't reattach those as well?"

Ayslic did not look away from her work. "No. I can only sew the skin together."

Klaris frowned. She glanced at Jax and found his eyes on her. "Will you let me try something?"

"Maybe," he said briefly. She could see the muscles of his stomach and neck taught with pain.

Klaris cocked her head to one side and questioned the priestess: "Why don't you allow him some poppy?"

Ayslic's eyes betrayed a deep sorrow. "Poppy is highly addictive, Weaver. We use it only for the most desperate situations."

Klaris considered what she was about to attempt rather desperate, and she didn't know if it would hurt him or not. Clearly, he was already bearing a great deal.

She gathered her magic. "I'd like to try some construction," she said softly. "Tell me if it causes a problem."

"But magic can't heal," one of the druids protested.

"I know."

Jax felt the severed bone move. He cleared his throat and shifted in his chair.

"Steady, my lord," said the other druid, wiping sweat from his brow.

Klaris's Mystic wove within him. Things pulled and stretched with sharp needles of pain, but the Mystic soothed him, stroked him. The more she worked, the more the pleasure flowed into other parts of his body.

"Goddess, Klaris," he breathed. On the other side of the room, Bryx frowned at the thickness of his brother's voice.

"Almost done," Klaris crooned.

Jax closed his eyes. Her magic, warm and soft, rubbed him deeply. This was the most erotic thing he had ever experienced.

"There," she said finally. He felt her withdraw the Mystic, but he remained inflamed.

"What did you do?" Ayslic asked.

"I pulled together the nerves and the bone. Really, it's not so different from moving rock and earth and water to create a building." She looked at Jax's face. He was watching her with such intensity her heart fluttered. "Let's hope it heals so you can play the Oracle's instrument."

"Why is that so important?" Bryx stepped toward them. He too had seen the look on his brother's face. "I can find you any number of Dragons to make music for you, Weaver. Why do you keep insisting that you need the admiral to entertain you? Especially as you must understand he has other, more important responsibilities, although I'm sure they are less enjoyable."

Klaris turned on him, and as she did so, she realized how many other people were present in the room: druids, servants, even Lad Yob. "Perhaps, your Majesty, you will allow me a moment to speak to you and your brother alone."

Bryx nodded and the others left the room.

Jax exploded out of the chair, stumbled to Klaris, grabbed a fistful of her curls, pulled her head back and bent to kiss her, frantic with desire. She responded in kind. Her fingernails gripped his naked back.

He wanted to get even closer. A table crashed over as they came up hard against a wall. Jax had never wanted, needed anyone with such intensity. He felt his own desire returned in her kisses and in the way she pressed against him.

"What are you doing?" Bryx's cold voice barely intruded upon Jax's consciousness. But Klaris made a growling noise deep in her throat. Jax moved his lips down, ripping away her silken dress.

"Yes, yes, yes." Klaris encouraged him.

"Stop! You're hurting her!" Bryx pounded Jax's shoulder. The sealord pulled an ornamental dagger from the wall with one hand. With the other, he grabbed a handful of his brother's pale hair and pulled Jax's head away from Klaris's breasts. He pressed the knife hard against Jax's throat.

"You will let her go. Now."

"Leave us alone," Klaris panted.

Jax's breathing was harsh. His eyes never left Klaris's.

"I'll strip you of your titles, my dear brother," the knife pressed closer, drawing blood. "I'll confiscate your ships, seize your rents. I'll take everything!"

Jax finally stepped away from Klaris. He faced Bryx, and when he spoke, Klaris felt herself melting at the roughness in his voice. "Aye. Strip me. Make me nobody. And then the Weaver can have me."

37

Jax dropped onto a sofa. Bryx plunged the knife into a cushion less than a foot from his brother's leg.

Klaris straightened her dress. She turned to the sealord.

"I need Jax."

"Oh, for dragons' sake, Princess," Bryx snorted.

"Listen to me, your Majesty. The dragons are coming back."

"So you say."

"So I *know*. It is very likely that this will be the kind of devastating catastrophe that it was a thousand years ago. It certainly will be if you continue to ignore the fact that your brother here is critical to our efforts to avoid another dragon interregnum."

"Why him?"

"I don't know. But he is clearly the Paradox that the prophecy speaks of."

"That prophecy about a ruler going to his knees?" Bryx's voice was hard.

"Yes," Klaris stated.

Jax spoke finally. "Did the Oracle have the rest of it?"

"No. But," she glanced at Bryx, "they told me how it drove the dragons away and ended the last dragon interregnum. They used that pipe, Jax. They played the fairy song and the dragons left."

"What fairy song?"

"They didn't tell me."

"Of course not." Jax picked up the pipe and frowned again at the sting of it. "You're saying we defeat the dragons with music?"

"Evidently."

Jax fiddled with the pipe, a cold realization settling in his stomach. Klaris couldn't play music. "We'll be incinerated."

"Are you having those dreams, too?" Klaris's voice was husky.

"Yes."

"I am sorry for your nightmares, Klaris," Bryx said coldly. "But Jax has a duty to Baria. And he agreed to it."

Klaris shook her head. "If the dragons return, there may be no Baria to serve, no fleet to manage."

Bryx leaned toward her. "Jax showed me this prophecy before he set out to take you from Sageham. It's *not* coming true. I will *not* be brought to my knees."

Jax answered softly. "That's why I went into that crowd yesterday. To keep you on your feet."

Bryx snorted.

Jax adjusted the bandage on his hand and went on. "If the dragons return, Bryx, we'll all be boiled in the same stew, everyone, all across the Knownlands. Think what would happen if the dragons decided to settle in Kree this time? Klaris is right. The Oracle is right. We have to address the dragon threat."

"But how?" Bryx demanded. "Align the magic? What's that supposed to mean?"

"That is the problem," Klaris snapped. "The prophecy is incomplete."

"So maybe it's wrong." Bryx leapt into this loophole. "Maybe Jax should stay here and run the fleet and explain to the lords and ladies of the Floating Islands why he let bilge rats chew him up."

Jax was on his feet. "Bilge rats! They're your *people*, Bryx. They're suffering, starving, watching their babies die."

"They're poor. That's their fate."

Jax looked like he'd been hit.

Klaris took the sealord by his shoulders. She felt him shiver as she touched him, but she did not release him. "Fate entraps us all. You must leave Jax to his."

Bryx raised his hand to touch Klaris's face. Her skin was so smooth. "Not if his fate involves you."

Klaris firmly removed Bryx's hand.

Jax shoved between them. "*My* fate probably involves being cooked by a bunch of dragons," he snapped. "But it also involves Klaris. I can't deny it and you can't stop it."

Bryx looked at Klaris, then back to Jax. "Why must you always, *always* take everything from me? Why?"

Jax gritted his teeth and ran his fingers though his hair. The scabs itched. "I'm not taking the Helm from you."

"Aren't you? You know the lords and ladies are gathering out there right now to hear about your little excursion."

Jax smiled, and Bryx saw their father in his brother's face. "Of course, they are! That's the point of what I did. You were supposed to rescue me and be the hero. Don't you understand?"

"Be the hero? Isn't that what you were trying to do?"

"No! I was the bait." He paused, amazed at the sealord's lack of comprehension. "You should have gotten me out of the bilge before those poor folks had time to do me any real damage." He shook his head at the opportunity Bryx had wasted. "I'd like to get cleaned up and dressed, but it's better if the lords and ladies of the Floating Islands see me like this. They'll be enraged. And they will rally to the Sharkin rule of Baria. We need that."

"You speak insolence," growled Bryx.

"Fluently, my lord," Jax said distinctly. "But everything I do or say is for *us*. For the Sharkin hand on the Helm of Baria."

"Not everything."

Jax continued. "I will go to the Gather tomorrow as your lord admiral and review the fleet so I can give instructions to be followed while I'm gone."

"Where are you going?" Bryx and Klaris asked in unison.

Jax turned to Klaris. "You tell me. When the Oracle came to me in Kree, it said we were going somewhere together, you and I. It said it wished it was coming along."

"That damn Oracle never says quite enough," Klaris groused. She considered Jax for a moment. "I'll go to Sageham while you go to the Gather. There used to be a strange bit of Dragon force in one corner of the library. I know Caledra is a pile of rubble now, but I want to investigate."

Jax nodded and turned back to the sealord. "After the Gather, I'm going to Hanter Lake. I'm going to stop slavery in the iron mines."

"What?" Bryx was astounded and confused at the change of topic. "What does trollish slavery have to do with whether or not dragons are returning?"

"Nothing. But I owe a debt there and I want to pay it before.... Before Klaris drags me to a musical performance for a flock of dragons." He stared at Klaris thinking not of dragons, but of pleasurable things he wanted to do with her.

Bryx read the look on his brother's face. "You will not touch her. You gave me your word. You made your choice!"

"He doesn't get to make that choice," Klaris said, her voice hard.

Suddenly exhausted, Jax leaned on the back of a chair. The other two barely heard his whisper: "None of us is free."

The lords and ladies of the Floating Islands, hearing the news that Prince Jax had returned, flocked to the Cabyn and had been troubling the servants while they waited for their audience. When the door to the parlor finally opened and they faced their rumpled and bandaged lord admiral, their outrage was palpable. They bowed to the sealord, who sat in the largest chair and they eyed the Weaver who stood by a window, but their focus was absorbed by the younger Sharkin.

They noted the cuts and bruises. Goddess knew what would happen to Baria if they lost him again.

"Come sit, my lords and ladies," Jax invited. "Let me share my interesting findings."

"Findings, Admiral?" Doubt soured Lady Koralixa's tone. "As if you went willingly."

"I did go willingly."

"You risked your crazy neck," Neben grumbled.

"I risked *their* necks. They're the ones who will pay for showing me the truth."

"What truth?" Lady Esmee demanded.

"The truth that no matter how bad it is in the upper holds, they live a much darker, grimmer life down there. We must do more for them."

"Your Highness," protested Janil. "We are all horrified by this incident, but this is the fault of a couple of bad fish. It doesn't have anything to do with us!"

"It has everything to do with us," Jax retorted. "No noble will be safe if we continue to ignore our duty."

"What do you expect us to do, my lord?" asked Lady Koralixa.

"I expect us all to earn our silk shirts and fine wines. The captain gets privileges because he or she bears responsibility for the ship."

"You sound like Admiral Hix lecturing to group of midshipmen." Neben half smiled.

"I apologize if I'm patronizing anyone." Jax glanced coldly at his old friend. "But you have all been here. You have all seen the mess on the decks; you must all know that people are in trouble in the bilges."

"People are always in trouble in the bilges," said Lady Villar, with a negligent wave of her hand.

"I see." Jax answered. "I hope you can sleep well in your cabin on Ayx, my lady, knowing that the people who attacked me are lurking in the holds below you, thinking about you."

"Thinking about me?"

"Sure. Wondering if they could just snitch a bit off that golden fountain in your courtyard, or take a crate of fruits from your kitchen yard, or maybe break a window to find some valuable bauble sitting on a bureau."

Lady Villar frowned, her imagination whirling.

"Look," he continued. "The people in the bilges don't want trouble any more than we do."

"Except the ones that chopped you up," Bryx noted.

Jax shot him a quelling glance. "The one who held me is a bully. No one will follow him or his ilk if we do our duty. It is clearly our responsibility, my lords and ladies, to look to the needs of our people, to clean up the trash on the streets, to repair ships so the people can earn a living again."

"But I don't have the money to do it!" Janil said with exasperation. "None of us does, my lord. That's the problem."

Jax paused. "The problem isn't the lack of money. The problem is how we spend what we have."

He surveyed their faces and saw a mixture of shame, shock, and calculation.

When he spoke again, his voice was low. "I have spent a lot of time lately among the poor and disenfranchised peoples of the Knownlands. Some of what they need depends on money, but what they really need is someone to hear them and work with them to solve their problems. They need to know that their leaders care for them, worry about them, and do what they can for them."

Jax had known these nobles all his life. He had watched his father manage them. He remembered the way Rax would speak, and when he continued, he heard the cadences of the old sealord in his own voice. They heard it too. "Our privileges as nobles can only be justified by sacrifice and service. I will review and adjust the fleet tax during the Gather, because clearly you aren't able to find the resources to serve our shipmates within the holds."

"Are you defending those criminals who harmed you?" Esmee asked.

"I'm not condoning their actions, but their grievances are valid."

"Their losses are your fault, Jax!" Bryx interrupted. "You are the one who got us locked out of Kordon. And it's your *prophecy* that called up the Great Wave."

"I might debate you on whether or not any of these things is my fault, but solving the resulting humanitarian disaster is certainly my responsibility, our responsibility, your Majesty, my Lords and Ladies."

No one spoke for a minute. The nobles observed their sealord's sneer.

"You can try to raise funds by taxing an empty hold, my lord," Janil complained, "but you won't get much."

"No. You should let us solve these problems with our own resources," Lady Villar suggested.

"That opportunity was already given to you." Jax snapped. "And you didn't do it. I don't know why you let rubbish rot in the streets. I don't know why you didn't find reserves to support people who lost their homes or their livelihoods. But Haven is a mess. And I am appalled."

"You weren't here! You don't have the right to judge us!" Koralixa rose, furious.

Jax stood to meet her eyes. "This is not about rights, my lady. This is about responsibilities."

He considered their faces. "Look, we are on these Islands together. I know you don't want your crewmates to suffer. Let's listen to them and then solve these problems together."

"I'm not going down in the bilges until those traitors who harmed you have fed the shark!" Lady Villar announced.

"Then invite them to your cabin," Jax said, fatigue finally overwhelming him. "Good day, my Ladies and Lords."

The nobles bowed and left.

"Well," Bryx smirked. "You certainly rallied them all to our cause."

"We have Neben and Esmee," Jax said. "Villar will come along once she gets over her embarrassment that it was Axyans who harmed me. You could probably get Janil to come around by offering him a vice admiralship."

Bryx stared at him, wondering how Jax seemed to know so many things that hadn't been said. "Where does that come from? Didn't you listen to them?"

"I heard them, Bryx." He looked down at the bandage on his hand. "I need some food and a nap." He bowed to the sealord, cast one last longing glance at silent Klaris, and returned to his own rooms. No rest awaited him there. The senior staff of the admiralty and the fleet captains had sheaves of papers with questions he had to answer in order for Baria to be ready to sail to the Gather tomorrow.

He managed to get a bite to eat and a clean shirt, but by mid-afternoon he could no longer concentrate and knew he needed both a bath and a nap before the sealord's banquet that evening. He excused his staff, took a quick bath, let a druid re-bandage his wounds and fell into bed.

The nightmare ripped him out of sleep. He lay in his bed watching the late-afternoon sun move shadows across the familiar ceiling. He ached for Klaris. Rolling over, he buried his head in his arms. The movement pulled at his bandages and reminded him of the bilge slums, of Thyl and Logil. What choices did they have? What luxuries? What loves? Duty propelled him out of bed, calling for Bolo.

38

Jax took six men of his household, including Bolo, to walk with him across the Floating Islands and over the bridge to the mainland and Valla's Palace, but as he expected, guards were not necessary now.

People cheered him heartily.

"Oy, Prince Jax!"

"Blessings, milord!"

"Greetings, Admiral."

Bolo shook his head. "They're sure singing a different tune today, aren't they, my lord?"

"I told you they would," Jax answered, waving his bandaged hand to a cheering group of sailors who had gathered outside a tavern. "People might be miserable, but most of them don't want to change the world."

The steward appraised his prince with sharp sea blue eyes. "You gambled your life on that, sir."

"No. I gambled their lives, and I lost."

Bolo shared a glance with the other household staff, their slanted islish brows raised in surprise. Ahead of them, Jax Sharkin strode, smiling at his people, the late sun glinting off his shiny hair, the Royal Barian Blue silk of his fine cloak billowing behind him.

Neben de Rillt came down the steps of Valla's Palace to greet them. "Good news, Jax! Lady Villar just sent word that her people have found and arrested the traitors."

Jax nodded and walked side by side with Neben into the great hall. Wide windows opened to the balcony overlooking the harbor and the Floating Islands, letting in the light and breeze of the mild spring evening. Three musicians played softly in a corner. The nobles, glittering in their silks and satins, raised a cheer for Jax as he entered the room.

He raised his cup to them in a salute then began his work. One by one he cornered the lord or lady of each Floating Island, quietly reviewing the meeting of the morning and discussing their specific goals for improvements. His secretaries followed him making discreet notes of these exchanges.

When Klaris arrived, she saw him conversationally impaling Lady Villar, so she slipped out to the balcony and joined Wexalay, who was seeking refuge from the Dragon force coming from the musicians.

"I found the child, Weaver," Wexalay said carefully. "It was his father, apparently, who was behind the abduction."

Klaris cocked her head to one side, considering the implications of this information. "So, he'll soon be fatherless."

Wexalay nodded, soberly. "The boy is only four years old, but he has a lot of potential."

"I noticed."

"We'll keep an eye on him."

Klaris looked at the harbor, purple under a lavender sky. "He'll need watching if he's going to be able to pass the soul test someday," she said softly.

"That was my thought," agreed Wexalay.

Finished with his rounds of the nobles, Jax joined Klaris on the balcony. She smiled uncertainly and reached out to touch him. He took her hand and held it, looking down at their fingers.

Wexalay watched, uneasily. After a moment, Jax turned his eyes to the Royal Mystic. She dropped a hasty curtsey and fled.

Klaris raised her other hand to Jax's cheek. "I thought we'd lost you."

"We?"

"Me. But then, I have lost you, haven't I?"

"Klaris. I've sworn oaths to the king of Kordon and to the sealord to serve and obey them." His voice dropped to a whisper. "I must keep my word."

"But what about the Oracle?"

"I have its chain around my neck."

"And what about me?"

He couldn't help his smile. "You, my lady, are the power of the sea and the glory of the wind. Bright and...." He was kissing her in spite of himself. She wrapped her arms around his neck and tangled her fingers in his hair.

"No," he choked, finally pulling away. "Sweet goddess, no, Klaris."

"No?"

His eyes pleaded. "You are the Weaver. You're law unto yourself. I have others to answer to."

"Yes. Like the Oracle. Like me." He felt her gather herself before she continued. "You have to figure out how to be master of your own destiny."

"My lord?" The chamberlain cleared his throat delicately. "Everyone is seated. The sealord requires your presence."

Jax looked into Klaris's green eyes for one more moment, grieving at the pain he saw there. He took her hand and followed the chamberlain to the banquet hall.

The crowd, seated at long tables in the great hall, cheered as they entered and took their seats with the sealord.

Lady Villar, on the other side of the sealord, was leaning across to talk to Jax. "The mob is after them, I tell you, Admiral. I've got guards posted all around my palace, but it's a decoy. I've moved the criminals to my flagship, in the harbor. I think they'll be safer there."

"Safe for their execution," Bryx growled.

"Aye, your Majesty," said Neben, swallowing quickly. "The entire port's out for their blood."

Neben's wife, Shallyx, put a familiar hand out to touch the bandage on Jax's hand. "People on both Rillt and Callisto cheered for me today because they know we were old... friends."

Jax looked for a long minute into the blood red wine in his goblet. He'd used Dury, knowing that the man's open display of malice would unite the nobles and the people behind the Sharkins. It had worked, but Jax regretted the cost to Logil, Thyl and the boy. He took a deep drink of the wine, it was awful. "Sweet goddess, your Majesty, I'm going to supply you with some Darkwood wine. This stuff must have come from Brakkle."

As the tables were cleared following dinner, the sealord rose to address the nobles of Baria.

"My lords and ladies, as you know by now, we have captured the traitors who dared to spill royal Barian blood. They will die tomorrow, even as most of you will set sail for the Gather."

Great cheers greeted this gruesome announcement.

"My brother, the Lord Admiral Prince Javix, will oversee the Gather this year at the Back of Baria."

More cheering. Jax noted that the poor quality of the wine had not deterred anyone from drinking lots of it.

The sealord waited until the crowd settled a bit then he continued. "The Gather is always a time of celebration, but this year we must focus ourselves to work to rebuild Baria. Especially as we may face a new and even greater threat."

The nobles were silent, listening. "We believe that dragons are returning to the Knownlands."

The crowd murmured in dismay.

"Clearly, we must prepare. Stores will be sent to the hard ports and we must also fill our holds on the Floating Islands, in case we have to cut them loose again."

Jax sat and stared. This was good, but he wondered who would organize these measures.

The sealord paused for a moment. "It is because of this new threat that I will not be joining you at the Gather this year."

Jax kept his face impassive, but his heart went cold. He watched the nobles at the tables below him quickly hide their expressions of amazement and derision as the sealord continued: "I will sail for Kree. I will secure our alliances with the Kordish and make sure that if the dragons do come, we are not once again banished from Kordon."

After a moment of shocked silence, the nobles realized that the sealord was finished and they cheered him mechanically, turning back to their wine cups with eyes like spooked animals.

The musicians began again, and the party soon became loud and chaotic.

"What's the matter?" Klaris whispered to Jax.

"The sealord can't miss the Gather. It just doesn't happen. No matter how sick or how old or troubled, the sealord or seaqueen always goes to the Gather. It's kind of the whole point of the Gather: to be together as a people, from sealord to cabin kid." He paused and scratched delicately at the scabs in his hair. "Baria needs its sealord. He can send ambassadors to Kordon."

"He disappoints you, doesn't he?"

Jax swirled the wine in his glass. "I just keep expecting him to be something he's not."

She watched his blue eyes survey the crowd, noting who was talking to whom and the isolation of the sealord over by the windows.

"It's my problem," he said finally. "Not his."

"I'm pretty sure it's his problem, too."

Jax took another sip of wine, but its sour finish disappointed him.

Klaris saw him come to a decision. He turned to her.

"I am not master of anything, Klaris. I have to choose how to fulfill a lot of responsibilities, and I'm not really sure I'm making any of the right decisions."

"I could offer you an opinion."

He laughed "Goddess, but I—." He stopped suddenly, amazed at what he'd almost said. He continued to stare at her for a moment.

"You what?"

He cleared his throat. "I have to talk to Bryx."

Then he was gone, slowly making his way through the crowd to where the sealord sat alone in a great carved chair, staring at the dance without seeming to see it. Klaris didn't realize she was crying until Wexalay came up and gently offered her a handkerchief.

Jax pulled up a stool and sat, ignoring the sealord's raised eyebrow at this familiarity. "It's a great idea to build up the stores, my lord."

"I'm glad you think so. You see to it."

Jax nodded. He paused a moment, looking into his brother's round landish eyes. "Come to the Gather, Bryx. Please."

"Why? You don't need me there. No one wants me there. And frankly, I hate those Back of Baria Gathers."

"Everyone wants you there."

Bryx snorted. "You've been back in Haven for one day, half of it spent in the bilge. What do you know about what everyone wants?"

"Didn't you hear them at dinner?"

"I heard them cheering for you."

Jax shook his head. "They're cheering my leadership, that's all. They want someone to lead them, to tell them what to do."

"You don't."

"I...." Jax looked away. "No, I don't. But that doesn't stop everyone from the Oracle to the poor folk in the bilges from giving me orders."

"I'm going to kill those traitors who abducted you. Slowly."

"Are you executing them for what they did or for what they didn't do?"

Bryx frowned in confusion.

"I saw your response to the ransom note."

"Ah." The sealord grinned. "Did you appreciate that type of leadership?"

"If you weren't going to get me out of there, it was the next best thing you could do. You devalued me as a hostage, and there was little chance they'd actually do your bidding. Of course, if they had, it wouldn't really have bothered you."

Bryx shrugged. "Hix would be despondent. But then the Weaver would be free."

Jax stood up and shifted the conversation. "None of us is free. And only Dury deserves a traitor's death."

"Don't they all? Aren't they all traitors?"

"Dury is the only one who intended to commit treason. He's a bully. The others were just desperate. We need to remember that they fell victim to a bully because we left the opportunity open."

"Fine. I'll be merciful: the followers can die quickly. But the ringleader will feed the shark." Bryx shifted in his chair to look up at his younger brother. "You will be there, of course."

"No one has fed the shark since Sealord Rovix put down the Rillian Conspiracy 600 Risings ago."

Bryx gave his brother a very chilly smile. "Perhaps it's time to remind people what a traitor's death looks like on Baria."

"Executing traitors is never a win, no matter how the people cry for blood."

"You have the queerest ideas about politics, Jax. Were you always like this or did the slave pens give you this weird perspective?"

"The slave pens gave me...." He paused. He'd been going to say 'nothing.' He didn't want to admit that he had gained anything from those horrible years, but he'd suddenly thought of Jolira. "Empathy. Perhaps. By your leave, my lord?"

"Yes, go. I'll see you in the morning."

Maybe it was the bad wine or just complete exhaustion, but Jax slept that night without a nightmare. He awoke thinking of Klaris, then remembered all this day held before the tide turned and he could sail the *Sharkin* for the Back of Baria. Finally, he pushed aside the covers and walked out to the private dock. As the sun rose out of the sea, he dove in. Ignoring the stinging of his cuts, he set off down the shore.

Small fishing dories rowed in with their night's catch. Gulls wheeled and screeched overhead. He breathed the salty air over and under the gentle summer waves, his body warmed by the rhythm of stroke and kick.

Swimming forced him to steady his breath. As the sun rose to glow on the waves, he thought of Klaris's advice to be master of his destiny. Arm over arm he went, thinking about the times he had attempted to take hold of his own fate. First, he had resolved to sink Oblek's ferry and drown both the troll and himself. He'd failed, of course. The second time was when he'd walked into Rippsgate to save Mother Marith, knowing that he'd likely face a traitor's death as a result. The Oracle had saved him from that experience only to burden him with a doom just as harrowing.

He ducked under the cool waves and saw Jolira's happy face before his eyes. Her dark eyes were laughing at something, and that laughter there in the grim depths of the Hanter Iron Mines held a power as great as all of Mystic and Dragon combined.

Together, he and Jolira had tried to control their own fates, and in a paradoxical way they had succeeded, because one of them had died. He gulped grief with a wave and had to force himself to the surface against the heavy hollowness of her absence. He would always regret that he had never told Jolira how she brightened the darkness of his life as a slave. She had died alone in the dark of a mine tunnel, thinking she was unloved, forsaken.

Finally, he turned back to the dock, ready to face the exigent tragedies of the day. He pulled himself out of the water and went dripping back to his rooms. His stewards and valets got him dressed, groomed, and fed, and it was still early when he walked, alone this time, to Valla's Palace. The few people in the streets greeted him cheerily.

In the palace, he climbed the stairs to the guest wing. He let Klaris's Mystic lead him to her door.

After the Sealord's feast Klaris had found Wexalay and asked for another session of moon salutations. Exhausted by the exercises she slept deeply, undisturbed by nightmares, and awoke to the light chime of a druid summoning the morning sun salutations.

Klaris rose almost automatically, still half asleep and moved through the poses coming awake with the beat of her heart and the warmth of her flowing blood.

Back in her room, she gazed out the window at the pine covered mountain and sipped her tea. How could she extract Jax from the very things that made him whole? His sense of duty and love for everything Barian? Watching the sunlight slide down the mountain, she understood that love meant letting go and holding tight at the same time.

She turned at the brief knock on her door and faced these paradoxes.

"I wish you wouldn't look at me like that," Jax said.

She stared at him, standing there, with his sea blue eyes and his hair still a little wet. "I can't...." Humiliated, she choked to a stop. "You chose Baria."

"Klaris," he reached out, but didn't touch her. "Yes, I chose Baria. For the moment. These people need me."

"Read the prophecy, Jax. The entire Knownlands *needs* you."

"Aye, but they don't all want me."

"I want—." She stopped, frowning at his smile.

"Klaris...."

She could not breathe. "What?"

"I have something I want to give you." He held open a small box. A large, square cut sapphire sparkled on a white velvet cushion.

Klaris looked up into the vulnerability in his eyes.

"This is a Sharkin heirloom. I earned my captaincy early, you know. That same year, I won the regatta too. My father was...proud, and he gave me this. It's the ring my mother wore."

Klaris gulped, terror and joy pounding through her.

Jax continued, speaking quickly. "I would like you to wear it."

"You would?"

He nodded and pulled the ring from its velvet nest. "All Baria will know what it means."

"What does it mean?"

His smile warmed her soul. "That there's a Master in my destiny?"

She laughed a little and realized that tears were spilling from her eyes.

He desperately wanted to kiss her, but he took a deep breath instead. "I can't kiss you. I can't touch you. I can't lie with you, but I can't deny that I love you, Klaris. I want you to know it, and everyone else." He took her hand and held the ring, but he waited, watching her.

She whispered, "I have nothing for you."

She felt this pierce through him.

"Nothing?"

"I don't have a ring, a talisman for you."

He took a rather shaky breath. "Just give me your heart."

"It's yours already."

At last, he slipped the ring on her finger and smiled. "Good."

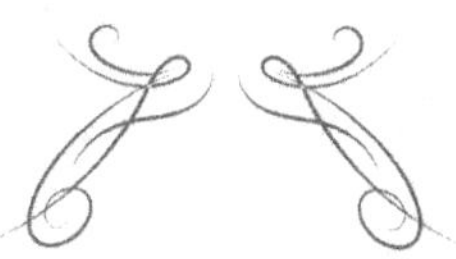

Character Names, Titles: Relationships

Ansyn Bil, Queen of Kordon: wife of King Kodill

Aric: inn keeper in Hilsen Vale

Aychex: Duke Frinz Ellswyth

Blanx, Captain of the Sharkin

Bolo Powluna, Jax's steward in Baria

Borrel Starrish: Mystic, Florin's twin

Boss Taint: Director Hanter Iron Mines

Bryx Jorvan Sharkin, Sealord: Jax's older brother

Carden Yemmel, Lord of Traik: betrothed to Tallyn of Kordon

Carte Serge, Royal Mystic: Kordon

Cheshir Griffyn, Lady of Deepford: foster sister to Tallyn, Jax and Foby

Chevvain: Duchess Patrice Gracevine

Clairo: Duke Von Houghlow

Corvyd Cale, Lord of Cale: slave from Ily

Dayne Kora, heir to Rippsmarch: siblings: Foby and Thessaly

"Doc", Mrac Appendel: child of Marith/spouse to Adgar

Dowager Stylla, Dowager Queen: Grandmother of Jax

Dury Axian: Troublemaker

Dylith: friend in Hilsen Vale

Earl Oklan Kora, Rippsmarch

Earla Stona Swansee, Earla Tarron March

Eleeza St. Clare, Eldar Chieftess: Lexy's sister

Elmore Aethelyn, Earl of Vobury

Esmee Choles, Lady of Callisto

Essa of Farsouth, dec Queen of Farsouth: Klaris's grandmother

Estyl Pexborn, Duchess of Midipex: wife of Thorag Addle

Fairy Queen: rules the Fae

Father Mallix, Priest to Sageham

Florin Starrish: Borrel's twin

Foby Kora, Lord of Rippsfell: son of Earl Kora, foster brother

Frinz Ellswyth, Duke of Aychex: fostered with Dayne and Bryx
Grisham: Ambassador of Baria
Grobber Vloggan, Magistrate Hilsen Vale
Hix Sharkin, Lord Admiral: cousin to Sealord Rax
Janil Embay: Lord of Phlyx
Jax: see Javix Sharkin, below
Jeress de Farsouth, Queen of Farsouth
Jolira: slave from Ohe
Juna, Oracular Priestess
Karric: Captain of King's Guard/Tutor
Keffex: Duke Kevlor Brondon
Kevlor Brondon, Duke of Keffex: cousin to King Kodill
King Kodill, Kodill Brondon: Tallyn's father
Klaris de Farsouth, Princess of Farsouth: Tower-tested Mystic
Kodill Brondon, King of Kordon: Jax's uncle (mother's brother)
Koralixa Windis, Lady of Jeff
Lad Yob: Saghamite servant to Klaris
Lady Mollish, Priestess to Kree: druid
Lexyl St. Clare, Speaker's Heir: Mystic, sister to Eleeza St. Clare
Lord of Traik: see Carden Yemmel
Logil Lowax: Friend of Dury Axian
Marith Appendel, druid in Hilsen Vale: Doc's mother
Master Illat, Captain of the Flagship *Drixa*
Midipex: Duke Thorag Addle
Mother Ayslic, Priestess to Baria
Neben de Rillt, Lord of Rillt: Spouse to Shallyx of Callysto
Oblek, overmaster
Oklan Kora, Earl of Rippsmarch: kids: Dayne, Foby, Thessaly
Oracle, Speaks for the Goddess
Patrice Gracevine , Duchess of Chevvain
Prina, Eleeza's wife
Professor Essen, Bricks and Mortar Tutor
Professor Hiddicot, Dock and Portal Tutor
Professor Lellyn, Tower Tutor

Raggar, Dragon Highlord

Raisha Allanaugh: Kordish courtier

Rax Sharkin VII, Sealord of Baria: Bryx and Jax's father

Rippsmarch: Earl Oklan Kora

Ryxa, 1st Lieutenant on *Drixa*

Shallix of Callisto: preeminent Barian sailor

Shaloh: Foby Kora's favorite dog

Shaman Ashande, Shaman in Arandy

Slave Wrangler: Hanter Iron Mines

Stona Swansea, Earla Tarron March

Stylla Aethelyn, Dowager Queen: grandmother to Jax, Tallyn and Bryx

Tallyn Brondon, Crown Princess: Jax's cousin and foster sibling

Thessaly Kora: Foby's younger sister, druid

Thorag Addle, Duke of Midipex: Chancellor of Kordon

Thyl Axian: wife of Dury

Trajan, Consort of Farsouth: husband of Queen Jeress

Valla Brondon, dec., Consort of Baria: child of Stylla; mother of Jax

Vigo Axian: child of Thyl and Dury Axian

Vobury: Earl Elmore Aethelyn

Von Houghlow, Duke of Clairo

Allynor of Caer Keff, Duchess of Keffex

Expanded biographical information:

Javix Brondon Fellix Sharkin: Prince of Baria, Prince of Kordon, Viscount Norbay. Nephew of King Kodill of Kordon; Son of Sealord Rax Sharkin and Valla Brondon of Kordon; foster siblings, Koby Fora of Rippsfell, Cheshire Griffyn of Deepford and Tallyn Bondon of Kordon. He dislikes the name Javix, especially because it's usually mispronounced in Landish.

PROPHECY

Titles and Names:

Thorag Addle, Duke of Midipex, Lord Chancellor:

> Referred to as the Duke of Midipex, Lord Thorag, or simply by his territorial name: Midipex.
>
> He would be addressed formally as: Lord Thorag, Duke Thorag, or Your Grace.
>
> Less Formal: my lord. His peers might call him Thorag, as could his wife, but she doesn't (this is explained in PROPHECY).

Crown Princess Tallyn Brondon:

> Referred to as Princess Tallyn.
>
> Addressed formally as your royal highness (because she's heir to the throne), then Ma'am or my lady.

Prince Javix Sharkin:

> Referred to as Prince Javix or Prince Jax.
>
> Addressed formally as your highness, my lord, or sir.
>
> Might be referred to as Norbay (his territorial name) but since it's less important than being a Prince of the Blood, he'd more likely be called prince.

Kordish Royal Council:

> King Kodill
>
> Dowager Stylla (non voting)
>
> Crown Princess Tallyn
>
> Lord Chancellor, Duke of Midipex, Thorag Addle
>
> Duke of Keffex, Kevlor Brondon
>
> Duchess of Chevvain, Patrice Gracevine
>
> Duke of Aychex, Frinz Ellswyth
>
> Duke of Clairo, Von Houghlow
>
> Earl of Rippsmarch, Oklan Kora
>
> Earl of Vobury, Elmore Aethelyn
>
> Earla of Tarron March, Stona Sweansea

Floating Islands:
    Helm, Bryx Sharkin
    Jeff: Koralixa Windish
    Rillt: Neben de Rillt
    Callisto: Esmee Choles
    Phlyx: Janil Embay
    Ayx: Villar d'Ayx

Mystic Studies at Caledra:
    Dock and Portal Acolytes, Professor Hiddicot
    Bricks and Mortar Novices, Professor Essen
    Foundation Firsts, Professor Visidor
    Corridor Cadets, Professor Ancellin
    Tower Tested, Professor Lellyn

Acknowledgements

I'm grateful to the many friends and family who have read this story, sometimes more than once, and made it so much better: Bill Stearns, Cathy Calhoun Damon, Warren Fox, Robbie Fox, Norma Staley, Kristen Gould Case, Mark Menlove, Andy Cier, Joe Totten, Lisa Cilva Ward, Karri Dell Hayes, Asha Rehnberg, Evan Gregory, Gloria Rice, Willoughby Staley and David Staley. I am deeply indebted to my cousin Valerie for introducing me to Starhawk and non-patriarchal religion. Starhawk continues to work in this space and can be found on Instagram. Adrian Fox Staley manages my online presence at *CAFoxBooks.com*. Check it out for information on the backstory and upcoming books. I wouldn't be able to share the story without the amazing support and talent of Katie Mullaly at Surrogate Press and Michelle Rayner of Cosmic Design. Any errors in the text are entirely my own.

About the Author 

C.A. Fox has taught skiing, sold books, encouraged critical thinking among college students, and raised two free thinking kids, not always with appreciation for their independent thoughts. Home is a place that requires high-elevation modifications for baking and the expectation that it may snow on any day of the year. Like the fictional poet, Featherfetch, Fox casts nets of words to catch the downy bits out of the wind. Visit *CAFoxBooks.com* for more information and follow on Facebook, *@Paradox Trilogy*.